Fisher's Light

Other books by Tara Sivec

Fisher's Light

By
Tara Sivec

Fisher's Light
Copyright © 2015 Tara Sivec
Print Edition

Disclaimer

Editing by Nikki Rushbrook

Cover Design by Michelle Preast
www.MichellePreast.com

Drawings by Danielle Torella of Pushy Girl Paintings
www.pushygirltorella.deviantart.com

Interior Design by Paul Salvette, BB eBooks
bbebooksthailand.com

A Note to Readers

My father is a Vietnam Veteran. For as long as I can remember, he has NEVER spoken about his time in the war and we've always just known not to ask him about it. One day, out of the clear blue, he started talking about PTSD and how even after forty plus years, his time overseas still has a deep impact on him. The following day, I had a dream about Fisher and Lucy. A dream about a couple dealing with deployments and the effects that it has on a relationship. This dream hit me so hard that I woke up and immediately started writing.

As with any type of fictional story, there are liberties that need to be taken in order to bring it to life and have it flow the way that an author needs it to. I have done extensive research on the military and military families and I've spoken to several of them while I wrote this book. Please keep in mind that any inconsistencies in regards to the timeline of deployments, where the soldier is stationed, etc. etc. are only there to make this story move in the direction that I needed it to.

Thank you so much for reading and I hope you enjoy Fisher's Light!

For James – my light in the darkness.

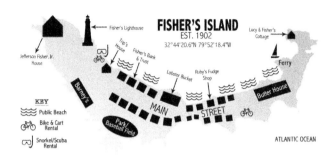

FISHER'S ISLAND
EST. 1902
32°44'20.6"N 79°52'18.4"W

Fisher's Lighthouse

Lucy & Fisher's Cottage

Jefferson Fisher, Jr. House

Trip's House

Fisher's Bank & Trust

Lobster Bucket

Ruby's Fudge Shop

Ferry

Butler House

Barney's

MAIN   STREET

Park/ Baseball Field

ATLANTIC OCEAN

KEY

〰️ Public Beach

🚲 Bike & Cart Rental

🤿 Snorkel/Scuba Rental

Prologue
Fisher's Journal

AT THE END of a long, dark hallway, there's a door. It's the same average, everyday wooden door that can be found in almost every house, condo or apartment anywhere in the world. Just looking at this door, there's nothing special about it. Made of oak, it has a few nicks and scratches from years of wear and tear, it creaks when you open it and sticks when it's humid outside and the wood expands. Locked away behind the door, though, is the shit no one wants to know about. The memories, the nightmares and all the reasons my life is a fucked up mess lie just inside that door in a pile of regret. I lost everything because of that damn door, because my mind splintered into a thousand pieces and I couldn't tell the difference between dreams and reality. I became a different man.

A dangerous man.

A suicidal man.

Some days, I think of that door as a barrier between me and the dark corners of my subconscious, a place to stockpile the skeletons of my past so that I don't have to look at them or think about them. Other days, that door busts wide open and I am forced to relive every mistake I've made. I can walk into the room, sweat running down my back, and run my hands over each item that carved me into the man I've become. I can dig through the shoebox on the end of the bed and run the tips of my fingers over each letter she sent me, I can pick up the Purple Heart from the top of the dresser and feel the cold weight of the bronze medal and the satin purple ribbon in the palm of my hand, and I can lift the backpack off the floor in the corner of the room and smell the heat from the desert and the metallic hint of dried blood splattered on the camouflage design.

It's not long before the sounds of war fill my ears and only seconds until I'm clutching my head with shaking hands and a pounding heart, trying to determine the source of the most tormented, heartbroken noises I've ever heard, the crying and the begging so loud that they can be heard even over the gunfire. It's only when I realize that the horrified screams are coming from me, that *I'm* the one pleading for mercy, that I slam shut that door in my mind, begging anyone that'll listen to take away the grief and the pain so that I never go back inside that room.

This is where my story begins.

Or ends.

I can never really decide.

The mind is a great and powerful thing, bisected with hallways of darkness and corners of light. Memories can alternately fill your life with joy and happiness and cloud every moment with nightmares and fear, making you second-guess all of the good things and wonder if they were ever real. Was I happy? Did I ever smile and laugh easily without a care in the world? How do I get that back when the darkness is hell bent on taking over, holding me in its clutches and making sure I never see the sunshine again?

I'm going to figure it out even if it kills me. I will piece together the fractures in my mind and take back what's mine. I don't blame her for walking away; I shoved her out the door and told her to go. I should have realized that *she* was my light. She was everything bright and beautiful about my life and it went to shit after she left.

I'm going to fix this. I *have* to fix this. I hate being in this place filled with people who think they know everything about me. I hate every moment that I'm away from her, but I will do whatever it takes to find the man she once loved and bring him back to her.

I'm going to kick down that fucking door at the end of the long, dark hallway and show everyone that I deserve the light.

Chapter 1

Lucy

March 24, 2006

S CREAMS FILL MY ears and I jerk up in bed with my heart pounding. The moonlight shines through the bedroom window, illuminating Fisher's body as he kicks at the covers and punches his fists into the mattress on either side of him. His screams are so loud and painful that I want to cover my ears and cry for him.

"Fisher! Fisher, wake up!" I shout over his yells and curses.

His eyes are squeezed shut and sweat drips down his chest, soaking the t-shirt he wore to bed. I quickly reach over and flip on the lamp on my nightstand, yank the covers away from us and move close to him, pressing my hands to either side of his face to turn his head towards me.

"Please, baby, wake up. It's just a dream, it's just a dream," I chant softly, running my hands soothingly down his face.

He stops screaming, but the words that come out of his mouth next are almost worse than the screams.

"I'm sorry, I'm so sorry. I didn't mean to kill him, he got in the way. Oh, God, I'm so sorry!"

I sob for him and the agony that rips through his

voice as he continues to thrash against me and cry out, shoving my hands off his face and pushing me away from him. He's lost in another world, another time, and I can't stand seeing him like this. He's hurting so much.

God, please make him stop hurting.

"Please, Fisher, wake up. Come on, baby, open your eyes," I cry, throwing my leg over top of his and using all my strength to get him to calm down and wake him up from this nightmare.

His hand flies out and connects with my cheek and I let out a yelp of pain, but I keep going. This isn't Fisher; he would never hit me if he was awake and in his right mind. I have to wake him up. I need him to wake up.

Oh, God, I don't know what to do!

As quickly as I can, I climb on top of him, straddling his waist and taking hits to my arms and chest before I can grab his wrists and hold them down at his sides. I kiss every inch of his face, my tears dripping down off of my nose and onto his cheeks as I whisper his name over and over and beg him to come back to me.

He suddenly goes completely still and his eyes pop open. I hold myself above him and stare into his eyes until they finally focus on me.

"You're okay, baby, you're okay," I tell him softly as I rest my forehead against his.

I let go of his arms and he quickly wraps them around me, pulling me down fully on top of him. His heart beats like a drum against my chest as he tries to slow his breathing. After a few seconds, I pull back and look into his eyes. They immediately go wide and he gasps in horror, bringing his hands up to my face.

"Oh, God, what did I do? Baby, what did I do?" he cries as he examines my cheek and the bruise I'm sure is forming there.

I cover his hand with mine and shake my head at him. "It's okay, I'm fine. I promise, I'm fine, Fisher."

"I'm sorry, I'm so sorry," he softly sobs as he leans up and gently kisses my cheek. "Lucy, my Lucy. I'm so sorry."

I move down to rest my cheek against his chest, listening to his heartbeat as I wrap my arms around his body and squeeze him as tightly as I can.

"You didn't mean it. You were just having a bad dream. It's okay, I'm fine," I whisper again.

We've only been married for two of the six months he's been home after his second deployment, but this isn't the first nightmare he's had. Each one is worse than the last and I don't know what to do to help him anymore. I want to take away his pain, to stop the hurt that fills his heart and his mind, but I feel like I'm so far out of my depth that I'm drowning.

"Please, talk to me, Fisher. I want to help you, but I need to understand," I speak softly against his chest.

"There's nothing to understand, Lucy. It was just a bad dream. They'll go away after a little while, just like they always do," he promises me, running his fingers gently through the long strands of my hair.

"I need to know, Fisher. You don't have to go through this alone."

He slides out from under me and pushes himself up

to lean his back against the headboard. I get up onto my knees and scoot closer to him, hating the distance he's trying to put between us.

"Don't ask questions you don't want to know the answers to," he speaks softly, thumping his head against the headboard to stare up at the ceiling.

"That doesn't make any sense. Of course I want answers. I want to know everything. That's why I'm here. I'm your wife, Fisher, and I love you more than anything. We're in this together, every step of the way," I remind him.

He's quiet for a while and I see every emotion from sadness to frustration skate across his features before finally settling on anger. I don't want him to be angry with me for asking him to share his troubles, but I don't know what else to do. How can I help him shoulder his burdens if he doesn't share them with me?

"So, what do you want to know?" he finally asks, the sarcasm lacing his voice making the hair on my arms stand up. "Do you want to know what it's like to find the mutilated body of the little girl you brought food to yesterday lying in the street? What it's like fighting a war against people who will kill children to drive home a message? Or do you want to know what it's like to be walking down a deserted street on foot patrol, making sure it's clear for the convoy, talking to one of your friends about football and then mid-sentence his head explodes and his blood and brains are splattered all over your face?"

He speaks in a monotone voice that is like nothing

I've ever heard before. Tears flow down my cheeks and I have to hold my hand against my mouth to stop myself from sobbing. I shake my head back and forth, wanting him to stop, but knowing that I asked for it. I wanted to know everything and now he's giving it to me.

"Maybe you want to know what it's like to get orders to take out an enemy sniper and right when you pull the trigger, a nine-year-old boy runs in the line of your shot. I'm sure you'd like to know what it's like to watch his mother hold his lifeless body in her arms while she screams and cries and tries to hold together the hole in his head with her hands. Do you know how hard it is to try and shove someone's brain back into his head after you've blown a hole in it the size of a softball?"

He finally stops talking and I squeeze my eyes closed, trying to block out the visions of what he's told me from my mind. I can't breathe, I can't make my heart stop hurting and I can't stop crying. He warned me and I didn't listen. I just wanted to live in his mind for one second, learn more about him so I could be a better wife and give him whatever he needed, but I can't help him with this and it kills me. I can't take away these memories because they are burned into his brain and his soul. I've always known he lives an entirely different life when he's away from me, but this is almost too much to handle. I don't know if I'm strong enough to get him through this. I don't know if I'm *enough* to make him forget.

"Oh, Jesus. Fuck, Lucy. I'm sorry. I shouldn't have said any of that. What the hell is wrong with me?"

When my sobs break through the hand clamped over

my mouth, he suddenly comes back from whatever trance he was in. He moves towards me, sliding his legs around either side of my knees and wrapping his arms around my body. He cradles the back of my head and brings it down to his shoulder, smoothing my hair down my back as he rocks us back and forth.

"I shouldn't have asked. I'm so sorry I made you tell me. I'm so sorry you've had to go through that," I cry softly into his shoulder as he continues to slowly rock us from side to side.

I'm ashamed of myself for crying. I have nothing to cry about. When he's gone, doing all of these awful things to protect our country, I'm safe and content in my own little bubble on this island, surrounded by the ocean and family and friends.

"Don't, Lucy. Don't ever apologize for something like that. I'm going to be fine, just give me time, okay? Just keep loving me and being here, that's all I need."

We fall asleep in each other's arms and Fisher doesn't wake up again that night or any night for the next few months. I try to tell myself that everything is fine and he's getting better each day he's home, putting distance between himself and the war. For a while, it's an easy enough lie to believe. For an entire year, I have him all to myself, and we're so happy and settled that I actually believe he'll never leave me again.

Then he tells me that he *volunteered* to go back there for a third time.

"I don't understand, Fisher. Why? Why would you go back there?" I ask, trying not to let him know that this decision is killing me. I choke back the tears as he paces around the kitchen like a caged tiger. I should have known this was coming. Each time he sees something in the news about the war, he gets so anxious that he can't sit still.

"I have to go back, Lucy, I have to. I can't be here when my friends are over there fighting for everything I believe in and risking their lives," he explains.

Hearing him say that he can't be here breaks my heart. Why isn't our life together on this island enough for him? I love that he has this need to protect our country and our freedom, but at the same time, I hate it because it takes him away from me.

And sends him back just a little more broken every time.

After all the things he's been through, he asked to go back. I want to be angry, I want to scream and cry and beg him not to leave me again, but I can't do that. Deep in my heart, I'm still so very proud of him for fighting for our country. I admire him for doing something so scary and selfless, and the very idea that he would willingly return to that hellhole reminds me of how strong and amazing he is. It also makes me dread what will happen the *next* time he comes home, makes me fear which pieces of the man I love will be claimed by this war. I worry things will only get worse, and that scares the hell out of me.

"I just don't understand why you keep doing this to yourself. Why you keep putting yourself through this. What about us? What about *our* lives? We talked about starting a family, but how can we do that if you aren't here?" I ask him, hating the weakness in my voice.

"Jesus, Lucy! How can you even *think* about bringing children into this world right now? What kind of future would they have if this shit never ends?" he argues.

There's no use in trying to hold back the tears at this point. They fall down my cheeks and Fisher immediately comes over to me and pulls me into his arms.

"I'm sorry, baby. I didn't mean to yell," he tells me softly as he kisses the top of my head. "I just need you to understand how important this is to me. I can't stand the idea that my men, *my brothers*, are over there without me. They leave their families and they put their lives on hold to fight this war and I need to do the same. I HAVE to do the same. I love you, Lucy, but I need to do this. Please, tell me you understand."

I hold onto him as tightly as I can as we sway back and forth in the kitchen and I give him a silent nod. He loves me, we're building a life together and nothing else should matter. We're strong and we can make it through anything. We *will* make it through anything because Fisher has always promised me that he will find his way back to me. I believe him with every piece of my heart and I will support whatever decisions he makes because I have faith in him and in us. This is just a tiny bump in the long road of our lives together. We'll get over it and everything will be fine, I know it.

Chapter 2

Lucy

Present Day

Dear Fisher,

I guess this is it, huh? After almost fourteen years together, starting a life of our own on this island, five tours of duty and countless letters I've written you through it all, I finally go out to the mailbox and see something I've always dreamed of: an envelope with your handwriting on it. For one moment, I actually thought you'd changed your mind. That all the awful things you said to me were just your way of coping after everything you'd been through. I was still here, Fisher. I was still here, holding my breath, waiting for you to come back even though you told me you never would. You always said you'd find your way back to me. Out of all the lies you've told me, this one hurts the most.

Enclosed you will find the signed divorce papers, as requested. I hope you find what you're looking for. I'm sorry it wasn't me.

Lucy

I STARE AT the note in my hand, the creases that run through the words so worn from the number of times I've folded and unfolded this thing that I'm surprised the paper doesn't tear right in half. I can still see little smudges in the ink where my tears fell on the page as I wrote the note last year. I can remember that day like it was yesterday and the pain in my heart is still just as fresh as it was then, even though I've convinced myself that I'm fine and I'm happy and I've moved on.

I *am* fine.

I *am* happy.

I *have* moved on.

Dammit.

Looking around my teenage bedroom, complete with the same pearlescent wallpaper with tiny pink roses, white, four-poster canopy bed and plush rose-colored carpeting, I realize maybe that's not exactly the case. Moving back home after my divorce probably wasn't the best idea, but there was nowhere else for me to go and nothing else for me to do. I've worked at Butler House Inn since we moved to the island when I was a teenager and my parents took over running the family business. Butler House was my grandparents' legacy and my parents' nightmare all rolled into one. When both of my grandparents passed away the year I turned sixteen, my parents thought a fresh start in a new place was just the thing our family needed. They uprooted me from my quiet little life in the city right before my sophomore year of high school, moving me out to an island where I knew no one. Little did they know, my grandparents didn't leave Butler House in the best condition when they died. It took a lot of years and every penny in my parents' savings just to get it back into the black, and by that point, my parents had had enough. Butler House was situated on a prime piece of island real estate, so there were quite a few investors who came sniffing around at that time, offering to purchase the inn. Even though my parents were exhausted and at an age where they just wanted to retire and relax, they couldn't imagine handing over our family's legacy to a stranger.

I gave up my dreams of seeing the world to take online college business courses, and as soon as I turned twenty-one, Butler House Inn became mine. I let the man I gave my heart and soul to travel the world in my stead and I stayed behind to make sure he had someplace to come home to.

Now, I couldn't imagine living anywhere else. Well, I could definitely imagine moving out of my teenage bedroom in the inn's attached living quarters and finding a place of my own, but Butler House barely makes enough money to stay open as it is. Even right now, at the start summer peak season, some weeks I don't pull in enough money to give myself a paycheck.

Glancing back down at the note in my hand, I hastily fold it up and curse myself for reading it. I was too chicken-shit to send it when I wrote it and who knows why I've kept it all this time. I was hurt and angry and my heart felt like it was being ripped out of my chest. After I tore open the envelope that day and found the legal papers inside, I penned this note through the tears, wanting to hurt Fisher as much as he hurt me. In the end, I didn't enclose my note when I sent the signed divorce papers back. Even though what he did was the equivalent of shoving a knife right through my chest, I couldn't deliberately hurt him. That has always been my problem where Jefferson Fisher III was concerned. I would do anything for him, even if it meant sacrificing something of myself. I let him go not once, but five times when he had a duty to perform for this country, even though I wanted nothing more than to beg him not to leave. I supported his decision and praised his honor for being so selfless. I wrote to him every day and made sure he never had to worry about the island or the people he loved and promised him we would always be waiting here for him when he came home to us.

When he came back the first time, he was only a little bit different. More serious, more intense, not so quick to laugh like the smart-ass eighteen-year-old I'd first fallen in love with. I knew that war could change a man, and I loved him even more through those changes. He helped me with the inn when he was home and I kept the memories and the love we shared alive for the both of us while he was gone, protecting our country. I showered him with all of it when he returned, doing everything I could to erase the memories of the things he'd seen while he was away from me, away from our island, away from the physical proof of my love.

I naively thought all of that was enough. I never expected more and more of him to be chipped away each time he left me, but after he came home the last time, there was nothing left of the man I'd loved since I was sixteen years old. The boy who'd confidently kissed me for the first time at the base of Fisher's Lighthouse and asked me to marry him a few years later in the exact same spot by stating all the reasons he loved me no longer existed. In his place was an angry, depressed man who couldn't break free of his nightmares and blamed me for being stuck here where it seemed his darkness flourished instead of faded away.

We'd been together for fourteen years, but if you add up all of the time we *actually* spent together through those years, living together, working together, growing together side-by-side…it only equals a little over six years. A handful of months here and there in between basic training and five tours of duty over a fourteen-year span. When things began going downhill after his fifth tour, I started believing all of the hateful, hurtful shit that came out of his mouth. I'd even started to wonder if he'd ever really loved me. If you think about it, how in the hell is it possible to love someone who occupies the tiniest portion of your life? Did he even know me? I thought I knew him, but I also thought nothing could take down the strongest man I'd ever met.

Glancing down at the shoebox where I'd tossed the note, thirteen identical envelopes from Fisher's Bank and Trust stare back at me. I think about the savings account in my name at the bank that has received an automatic deposit on the last Friday of every month for the last thirteen months. I can still recall receiving the very first statement, which arrived during a time when I was still mourning the loss of my marriage. Looking back, I realize that it was my rage over the fact that the man I loved sought to placate me with money that pulled me out of the grief I was drowning in. Since then, I've tossed the unopened monthly statements into this box as soon as they arrive, so I have no idea what the balance is. Based on that initial deposit, however, I'm sure it's more than enough money to finish all of the repairs that need to be done around this place and probably even construct the addition I've been dreaming about for five years that would add two extra bedrooms and a game room for kids.

Smacking the lid down angrily on top of the shoebox, I shove it under my bed. I hate the mere idea of that damn savings account almost as much as I hate the man who opened it for me. He broke my heart and damaged a piece of my soul that will never heal and he thinks throwing his family's money into a savings account makes up for what he did. It may have pissed me off initially, but now it just hurts. Those bank statements are a constant reminder that he's still out there, living a life that doesn't include me. A better life. A peaceful life. A life that doesn't give him night terrors and pain. Just when I think I've gotten over the hurtful words he threw at me the last time I saw him, another statement comes in the mail and I have to live through that day all over again, realizing I wasn't good enough, wasn't strong enough, wasn't…*enough*. I wouldn't touch that money even if the bank foreclosed on Butler House and I was facing a life on the streets.

A doorbell rings through the intercom attached to the wall in my room, indicating there's someone at the front desk at the inn. Pushing myself off the bed, I quickly check my reflection in the mirror hanging above my dresser. My long, strawberry blonde hair is pulled up into a messy ponytail, and even though we're only a few weeks into summer, my skin is already lightly tanned from working outside. I like the healthy color it gives me and that it makes the dark circles under my eyes less noticeable, but it also brings out the stupid freckles on my nose and cheeks that I absolutely hate. Freckles scream cute and adorable, not sexy and hot. Taking in my reflection, I flick at the frayed edges of my cut-off jean shorts and attempt to smooth the wrinkles in my red, faded Lobster Bucket tank top that advertises my favorite restaurant on the island and is covered in dirt and sweat. Sexy and hot is going to have to wait for a day when I don't have clogged sinks in two guest bathrooms, a washing machine that won't drain, a freezer that won't cool below thirty degrees and fifteen new guests checking in this afternoon who will expect all of these things to be in working order.

The bell dings through the intercom again and I race out of my bedroom and down the stairs, my flip-flops slapping against the hardwood as I go. One of the downsides of living on Fisher Island is just that. Living on Fisher Island – a town named after the family of the man who broke my heart. Everywhere I turn, I have to see his name on business signs, street signs or beach signs. It also doesn't help that his grandfather, Trip Fisher, is the island's only handyman. Trip's parents founded this island and, while his father was a successful fisherman turned financier whose money helped establish many of the shops that still thrived on the island, Trip decided at an early age that he wanted nothing to do with the business side of things. He preferred getting his hands dirty and working side-by-side with the rest of the islanders who made this place their home. I smile to myself despite my earlier walk down memory lane as I stomp down the stairs. Trip is the only member of the Fisher family who ever truly embraced me and made me feel like I was worthy of the Fisher name. At eighty-three-years-old, he's still just as active and hard working as I imagine he was as a young man, and whenever I'm having a problem here at the inn, he drops everything he's doing to help me. It doesn't hurt that he's got the mouth of a trucker, flirts like a frat boy and never fails to make me laugh when I see him.

He made good time, considering I left him a message about all the problems that cropped up this morning only fifteen minutes ago. Even though each new issue I came across as I ran through my daily checklist while I drank my first cup of coffee made me want to scream in frustration, at least all this shit gave me something to keep my mind off of the *real* issue. There was one thing sure to push me over the edge, even more so than a few clogged drains, and the only reason I pulled that stupid shoebox out from under my bed when I haven't touched that thing in months, other than to throw the bank statements inside.

Everyone has been talking about today ever since Trip made the announcement at the town meeting two weeks ago. The events that took place thirteen months ago didn't just affect me, they affected everyone who lives here. We're a small, tightknit community and everyone knows everyone else's business, whether we want them to or not. When the prodigal son of the town's wealthiest family very loudly kicks his high school sweetheart and wife out of their home, goes on a drunken bender, trashes several business and gets into fist fights with more than a few men on Main Street, it's front page news. Literally. The story was on the front page of the Fisher Times even though the family owns the damn paper.

When Trip announced to the town that Fisher was coming home, the calm, cordial meeting that was supposed to be about zoning permits turned into complete anarchy. I got up and walked out without a word, and for two weeks, I tried not to think about today. I tried to keep myself busy at the inn and with the social life I was finally attempting to have. I refused to look at the indentation on the third finger of my left hand where a wedding ring used to wrap and sparkle against the morning rays of sun when I stretched in bed. I politely smiled when people in town stopped and asked me what I was going to do when *he* came back to the island. I went about my business, refusing to allow myself to fall down that stupid rabbit hole of sadness and depression.

I might not have been born here, but this is *my* island. I've made a name for myself, I have friends and family here and I've built a life here, such as it is. I've cleaned up the mess he left behind and I've moved on. As strong as I'd like to believe I've become, though, even I can admit it's not a good sign that the very thought of running into him sends chills running throughout my body. This isn't a huge island and, unfortunately, I have to shop at several of the businesses his family owns. It's only a matter of time before I have to see him again, and I hope that I'm strong enough not to allow his presence to ruin me once more. I won't let Fisher crack the walls I've spent so long and worked so hard at reconstructing. I don't know why he's coming back and I don't care. I have my own life now that has nothing to do with Jefferson Fisher, just like he wanted.

Pushing through the door connecting the living quarters to the inn, I stop short when I see the ass-end of a man on all fours, smacking his hammer against my floor right in front of the registration desk.

"Enjoying the view, pretty lady?"

Trip stops hammering and grins at me over his shoulder.

I shake my head and laugh as I walk into the room, holding out my hand to help him up from the floor, but he bats it away and grumbles at me.

"I'm not that fucking old. The day I need help getting up from the ground..." he trails off as he grunts and groans while he pushes himself to his feet. Just like his grandson, Trip Fisher stands well over six-feet. Between his full head of salt and pepper hair and the body he keeps in shape walking all over the island and performing manual labor, I'd know even without seeing old pictures that he was a very good looking man in his day.

"Why are you beating up my floor, Trip?" I ask as I lean forward and peck his cheek with a kiss.

"That board has been loose for weeks. It's a lawsuit waiting to happen when one of those yuppies comes in here and stumbles over it," he explains, shoving his hammer into his tool belt. "How you holding up, Lucy Girl?"

We haven't talked at all about the bombshell he dropped during the town meeting, even though he's tried countless times. I know he's worried about how I'm feeling about Fisher's return, but I still don't want to talk about it, especially with him. I love him like he's my own grandfather, but he was always our biggest supporter and was almost as heartbroken as I was after our marriage fell apart. No matter what I say, Trip will turn it around and try to play matchmaker.

"I'm fine, Trip. Just worried about all the crap around here that keeps falling apart. I've got fifteen new vacationers coming in this afternoon and I'd like them to be able to use their sinks."

His brown eyes narrow as he looks me up and down. "Fine, my ass. When was the last time you ate? Get out of here and go up to the Lobster Bucket and tell Carl to make you a lobster roll. Scratch that, make it two and put it on my tab. Don't come back until your belly is full. I'll have your sinks working by then and I'll keep an eye out if anyone stops by."

I start to argue, thinking about the laundry that isn't going to wash itself, but quickly realize there's no sense in going to battle with Trip Fisher. It's not like I can do the laundry with a busted machine that won't drain, anyway. It's not very often that I get a chance to get away from the inn and take some time for myself, so I grab the offer and run with it. With another kiss to Trip's cheek, I grab my purse from behind the counter and make a quick call to my best friend, Ellie. I need to forget about the man who forced me out of our home and his life over a year ago and concentrate on my date tonight. I'm fine, I'm happy and I've moved on. Ellie will help me keep my mind off of the past and focus my future. Or, she'll just get me drunk. Either way, I refuse to spend the rest of the day worrying about running into Fisher.

Chapter 3

Lucy

February 25, 2014

P ULLING THE PAN of lasagna out of the oven, I turn to walk it over to the counter and stop in the middle of the room. The pan slips from my hands and crashes to the floor as my eyes cloud with tears while I stare at the open kitchen door.

"You're home," I choke through my tears.

He was gone for sixteen months, five days and twelve hours this time. He was able to call every couple of weeks, but sometimes hearing his voice made things harder, driving home the fact that I would have to go to bed alone and wake up without him beside me.

Fisher doesn't move from the doorway. He's still wearing his Marine BDU's and his camouflage backpack is slung over one shoulder. I'm not used to seeing him like this. He never lets me see him off, always saying good-bye the night before in civilian clothes and stopping at a hotel halfway home to change, clean up and shave before he sees me again. He jokes that he likes to get the "stink of war" off of him before he touches me again, even though I've assured him that I don't care about any of that, just as long as he comes home.

I take in every inch of his six-foot-four frame, from

the new muscles he seemed to have developed while he was gone to the beard that covers his cheeks and chin. Between the letters that I write to him when he's away and the news about the war I have to constantly see on TV, not a day goes by that I'm not reminded of the fact that I'm a military wife and my man is a Marine. I'm so very proud to call myself *his*, but fear and worry are my constant companions. Every time the phone rings or I hear a knock at the door, there's that niggle of uncertainty, but nothing hits home harder than seeing Fisher standing here in front of me, fresh from a flight from Kuwait with desert sand still clinging to his black hiking boots. The sight of the man I love looking like he just stepped off of the battlefield in the middle of this bright, cheery, yellow kitchen makes me want to drop to my knees and sob, knowing that I could have lost him. This could have been the time that military personnel stood in my kitchen doorway instead of him.

I need to touch him and reassure myself that he's real, he's here and he made it back to me in one piece. As my feet start to move in his direction, he drops his pack from his shoulder and charges across the room to me. He steps over the lasagna mess, wraps his hands around my upper arms and walks me backwards until my ass hits the wall next to the fridge. I try to shake my arms out of his grasp so I can run my hands over his face, slide my fingers through his hair and kiss the lips I've missed for far too long, but he quickly spins me around, pressing his body against my back and pushing me more firmly into the cold wall.

I should be afraid of the manic look I saw in his eyes when he charged across the room or worried that he hasn't spoken a single word. Something about this is extremely different than all of his other homecomings, and I should probably be a little wary of this man who's not behaving at all like my Fisher.

But I'm not.

"I missed you so much," I whisper as his hands roughly yank my yoga pants and underwear down my thighs.

I'm not afraid, I'm turned on, more than I ever have been in my entire life. Aside from the sixteen months without sex, there's something about this that excites me and makes me wet. I want whatever he's going to give me and I want it now.

I hear the rustle of his pants being pushed down and I know I should try to speak again, try to make my voice louder so he'll hear me, slow down, let me touch him and calm whatever storm I feel is brewing in this kitchen right now, but I don't want to. I want the thunder and lightning, I want the crash of the storm and I want whatever destruction it will leave behind.

I don't have time to prepare or even think of something else to say before the shock of him slamming inside of me steals the breath from my lungs. He clutches onto my hips and I brace my hands against the wall as he pounds into me without a word or a sound. I was wet for him as soon as he stalked across the room to me, but I still feel a sting of pain after having gone so long without him inside of me. It's delicious and perfect. The pain reminds me that he's here, he's alive and he's home. He's inside of me where I've needed him for sixteen long months and I never want him to stop.

He thrusts into me roughly and his hips slam against my ass each time. My body smacks into the wall with each hard drive of his cock inside of me, and I can already feel bruises forming on my hips from how hard he's holding onto me so he can move faster, go deeper, fill me completely.

His hot breath against the back of my neck is something I've dreamt about for sixteen months, something as familiar to me as my own reflection. Fisher feels the same and smells the same, but nothing about what is happening right now is anything like him. He's different every time he comes back from the war, but this is like nothing he's ever done before. He always talks to me when he gets home, says my name over and over, tells me how much he loves me and how much he missed me. He holds me and touches me lovingly and I always feel cherished. This time, I feel wanted. I feel craved and I feel *needed*. He's taking me like an animal and I want more. I want it harder, I want it faster, I want to know without a shadow of a doubt that he's been dreaming about this, dreaming about *me* while he's been gone and needing me as much as I need him.

I arch my back and tilt my hips to meet each of his thrusts and pull him in deeper. I remove one of my hands from the wall and push it between my legs, sliding my fingers around where we're joined and bringing the wetness up to circle around my clit. Bracing my feet against the floor so I don't fall to the ground with the force of him fucking me, I rub my clit with the tips of my fingers. I want to moan and scream at how good it feels, but my breath gets caught in my throat each time he slams into me. I wish I could turn around and see him. He must look like a wild beast rutting against me, and as crude as that sounds, that knowledge makes my sex throb and causes my orgasm to explode out of me in a rush of heat and pleasure. I come against my fingers with my face pressed against the wall while Fisher fucks the hell out of me. It's not even fucking at this point, it's *taking*. He's taking me, he's owning me and he's punishing me with his body and his cock. I want the punishment. I want the pain. I want to hurt for all the months I forced myself to shut down and turn off my emotions so I wouldn't go crazy with worry for him. I want to wake up tomorrow with pain between my thighs reminding me with every step I take that he kept his promise and he found his way back to me.

He's unrelenting as he fucks me, never slowing down, never easing up. He's racing to the finish line and I can feel the sweat dripping down his face and onto my shoulder. He slams into me roughly one last time before holding himself still while he comes inside of me.

WE'VE BARELY SPOKEN two words to each other in a

month. I look at my husband across the dinner table and I feel like I'm looking at a stranger. This is my husband, my love, my Fisher. He's the man who leaves me every once in a while, but always, *always* comes home to me. He loves me, he takes care of me and he does everything in his power to make me smile.

Except lately.

The last four weeks have been filled with one-word answers and grunts when I ask him a question. We've haven't had sex since that night in the kitchen and every time I've tried to touch him, he gets up and leaves the room. I feel like I did something wrong, but I have no idea what it could be. I need to hear his voice, I need to know he's still the same man who named all of my freckles, even though I hated it, and sings *Lucy in the Sky with Diamonds* in a loud, off key voice whenever he says my name. I won't pretend to know what kind of demons he's trying to chase away, and I won't pretend to understand what's going on in his mind. All I can do is let him know that I'm here and I'm not going anywhere.

I don't say anything when I see him grab a beer from the fridge or pour a glass of whiskey from the cabinet above the dishes. It's been happening more frequently during the day, but who am I to say something to him about it? He goes off to war, fights for our country and then he comes home to me and works his ass off around the inn. I can't pick a fight with him just to get a reaction out of him, even though I want to. I want to see something spark behind his eyes instead of the cold, dead stare he seems to always have lately. I want to smack him across the face, push him so hard in the chest he stumbles. Something, ANYTHING to get some kind of emotion out of him. I want the man back who took me in the kitchen the night he came home. The man who needed me so much he couldn't even say one word before he buried himself inside of me.

His nightmares have been getting worse lately. Almost every night, he wakes up covered in sweat and screaming. He's always had bad dreams when he gets home from a tour and he's always let me hold him, run my hands through his hair and do whatever I could to calm him until he was able to go back to sleep, telling me I was the only thing that could make it all go away. Now, he jumps out of bed and goes to the spare bedroom, slamming and locking the door behind him. I've never felt so alone, even when he was halfway across the world. I'm living in this house with my husband and I get to see him every day, but it feels like I'm living with a ghost. He's been honorably discharged due to permanent nerve damage from some shrapnel he took to the shoulder during this last deployment, an injury I didn't find out about until after he came home. I'll never forget the fear that clawed at my throat seeing those scars on his back, realizing how very close I'd come to losing him. Even then, when I'd broken down in tears and raged at my husband for refusing to allow his commanding officer to contact me when he'd been injured, Fisher showed absolutely no reaction. The man who couldn't stand to see me cry was totally and completely blank, walking calmly out of our home as I sobbed.

It was after a military doctor declared the damage to his nerves too severe to resume his duties that Fisher's drinking started to escalate. I want to be happy that he'll never be taken from me again and he'll never voluntarily leave me for a year, but it's obvious he's not happy about never going back to combat again. He watches the news every hour of the day, waiting for information on the war and the friends he left behind and curses his shoulder for messing up his chance of going back and helping them. Doesn't he understand that his life and his mental health aren't worth it? Leaving our life together isn't worth it? Every time I get the nerve to tell him that I'm happy he'll never leave again, I stop myself at the last minute. Being a Marine was his life, this war was something he believed in and protecting this country was what he'd wanted to do from the first time I met him. I can't be happy about him losing something that is such a huge part of him. I just want him to talk to me, to let me take away some of his demons, but I don't know how anymore. I don't know how because he won't let me in. Every time he moves into the spare bedroom and slams the door, I feel like he's slamming a door to his heart and I no longer have a key that opens it anymore.

Chapter 4

Fisher

I DON'T CARE if you don't drink anymore, man, you still have to come up to Barney's and say hi to everyone," Bobby argues as he watches me run a piece of sand paper over the arm of a rocking chair I started working on this morning. My shoulder is killing me, but working with wood is one of the few things in my life right now that brings me pleasure. Since the shrapnel from an IED damaged the nerves in my shoulder on my last deployment, I've had to limit the time I spend in my makeshift workshop. If I work for more than a few hours at a time, the pinch in my shoulder either travels down my arm and hurts like a bitch or makes me lose all feeling in my hand. Numbness plus power tools is never a good equation.

Tossing down the sandpaper, I roll my shoulder and rub the kinks out, cursing myself for not taking a break earlier. As I continue to stretch out the tight muscles, I head up the stairs of Trip's house and Bobby follows. When I decided it was time to come home, I naturally assumed I'd just go back to the house Lucy and I shared that's been sitting empty for over a year. A small, yellow cottage with white trim in a quiet part of the island that overlooked the ocean and provided us with our own, small private beach, I surprised Lucy with it when I came home from my second tour, right before we got married. Surrounded by trees and flowers in the front to provide privacy and nothing but a view of the ocean and a boardwalk leading down to our beach in the back, it was the perfect home for the two of us to start our lives.

I walked into the place last night when I arrived on the last ferry to the island, nearly losing my dinner as I looked around at the empty shell of a home that had been wiped clean of every trace of her. I knew Bobby had cleaned out the house, putting my furniture and extra clothes in storage, but I wasn't prepared to walk in and see our house devoid of my Lucy. Everything that made this place a home and every memory of the life we'd built together was no longer there. It was like she never even existed, like the eight years we spent living under that roof never happened and I couldn't stand being in that place for one more second. I backed out of the house, locked the door behind me and went running to my grandfather's house like a fucking pussy. He told me I could stay for however long I needed, as long as I helped him out with odd jobs around the island when I had time.

I wipe my hands on my jeans and turn to face my best friend once we get up to the kitchen. It's kind of surprising that we're still friends after all these years and all the shit that's happened in between. I practically ditched him for Lucy in high school and I was so caught up in her and my life with the Marines that it didn't leave much room for anything or anyone else, but Bobby was always here, on the island, waiting for me whenever I needed him. He was the best man in my wedding, kept an eye on my grandfather and Lucy whenever I was out of the country and he knocked me on my ass last year when I lost my shit all over the town, dragging my passed-out body two blocks to the ferry and then right up to the front doors of the VA's rehab facility.

"Look, we're just going up there to throw some darts and unwind. It's Friday night during peak season, man. Do you have any idea how many hot, barely legal chicks will be walking around town looking for a couple of locals to show them a good time?" Bobby asks with a laugh. "It will be like shooting fish in a barrel."

"You know that's not why I came back here," I argue, wanting nothing more than to go back downstairs and continue with the piece I was working on. My woodworking started off as a hobby when I was young and my grandfather first taught me how to whittle, carving intricate designs out of spare pieces he had lying around. When I mastered that skill, he taught me how to use a table saw and measure and cut wood. While he was busy working on window frames or crown molding and I got bored with whittling, I would take those spare pieces of wood and start hammering them together. Pretty soon, I'd built my first rocking chair. It was a rickety piece of shit that probably wouldn't hold a kitten without falling apart, but it made me feel good to create something from scratch. After that, I checked out every book in the library I could find on building wood furniture and taught myself how to do it right. It wasn't too long before people on the island saw my designs and started asking me to make things for them. I made everything out of old pieces of wood, adding my own artistic designs and carvings to all of them. People ordered everything from kitchen tables and rocking chairs to king sized beds and bookcases. It turned into a pretty lucrative business and kept me plenty busy when I was back on the island in between deployments.

"I know, I know, you came back to get your woman and all that shit. At least be my wingman. Can you do that for me?" Bobby begs.

"Fine. One game of darts and them I'm out of there. I don't think I can handle that much staring and finger pointing from all the fucking townies," I tell him as I wash the wood dust off of my hands at the sink.

Bobby sighs as he tosses me a towel. "They're a bunch of busybody fucks who have nothing better to do with their time. Give it a few days and everything will go back to normal. It's kind of a big deal, you being back here and all. You didn't exactly leave the island quietly, you know."

He doesn't have to remind me. Unfortunately, I wasn't one of those drunks who could do stupid shit and then pass out and forget it all. I could remember with perfect clarity every word I screamed as I walked through the town, every local I'd picked a fight with and every window I'd thrown a rock or a chair through. I knew it was wrong when I was doing it, but there was nothing I could do to stop it. I was so lost in my own mind, not able to tell if I was walking down Main Street or walking into the middle of an ambush in Afghanistan, that everyone looked like the enemy to me. Every terrifying thing I'd ever seen or done flashed through my mind and I didn't care about anything but lashing out at anyone who came in contact with me. I hated myself, I hated my life and I hated what I'd become and I wanted everyone to suffer that agony right along with me.

"I knew coming back here would be hard, but Jesus. I stopped by Sal's Diner this morning to grab a cup of coffee and as soon as he saw me, he ran into the kitchen and refused to come back out. That guy taught me how to ride a bike and bought me my first case of beer when I turned twenty-one," I tell Bobby.

"Well, you did punch Sal in the gut and tell him you hoped he fucking died like the dog he was," Bobby adds.

I wince as I finish drying my hands and toss the towel on the counter. I had been in the throes of one of the worst flashbacks of my life when that happened. To me, Sal looked like a fanatic jihadi holding a gun to my head instead of the owner of the town diner with a spatula in his hand. I had a lot of fucking apologizing to do before anyone in this town would trust me again.

"It will be fine, I promise. Two games of darts and then you can go home," Bobby says with a smile.

"I thought I said one game."

Bobby turns and heads for the front door.

"That's what I said. Three games of darts and then you can go home."

THIS WAS A bad idea. A really, really bad idea. Walking into Barney's was like something out of a fucking movie where the jukebox screeches to a halt in the middle of a song and the entire place turns and looks at you in one big wave of prying eyes. Under normal circumstances, Barney's is never crowded, even during the summer season when the tourists are out in full force. A little ways from the edge of town, Barney's is a bit off the beaten path. A building that is longer than it is tall, the front of the establishment still has all of the original cedar wood planking. A huge awning runs down the entire length of the building so people can stand outside and shoot the shit or have a smoke. With its 1950's décor and a bar that only serves beer, Jim, Jack, Johnny Red and Jose, it's a favorite for the locals, who prefer it to spots that cater to young partiers looking for fruity drinks with umbrellas and that techno shit music piped through a sound system so they can dance. The only music you're going to find at Barney's is whatever is on the jukebox, also from the 50's and 60's, and the only dancing done around here is when someone presses E14 and Patsy Cline's "I Fall to Pieces" blasts through the tinny speakers. If Buster and Sylvia Crawford have had too much to drink (which is every time they're in here), Buster always asks Sylvia to dance, and when you put two drunk eighty-somethings who have more metal in their hips and knees than a steel manufacturing plant together, dancing in the middle of a crowd of tables, people always watch. Mostly to see if Buster will grab Sylvia's ass or trip over a chair.

I've never seen Barney's this packed and it's not even full of tourists. Word must have traveled pretty fast that I was going to be here and everyone with two working legs came out to see if anything exciting would happen in this otherwise boring town.

Located fifteen miles off the coast of South Carolina, in the middle of the Atlantic Ocean, Fisher's Island was purchased by my great-grandfather in 1902. At that time, the island was just a place for boats to wander when they were lost getting back to the mainland, but my great-grandfather saw potential and used what little money he had left after buying the island to build it into a fishing village that caught and harvested seafood for the surrounding coastlines. It wasn't long before he made enough money to turn this place into a tourist attraction with restaurants, inns, parks, public beaches and a ferry system to move people back and forth. We have one elementary school, one high school, one bank and a population of 3,044 at last count. My father, Jefferson Fisher Jr., owns half of the businesses on this island and is jokingly referred to as King Fisher. I'm sure it's eating him alive that I've come back to town and I'm sure he's going to hear all about how I showed my face in public tonight. The fact that I love nothing more than pissing my father off is the only thing giving me the strength to continue moving through the bar when everyone is whispering and pointing at me.

"DON'T WORRY! HE PROMISES NOT TO PUNCH ANYONE IN THE FACE TONIGHT!" Bobby yells to the crowded bar, lifting both of his hands up in surrender.

Everyone shrugs and goes back to their drinks and conversations with just a few stragglers glancing at me nervously as we make our way to the back of the bar where the dart boards and pool tables are set up.

"Gee, thanks for putting everyone at ease and making me feel at home," I grumble.

"I aim to please, my friend. I'm going to grab a beer. What's that sissy shit you drink now?" he asks.

"San Pellegrino with a slice of lime, asshole," I remind him.

He claps me on the back before heading off to the bar. It really *is* some sissy shit, but drinking it makes me feel a little more comfortable when I'm around people consuming alcohol. It looks like a glass of vodka and I don't have to deal with people asking me why I'm not drinking or any other multitude of questions that will eventually lead to me having to explain that I'm a recovering alcoholic with severe PTSD who went a little batshit crazy a year ago and fucked up my entire life.

While Bobby is ordering the drinks, I say hello to a few guys from high school that don't seem to be cowering, afraid that I'm going to attack at any moment. When Bobby comes back, we start a game and shoot the shit for about an hour. Even though I dreaded everything about coming here tonight, it feels good to be in this place, surrounded by the people I grew up with and doing something normal. For the last year of my life, every waking moment was spent talking to counselors, dealing with my issues and rehashing the things I'd experienced overseas that fractured my brain and turned me into a monster. This is a step in the right direction, coming here. I have a long way to go to prove to these people that I'm not that man anymore. Maybe I'm not fully healed, maybe I'll always have nightmares and regrets, but I can't keep living in the past and I *am* a different person than I was a year ago. I can't ignore things and hope they'll eventually go away. I did that with Lucy and look where that got me.

"Damn, she looks better every time I see her. Who the hell is that lucky fuck that convinced her to go out? I've been trying to tap that for months and all I got is the cold shoulder."

Eric, a web designer and tourist from last season who cashed in an inheritance and bought a cottage on the beach and became a transplant, stares at someone behind me. Eric's arrival came after my departure, so luckily I didn't have to deal with any weird stares or fear from him. Bobby gave him the gist of the story when he noticed how everyone was gawking at me, and he just shrugged and said, "Whatever. Everyone loses their shit now and then. Who wants to play some darts?"

I decided right away I liked Eric, but as I turn around to see who the hell he's making a fuss over, I realize it's probably a good thing it wasn't my turn and I don't currently have a sharp object in my hand.

Perched on the edge of a stool in the middle of the

bar is my Lucy. She's curled her long hair in soft waves that frame her beautiful face and my heart cracks in half. She only curls her hair for special occasions. She curled it for our wedding, for our first anniversary, for four homecomings and now, she's sitting at a table with another man with her hair fucking curled. Anger and jealousy simmers below the surface as I stand here staring at her like a schmuck while she rests her elbows on the table in front of her and leans closer to that asshole. He kisses her cheek and whispers something in her ear that makes her scrunch up her nose and laugh in that God-damn adorable way that I love so much.

"Deep breaths, man. In with the good, out with the bad," Bobby coaches as he comes up to stand next to me.

"What in the fuck is happening right now?" I growl through clenched teeth.

Bobby lets out a loud, over-exaggerated sigh as he takes a sip of his beer and then points the bottle in Lucy's direction.

"Allow me to introduce you to Lucy. Your EX-wife. You know, the one you divorced and then walked away from a year ago? Looks to me like she's on a date. And since she's DIVORCED and all that, I'm pretty sure she's free to go on said date," Bobby states sarcastically.

Refusing to take my eyes off of the woman across the room, the one I walked through fire for just to make myself whole again so I could come back to her, I reach over and grab onto the front of Bobby's shirt and pull him into my line of sight.

"You knew about this when you told me it was high

time for me to come back here, didn't you?"

Even though I planned on coming back as soon as I started healing and realized I could live a normal life if I wanted to, the phone call from Bobby urging me to do it soon because it was "time" was enough to get my ass in gear and start the process of getting the okay from my counselors to go back into the real world.

Bobby just shrugs, taking another sip of his beer and ignoring the furious clutch of my hand on his shirt and the daggers I keep shooting his way in between glances over at Lucy and her fucking "date".

"Dude, you've lived on this island all your life. People can't take a shit without their next-door neighbor knowing what size and color it is. Do you really think Lucy would be able to start dating someone and the whole island wouldn't know about it five seconds after it happened?"

I tear my eyes away from Lucy when I see her rest her hand on top of that douchebag's she's sharing a table with.

"I thought you said she was 'on' a date, not 'dating.' Which is it? Is she on a date or is she dating him? There's a big difference between those two things, so pick your words wisely," I tell Bobby, trying not to let my voice rise to shout level, even though I'm about two seconds away from screaming my fucking head off.

Bobby calmly removes my hand from his shirt and takes a step back, crossing his arms in front of him. "His name is Stanford and he works for your father at the main branch of the bank on the mainland. Your father hired him to do some auditing work for a few of the businesses and Trip asked him to take a look at Butler House's books while he was here. He asked Lucy out a month ago and she said yes. They go out every time he's on the island, which is pretty fucking often, if you ask me," Bobby rambles. "And really, what kind of a fucking name is *Stanford*? It's a school, not a dude. Fucking pussy."

Bobby keeps complaining about that asshole's name, but I tune him out, staring at Lucy across the room and wishing I could hate her. She moved on. She wasn't supposed to move on. She was supposed to love ME forever, be with ME forever. She's even more beautiful than every memory or photo I have of her. In a light blue wrap-around dress, I can see every curve of her body and the color of the dress highlights her summer tan, showcasing the freckles she always tries to hide with make-up. She crosses her slim legs to the side of the table and my hands itch to run my palms up the smooth skin of them and feel them wrapping around my waist. I miss her smell and her laugh and her touch so much that I want to drop down on my knees in the middle of this fucking bar and sob like a baby.

Of course she moved on. Of course she stopped loving me. I looked her right in the eye and told her didn't deserve me and that she was weak and pathetic for sticking around, waiting for me as long as she had. I broke her and I hurt her in the worst imaginable way and then I walked out. I never deserved *her* and she should have always known that, always felt that, always believed that. I just want her to be happy. I want her to smile easily and laugh often. I see her doing it with that fuckwad across the bar, but I don't care. I know it's selfish and I know it's weak, but I don't fucking care. If I were a better man I would walk away, leave this island and never look back. I would let her have this happiness that she deserves even if it killed everything inside of me.

Too bad I'm not a better man. It should be *me*. It was always me and it's still going to be me, dammit.

With Bobby calling my name and telling me not to do anything stupid, I clutch my drink in my hand to keep me from throwing any punches and make my way across the room to MY Lucy.

Chapter 5

Lucy

April 8, 2014 - 1:45 PM

"FISHER, PLEASE, DON'T do this!" I beg through my tears as I stand in the doorway of our bedroom with my arms wrapped around my waist and watch him stalk around the room.

He yanks my clothes from the hangers in the closet and rips them out of the drawers of my dresser, shoving everything into the two open suitcases he has lying on top of the bed.

For two months he's barely said more than a few words to me and now he's done a complete one-eighty, saying more than I ever wanted to hear.

"We're done. This is over. I'm packing your shit and you're leaving!" he barks, grabbing my books and reading glasses off the nightstand and tossing them on top of the clothes.

I race across the room and grab onto his arm, determined to make him see reason, but he jerks out of my grasp and goes back to the closet, snatching up my shoes and piling them in his arms.

"Will you stop and just talk to me?" I yell, coming up behind him and reaching for the shoes in his hand.

He side-steps me, never even glancing in my direction.

"There's nothing to talk about. It's perfectly clear what's going on here. Everything is fucked up, don't you get that? It's ruined, all of it is ruined and you need to fucking leave!" he yells as he slams the armful of shoes into the suitcase.

My body shakes with fear and the sobs that I'm trying so hard to contain. I've done everything I could. I've tried talking, I've tried ignoring things, I've tried reading books and speaking to other wives whose husbands have been deployed and nothing has worked. No suggestion was good enough and nothing I've done has broken through whatever walls Fisher has put up in his mind to keep me out. I made the mistake of casually suggesting over breakfast that maybe it was time for him to talk to a counselor and that's when my world came to a screeching halt.

"It's not ruined, Fisher, it's just a little broken," I whisper through my tears. "After all these years, after everything we've been through together, you can't just shut me out. I only want to help you, I want to see you smile and laugh again, I want to make you happy."

He laughs cynically, finally turning to face me. He crosses his arms over his chest and stares at me. The look in his eyes makes my skin crawl. I don't recognize this man scowling at me with so much animosity and hatred.

"You can't help me and honestly, I think it's pretty pathetic that you keep trying. Jesus, you really need to get a life. You've spent how many years now, sitting on this shitty island just waiting around for me? All your life, just sitting here like a good little girl, waiting and waiting while life passed you by."

My lip trembles with the tears I'm trying to hold back. I want to scream and argue with him, but a part of me knows that he's right. I *have* just sat around here, waiting for Fisher. My life has been spent waiting for this man to come back to me. I know I should just walk away and give him time to calm down. He's been drinking and I know on top of the nightmares and the memories that always haunt him, the alcohol is only making things worse. I should step back and let him decompress, but I can't. I've never been able to walk away from him, and there's no way I can do it now when he's broken and hurting. Regardless of what he says, I know he needs me. He's always told me I'm the only one who can take it all away when he's at his lowest. He's lower than low right now and I refuse to leave him, even though he's doing everything in his power to make that happen.

"You don't mean that," I mumble, worrying at the hard look in his eyes that maybe I'm wrong. Maybe this time he really does mean all the nasty things he's saying.

He laughs cruelly, dropping his arms to his sides and stalking across the room towards me. I back away from him, stopping only when I feel the bedroom wall behind me. I'm not afraid of Fisher, I could *never* be afraid of Fisher, but this isn't Fisher right now. This is a stranger, a man intent on breaking my heart in the worst possible way.

"I've seen things you wouldn't believe and experienced things you couldn't even imagine while you were rotting away on this Godforsaken island, wasting your time writing me all those fucking letters, week after week. All those sad, pathetic letters about how you missed me, you needed me, you loved me."

He laughs again and shakes his head like he pities me. I hate him for bringing up those letters. Years and years worth of letters that I never stopped writing and sending to him, even when the internet and email would have made things easier. I took the time to write him *real* letters so he could get a piece of home to touch and hold onto when he was so far away. Week after week, year after year, I poured my heart and soul into those letters. When I asked him why he never wrote me back, he told me that he didn't have time, but that I shouldn't stop writing them because they gave him the strength to do his job and come home to me.

"Do you want to know why I never wrote you?" he asks, almost like he's looking right through my eyes and into my soul, knowing exactly what I was thinking. "It wasn't because I didn't have time. Plenty of guys over there write to their wives or their girlfriends. The problem was, I just didn't want to."

I shake my head back and forth and swipe angrily at the tears falling steadily down my cheeks.

"Stop it. Just stop it. I know what you're doing. You're trying to be cruel to get me to walk away and it's not going to work. You can say whatever you want, throw whatever hurtful words at me you think will hit the right mark to make me hate you, but it's not going to work."

Pushing myself off of the wall, I press my palms to

either side of his face and force his head down so he's looking me in the eyes.

"You and me against the world, Fisher. It's *always* been you and me, and it always will be. I shouldn't have brought up counseling out of the blue like I did. Whatever you want to do, however you need me to help, I will do it. I will always do anything for you. Let's just calm down and forget about this for right now. We can go for a walk to the lighthouse, we can do whatever you want. We don't have to talk about this right now."

I don't want to come right out and say that we shouldn't do this when he's been drinking, but it's definitely implied. He's so quick to anger lately and I never know what's going to set him off. All I can do is apologize afterwards and pray that he'll get better, that it won't always be like this and eventually he WILL get better.

Fisher brings his hands up and rests them on top of both of mine against his cheeks. He leans forward and presses his forehead against mine and I'm able to take a breath for the first time since I came up to the bedroom and saw him packing my things.

I move my hands from his face to the hem of his shirt, sliding my palms underneath the material to feel the hard, warm skin of his abs and chest. Kissing my way down the side of his face, I lightly nip at the skin of his neck, doing whatever I can to bring him back to me, to see me, to *feel* me. I miss making love to him. I miss the closeness we always share when we connect on that level. All of our problems go away and nothing matters but the two of us. Maybe it's wrong to try and seduce him now, but I'm out of ideas on how to break through to him. My hands slide over his chest underneath his shirt and my thumbs graze over his nipples as I move my body closer to him.

I should have known better than to let my guard down.

"Oh, Lucy. Sweet, innocent, pathetic Lucy. It's really cute how you honestly think you've been the only one all these years. You were a virgin when we met and sorry, but I prefer a woman with a little more experience to get me through the nights away from home."

I jerk my hands out from under his shirt, take a step back and stare at him in shock and horror. I've always, ALWAYS lived with the insecurities that I've never been enough for him physically *and* sexually, but he's never made me feel like I was anything but absolutely perfect for him. Is he honestly telling me right now that he hasn't been faithful? That some other woman warmed his bed and gave him things I couldn't give while he was away from me? Sure, he had a lot more experience than I did when we met and I hated it. He's right, I was a virgin, but he helped me lose some of my insecurities by teaching me all the ways to please him and make things feel good for myself. Over the years, we learned each other's bodies and our sex life has always been good, but I never quite learned how to ask for more, never really understood what *more* meant. It wasn't until that night in the kitchen two months ago, the night when he took me with all-consuming passion, that I realized what I truly needed from him. Maybe that's what he's always wanted and he hated that I didn't give it to him. I *would* have given it to him. I *wanted* to give it to him more than he even knows, and it kills me to think that he shared that with another woman.

"Congratulations. You did it. You made me hate you," I tell him as the tears fall silently down my face and he goes back to the bed, closing the lid on the suitcases and zipping them shut.

"Took you long enough," he says with a sarcastic laugh. "Jesus, how much more shit were you going to put up with before you realized that? You just thought we could live happily ever after on this shithole island, grow old and die here? This place is eating me alive. Every time I come back here, I want to burn the entire fucking place down. It doesn't get better when I come home to you, it gets fucking worse. You and your positivity and always trying to 'fix' me. This is it, babe. What you see is what you get, and every time I have to come home it gets darker and darker and I hate this life more and more."

He lifts up the suitcases, walks them to the doorway next to me and tosses them out into the hallway.

"Get out so I can finally fucking breathe without you always trying to 'help' me. I don't want or need your help. You better be gone by the time I get back."

He walks past me and out the door, stepping over the suitcases as he goes. I hear his shoes pounding against the hardwood floor and then seconds later, the slamming of the front door.

I sink to my knees and then crumble to my side on

the carpet, curling my body into the tightest ball I can. If I make myself small enough, maybe it won't hurt as bad. Maybe I won't feel like my heart has been ripped from my chest and stomped to pieces. Maybe if I'm small enough, this won't feel like the biggest betrayal and most soul crushing moment of my entire life.

If I'm small enough, maybe I won't want to die from the enormity of the pain.

If I'm small enough, maybe I won't feel like such a failure.

Chapter 6

Lucy

Present Day

"YOU ARE SO beautiful, it takes my breath away," Stanford whispers in my ear after he places a kiss on my cheek.

I laugh uncomfortably and rest my hand on top of his on the table. It's been a long time since anyone called me beautiful, and I try my best to accept the compliment and not brush it off. I know I'm not classically beautiful. Contrary to what Trip said this morning, I'm not all skin and bones. I have curves and thighs that I hate, freckles on my face that piss me off and a nose that's too small for my features. I'm small and short and most of the time, people call me cute. Fisher used to always tell me I was adorable, that he wanted to put me in his pocket and carry me around with him everywhere. But when we were alone, naked in bed, he worshiped every part of my body. He was the only one who could get away with calling me beautiful and sexy and actually make me believe it.

Get it together, Lucy. You're on date with another man. Stop thinking about Fisher.

While Stanford tells me about his day clearing up accounts at Fisher's Bank and Trust, I take the time to study him. Six years older than me at nearly thirty-seven, with short blonde hair he keeps slicked back from his forehead, light blue eyes and a clean-shaven face, he's definitely a good-looking man. He's not the type of man I ever thought I'd be attracted to, but I also never thought I would be out in the dating world again, so none of that really matters. He always looks put-together, wearing clothing that probably costs more than the monthly upkeep fees on the inn and he never has a hair out of place, but he's also funny and treats me well. He's incredibly smart and a huge book nerd just like myself, even though my book preferences have been the cause of his raised eyebrows on more than one occasion. It's only been a little over a month, but I already feel like I've known him for much longer. He's easy to talk to and he always has great suggestions and ideas for things I can do at the inn to bring in more revenue and increase business. As I tick off all of his qualities in my head, I realize he's everything that Fisher isn't. Regardless of his family's wealth, Fisher is a blue-collar worker at heart. He likes to get dirty and he never cared if his clothes were name brand or from Target. He was a Marine through and through – intense, focused, direct, loyal…well, I guess not always loyal.

Thinking about my ex-husband is definitely not ap-propriate when I'm on a date with another man. A good man, a steady man, a man I feel like I already know would never throw words at me that were sure to cut me in half. It's been a damn year, why can't I just forget? A year where the only contact was via an envelope filled with divorce papers. Even after all the things he said to me, I still thought he might come back. He'd get better, he'd get help and he'd come back to me. Those divorce papers were the end of everything. Every dream, every hope and every idea I'd ever had about love.

I hate that everything on this island reminds me of him. Everywhere I go, everywhere I look, there's a memory of the two of us together. It doesn't help that I know he's close. He's in this town, breathing the same air as me, looking out at the same ocean and walking the same streets. Shoving those thoughts firmly from my mind, I flip Stanford's hand over and intertwine my fingers with his. He stops talking and leans closer to me.

"Is everything okay, Luce? You seem a little distracted tonight."

There it is, the one thing in the negative column for Stanford. I really hate that he calls me *Luce.* I know it's a common nickname for Lucy, but I feel like he's calling me *loose.* Every time he says it, I inwardly cringe. Seriously, though, if that's the only thing I don't like about him, I need to count myself lucky. I wet my lips with my tongue and I watch as he stares at the movement, his eyes narrowing as I glide my tongue across my bottom lip. It makes my body heat with excitement, knowing that he wants me. He's told me more than once, but seeing it is better than hearing it.

"I'm sorry, I'm just a little tired," I lie, answering his question distractedly as my thoughts continue to wander while he flags a waitress down and orders us drinks.

I really had no idea what I was doing the first night I went out with Stanford. Fisher had been my first everything. I didn't know the one thing about satisfying someone other than the man I'd married and, based on the last words he spoke to me, I didn't even do *that* well. I let all of those old, teenage insecurities blossom once again and I spent a year wallowing in misery, wondering what the hell was wrong with me. Then Stanford came along and swept me away with romance and sweet words, soft kisses and light touches, making me feel cherished and worthy of the affection he gives me. I like the way he makes me feel, even if something I can't quite put my finger on is missing. It's the reason I keep putting him off when he attempts to go beyond second base.

Stanford pulls his phone from his suit pocket when it starts to buzz with an incoming call. Turning away from me, he starts talking rapidly to someone about interest rates and refinancing. He chews on his bottom lip during a pause in the conversation and I can't help but stare at his mouth. I like kissing Stanford, I like feeling his hands on me, but I don't crave it. I don't dream about it when I'm away from him and I don't feel like I'm going to explode if I don't get him inside of me. Try as I might, I can't help but crave that feeling, the twinge of nerves coupled a touch of fear that you're about to do something unexpected and thrilling, elicit and a little dirty.

But I had that once.

And look how *that* turned out.

It went to shit and was I left feeling ashamed of who I was and the things I wanted.

So *pleasant* is my new normal.

This is what falling in love is supposed to feel like. It

should be easy to be with someone, as natural as breathing, and it should leave you content, exactly the way I feel with Stanford. We barely know each other, so I'm sure that the rest will come. Six weeks of dating really isn't that long when you think about it. Maybe it will just take time for the passion and butterflies to kick in. Hell, maybe I need to start being a little more forward with him and try my hand at making the first move.

Reaching across the table, I run the tips of my fingers over the top of his hand to try and get his attention. He turns his head and looks at me questioningly while I give him my best sultry smile.

"Do you need something?" he whispers, moving his hand to cover the mouthpiece.

"Just you," I tell him softly with a wink.

"What do you mean there isn't time to lock in that rate? I gave you that paperwork four days ago," Stanford argues into the phone, turning back away from me and ignoring my attempts at flirting.

Make that two things in the negative column.

When Stanford is working, he doesn't pay attention to anything around him, including me. It's a little hard to get used to after being married to a man who made me feel like the center of his world when he was home from a deployment…until the next time he'd volunteer to go back and I started to wonder if he loved his fellow Marines more than me.

I haven't told Stanford everything about Fisher. He knows the basics – that I was married to his boss' son and we got divorced. He knows I've been single for a year and he knows I had no intention of getting serious with *anyone*, least of all someone who didn't live here permanently on the island. I've been with one man my entire life, and I wasn't about to start having flings with vacationers. Who knows what kind of gossip he's heard around the island since he's been here? I haven't asked and he hasn't offered it up. I don't know where this thing will go with the two of us, but there's no way I could taint a new relationship right off the bat with my sob story. I let him think I'm just a single, shy island resident who lives a sheltered life and he goes along with it. I don't tell him that I still fantasize about my ex-husband and worry that I'll never find another man who can make my body feel the way he did. I don't admit that I think I'm damaged and will never be able to feel comfortable enough to let go and be the woman I've always wanted to be with someone else like I did with Fisher. I certainly don't tell him that I'm neither shy, nor sheltered when it comes to sex and that I'm afraid of the things I fantasize about, the things I want and the things I need.

Stanford finally ends the call, scooting his chair closer to mine and rubbing his hand up and down my arm as he smiles at me. He doesn't have any dimples, but that's just another checkmark in his favor. Women turn stupid for dimples and I'm not about to be a stupid woman ever again.

"How about we finish our drinks and then head back to the inn? I can build a fire, and hopefully all of the guests will be in bed by then so we can be alone."

It's time to stop being a wuss. I can't hold Stanford at

arms-length forever. I like kissing him and I enjoy him touching me. My body doesn't burn when he does it, but it's nice and I need a little nice in my life. Maybe sex doesn't need to be punishing, frantic and desperate all the time. Maybe soft and sweet and loving is normal. Looking at Stanford, I know he can quiet that part deep inside of me that screams for something more, something illicit and dangerous. I won't let myself even think the word "boring." Stanford is NOT boring. He's dependable and constant. I'm a thirty-year-old woman who owns her own business and I have an image to uphold in this small town. I need a man like Stanford to keep me grounded.

We finish off our drinks and Stanford comes around behind me to pull out my chair. He holds my hair off of my neck as I secure my wrap around my shoulders. As we turn towards the door and he holds his arm out for me to take, a voice from my dreams and my past resonates from behind us. A deep, raspy sound with a touch of a southern accent that never fails to make my legs weak and my stomach flop.

"Lucy In the sky with diamonds. Aren't you just a sight for sore eyes?"

Chapter 7

Lucy

April 8, 2014 - 9:12 PM

"YOU DON'T HAVE to do this, you know. He's not your responsibility anymore. Not after today. Not after the bullshit things he said to you."

I glance over at my best friend, Ellie, as we quickly walk through town to Barney's. As soon as I managed to pull myself up from the floor of our bedroom, I grabbed my suitcases and went right to Ellie's house. We became friends years ago when I went to my first support group meeting on the mainland for wives of deployed soldiers. She was the most vocal person in the room, always quick to help another wife out when they needed it, and she protected the people she cared about like a rabid pit-bull. I found out at my second meeting that she was a widow, losing her husband at the age of nineteen during his first deployment. It amazed me that, after everything she'd been through, she still took the time to go to those meetings and help other people. After a few visits to the island, I managed to convince her to move here permanently and help me out at the inn. She does all of the cooking for the guests, all of the website maintenance and anything else I ask her to do.

"He's sick, Ellie. That doesn't excuse the things he

said to me, I know that, but I can't just turn my back on him. We have too much history, too many years together for me to just give up."

She wraps her arm around my shoulder as we walk and pulls me against her in a quick hug. "You're too good a person, Lucy. I'm still going to kick Bobby's ass for calling you. He should have taken care of the situation himself."

Bobby called my cell phone in a panic fifteen minutes ago telling me Fisher was holed up at Barney's, drinking his weight in Jack Daniels. When the bartender cut him off an hour ago, Fisher started getting combative and belligerent. Bobby obviously had no idea about what happened earlier in the day or that I would be the last person Fisher wanted to see, so I couldn't blame him for calling me. He was worried about his best friend and couldn't get him to calm down. I'd always been the one to get through to Fisher, to calm his fears and ease his pain. He naturally assumed I could work my magic again.

"I'm not going to stay long. I'm just going to see if I can get him to leave Barney's and sleep it off," I tell her as we cross the street in front of the bar.

I don't tell her that everything inside of me is hoping that, as soon as he sees me, he'll apologize and take back the things he said earlier. I don't admit that I'm still holding onto hope that I didn't lose him completely.

Ellie pushes open the door to Barney's and holds it for me to enter. A country song is blasting on the jukebox and the air is filled with the usual smell of stale beer and old cigarette smoke. It's not very busy in here, but it still takes me a few seconds to find Fisher through the small crowds of people gathered around tables and walking back and forth to the bar. He's sitting on a stool at one of the tall tables and Bobby is in front of him. I can see Bobby throwing up his arms every few seconds while he speaks to him, and I can tell he's getting frustrated that Fisher most likely isn't listening to a word he says. Fisher's hair is a scattered mess on top of his head and I can just picture him running his hands through it all night while he sat here, trying to drown his misery. His face is flushed from the alcohol and his shirt is soaked through with sweat. My heart starts hurting all over again seeing him like this, so lost and unable to focus on Bobby's face as his body sways a little from side to side.

My feet stay rooted to the stained, dirty hardwood floor as I stand here, staring at the man I fell in love with at sixteen and who has held my heart in the palm of his hand ever since then. That heart is beating nervously in my chest and I'm surprised that it still functions. Maybe he didn't squeeze the life out of it earlier today. Maybe we can still make it. He'll look at me and he'll *see* me. The haze of alcohol and the demons trying to take over his mind will fade away and he'll remember. I just want him to remember everything good and amazing about the two of us. He'll remember and he'll feel horrible about the things he said to me, the lies he told me to push me away for good. Having had time to think it through, I realize it was all lies. I have to believe that or I won't be able to take another breath, move another inch or go on with this life without him.

He'll feel bad and he'll apologize and he'll finally realize he needs to get help. I don't want him to believe that I think he's damaged. I told him things were just broken and I truly believe that. Pieces fall apart, but they don't disintegrate. You can pick up those pieces and you can put them back together until everything is whole again. There might be a few cracks, but nothing is ever perfect. Anything that's worth living for, worth dying for, has a few cracks. I believe our cracks can hold and we can keep it all together. I can give him another chance to breathe some life back into the part of my body that feels like it only exists with him, only beats for him and only lives for him. I can do this. He's taught me how to be strong and how to be a fighter and I will fight for him until the day I die.

Bobby steps away from Fisher and his eyes catch mine across the room. He walks away from Fisher and makes his way up to Ellie and I.

"Thanks for coming, babe. I don't know what the fuck to do. He won't listen to me, he won't stop arguing with people and he's pretty much decided to drink himself into a coma," Bobby explains with a sigh.

"You should have just let him do it. Let him pass out in a pile of his own vomit and regret," Ellie states angrily.

"Pipe down, hardass," Bobby tells her. "He's my best friend and he's hurting. I know Lucy will be able to get through to him."

Ellie scoffs and shakes her head at him. "He kicked her out of the house this afternoon and told her he's been fucking around on her all this time. No one is going to be able to get through to that asshole right now."

Bobby's eyes go as wide as dinner plates and he runs a hand through his short, curly hair. "Jesus Christ, Lucy. Fuck. I'm so sorry. You know it's all bullshit, right? He's going through some shit right now. He would never, ever do that to you. He loves you more than anything."

I nod, hoping to God he's right. "I know. It's just…this is really hard, Bobby. It's hard to see him like this when I don't know how to help him. I brought up therapy this morning and he completely lost it. I don't think he's going to want to see me right now."

Bobby shakes his head in denial, resting both of his hands on my shoulders and squatting down to look me straight in the eye. "You're his entire world, Lucy, no matter what kind of shit he spouted earlier. Don't believe any of it, you hear me?"

I nod at him again and he drops his hands from my shoulders.

"Oh, shit," Ellie mutters from beside me.

She quickly moves in front of me, pressing her arm against Bobby's before reaching up and cupping my cheeks in her hands. "I think we should go. Just turn around and leave and let him sleep it off. You don't want to try and talk to him now when he's had a shit ton more alcohol than earlier today. Let's just go, Lucy."

I know she wasn't happy about my decision to come up here, but does she really think I walked all the way into town to tuck my tail between my legs and leave before I've even tried?

Bobby and I both look at her in confusion. Bobby

looks behind him, over his shoulder, and then quickly back to me, moving closer to Ellie.

"You know what, I think that might be the best idea. It was stupid for me to call you. I'll take him back to my place and we can figure out something tomorrow when he's sober."

Ellie drops her hands from my face and Bobby grabs my shoulders again, but this time he turns my body around and starts pushing me towards the door. I pull away from him and put my hands on my hips as I glare at both of them.

"What the hell is wrong with the two of you? I'm not leaving until I talk to him."

My eyes move to the space between Bobby and Ellie that they had been trying so hard to keep covered from my line of sight. My hands drop from my hips and I start walking forward blindly, shoving the two of them further apart so I can walk in between them.

This isn't happening. This can't be real.

I keep moving, one foot in front of the other, even though all I want to do is take Bobby and Ellie up on their suggestion and turn and run as far away as I possibly can.

On the other side of the room, Fisher is still perched on his barstool, but now he has an extra person helping him fill the seat. Straddling his lap with her arms draped loosely around his shoulders is Melanie Sanders. She's been a thorn in my side since high school, when she shamelessly flirted with Fisher right in front of me, even after the two of us became a couple and he obviously wasn't interested in her anymore. Over the years, she's gone through three husbands, but it never stopped her from blatantly telling Fisher she'd always be available to him whenever he was in town. Fisher told me they only slept together once in high school, right before I moved to the island, but it was enough to keep the jealousy alive and kicking in my veins over the years.

It hurt that he'd had so much more experience before we slept together and that I had to see constant reminders of his conquests around the island, but nothing stung my pride more over the years than Melanie Sanders. She is the epitome of everything I'm not. Big (read: fake) boobs, long legs, tiny waist, perfect skin without a trace of freckles, outgoing and the life of every party. She's made enough money through her divorces that she can travel the world whenever the mood strikes and she never has to work to make ends meet. Her hair and make-up are always perfect and she's always dressed in the latest fashions when she struts through town. Tugging at the hem of my Butler House t-shirt that is dirty and stained from cleaning the bathrooms this morning at the inn, I try not to feel like less of a woman thinking about how my hair is a mess in a loose ponytail and I don't even remember the last time I put on make-up.

Even though my brain and my heart are screaming at me to look away, I can't do it. I keep walking in a daze through the bar until I'm only a few feet away from Fisher, who now has his hands wrapped around Melanie's ass.

I watch her run her tongue over his lips. The same

lips I've kissed for fourteen years, the same lips that have kissed every inch of my body and spoken words of love and desire. My heart feels like it's breaking in half. I bend over at the waist and wrap my arms around myself, trying to hold it all together. I feel like any second, my insides will spill all over the floor at my feet. A strangled cry escapes my mouth as Melanie shifts her hips in Fisher's lap and I hear him groan.

Both of their heads turn in my direction at my guttural sound and I want a hole to appear in the floor so I can fall through it and disappear forever.

Melanie smirks and Fisher stares right through me with cold, dead eyes.

"Sorry, sweetheart, it looks like you just didn't have what it takes anymore," Melanie sneers as she keeps her eyes on me while she leans forward and runs her tongue over Fisher's lips again.

I feel someone's arms wrap around me from behind. I don't even struggle as they pull me backwards, away from the nightmare I'm living through right now.

"Come on, Lucy, let's go home," Ellie says softly next to my ear.

"Yeah, get out of here, I'm a little busy," Fisher finally speaks as he wraps his arms around Melanie's waist and turns his head to look at her instead of me.

"You're a fucking asshole, you know that?" Ellie shouts as she continues to pull me through the bar.

"Been trying to get everyone to realize that for a while now," Fisher yells in response, still gazing at Melanie.

I try to look away from the two of them, but I can't

do it. It's like driving by a car accident and not being able to tear your eyes away from the devastation because you just have to see, you have to know that it's real and that it actually happened.

"What the hell are all of you looking at? Mind your own fucking business!" I hear Bobby shout as his arms wrap around me, as well, and he helps Ellie usher me out of here.

I suddenly notice that the bar is silent. Someone turned off the music and everyone is looking between Ellie, Bobby and I over to what Fisher is doing at his table. It's mortifying and I want to die. I feel like a bug under a microscope, like everyone is examining every detail of my life just for the fun of it. I don't want to be the source of entertainment for this town. I've kept what's been going on with Fisher a secret for years, never admitting to anyone but Ellie about how I felt like he was slipping further and further away from me. Too many people wanted our relationship to fail. Too many people tried to tell us that high school romances never work, especially when one of those people is a Marine who spends more time deployed than he does at home. I don't want them to be right. I don't want them to talk about me behind my back, satisfied that their predictions came true and that they were right along.

I can't pretend like the things he said to me earlier were all lies, a way for him to push me away so I wouldn't have to continue watching him fall down that deep, dark well. I've seen it with my own eyes. I've seen the betrayal and the hard truth of the words he spoke to me in living color.

My legs give out as we make it through the door of Barney's and out onto the sidewalk. I don't know who is holding me up or who is helping me walk at this point. Ellie and Bobby have a tight hold on me, both of them giving me words of apology and reassurance that I don't even bother listening to as they take me away from the bar and my shattered hopes.

I've lost him. Everything he ever promised me was a lie. He was never going to find his way back to me.

Chapter 8

Fisher

```
Present Day
```

LUCY TURNS AROUND and glares at me when I say her name. I might have added a little song to my voice when I said it, just like old times. I want to get a rise out of her. I want some sort of proof that she still feels something for me. I hate the fact that she's clinging to this asshole's arm so tightly that she's probably cutting off circulation, practically begging him to keep her safe from the big bad wolf.

I want to say something cocky. I want to smirk at her and make some sort of joke about how I'm back and she can kick this jerk to the curb, but I can't find my fucking voice. Jesus, how in the hell did I stay away from this woman for over a year? I didn't want to, that's for damn sure, but I had to. I was headed down a path that neither of us would have recovered from, and I couldn't take her with me. I'd already done more damage to her than I cared to admit when I pushed her away, more harm than I ever wanted to think about, but that's why I'm here. I have to relive all of that shit and I have to find a way to erase all of the pain I inflicted on her. It's part of my recovery and it's the only way I stand a chance in hell of proving to her that I never meant the things I said to her a year ago. I never meant to do what I did to her in that kitchen the last time I came home. It was a mistake. Every word I spoke and everything I did was a mistake, and I want to take it all back and make it right again. She just has to give me a chance to make it right.

"*Jefferson.*"

My first name on her lips sounds like a curse. I've never gone by that name since I share it with my father and my grandfather; it's too confusing. I hate that damn name, but it's still the most beautiful fucking sound in the world coming from her mouth, so I don't complain.

"If you'll excuse us, we have somewhere else to be," she says in a polite, pissy voice as she starts to move away.

"Aren't you going to introduce me to your friend?" I ask, nodding to the fancy asshole in the suit with his arm wrapped protectively around her shoulder, touching my girl. Standing close to my girl. Doing God knows WHAT with my fucking girl.

I will not lose my shit, I will not lose my shit.

I've come too far and worked too hard to go back a thousand fucking steps right now. I take a few deep breaths to calm myself down and put an easy smile on my face that I sure as hell don't feel.

Lucy sighs and closes her eyes briefly. "Fisher, this is Stanford Wallis, Stanford, this is Jefferson Fisher."

Dipshit actually has the foresight to remove his arm from Lucy's shoulders when she says my full name.

"Wow, so you're Jefferson Fisher. I've heard a lot about you from your father," he says, his eyes widening as he holds his hand out to me.

I grab onto it, squeezing it a little harder than I probably should, but what the fuck? "That's right, Stanley, I'm Jefferson Fisher. My friends call me Fisher, so you can call me Jefferson."

"Oh, good Lord," Lucy mutters quietly.

"Actually, it's Stanford. No one calls me Stanley," he laughs nervously.

Gripping his hand just hard enough to feel his bones rub together, I drop it quickly and nod. "Good to know, Stanley."

I bring my drink up to my lips, pausing before taking a sip. Lucy eyes the drink and I don't miss the look of worry that flashes across her face. She might not want to, but she still cares, and it warms my cold fucking soul and stops me from shoving my fist into Nancy Stanley's mouth.

"Don't worry, sweetheart, it's just sparkling water," I tell her softly.

Her eyes jerk away from the glass and meet mine. She scrunches up her nose and it takes every single muscle in my body to keep myself from closing the space between us and kissing that damn nose.

"What you drink is no business of mine," she says flippantly.

I might have believed her a year ago. Sobriety is nothing if not a great excuse to think clearly for once and see the truth of what's happening right in front of you. For instance, Lucy keeps running her fingers through her hair and then fidgeting with the neckline of her dress. I know for a fact she does that whenever she's nervous. The first time I kissed her, I had to hold her hands down at her sides so she'd stop messing with her hair. On our wedding day, she kept tugging up the white, strapless gown even though that thing molded her perfect body like a glove and wasn't going anywhere. I still make Lucy nervous, and that's all the information I need for tonight.

"Well, we really do have to be going," Lucy states, grabbing onto Fuckford's hand and tugging him towards the door.

"Hey, Stanny-boy, can you give us just a second?"

He looks between Lucy and I, raising his eyebrows at her questioningly. Lucy runs her fingers through her hair and then nods.

"It's fine. Go on outside. I'll meet you there in a second," she tells him.

I lift my glass in his direction in a silent toast and smirk. He leans down and kisses her cheek without taking his eyes off of me before backing away and out the front door.

"Was that really necessary?" Lucy asks in irritation, bringing her eyes back to me and away from the door where Stick-Up-His-Assford just exited.

"I have no idea what you're talking about."

She folds her arms across her chest, pushing her tits up through the deep vee until I can see so much creamy cleavage that my mouth waters. I quickly toss back the rest of my drink, clinking my glass down on the table next to us.

"Stop calling him *Stanley* and stop trying to piss all over me like I'm your property!"

My dick instantly springs to life inside my jeans. I can't help it. When Lucy gets fired up, I get turned on. It's like some Pavlov's dog shit.

"You're seriously going to pick some fuck named Stanford over me?" I ask indignantly.

She takes a step forward, moving so close that I can feel the heat from her body and smell the coconut on her skin from the suntan oil she uses. No matter how hard she tries to wash it off, that scent always lingers on her and it's the best damn smell in the world. She always smells like summer and beaches and fresh ocean air.

"I'm not *picking* anyone. *You* walked away, Fisher. You're the one who made the choice; I just had to go along with it."

My hand moves of its own accord, my fingers sliding through the long bangs that hang down over one of her eyes. I brush them out of the way and hear her intake of breath when I inch even closer, moving right into her personal space and pressing my body against hers. I feel her thighs against mine and her breasts brushing against my chest. Every breath she takes pushes them into me and my hands shake with the need to cup them in my palms, feel the weight of them in my hands and run my thumbs over her nipples. This feels worse than being in detox after I quit drinking. It's worse than the night sweats and the stomach cramps, worse than puking up my guts and blinding headaches that made me want to shove a knife in my eye. I want this woman more than any drug or bottle of booze, and being without her is almost killing me.

"I chose wrong, Lucy. You have to know that. You

have to *feel* that," I whisper as I stare into her ocean blue eyes.

Her eyelids flutter closed and she leans into me.

"Tell me you still feel it," I beg softly, moving my face closer to hers, focusing on her lips, already able to taste their sweetness on my tongue and their wet warmth against my own.

"FISHER! GET YOUR ASS OVER HERE! IT'S YOUR TURN!"

Bobby's shout from across the room has Lucy jumping away from me guiltily, her eyes flying around the room to make sure no one saw us.

Of course, every eye in the place is on the two of us, standing in the middle of the damn bar. I didn't think about them, I didn't care about them, I only cared about touching my girl, getting close to Lucy and reminding her that I'm still here.

"I...I have to go...I have..." Lucy cuts herself off mid-mumble, turns and walks quickly out of the bar without a look back.

Running my hand down my face, I blow out a frustrated breath before turning around and walking over to Bobby and the guys.

"Nice timing, dick head," I admonish him, punching him in the arm.

"Hey, I was helping you out. Did you really want all of Fisher's Island watching you kiss her for the first time in a year? That's just depressing. And here I thought you had moves," he tells me with a sad shake of his head.

He's right, and I hate that our first encounter had to

happen in a public place, but it was probably for the best that I wasn't able to go through with that kiss. If we would have been somewhere alone, there's no telling what the hell I would have done. I've gone more than a year without her too many times to count since we've been together, but never once was she not there waiting for me when I came home so I could sink myself into her and forget what I'd done when I was away. It bruises my pride and hurts my heart that she wasn't waiting this time, but I deserve her brush off and more. I want her to scream and shout at me and call me every name she can think of. I want her to remind me of every shitty thing I said and did to her so I can make it right and take it all back. I'm still a sick fuck, but only when it comes to her. I need to do this the right way for once. I can't let my needs and my fucking dick lead the way and screw this all up before it even begins. I'm going to remind her why we're perfect for each other. I'm going to show her that there's no one else on this earth that can love her like I can.

"I'll give you this, though. Stanford definitely isn't getting any tonight. Nice cock-blocking moves, my friend," Bobby says with a laugh as he holds his fist up for me to bump. "Let's get back to these darts so you can tell me what your plan is for getting her back. I seriously hope it's better than the shit show you just put on for all of us."

Before heading over to the dartboards, I take one last look at the door Lucy left through. As much as I wasn't looking forward to coming back to this island and all of the judgy looks I'd get from everyone here, it's the best place for me to be. It's where Lucy and I began, and I'll be damned if it's where we'll end.

Chapter 9

Lucy

April 30, 2014

H<small>E'S BEEN GONE</small> from the island for three weeks and one day. I know he's gone only because everyone on the island got a front row seat of his breakdown after I walked into Barney's and had to see him with Melanie, and that's all they've been talking about since. They saw him trash businesses on Main Street, get into fights with people he's known all his life and then witnessed Bobby drag him to the ferry and take him off the island. He hasn't been back since.

Bobby has stopped by to check up on me a few times, and as much as I want to ask where he is or what he's doing, I won't let myself do it. It's bad enough that I spend every second going over our last words to each other, wondering if I could have said or done something differently to get a better outcome, but at this point it doesn't even matter. I saw the truth of his words with my own two eyes. I don't want to know where is. If I knew, I might be tempted to hunt him down, ask him how he could have done what he did with *Melanie Sanders,* of all people, lash out at him and hurt him like he hurt me. I'm not that person. I'm not the kind of woman who screams and shouts and makes a scene. He kicked me when I was down and I know better than to try and stand up again right now. I don't know where he is and I don't care.

There are rumors floating around that, even though he was honorably discharged with a Purple Heart for an injury he sustained on his last tour, the Marines called him back to active duty, that he met someone else and went to live on the mainland, that he actually had an entire other family in another town and he finally went to be with them, and that he checked himself into rehab. Every day there's a new, outrageous rumor and I try not to listen, but it's hard when everywhere you go, everyone is talking about what happened that night. He'd been drinking all morning when we got into it in the bedroom, and Lord only knows how much more he consumed after he left me. I can't imagine him doing something so destructive and out of control, but the proof is all around me. The devastation Fisher wrought could be seen in everything from the boarded up front window of the Lobster Bucket to the black eye Randy Miller, the security guard at Fisher's Bank and Trust, sported for over a week.

I've tried so hard to continue hating him as much as I did the day he said all of those nasty things to me and I saw him with Melanie, but my brain and my heart are in an epic battle of wills. I know I should hate him. He broke my heart and said things he knew would tear me in half, but how do you turn your back on all the years you've spent loving someone, growing with him and building a life together? It wasn't all bad. Actually, it was rarely bad; only when he returned from a tour were things a little dicey. I had to walk on eggshells the first few months he was home, but I was willing to do all of that and more to make sure Fisher was happy.

Taking a break from dusting the counters in the registration area, I call upstairs to Ellie, who is changing sheets in the guest rooms, to let her know I'm going outside for the mail.

As soon as I open the door, my nose is filled with the salty ocean air and my skin warms with a gentle breeze that floats in off the water. Even though the ocean is on the backside of the property and I can't see it as I walk down the front sidewalk to the mailbox, I can still hear the waves crashing against the shore and the cry of seagulls as they skim the water looking for fish. So many times I've thought of moving off this island, selling the inn and doing something new and exciting. Those thoughts have plagued me every day for the last three weeks as I wondered how I'm going to be able to stand living in the place where everywhere I look, I see and remember something about our life together.

Smelling the ocean air, listening to the call of the birds, feeling the sand between my toes and being woken up every morning by the sun rising over the ocean water is like nothing I've ever known. I lived on the mainland for sixteen years, surrounded by tall buildings and bustling traffic, everyone rushing past and shoving you out of the way because they're always in a hurry. I go over there every once in a while for meetings or dinner with old friends, and there's absolutely nothing that I miss about it. Island life is like living in your own piece of heaven.

Everything is slower here, everything is quieter here and everything is more beautiful here. During the summer months, cars are banned from Main Street because of all the tourists. The only way to get around is by golf cart or bike, both of which every permanent resident on the island own at least a few of. I wave to a couple people as they bike or putter by in carts as I stroll down the long, bricked walkway to the mailbox.

This island might be filled with ghosts and memories of things that I'd rather forget, but it's also my home. It's jam packed with all of the people I care about and the business I love to run, even if it exhausts me.

I open the door to the mailbox and grab the letters from inside, taking a moment to breathe deeply, close my eyes and enjoy the sun on my face. Everything is going to be okay. My pride is hurt and my heart is broken, but I live in one of the most beautiful places in the world. I have supportive family and loving friends and they will help me get through this. Maybe Fisher will find what he's looking for away from this island, but maybe he'll get better and come back to me. The damage that has been done doesn't have to be permanent. Holding out hope probably makes me as weak and pathetic as he accused me of being, but I like to think of it as having a big heart that knows how to forgive. The Fisher of the last few months was not the boy I fell in love with or the man I married, and I know that person is still in there somewhere. He just has to want it bad enough to break free of the prison in his mind.

With one last deep breath, I open my eyes and make

my way back up to the inn, flipping through the bills, coupons and other items that came in the mail. As I walk up the steps and push through the front door, I toss all of the mail except for one large, white envelope on the registration desk. My heart starts beating erratically in my chest when I see the handwriting in the middle. Tracing my fingers over my name and address written in Fisher's small, neat block letters, I try to ignore the words running on repeat in my mind. Forcing memories of the cold, empty look on his face as he told me he never wrote to me when he was overseas because he *just didn't want to* from my head, my eyes fill with tears and I smile to myself as I flip the envelope over and quickly tear it open. He finally wrote me a letter. I almost can't believe it. I knew I shouldn't give up on him. I knew that no matter what, he would find that person inside I fell in love with and come back to me.

I reach inside the envelope and pull out a stack of papers stapled together. Flipping them over, my smile falls and my hands shake when I see the computer printed pages with the words *Grayson & Smith, Attorneys at Law.*

Scanning through the pages, I see the words *no-fault divorce* and *irreconcilable differences.* On the very last page, in dark blue ink, is Fisher's signature.

I let the pages flutter to the ground and I brace my hands on the desk in front of me, holding myself up so I don't crumple to the floor with them.

"Alright, all the beds are clean and ready to go. Do you want me—"

Ellie's voice cuts off when she walks into the room.

She rushes over to me, picks up the papers at my feet and I hear her flipping through them as I take deep breaths and hold back the tears.

"That worthless piece of shit! I'm going to kick his motherfucking ass," she curses as she clutches the papers in one hand and wraps her arms around me.

Refusing to break down, I swallow back the tears threatening to choke me. The anger at how quickly he's cut me out of his life simmers just below the surface and I let it take over, bubbling to the top and exploding out of me. I move away from Ellie's arms and stomp around to the back of the desk, shoving folders, invoices, cups of paperclips and a stapler out of my way as I rummage around for what I'm looking for.

When I find it, I hold the pen up in front of me as well as my outstretched hand.

"Give me the papers," I tell Ellie in a low, pissed-off voice that I barely recognize.

"Sweetie, take a breath. You don't have to sign these right now. Let's go out and have a few drinks and come back and deal with this later," she tries to reason with me.

"Give me the *fucking* papers," I growl at her.

She quickly shoves them towards me, staring at me with her eyes wide and her mouth open. I snatch them out of her hand, flip to the last page and sign my name on the line right next to Fisher's. When I'm finished, I thrust them back at her. "Send them back FedEx. Next day."

Tossing the pen on top of the desk, the fingers of my right hand wrap around the wedding and engagement rings on my left hand. It takes a little effort to twist and turn and pull them, but after a few seconds, I manage to tug them off and smack them down on top of the desk. "Throw those in the envelope, too, while you're at it."

Walking around the desk, I head towards the front door.

"Where are you going?" Ellie shouts after me as she chases me out the door and onto the front porch.

"I'm going to Barney's. I'm going to buy an entire bottle of vodka and sit there until I am completely fucked up wasted," I inform her as I stomp down the stairs.

"Well, Jesus! At least give me time to get my purse!" she shouts back.

Chapter 10

Lucy

```
Present Day
```

STANFORD'S SOFT HANDS slide into the vee of my dress and move with confidence until he's cupping one lace-covered breast in his hand. His tongue teases my lips and I open for him, letting him circle his tongue around my own. The fire he lit when we got back to the inn crackles in the hearth a few feet away and warms the chilly room. Even though it's May, the breeze from the ocean when the sun goes down drops the temperature significantly, and with the windows open, the fire is a nice comfort in the room. I wish I could say Stanford is responsible for the warmth on my skin, but that would be a complete lie. Sure, it feels nice to be touched and held and kissed, but that's the problem—it just feels *nice*. His face is too smooth against my jaw, his hands too soft. With my eyes closed, I can easily picture hands that are rough with blisters and callused from years of working with wood and holding firearms touching my breasts. I can feel the scratch of a month's worth of stubble stinging the skin of my cheek as it slides against it down to my neck.

My hands tangle in the hair on the back of Stanford's head and I clench it between my fingers as he moves away

84

from my mouth and kisses his way across my cheek and down to my neck. I'm sitting sideways on his lap and I can feel his erection pressing against my ass. I move subtly and hear him groan softly as he nips at my skin where my neck connects to my shoulder. His thumb brushes over my nipple and I squeeze my eyes closed even harder, picturing another thumb, another mouth, another voice whispering how good my skin tastes.

I press his head against my neck and will him to open his mouth and sink his teeth into my skin, squeeze my breast harder, say something crude instead of something sweet. The feel of his hands and his lips on me, though different and not what I need, are enough to confuse my mind between the past and the present until I'm so lost in old memories and old feelings that I can easily imagine something else...*someone* else, doing all of these things to me.

The smooth, clean-shaven face suddenly becomes rough and course with stubble and I moan loudly when I feel it slide up my neck and back to my waiting mouth. The gentle tongue that slides past my lips immediately becomes a punishing and forceful one, claiming my mouth and swallowing me whole. The manicured hand that has never even picked up a hammer turns into a rough touch, pinching my nipple between callused fingers. I'm so lost between fantasy and reality that it doesn't even occur to me that none of these things are happening. My body is already ten steps ahead and the tingling between my legs is so strong, I feel like I could come without any help. I don't realize how far gone I am when I quickly twist my body around so that I'm strad-dling thighs that are slimmer than the muscled ones in my mind. With my hands still clenched in his hair, I yank his head back roughly until he's staring up at me. Even with his clear blue eyes looking at me in shock instead of the brown ones I see in my mind, it still doesn't penetrate the haze of lust and need that has consumed me.

With quick hands, I grab onto the front of his but-ton-down shirt and yank it open, buttons flying off and falling *clickety-clack* all over the floor. I need this. I want this. I need to feel how much he wants me, how much he needs me. I need him to take me and claim me and bruise me with his hunger for me.

"Whoa! Jesus, Lucy, slow down!" Stanford shouts in surprise and a little bit of irritation.

His smooth, cultured voice is what brings me back to the present, brings me back to myself. It's not the raspy Southern drawl I was hearing in my mind. His thin lips are not the full ones I was feeling against my mouth and his smooth hands are definitely not the rough ones I was feeling against my breast. My face heats with mortifica-tion and shame as I quickly scramble off of his lap and take a few steps back from the couch.

Stanford stands up, holding his ruined shirt together with his hands as he looks at me like I'm insane. I probably am. Screw that, I *definitely* am. My total loss of control is a direct result of seeing Fisher tonight. Seeing him again, even though I knew it was coming, threw me for a loop, invoking feelings in my body that had long been dormant. He shouldn't be allowed to look even better than he did the last time I saw him. It was the stubble, that's what it was. That fucking stubble and those damn dimples that popped out when he smirked at me. His face was covered in coarse, dark hair and it reminded me of that day in our kitchen when he came home from his last deployment. It made me think about everything that I dreamed about, fantasized about and craved that I kept to myself. I'd become a sex-starved, bumbling mess of hormones and I'd attacked Stanford like he had the magic stick that would cure what ailed me.

"That was…unexpected," Stanford says with an awkward laugh.

Bringing my hands up to my heated cheeks, I try to cover the redness I know is there.

"I'm sorry. I don't…I didn't."

I stammer, completely humiliated and having no clue how to talk myself out of this situation.

"It's okay, Luce. I just wasn't expecting that. I thought you wanted to take things slow and you caught me off guard. You don't seem like the type of girl to do something so…*crazy*," he says as he runs his hand over his hair to flatten down the mess I made of it when I was practically ripping it out by the roots.

He's so busy trying to fix his hair and hold his shirt together that he doesn't see the irritated look on my face. Why the hell does a woman have to be considered crazy because she wants a man and isn't afraid to show it? Granted, it wasn't Stanford I was so hot for, but that's beside the point. Unless my hearing is as off as my mind tonight, the guy I'm dating just called me crazy.

"I think you should probably go," I inform him, crossing my arms in front of me and trying not to tap my foot.

"Yeah, that's probably a good idea."

He closes the distance between us and kisses my cheek, running his hand down the top of my head, and I have to force myself not to jerk away from his touch. I'm being a bitch and I know it. Stanford's right, I acted completely unlike myself tonight and I can't really blame him for being a little shocked by my behavior. We've made out, we've done a little light petting above the clothes and I've always stopped him when he's tried to go further. All of a sudden tonight, after running into my ex-husband, I practically maul him on the couch. In the middle of the sitting room at the inn. Where any of the fifteen guests in residence could have walked in.

Yep, definitely losing my mind.

I push the attitude and anger deep down and put a smile on my face, walking him to the front door.

"How about I take you to lunch tomorrow?" Stanford asks. "I have a meeting at the bank at eleven and it shouldn't take too long. Maybe we can have a picnic on the beach or something."

I smile and nod. "That sounds wonderful. I'll make sure Ellie can cover things here and I'll meet you at the bank. Say, around noon?"

"Perfect," Stanford agrees. "Sleep tight, Luce. And really, don't worry about tonight."

I keep the smile pasted on my face as he gives me another quick peck on the cheek before walking out the door. I make sure not to slam it behind him and take a deep breath as I pace anxiously around the sitting room.

Damn you, Jefferson Fisher. Why in the hell did you have to come back now, when things were finally starting to look good in my life? Stanford is a good, stable man and he treats me well. I have no business fantasizing about a man who shoved me aside and didn't want me. The only reason he pulled that shit tonight at the bar was because he saw me with Stanford and couldn't handle it. Why the hell he thinks he has any reason to be jealous is beyond me. His ego probably couldn't stand the idea that someone else would actually want me after he ripped me apart. The next time I see him, I'm going to make it perfectly clear that he needs to stay the hell away from me. I'm sure *Melanie* would be more than happy to pick up where they left off last year.

Chapter 11

Fisher's Therapy Journal

Memory Date: February 25, 2014

I'M A MONSTER.

If there was a stronger word to describe the person I've become, I would use it, but this will have to do until I can come up with something better.

I shouldn't have turned the light on. I should've remained in the dark and tried to convince myself that what happened tonight wasn't real, but lying here with the soft glow of the bedside lamp illuminating the room, I can't take my eyes off of the evidence of my disgusting behavior.

Not even an impromptu dip in the ocean after Lucy went upstairs to get ready for bed could clear the horrible images from my mind. As soon as she left the kitchen, I walked right out the back door, down the steps to the beach and into the ocean, still wearing my military hiking boots and camo pants. I dropped down into the water, fully clothed, and wished for the water to wash away the shit I'd just done to my wife.

For the first time, my head is filled with the horror of what I did to Lucy instead of what I did overseas, and I want to scream until my throat is raw.

Lucy sleeps peacefully next to me on her stomach and

I gently trail my hands down her naked back, stopping when I get to her hips.

The hips that are covered in bruises roughly the size and shape of my fingers.

Jesus, I left marks on her. My beautiful, perfect girl and I marked her with my anger and the need that consumed me so completely when I walked in the door and saw her standing there that I couldn't control it. The entire plane ride home, all I could think about was wrapping her in my arms and letting her skin and her soft touch wash away all the dark and evil things I saw the past year. I didn't even stop off at a hotel like I usually do to change into civilian clothes. I didn't shower, I didn't shave; it was all I could do to get to her as fast as possible before my mind ripped in half.

I walked through that door and saw her standing there in a pair of drawstring pants that hugged her hips and legs and a tight tank top with no bra and all I could think about was being inside of her. All I could concentrate on was burying myself in her so deep that all the bad thoughts went away. I charged at her like an animal and I took her against the wall like a rabid beast. I was punishing her for being so soft and sweet and beautiful when all I'd known for the last year was hard and awful and ugly. I don't deserve her. I don't deserve to have her sitting here waiting for me, day after day, month after month. I don't deserve to come home to someone like her who loves me so completely, even when my body and my mind take me away from her and make me forget how good I have it.

I try to swallow past the lump in my throat as I gently

run my fingers over the bruises on her hips, but it's no use. The tears pool in my eyes and fall down my face. I love her so much and all I'm doing is hurting her. The one person in my life who never lets me down and all I keep doing is breaking her apart. I let her down every time I leave, I let her down every time she has to handle something alone, I let her down when I come home and I'm not myself because I'm still stuck in a place halfway across the world and I let her down by touching her with anything other than loving hands and worshipful kisses.

I never even got a chance to say her name or tell her I love her or how much I missed her. I didn't say a word to her tonight, so afraid that I would scream and cry and break down right in front of her if I opened my mouth. She puts up with so much from me, I can't add that to the mix, as well. She would want to fix me, to put her life on hold to help me, and I can't allow that. She's already sacrificed so much. How can I continue doing this to her? How can I continue putting her though this when I'm not sure the bullshit in my head will ever go away? In the past, a few months between me and a combat zone and my Lucy were all it took to battle the demons that crawled into my head, but this go-round, the nightmares are getting worse instead of better with each mile I put between myself and the war. I won't be going on another deployment thanks to the shrapnel I took to the back of my shoulder and the resulting nerve damage, but that doesn't mean I'll start to forget. It doesn't mean the horrors I've witnessed all these years will just suddenly disappear from my mind.

I choke back sobs as I lean forward and press my lips against the bruised skin of her hip. Lucy sighs in her sleep and I hold perfectly still, not wanting to wake her. I came up to bed after sitting in the water, stripped out of my wet clothes and curled up against her, willing sleep to come, but it never did. I just held onto her sleeping body and tried to forget about what I'd done until it was too much to take and I had to turn on the light to make sure it really happened.

I wish she had screamed at me when I took her like that against the wall. I wish she'd told me to stop, pushed me away, forced me to look into her eyes and see her and realize what I was doing to her. I'm consumed with so much guilt that I don't even know how to breathe. My chest feels tight and my heart rate starts picking up, feelings I've come to recognize as the beginning of a panic attack.

Moving as quietly as I can out of bed so I don't disturb her, I try to slow my quickening breaths as I hurry out into the hallway and to the bathroom. My hands shake so hard that I can barely get the door closed and locked behind me. I flip on the light and take huge, gulping breaths as my heart beats faster and faster until it feels like it's going to explode out of my chest. I run cold water and cup it in my hands, counting to a hundred in my head as I repeatedly splash my face. I glance up into the mirror and, instead of seeing just my own reflection with water dripping down my face, I see a man standing next to me wearing a white and black checkered scarf over his head, nose and mouth with a machine gun pointed right at my skull.

I let out a panicked shout as I whirl around and throw my hands up over my head to protect myself from the enemy. When I turn, I'm met with nothing but an empty bathroom behind me. Sobbing, I drop to my knees on the cold, tile floor. With my head in my hands, I rock back and forth, making a vow to never again allow Lucy to suffer because of my demons. I can't do this to her anymore. I can't trust myself around her and I refuse to hurt her again like I did tonight. God only knows what will happen if things get worse, and I *do* feel like they're getting worse. It's too hard to distinguish reality from fantasy. I've already hurt her countless times in the middle of the night with nightmares I can't control, and I continue to hurt her every time she tries to help me and I push her away. She is my heart, my soul, my everything and I know it's only a matter of time before I do something that could possibly kill her. The tears come fast and hard at the thought that my beautiful, amazing wife could be taken from this earth by my own hands. I won't let that happen. I won't let her fall down this hole with me. If I have to fall, I'm going to do it on my own where I won't hurt anyone, especially her. I know she'll never leave me on her own. She loves me too much to turn her back on me when she knows I'm hurting, so I'll have to push her away.

I have to *make* her leave so that I can never hurt her again.

Chapter 12
Lucy

"DAMN, BITCH! YOU look hot!"

I smile at Ellie when she whistles at me as I walk into the registration area of the front room. I do a little twirl and curtsey for her, laughing when she gives me a slow golf clap. With a teal, form fitting tank top that comes to a vee in the front and ties up around my neck, my boobs look pretty good, if I do say so myself. The incredibly short, white jean shorts I have on make my tan legs look longer than they normally do and the teal and white wedges on my feet bring me up a good three inches, adding to the illusion. I left my strawberry blonde hair straight, hanging around my bare shoulders and down my back, and I added a few peach bangle bracelets to my wrist. It's not much, but aside from wearing a dress last night, it's more fancy than my usual.

"Nice, very nice. Stanford won't be able to keep his hands off of you," Ellie informs me.

I blush, thinking about what happened last night over there on the couch in this very room. I'm pretty sure Stanford will be keeping his hands off of me for a while after *that*. It doesn't matter, though. I'm going to relax with a picnic on the beach with the man I'm dating. The sun is shining and there is only a light breeze coming in off the ocean, so we won't have to worry about sand flying all over the place, getting into our food. It's a perfect day on Fisher's Island, and I'm not going to let anything ruin it.

"That little weasel better keep his hands to himself," Trip grumbles as he walks in from the front porch and stands in the middle of the room, looking me up and down.

"Oh, please. Like you weren't just like that little weasel back in the day," Ellie laughs at him. "I'm sure you had a line of ladies just begging you to put your hands on them."

Trip raises his eyebrow at her and harrumphs. "Of course I did. Have you looked at me lately?"

Ellie laughs even harder, skipping around the counter and throwing her arms around Trip's neck. "You are the best grandpa in the entire world. I'm going to adopt you."

Trip shakes his head at her behavior and then eyes me again. "I take it you're going to see Salamander?"

I roll my eyes and shake my head at him. "It's Stanford and yes, we're going on a picnic after he gets out of his meeting at the bank."

"Heard you ran into Fisher last night at Barney's," he says nonchalantly as he runs his hand over the top of a side table and tries to jiggle it, pretending like he's checking it for a loose leg.

"Don't play coy, it's beneath you," I tell him. "The entire town knows I ran into Fisher last night, Trip. What's your point?"

He shrugs, folding his arms across his chest as he looks me in the eye. "Don't really have a point, Lucy girl. I'm just wondering about all the sparks I heard were flying between the two of you, that's all. If I were Santana, I wouldn't take too kindly to my woman getting all hot and bothered over another man."

"Oh, my God," I mutter. "STANFORD. His name is Stanford and I didn't get all hot and bothered."

"Yeah, you were pretty hot and bothered," Ellie agrees.

I glare at her. "You weren't even there, how do you know?"

"Word travels fast in this small town, my friend. Also, Bobby called me right after you left the bar," she informs me with a sneaky smile.

"I'm leaving. To go on my date with STANFORD. You two yentas enjoy gossiping like a bunch of little old ladies," I tell them with a huff as I grab my purse from the desk and walk around them, out the door. "You can also be prepared to explain to me why Bobby has your cell phone number when last I heard, you couldn't stand the guy."

I watch Ellie's smile fall and a nervous look come over her face. She's definitely going to explain *that* shit later. Bobby's been hitting on her since the day I brought her to this island and all she's ever done is complain about how annoying he is and how she wouldn't date him if he were the last man on earth. Unless the Apocalypse hit and I didn't hear about it, something is going on with those two.

Leaving Trip and Ellie behind to most likely talk about me, I decide against taking one of the inn's golf carts into town and walk the ten blocks instead. It's a gorgeous day and I want to enjoy it. I still have a half hour before Stanford will be out of his meeting, plenty of time for a leisurely walk.

I quickly realize the error of my decision as I walk down Main Street. The sidewalks are filled with the first crowd of vacationers window-shopping since this weekend is the official start of our busy season, but they are also filled with busybody townies. They stand in doorways or sit on lawn chairs and benches in front of businesses, chatting back and forth about the happenings on the island. Clearly, what happened last night at Barney's is the only exciting thing going on right now, even with the island overflowing with out-of-towners constantly doing stupid shit. I hear my name and Fisher's name whispered several times as I walk by, smiling and waving at people uncomfortably. I hasten my steps until I get to the front of Fisher's Bank and Trust right as the front doors open and Stanford walks out to meet me.

"Good timing, I just got finished," he tells me, leaning in to kiss my cheek. "You look beautiful."

He grabs my hands and holds my arms out to the side so he can look at me.

"Absolutely beautiful," he reiterates. "But do you think those shorts are a bit…short for you?"

I look down at myself and try not to roll my eyes. They're called *shorts* for a reason. There's not much length to them, but my ass isn't hanging out and they fit me perfectly. Stanford isn't the type of man to ever dress casually, even for a picnic on the beach, so I just smile at him and shrug, letting his comment slide rather than get into an argument with him about my clothing choices.

He keeps hold of one of my hands as we cross the street and head over to the outdoor farmer's market. "Listen, about last night…"

I bite down on my bottom lip to keep myself from telling him that we should never, ever talk about that again.

"I'm sorry about the way I reacted," he continues. "I wanted to kick my own ass when I got home."

I let out the breath I was holding, assuming he was going to call me crazy again, and let him continue.

"Really, how stupid am I? I had a beautiful, sexy woman in my arms and I pushed her away when she finally gave me the green light," he laughs.

I don't correct him, even though I should. I really, really should. I don't want him to think that it's time to move this relationship into warp speed, regardless of my behavior the previous night.

"I'm an idiot and I'm sorry. I hope I didn't make you feel bad. I never want to make you feel bad, Luce," he tells me softly.

I smile up at him as we walk through the tables of produce, throwing things into a basket that we can take down to the beach.

"It's fine, don't worry about it. I was a little out of sorts last night, anyway," I explain as we make our way to the register.

"It was because of Jefferson, wasn't it?" he asks as I set the basket on the counter and start pulling our wares out of it.

"It's Fisher, and yes, he's part of the reason."

I have no idea why I corrected him when he called Fisher, Jefferson. Why do I care if he gets Fisher's name wrong? It's not like Fisher gave a rat's ass about saying *his* name wrong over and over. I even called him Jefferson myself last night, but that was just to piss him off. He hates that he shares a name with his father.

"It's hard running into an ex again for the first time, it's completely understandable. I just want you to know that I'm here for you. Whatever you need, I'm not going anywhere. I really care for you, Luce. I want to make this work and see where it goes."

I nod and smile without saying anything in return. I should agree with him and tell him that I want to make this work, too. I should tell him that he makes me happy and that it's been a long time since I've had a reason to smile, but nothing comes out of my mouth.

Out of the corner of my eye, I see my mother a few tables away and I lift my arm and wave, flagging her over to check us out. My parents had me pretty late in life; my mother was forty-five and my father was fifty-one when I was born. Even though running the inn soon became too much for them, my mother isn't the type of person who can just sit around and do nothing but fish all day like my father. She likes to stay busy, so during the summer months, she helps out at the farmer's market on week-ends.

"Lu-Lu, I didn't know you were coming by the market today," my mother tells me as I lean over the table and kiss the cheek that she turns up for me. I got both my short stature and my looks from my mother. In her late sixties, Evelyn Butler refuses to grow old gracefully. She still has the same dark, strawberry blonde hair as myself, though Mom's is now courtesy of her standing appointment at Sally's House of Beauty every six weeks. She wears her hair in the same short, straight bob that she has for all of my life and, even after years of baking her skin in the summer sun, she still has a great complexion, with freckles across her nose and cheeks that match mine.

"It was a last minute decision yesterday evening. Stanford and I decided to do a picnic on the beach, so we're just picking up a few things," I explain to her.

She finally notices Stanford standing beside me and her head jerks back and forth between us like she's at a tennis match.

"Oh! You're still…I thought…I mean, I heard…last night. I didn't realize you two were still together," she stammers awkwardly.

Oh, for the love of God. Now my mother is joining the gossip mill?

Moving closer to Stanford, I slide my hand through his arm and lean into him, resting my head on his shoulder.

"Yes, we're together and we're very happy," I inform her, giving her my biggest smile.

"It's nice to see you again, Evelyn," Stanford tells her with a warm smile. He's met my parents a few times over the last month and my parents have been nice to him, but a little standoffish. It's annoying and we're definitely going to be sitting down and having a talk about it soon.

Lifting my head, I push up on my toes and kiss Stanford right on the lips. Laying it on a little thick, I know, but give me a break. My mother, of all people, needs to cut me some slack. She knows what I went through with Fisher and she knows that dating someone else for the first time in my life scares me to death. Unfortunately, she and my father adore Fisher and all they talk about when I see them is whether I've heard from him and how worried they are about him. I know it's going to be much worse now that he's back home.

"Yes, well it's…very nice to see you again, too," my mother says with a tight smile as she adds up our total and Stanford pulls out his wallet to pay her.

I grab the bag from the counter and try not to give her the stink eye when I tell her I'll talk to her later. We say our goodbyes and Stanford and I walk away, heading across the street to the beach.

"I'm sorry about that. My mother is…"

"Protective of her one and only daughter?" Stanford asks with a laugh. "It's okay, I'm a big boy. I can handle it. As long as you're okay, I'm okay."

I tighten my hold on his arm and rest my head on his shoulder, just for myself this time instead of for show. This man really is charming and kind and I should be thrilled that he wants to be with me. I need to stop comparing him to someone else and enjoy learning about him and, like he said, see where this thing takes us. As we walk down the stairs to the boardwalk on the sand, I decide that is exactly what I'm going to do. I don't care what anyone in this town thinks, I'm going to do what makes me happy.

Chapter 13

Fisher's Therapy Journal

Memory Date: April 8, 2014 - 1:45 PM

"*M*AYBE WE SHOULD *look into counseling again.*"

Lucy's words over breakfast run on a loop in my head. Tossing back another shot of whiskey, I hurl the empty glass across the kitchen. It shatters against the cupboards and the pieces scatter across the floor.

I'm broken, just like those fucking pieces of glass. I know it, and now Lucy knows it. Counseling isn't going to work, nothing is going to work. She looked at me this morning with pity and I couldn't stand it anymore. I don't want her fucking pity.

I hear a loud bang outside and drop to the floor, covering my head with my arms. My breath comes out in gasps as I lie there waiting to hear the sound of gunfire and the sting of a bullet piercing my skin. When no sound and no pain come, I open my eyes and realize I'm lying on the kitchen floor.

"What the fuck is wrong with you, you stupid asshole?" I mutter to myself as I push up from the floor and stalk over to the counter to grab another glass and the half-full bottle of whiskey. I pour the amber liquid halfway up the glass and down the entire thing in one swallow.

She can't be here anymore, she can't see me like this. She's just kidding herself if she thinks me sitting in an office with some quack in a suit judging me and what I've been through is going to help me. I'm beyond help. The faster she realizes that, the faster she can get the hell out of here and away from me.

My hands shake as I forego the glass and just bring the bottle of whiskey right up to my mouth. A creaking from somewhere upstairs makes me jerk the bottle away from my lips. I smack it down on the counter, get into a crouch and quietly move through the house, darting in between doorways and silently racing up the stairs, just like I was taught. The only thing missing is the heavy weight of my rifle in my hand.

"WHO THE FUCK IS UP THERE?" I shout, as I get halfway up the stairs. "I WILL END YOUR SORRY LIFE, MOTHERFUCKER!"

Kicking in the bedroom door, I charge into the room, seeing desert sand and Humvees in front of me instead of a bed and a dresser. I drop to the sand and army crawl, knowing I'll be safe if I can just get to the convoy. Reaching down to my side to grab my gun, I feel nothing. I don't have my weapon. Why in the fuck am I without a weapon? A Marine should never be without his weapon. I hear gunfire and explosions in the distance and I crawl faster, keeping my body low and my head down.

"COVER ME! SOMEBODY FUCKING COVER ME!" I scream as I claw at the sand and move as fast as I can.

My head smacks into a desert rock and I close my

eyes and shake the pain away. When I open them again, I see cream carpet under my body and a king-sized bed covered in pale blue blankets right in front of my face. Not sand, not a rock, not a Humvee and not a convoy. Nothing but the bedroom I share with my wife.

"Oh, Jesus, oh, my God, what the fuck is happening to me?" I mutter as I push myself up from the floor and take in my surroundings, blinking to make sure what I'm seeing is real.

"I have to get her out of here. She can't be here anymore," I mumble as I race to the closet and pull two suitcases from the top shelf. Running over to the bed, I toss them on top and quickly unzip them, flipping them open.

I go to the dresser, pulling open the top drawer and grabbing socks, bras, underwear, whatever I can fit into my arms, before I race back to the bed and dump everything in to the first suitcase.

"Fisher, what the hell are you doing?"

The voice from the doorway startles me and I jump, automatically reaching down to my side for my gun. When I see Lucy standing there staring at me in confusion, I almost drop to my knees with the force of my shame. I reached for my gun. I reached for my fucking gun! If it had been there instead of locked up in a gun case in the living room, I could've shot her. I could've pulled it on her and put a bullet right through her chest.

"You're leaving. Right now. I can't do this anymore," I tell her, the vision before me flashing between her standing in the doorway and an insurgent standing there with a gun aimed at me.

The insurgent disappears as quickly as he came and all I see is Lucy, my beautiful Lucy, standing in the doorway with tears filling her eyes.

"Fisher, please, don't do this!" she begs as the first tear spills down her cheek.

I ignore her voice, even though it cuts right through me and makes me want to change my mind. I turn and run to the closet, ripping everything she owns off of hangers and piling the skirts and dresses, jeans and shirts in my arms. I come back out and stop again at the dresser, pulling open the bottom drawer and grabbing whatever else I can hold.

I toss all of that stuff into the second suitcase and watch as it morphs into an IED lying in the sand. I shake the image from my mind and try not to throw up all over the place.

"We're done, this is over. I'm packing your shit and you're leaving."

I'm sorry, I love you, please forgive me.

She grabs onto my arm and I yank it out of her grip. I can't let her touch me right now. Everything will come crashing down if I let her touch me. I need her touch, I want her touch, I don't know how I will live without her touch…

But I need to protect her more.

She begs and pleads with me, asking me to talk to her, just talk to her. She has no idea that I can't. I can't tell her all of the things that are so monumentally fucked up with me right now.

"There's nothing to talk about. It's perfectly clear what's going on here. Everything is fucked up, don't you get that? It's ruined, all of it is ruined and you need to fucking leave!"

I'm so sorry, I love you, please forgive me.

Her voice fills the room as she tries to get me to stop and listen to her. I can't take it. I can't take the sound of her voice, it hurts too much hearing all the loving words she gives me. They rip right through me and gut me like a fucking fish. I know she'll never leave. She'll never walk away from me like she needs to, like she HAS to. She needs to be safe, and I need her to understand that this is the only way I can protect her from what I've become.

Hurtful things, so many hurtful things I spit at her.

"You need to get a life."

I'm sorry, I love you, please forgive me.

"All those sad, pathetic letters…"

I'm lying, don't believe me, please don't believe me. I loved your letters, I kept them all and I cherish every one of them.

She presses her soft, sweet hands to my face and I rest my forehead against hers. I'm weak, I can't help it. I need to breathe her in one last time. I need to feel her close to me and remember why I'm doing this, why I'm doing all of these awful things to her. I need her to walk away. I need her to hate me enough to leave so she can be safe. I'll do anything to keep her safe. Every word I speak kills more and more of me, until I'm sure there's nothing left but an empty shell. She slides her hands under my shirt and I'm immediately hard for her. Her mouth makes its way down to my neck and I want to growl with my need for her when her lips and her teeth press into my skin. I need her. I love her.

But I can't have her or I will wind up killing her.

"I prefer women with a little more experience…"

I don't mean it. I don't mean any of it. Knowing I'm the only man who has ever been inside of you makes me feel like a fucking king and the luckiest man alive. I'm sorry, I love you, please forgive me.

She tells me she hates me and that empty shell crumbles to pieces and I know there's nothing left.

"It doesn't get better when I come home to you…I hate this life…"

I'm lying! Every word is a lie. I love our life and I wouldn't change it for anything in the world. I love you, I love you, I love you.

I grab her suitcases from the bed and toss them to the floor before I change my mind. I walk right past her, not saying a single word, even though I want to pull her into my arms and beg her not to leave me. It's too late for that now. Looking at the devastation on her face, I'm certain that all the lies I told, all the things I said to her to play on her insecurities and make her hate me…it worked. It worked just like I wanted it to. It worked so well that I know there's no hope of ever getting her to forgive me.

I don't deserve her forgiveness. I never deserved her to begin with, so now she'll be free to find security and happiness without having to worry about the broken man she married who can never be fixed.

Chapter 14
Fisher

Present Day

"HOW DOES IT feel to be the talk of the town? Again? Jesus, you're mister popularity," Bobby says with a laugh as I help him wash his gear down by the water.

Bobby runs his parents' snorkeling and scuba hut during the summer season as well as a golf cart and bike rental business, doing so well for himself that he doesn't need to work during the winter months. One of the perks of being friends with him is that I can dive anytime I want as long as I help him wash down all the gear when I'm finished. Bobby and I went for an early-morning dive before all the tourists woke up and it was a good way for me to clear my head. There's nothing like being all alone, down on the ocean floor, surrounded by fish and coral with nothing but the sound of your breathing apparatus filling your ears to think about things.

"It's not my fault this town has nothing better to do," I complain as we move all the cleaned gear to buckets to take back to the hut for the next diving tour.

"It's true, this place was pretty boring while you were gone," Bobby admits.

His phone beeps with an incoming text message and

he takes it out of the pocket of his cargo shorts, smiling and chuckling at what's on the screen.

"Who's that?" I ask, nodding towards the phone.

He looks up guiltily, wipes the smile off of his face and quickly shoves the phone back in his pocket.

"No one, nothing, it's nothing," he replies quickly.

"Really? It didn't look like nothing. You giggled like a little girl," I joke as we make our way up the beach.

"I do not giggle. I never giggle. Fuck off," he grumbles, shoving one of the buckets up on the counter of the hut.

I put my own bucket up next to his, turn and face him with my eyebrow raised, waiting for him to spill the beans. It only takes a few seconds for him to crack.

"Fine! It was Ellie. It's no big deal."

I stare at him in shock and then toss my head back and laugh. "Ellie? Are you serious? I thought you couldn't stand her. Why in the hell is she sending you text messages that make you giggle. And don't try to deny it, you totally fucking giggled."

He starts unloading the equipment from the buckets and lining it up on the counter so it's easy for the people in the tour to grab after they've received their instruction.

"Look, don't make a big thing about this. I like her, okay? She's not as big a bitch as I thought she was. She's actually kind of sweet," he says with a shrug.

"You are such a shitty liar," I laugh again. "You never thought she was a bitch. You've been trying to screw her since the first day you met her, and you got pissed when she blew you off."

"Of course I have. Have you seen that chick? Long, thick black hair, big blue eyes, tits that are more than a handful and an ass I want to sink my teeth into. Who wouldn't want to screw her?" he asks.

I raise my hand.

"Well, no shit. She's your ex-wife's best friend. And she hates you. She'd probably cut off your dick if you got within five feet of her."

We take the empty buckets inside the hut and stack them against the back wall.

"Let's get back to the more important matter at hand. What in the fuck are you going to do about Lucy? You know your window of opportunity is about ready to slam shut, right? As we speak, she is on another date with Sphincter. Sorry, I mean Stanford. I heard from Ellie that it's a romantic picnic on the beach," he informs me.

I close my eyes and take a deep breath, trying not to picture Lucy and Stanfuck snuggled together on a blanket in the sand.

"I'm trying to do this the right way. I don't want to invade her space or piss her off. Right now, I just want her to know that I'm back and I'm not going anywhere."

"I think it's high time you 'invade her space'," Bobby tells me, complete with air quotes. "Stan the Man is not about to back down. There's talk that he wants to buy Butler House from her and she's not really in a position to say no to him. He wants to partner with her and turn it into a resort, complete with a waterpark and spa. If they go into business together, you'll never be able to get close to her."

"What the hell do you mean she's not in a position to say no to him? Why in the fuck would she ever sell the inn? It's been in her family for three generations and she loves that place," I tell him, my anger on her behalf starting to grow.

The nerve of that ass fuck thinking he can come in here and buy Lucy's business right out from under her.

"Dude, the inn hardly makes any money. She's barely scraping by as it is, and with a place as old as that, there's always shit going wrong that she needs to fix. She's not going to be able to afford that place for too many more seasons before the bank takes it over. It's a fucking money pit," Bobby explains.

The inn has never turned much of a profit for as long as I've known Lucy, but it was always more than enough to cover her expenses and give her something to live on. Aside from that, she got half of everything I owned in the divorce. I would have given her every single penny I had, but the courts wouldn't let me. She should have plenty of money to do whatever she wants to the inn. What did she do with the money I sent her? Does she hate me so much that she refused to use it, even to make repairs to the place she loves? I'm angry and irritated, assuming that she never used the money just because it came from me. It was hers, all of it was hers to do with as she wanted. Why the hell didn't she use it? She could keep the inn in her family and avoid having to sell it to ANYONE, but especially that fucker who clearly has another agenda aside from getting in her pants.

"Well, would you look at that? A pretty lady all alone

on the beach," Bobby tells me, nodding his head over my shoulder.

Turning around, I see Lucy off in the distance, sitting on a blanket, staring out at the ocean.

Telling Bobby I'll talk to him later, I head in her direction. I watch as she leans back on her hands and turns her face up to the sun, her long hair cascading down behind her and brushing the blanket she's sitting on. She's so fucking beautiful it takes my breath away. I don't know where fuck face went and why she's sitting here all alone and I don't care. All I care about is getting close to her again.

I walk up in front of her, stopping when I'm blocking the sun from her face. Her eyes blink open and she looks up at me, a scowl taking over her face.

"Nice to see you again, too," I say with a laugh. "Mind if I sit down?"

I point to the blanket and she hesitates. I decide to plop down next to her anyway and deal with the consequences later. I sit close enough that her thigh presses against mine and her shoulder rubs against my arm. She scoots away with a huff and I keep my laughter to myself.

"Where's Sanford and Son? I thought you two had a date?"

She glares at me and shakes her head. "Is anything in this town private? And stop calling him names, it's juvenile."

"Did you really just ask if anything in this town is private? Are you new here?" I ask with a chuckle.

A laugh bursts out of her mouth and she finally smiles

at me. Fuck the sun shining down on us right now, this is a thousand times better.

"Yeah, you're right, silly me. Welcome to Fisher's Island, where everything is everyone's business and if you didn't already know that, you haven't been talking to the right people," she says with another laugh.

After a few quiet seconds she answers my initial question. "Stanford got called away to a meeting. We were already finished with lunch, so it's fine."

Fucking Sand-In-My-Crack-Ford. Who the hell leaves someone like Lucy in the middle of a date to go to a stupid meeting? I think back to all the times I left her over the years and it makes me feel like an asshole.

"So, how's the inn?" I ask nonchalantly.

She looks away from me to stare out at the ocean again. "It's fine, you know, the usual."

That's not really what I wanted to hear, so I try again.

"Everything good? You know, moneywise and shit?"

She purses her lips and looks back at me again.

"It's fine," she says through clenched teeth.

"I just…you know if you need any help, you can always ask, right? That place was as much a part of my life as it was yours for a lot of years. I care about it and I don't want to see anything happen to it."

She laughs cynically, shaking her head back and forth. "You are a real piece of work, you know that? You don't care about Butler House, so stop trying to feed me that bullshit. You hated everything that place represented and you hated that you were stuck here with me taking care of it. Give it a rest, Fisher."

"I never hated it, and I never felt like I was stuck here," I argue.

"Jesus, you just don't quit, do you? What do you want from me? Why are you even back here?"

I sigh, realizing quickly that this conversation is not going in the direction I wanted it to.

"I heard some things about you not being able to afford it and I'm concerned, okay? I mean, what happened to all the money I sent you? Why didn't you use it for that place?"

She pushes herself up from the blanket and snatches up her purse angrily. "Screw you AND your fucking money, Fisher. I got your money and it made me sick. Every Goddamn month for thirteen months, I got another bank statement in the mail about those stupid automatic deposits. It's bad enough your father always made me feel like the whore who took advantage of his son's money, I never thought *you* would stoop so low. I don't want your money. I NEVER wanted your money. You can take your money and shove it up your ass. Why don't you concentrate on making things right with the people on this island who still love you and care about you? You know, the ones that you went ballistic on before you left? Do something constructive while you're here and stop pissing me off."

She turns and storms off across the beach, leaving me there with my mouth wide open. What the hell was she even talking about? Monthly deposits? Jesus, this is not good. Not only is it glaringly obvious that she still hates me, I have to worry about trying to hide a fucking hard-on when I get up from this blanket and retrieve my clothes from the hut, since I didn't change out of my wet suit before I walked over here. Fucking hell…she's never spoken to me like that before. Never really raised her voice and certainly never cursed a blue streak like that. My Lucy has gotten herself a backbone and it's the hottest fucking thing I've ever seen.

Getting up from the blanket, I yank it up from the ground and shake off the sand. Not only do I have to figure out a way to get Lucy to forgive me and fall in love with me again, now I have to figure out what the hell she was talking about and try to smooth things over with *that*. I've got some serious questions for my grandfather right now. I have a strange suspicion he's behind the deposits Lucy was talking about and I might just kick his ass. She had a good point, though, in the middle of her tirade. I need to make things right with the other people in this place I screwed over a year ago. In order for her to see that I've changed, I need to fix everything I messed up.

Not just with her, but with everyone.

Chapter 15

Fisher's Therapy Journal

Memory Date: April 8, 2014 - 9:12 PM

B OBBY IS YELLING at me, but I have no idea what he's saying. I can see his mouth moving, his arms flailing all over the place, but the only thing I hear is the sound of Lucy's cries from this afternoon. They echo through my brain, piercing my skull and forcing me take another drink just to try and quiet them. Everything is fuzzy and the room spins so quickly I don't know how I haven't fallen off the fucking chair I'm sitting on. I just want to go home. I want to go to our little yellow house on the water and tell her it was all lies. I want to crawl into bed with her and touch her face and tell her I didn't mean any of it. Then I look over Bobby's shoulder and see a group of insurgents holding their guns at us and I realize I can never do that.

"Go away. Just go the fuck away and leave me alone!" I shout.

I'm talking to the assholes standing behind Bobby with guns pointed as us, but Bobby thinks I'm talking to him and he walks away.

I need another drink. The drunker I get, the harder it is to focus on the swirling images around the bar that keep morphing into the enemy.

"You look like you could use another drink."

I sway a little to the side when I hear a female voice right in my ear. Maybe it's Lucy. Maybe she ignored everything I said to her and came back to me. I know it's wrong and she shouldn't be here, but I just need her right now. I can see her one more time and then I'll walk away.

Looking down at the table, I watch as a glass of whiskey is placed in front of me. I grab it before someone takes it away and chug the entire thing, slamming the glass back down on the table.

"I'm sorry, I love you," I slur as I reach my hands out to Lucy, grab onto her hips and pull her onto my lap.

She doesn't feel the same and she doesn't smell the same, but none of that matters. Her legs straddle my thighs and I clutch onto her ass, pulling her closer so she doesn't change her mind and leave me.

"Please don't go, I'm sorry," I mumble brokenly as I rest my head on her shoulder.

"I'm not going anywhere, sugar, don't you worry."

I don't like her voice. It's not the same soft, sweet cadence that always makes my ears tingle and my heart beat fast. It's probably because my heart died and there's nothing inside my chest but a shriveled up, useless organ. This voice is shrill and annoying. Lucy is changing right before me, but I don't care. It's my fault, anyway. It's my fault she's different and doesn't feel the same or smell the same. I changed her, I hurt her…all my fault.

I lift my head and try to focus on her eyes, but all I see are blurry images and swirling faces.

She rocks her hips against me and my dick is instantly

hard for her, just like it always is. I want to be inside of her. It's the only place where I truly exist and can forget about the things I've done.

I feel her tongue trace against my bottom lip and something makes me want to pull away. She doesn't taste the same and I hate it. I want *my* Lucy, not this drunken, morphed version of her.

I hear a strangled cry from somewhere in the distance and I turn my head towards the sound. I have no idea what it was or where it came from. Maybe it's the enemy trying to trick me. They're probably here right now, just waiting to take me down. I don't care anymore, they can have me. They can shoot my body full of bullets and it would probably be a relief at this point. It would stop the pounding headache, put an end to the shakes wracking my body and make it all go away. I don't want to hurt anymore, I don't want to be confused anymore, I don't want any of it. I want to die from the pain and I want to scream at them to just do it already, just end it. I try to open my mouth to let the screams and the shouts empty out, but I feel Lucy's tongue against my lips again and I focus on that instead. I turn my head away from whoever is standing next to us and squeeze my eyes open and closed to try and see her. She's in my lap, in my arms where she belongs, and I never want to let her go. I tell the person standing there to go away because I'm busy with Lucy and they need to leave me the hell alone.

I hear angry shouts and the shuffling of feet and the Lucy on my lap speaks again and it makes me wince. I want to tell her to stop talking like that. Stop talking in a different voice, stop smelling different, stop feeling different…just stop it. Be MY Lucy. I need MY Lucy.

Someone calls me an asshole and I can't help but laugh. I *am* an asshole. And a monster and a fuck up and a nightmare all rolled into one piece of shit package and I'm glad they finally noticed, so I tell them that. I'm not a hero, I'm not a good man, I'm not a good husband…I am none of those things and they need to see that.

I need another drink. I push Lucy off of my lap and stumble up from the chair. Her hands wrap around my arms to steady me, but I push her away. I don't want her to see me like this. She's not even supposed to be here.

Shoving my way through the crowd of people, I head towards the door and smack my hands against the wood to open it. I step outside and nothing but the hot, dry desert stretches out in front of me. I start walking, knowing I need to make it back to camp. I shouldn't be out here alone. Why in the fuck am I out here alone? A Marine should always be with his platoon in case the enemy ambushes us. I can feel sweat dripping down my back and my legs start to ache the further I walk through the unforgiving desert sand. I just have to make it back to camp. As long as there aren't any surprise attacks, I'll be fine.

A man suddenly appears in front of me and I'm so startled at the sight of someone else out here in the lonely desert with me that I pull my arm back and let my fist fly right into his face.

"DO NOT GET IN MY WAY! I NEED TO GET BACK TO CAMP!"

I start running then, but it's like trying to run through quicksand. Each time my foot hits the ground it sinks deeper and deeper into the sand until my legs start to burn with the effort of moving. I stop suddenly when I see an IED sitting on the ground right at my feet. I quickly scan the area and, when I don't see anything or anyone, I snatch it up in my hands and throw it as hard as I can. I hear a crash and the sound of glass breaking. It doesn't make sense. There isn't any glass in the desert. The IED should have exploded as soon as I threw it. I don't care; I did what I was supposed to. I got that damn thing out of the way so the rest of my team won't happen upon it by mistake. I can't lose anyone else on my team, I can't.

It's a long, tireless walk back to camp and I happen upon quite a few enemies as I go, but I take them all out quickly and efficiently, just like I was taught. I can't find my gun, but luckily, I'm just as good at hand-to-hand combat as I am with a firearm. I hear myself screaming and shouting as I go, especially when there are so many people suddenly cropping up in the desert with me. They look at me funny, they point and stare and I don't understand what they're doing. If they are on my side, they should be helping me, not standing there doing nothing.

I yell at all of them, tell them to get their asses moving. I shout so many obscenities and threats that it has all of them cowering in fear. Good! They should be afraid of me. I'm a motherfucking Marine in the middle of a war.

I turn away from them to keep moving and something as hard as a rock slams into my face. I try to shake away the pain, but it just makes the world around me tilt on its axis. I sway to the side and my feet stumble. I feel myself falling, down, down, down, and right when I think I'm going to hit the ground, arms wrap around me to keep me from crashing. I close my eyes and let the world fade away, saying Lucy's name over and over, hoping that she hears me.

Chapter 16

Lucy

Present Day

"STUPID, POMPOUS ASSHOLE," I mutter angrily to myself as I stomp along the sidewalk through town.

I don't even care if people are sitting outside watching me talk to myself. Let them look, let them see the shit that they are constantly talking about behind my back. If they see that I am irritated beyond belief at my ex-husband, maybe they'll get it through their heads that I don't want anything to do with him. I cannot believe he had the nerve to bring up the fucking money. He makes me let my guard down by getting me to laugh and then he throws that shit in my face. And really, why in the hell does he have to look so good? He distracted me wearing that damn wet suit, rolled down to his waist with his bare chest hanging out for the whole world to see. I can't walk around with my shirt off, and it should be illegal for Fisher to do so, as well. Sweet Jesus, that man is hot. He was always in good shape because of the Marines, but I swear to God, he must have done nothing but crunches and drink protein shakes for the last thirteen months. Where he used to be bulky and huge, now he's lean and cut. His bare chest is nothing short of a miracle and it took everything in me not to lick his abs and the indents at his waist when he sat down next to me. I hate myself for staring at him when he walked over and blocked my sun, but good Lord, I felt like a dying woman in the middle of the desert and he was the only glass of cold water left on earth.

It's not fair. It is so not fair that he can look so good and piss me off so much at the same time.

I'm so lost in my own irritation, staring at my feet and cursing Fisher as I walk, that I don't pay attention to what's in front of me until I slam into someone and stumble backwards. Hands come out to grab my arms and steady me and, when I look up to apologize, I let out an audible sigh.

"Ms. Butler, how nice to see you."

Jefferson Fisher, Jr., my ex-father-in-law and the bane of my existence for fourteen years, towers over me, smoothing down the front of his navy blue three-piece suit like a brush with me just made him dirty. He looks the same as he always does, and it surprises me that this man never seems to age. As tall as Fisher and just as good looking, but with salt and pepper hair and more creases around his forehead and eyes, Jefferson Fisher, Jr. looks like George Clooney. You know, if George Clooney never smiled and always spoke to you in a condescending manner and gave backhanded compliments out like they were cookies.

"How are you doing, Ms. Butler?"

The way he annunciates my maiden name with a touch of a smirk makes me want to punch him in the mouth, right here on Main Street. The day my divorce from his son was final and I went back to my maiden name was probably the happiest day of his life. God forbid someone like me continue walking around, tainting the Fisher name.

"I'm fine, Mr. Fisher, how about yourself?" I ask politely. Politely only because I'm not about to make a scene in the middle of town and further validate his theory that I'm poor white trash who only latched onto his son for the last name and money.

"Very well, very well," he replies distractedly, still trying to brush off the imaginary dirt on his suit coat. "I'm actually glad we ran into each other. I've been meaning to speak to you about Butler House."

Pulling the strap of my purser higher on my shoulder, I paste on a fake smile and nod for him to continue. He's always made it more than clear at town meetings that he thinks the inn is outdated and an eyesore on the island. He's been wanting to either tear it down completely or sell it off to someone else who can update it and turn it into something more *worthy* of his vision of Fisher Island. I've told him several times that he can shove his opinion up his arrogant ass, nicely of course. It's not very easy when Fisher's Bank and Trust holds the mortgage for Butler House Inn. If I have another round of problems at the inn like the ones I had this winter, problems that emptied out my savings account and then some, causing me to fall behind on the mortgage, they are going to swoop in like a pack of vultures and take it right out of my hands.

"As you know, we've had several interested buyers for that property over the years and you've never expressed any interest in working with them before. I know you've met Stanford Wallis and I've heard that you two have been spending time together lately."

The disapproval is loud and clear in his voice. He almost sounds more irritated that I'm with Stanford than he was when I was with his son, and that just pisses me off *for* Fisher. His father never appreciated him, never saw the passion behind the choices he made for his life and did nothing but badger him about not following in his footsteps.

"Stanford is a very intelligent young man with a good head for business. I'm quite proud of the work he's been doing for me lately, and he's shared with me that he's been doing some consulting with you on the side. The ideas he has for Butler House and its future on this island are nothing short of amazing. We need to step it up into the next century, give it an update, make it more appealing to the young people who frequent the island looking for the newest trends, the hottest nightspots and the most stylish décor," he explains.

What he's saying isn't news to me. Stanford has been completely open and honest since day one about his desire to buy Butler House from me and turn the place into an elaborate resort, complete with waterpark, nightclub and day spa. He knows how much I adore my family's inn and how I can't imagine changing anything about it, so he doesn't push it. That doesn't stop him from throwing out ideas now and then and attempting to change my mind, but at least he's not rude or pushy about it like Mr. Fisher.

"As you are aware, Fisher Bank and Trust holds the mortgage to Butler House and I've been reviewing the data Stanford has been compiling regarding your financial situation and putting into a spreadsheet for you. Let's be honest here, Ms. Butler. The inn is not doing as well as it should. As well as it *could.* You're sinking, and you're sinking fast. You may well have lost the inn to foreclosure had spring weather not come early this year and brought vacationers to the island before summer season. You're a young woman, and you could potentially make hundreds of thousands of dollars on the sale of this property. It's in a prime location right by the ferry and it's the first thing people see when they step off the boat and onto the dock. You could retire at the age of thirty and live a life of relative leisure. The business is struggling and you're in over your head. I think it's high time you reconsider the ideas that Stanford has, especially if the two of you are seriously going to make a go at this *relationship.*"

I hate the sound of disgust in his voice when he mentions my *relationship* with Stanford. It's none of his business who I choose to date and, regardless of the fact that his bank owns my loan, it's none of his business what I do with the inn as long as I'm not late again with my mortgage payments. It's been touch and go for a while now, but I'm making it work. I will do whatever it takes to make it work and he needs to back the hell off.

"I appreciate your concern, Mr. Fisher, but Butler House has always been a part of my family and that's where it's going to stay," I tell him in the nicest voice possible and try not to grit my teeth. "I think it's about time you worry about your own family instead of what I'm doing with my life. Maybe if you concentrated on the *intelligent* man that is your flesh and blood, you wouldn't have so much free time to worry about what I'm doing."

It feels so good to tell this man what I think of him that I don't even stop to think about someone overhearing. I've held my tongue for so many years out of respect for Fisher, but now that we aren't together, I don't have to do that anymore.

"You have a son who is smart, honest, creative and has a very good head on his shoulders. Just because he did something different with his life than what you planned for him doesn't give you the right to shit all over him and pretend like he doesn't exist. Fisher is a better man than you'll ever be on his *worst* day, and it's nothing but sad and pathetic that you can't even see what is right in front of your face. All these years, he's done everything you've asked except work in the family business. He's lied for you, put up a front for you for everyone in this stupid town and you've never once thanked him. Hell, your son served this country for almost thirteen years and you never *once* told him you're proud of him. No wonder he can't stand this place and everything it represents."

I finally stop to take a breath, noticing a vein sticking so far out of Mr. Fisher's forehead that looks like it's about to pop. His face is so red that I'm surprised there isn't smoke coming out of his ears.

He takes a menacing step towards me and sticks his

finger right in my face.

"How DARE you speak to me that way. You've been nothing but a thorn in my side ever since you sunk your claws into my son when he was a teenager. You and your poor, trashy family honestly think you belong on this island? The only reason my son and someone as smart as Stanford want anything to do with you is because they are easily swayed by loose women who spread their legs for—"

"That's enough. Get your finger out of her face before I remove it for you."

A low, furious voice from behind me cuts off Mr. Fisher, but I don't bother turning around. Even without recognizing the voice, the heat from his body radiating against my back and the light smell of his cologne combined with the salty ocean water that always sticks to his skin would have given him away immediately.

"Put your ex-wife on a leash, son," Mr. Fisher snarls through clenched teeth.

"I said that's enough!" Fisher shouts this time. "If one more word about her comes out of your mouth I will sweep the fucking sidewalk with your face in front of everyone in your precious town."

The barely concealed fury in Fisher's voice sends chills down my spine and goose bumps pebble my skin even as the bright, late afternoon sun shines down on us. The chills aren't from fear or worry that Fisher might do something crazy, they're from pure, unadulterated lust. He's always defended me to his father, but it was always in a quiet, pleading sort of way. This is straight up, alpha male, I-protect-what's-mine shit going on and it's the hottest thing I've ever heard.

This is not good. This is SO not good.

"Fisher, I—"

"Not another word," Fisher growls, cutting him off. "Lucy, how about you head home now?"

Going by his quiet, firm voice, it's really more of a demand than a question. I don't really appreciate him ordering me around, but I'm not stupid. I'm smart enough to know when to walk away, and right now, I *need* to walk away.

I don't say a word and I don't look back at Fisher as I bypass his father and continue heading in the direction of the inn. I refuse to consider that Fisher could have been standing there all that time, listening to me expound on his virtues. He doesn't need anything else feeding his already inflated ego, but it had to be done. I'm so sick and tired of my ex-father-in-law thinking he can push everyone around because he has more money than God.

I quicken my steps and make it back to the inn in record time, rushing through the front doors and into the living quarters without a word to Ellie and Trip, who are still in the front room, shooting me questioning looks as I brush right past them. I need a cold shower. A really, really long, cold shower. Maybe that will erase the sound of Fisher's voice and what it did to me from my mind.

Chapter 17

Fisher's Therapy Journal

Memory Date: December 30, 2005

"OH, FISHER, IT'S beautiful!" my mother exclaims as she pulls the sheet off of the bench I just finished for her. It was supposed to be a Christmas present, but I've had a hard couple of months ever since I got home from my deployment in September. It's taken me a lot longer than I expected to acclimate myself back into my life here on the island and I've been consumed with spending all my time with Lucy to make up for the year and a half we spent apart.

She runs her hands over the varnished oak with swirling patterns carved into the seat back around the name *Fisher* that I burned into the wood. It's the most intricate design I've ever done and the first time I worked with wood burning and it came out pretty damn good.

"I can't wait to show this to everyone. I'm going to put it right in the foyer so it will be the first thing people see when they walk in the door," she tells me excitedly as she wraps her arms around me and gives me a big hug.

"Are you still wasting your time with that nonsense?" my father asks in irritation as he walks into the living room and sits down on the couch, staring at the bench like it's a dead carcass that I dragged into the house and left rotting on his carpet. My mother pulls away from me and shoots an irritated look at my father.

"It's not nonsense, Jefferson, and it's not a waste of time, it's art. Fisher is incredibly talented. Just look at the detail he put into this bench!" my mother defends, running her hands over the bench lovingly.

"It's a hobby and it most certainly is a waste of time. He should be going to college and preparing himself for a real career, not some frivolous pastime that isn't going to make him any money, or going off to fight some stupid war that has nothing to do with us," my father says in annoyance.

I don't bother telling him that my "pastime" is making me more money than he could possibly imagine. After I dropped off a rocking chair as a birthday gift to Sal to put out front of his diner, I started getting phone calls left and right from people who saw it and wanted one just like it. After a while, people started asking me for other things, different designs, new pieces of furniture. It was exciting and amazing and I loved every minute of it. I'd been worried for a while now about how I was going to be able to support Lucy once we were married. I would never be ok with allowing my wife to shoulder the financial burden in our marriage, and I knew we couldn't live well off of my meager lance corporal salary, especially on the island, where everything is more expensive. This "hobby" made it possible for me to put a deposit down on a house for the two of us. It wasn't anything big or elaborate like my parent's home, but it was clean and right on the water and I knew Lucy would love it.

TARA SIVEC

I also don't bother engaging my father in an argument over his criticism of the war. He's been pissed at me since he found out I joined the Marines, and was even more livid when I was called to active duty. He's never been a patriotic person; the only thing he cares about is making money and there's no point trying to make him see that the only reason he's *free* to make the money he loves so much is because of the men and women fighting halfway across the world.

"Fisher, we need to go over the menu for the rehearsal dinner one last time. Can you and Lucy stop by for dinner one night this week?" my mother asks, trying to defuse the situation.

She probably should have known that, aside from talk of my unacceptable career choices, the only other thing that would set my father off was talk of Lucy and our upcoming wedding.

My father sighs from the couch. "I don't understand why you feel the need to get married so young. You're twenty-two and she's only twenty. What in God's name is the rush?"

I clench my hands into fists at my sides and take a few deep, calming breaths. I don't know why I even let him get to me at this point. He's been like this for as long as I can remember, never happy with my decisions and always thinking he knows what's best for me. The truth is, even though we shared a home for nearly eighteen years, my father knows shit-all about me.

"We're not rushing anything. We've been together for almost four years and we love each other. I have a dangerous job and we know better than to take a second for granted. What does it matter if we get married two weeks from now or two years from now?" I ask.

"What matters is that there are much better choices out there for you, son. Women with money and a social status befitting someone of the Fisher name. She and her parents are middle class, at best, as were her grandparents before them that opened that Godforsaken eyesore on the edge of the island. Why you would want to lower yourself to that level when you have so much more potential is beyond me," he complains.

"You don't know the first thing about Lucy or her family. She is an amazing, intelligent, wonderful woman who loves me. Her parents are caring and supportive and they accept me for who I am, not for what's in my bank account. You would know that if you took one second to get to know them instead of judging them from afar," I argue.

My father just shakes his head in annoyance and I turn my back on him, kissing my mother on the cheek and telling her I'll get back to her about a night that Lucy and I will be free for dinner so we can finalize the wedding plans before the big day in a couple weeks.

As I head out the front door of the giant home by the sea that I grew up in, I wonder why I continue to come back here and torture myself with my father's disapproval. I do it to see my mother, but even that isn't worth the arguments most of the time because she never defends me. She never sticks up for me in front of my father, even though in private she always tells me how proud she is of me.

Standing on the front walkway, I stare up at the huge, three story European-style mansion that my father likes to call "The Estate." It's a monstrosity a few miles outside of town that sits up on a cliff with a few acres of manicured gardens on one side and nothing but the ocean on the other. It looks down on the town so my father can feel like the king he believes himself to be. I never felt comfortable living in this house and the best decision I ever made was going to live with my grandfather the day I told my parents I'd signed up for the Marines instead of applying for college.

I will never be like that man. I will never value money over my own family and their happiness. My father makes Lucy feel like she's not worthy to walk in the door of their home and it fills me with so much rage. I hate that he makes her feel insecure about herself and her family. I hate that he refuses to see how happy she makes me and how good my life is with her in it. No matter what, I will never make Lucy feel like she is anything but perfect and worth the bullshit I have to deal with from my father. I don't care that he could buy and sell her family ten times over. The only thing I care about is that they are decent, caring people. There aren't enough people like that left in this world and I am lucky that I will get to call them my family in just two short weeks.

Getting into my truck, I drive as fast as I can through the narrow island roads until I'm screeching to a halt in front of the inn. I race inside and find Lucy standing in front of the desk with her back to me, going over some paperwork. She's wearing a short, charcoal grey wool skirt with tall black boots and a soft white sweater that clings to her chest and small waist, making my hands itch with the need to run them underneath the material and feel her skin. She looks over her shoulder at me and smiles and all of the tension from being around my father slowly trickles out of me.

"I'm almost finished here," she tells me, turning her body around to face me. "How did it go at your parent's house? How did your mom like the bench?"

"It was fine, and she loved it," I tell her, not wanting to get into all the shit my father said. I want to forget about my father and just concentrate on the woman in front of me who will soon be my wife. I want to make her happy and I want to make her dreams come true. Nothing else matters, especially what my father thinks.

She finally finishes with her paperwork and walks towards me, sliding easily into my open arms and resting her cheek against my chest.

"I missed you," she tells me softly as I kiss the top of her head.

"I missed you, too. Always," I reply, squeezing her tighter against me.

Even though we saw each other this morning, ever since I came home from this deployment, each moment we're apart makes both of us anxious and on edge.

I reluctantly pull away from her and grab both of her hands, tugging her towards the door. "Come on, let's go for a drive. I have something to show you."

We race hand-in-hand out to my truck and Lucy

badgers me the entire five minute drive, asking me where we're going and what I'm up to. I just smile and refuse to answer her until I pull down a driveway and up to the house I just signed the papers on a few days ago.

"What are we doing here?" she asks curiously as she follows my lead and we both get out of the car.

I meet her at the front of the truck and grab her hand, pulling her across the side lawn to the porch that over-looks the ocean.

"Um, should we be walking up on these people's porch? I think this is considered trespassing," Lucy whispers as she presses herself against my back and I lead us to the door.

I laugh as I let go of her hand and flip through the keys on my keychain until I find the one I'm looking for. I stick it in the lock and turn the handle, opening the door wide before I turn back around to look at her. The moon is shining bright and she's backdropped by the ocean behind her. She stares up at me in confusion and wonder and I can't stop myself from leaning down and kissing her. Mid-kiss, I bend down and scoop her up into my arms. She lets out a squeal and throws her arms around my neck, holding on tight.

I step through the doorway and smile down at the shadow of her face. "Sorry, I can't turn the lights on because I haven't paid the electricity deposit yet. But welcome to your new home, soon-to-be Mrs. Fisher."

I can see the whites of her eyes as they go wide in shock. I slowly set her on her feet and she turns in a circle, looking at the area lit by the glow of the moon shining through all of the windows along the front of the house.

"Are you kidding me right now?" she whispers in awe.

I laugh, walking up behind her and wrapping my arms around her waist.

"Nope, not kidding. I bought it, it's ours. I really, really hope you like it because I don't think I can return it."

She doesn't say a word as she continues to look around. We're standing in a combination living room/kitchen/dining room. It's a large, open floor plan where no matter what room you're in, you can see everything. The entire front wall is filled with floor to ceiling windows that look out over the ocean. It's a small, two bedroom-one bathroom home, but I loved everything about it the first time I saw it and I could picture Lucy and I starting a life here so clearly in my head that I had to buy it. Now I'm wondering if I did the right thing. She's been quiet for so long that I'm starting to get nervous.

"Seriously, if you don't like it, I'm sure I still have time to take back the offer. We can look at something else and you can-"

She turns quickly in my arms and presses her fingers against my lips. "I love it. It's so perfect I want to cry. I can't believe you did this."

I wrap my hand around hers and pull it away from my mouth, pressing a kiss into her palm. "Of course I did this. I would do anything for you. I know it's not much, but we can fix it up, paint it however you want. I just love the idea of waking up with you every morning, sitting out on the porch and watching the sun come up."

She leans up on her tiptoes and presses her lips to mine. I slide my tongue against her lips and she immediately opens for me. It's not long before the kiss turns from sweet to fierce, our tongues battling together while our hands roam frantically, touching every part of each other that we can reach. I lift her up against my body without breaking the kiss and she wraps her legs around my waist. Not being able to see very well in the dark, I walk us over to the closest flat surface I can find – the counter in the kitchen – and set her down on top.

Her hands reach for the button of my jeans and my hands slide up the outside of her thighs under her wool skirt. Right when she gets my pants undone, I slide my fingers in the edge of her thong and pull it down her legs, tossing it to the side. My hand immediately goes between her thighs and my fingers slide through her to find her wet and ready for me. I lose my concentration momentarily when her small hand wraps around my cock and starts sliding up and down the length.

I try to distract myself with thoughts of something other than how good Lucy feels so I don't blow my load right in her hand, and the first thing that pops into my head is my asshole father and the words he spoke tonight. It fills me with anger and I distractedly push Lucy's hand away from my cock, line myself up against her opening and push myself into her roughly. The sound of her surprised gasp brings me back to the present and I hold myself completely still inside of her.

"Jesus, I'm sorry, Lucy. I'm sorry, did I hurt you?" I

whisper brokenly as I start to pull out of her.

Fuck, I need to calm down. What the hell is wrong with me?

Her hands clutch my ass and she tilts her hips, pulling me deeper inside of her.

"No, no, don't stop. Please, don't stop," she whispers softly.

I rest my forehead against hers while my cock pulses inside of her. I need to move so badly it's killing me. She's so soft, so warm and feels so good, but I'm afraid to move. I'm afraid the anger simmering just below the surface is going to take over and I'm going to hurt her again. I know she's only encouraging me because she doesn't want me to think I shocked her and hurt her. I'm always slow and gentle with her. I've never just slammed inside of her without getting her plenty ready for me, taking my time, showing her how much I cherish her.

She keeps her hands on my ass, tugging me forward and I have no choice but to move before I explode. I make it up to her by taking it slow, pushing and pulling my cock out of her gently, the way she deserves. I bring my hand down between us and slide my thumb over her clit exactly the way she likes until she's moaning and whispering my name. The sound of my name on her lips when she's coming is the one thing that keeps me grounded and keeps me in the here and now with her. I feel her clench around me and her thighs squeeze tighter around my hips as I work in and out of her achingly slow. She holds me tightly to her and rocks against me through her orgasm and I follow right behind, whispering her name against her ear and telling her how much I love her.

We stay against the kitchen counter for as long as it takes to calm our racing hearts, our arms wrapped around each other as I continue to whisper words of love and remind her how lucky I am to have her.

My father will never approve of the choices I've made in my life and I can't keep letting his opinions get to me and fuck with my mind. I'm just going to have to live with that and find my own happiness without him. Right here, in this kitchen, is the only happiness I need.

Chapter 18

Fisher

Present Day

"EXPLAIN YOURSELF, OLD man."

I'm standing in Trip's kitchen with my arms crossed and my foot tapping against the floor.

"Watch your mouth, boy. I can still wash it out with soap," he replies with a huff as he shuffles around the small room, fixing himself a sandwich.

"You're forgetting that I used to like the taste of soap," I tell him with a hint of a smile.

"You always were a cocky little shit. You'd swear, I'd put soap in your mouth and you'd tell me it was delicious. Remember that time—"

"Quit stalling," I interrupt him. "I know you had something to do with those monthly deposits for Lucy. She thinks it was me and I had no idea what she was talking about and now she's pissed at me."

Trip laughs, opening up the fridge to put the mayo and bologna away. "The day you do something that DOESN'T piss that poor girl off will be the day hell freezes over."

He slams the door closed, takes his plate to the small table in the corner of the room and sits down. He then proceeds to take a few bites of his sandwich, chewing as slowly as possible just to piss me off. Right when I'm about to snatch that damn sandwich from his hand and chuck it across the room, he finally starts talking again.

"That girl has had it pretty rough the last year. You up and left and it damn near tore her in two. Ellie and I had to practically drag her out of bed just to get her to take a shower and eat. Then, she'd crawl right back in that bed and not come out for days."

His words tear *me* in two, but I know I need to hear them. I'd punished myself with visions of what Lucy went through after what I did to her, but hearing it all laid out for me and finding out it was much worse is torture.

"On top of that, your daddy kept showing up, telling her he knew it was only a matter of time before you came to your senses and kicked her to the curb and that you lasted a lot longer than he thought you would. Girl's heart was already broken and he had to go and ruin her pride on top of it. Should have sent *that* little shit off to the military when he was a boy," Trip mutters under his breath. "Right when she starts coming around, getting out of that damn bedroom, learning to be happy again, fucking pipe bursts at the inn and floods the place. Leaked clean through the floor to the ceiling downstairs until the whole thing almost caved in. It was a bigger job than I could handle, and we had to call in a lot of professionals from the mainland to redo everything. New plumbing, new ceiling and floors and all new pipes and bathroom fixtures. Thirteen bathrooms that all needed replaced. It was a big job, took a lot of money. More money than was in her bank account, including the lump sum you sent her during the divorce that she refused to touch. Seeing as I own the majority of Fisher's Bank and Trust, I went behind her back and took that money out and used it. Boy, that girl sure came to life after that. I've never heard her scream so loud or swear so much."

He pauses to chuckle, shaking his head while he sits there, probably remembering when it happened. I can imagine it perfectly in my head, especially after the talking to she gave me on the beach earlier, and I almost laugh myself until I remember that I wasn't there when I should have been. It should have been me helping her when something went wrong at the inn. The fact that my money helped is no consolation; it just makes me feel worse. I never wanted her to feel like the money I'd made could fix everything or that she couldn't do something on her own without my help. It pains me to know that she didn't want to touch that money and the choice was taken out of her hands. I can only imagine how much that would have hurt her already bruised pride.

"That doesn't explain the monthly deposits she mentioned. Where in the hell did those come from?"

Trip shrugs and goes back to his sandwich. "I might have said some things to your mother right after you left. You know, just throwing out how the girl was struggling and how she refused to accept anything from me. Might want to check with her."

I narrow my eyes at him, but he ignores me, finishing off his meal and taking his plate to the sink to wash it. He absolutely knows more than he's letting on, but he gave me enough information for now. Time to move on to the next responsible party.

"I CAN'T BELIEVE you've been back on the island for two weeks and this is the first I'm seeing you."

I kiss my mother on the cheek and she slides her hand through the crook of my arm, leading me into the front sitting room of my parent's home. We sit down together on the love seat and I turn to face her.

"I know, and I'm sorry. I've just been really busy. I meant to stop by right when I got into town, but things got a little crazy with work," I explain.

"I saw the new sign on the front of the Lobster Bucket this morning, it's beautiful," she beams, reaching over to pat my hand.

I took Lucy's advice and tried to figure out a way to make amends with the people whose businesses I fucked up the night of my meltdown. The windows I smashed had long since been repaired, so it's not like I could fix those, but I could at least do something else to show my appreciation for the support they've always given me and to apologize for what I did. I've spent the last two weeks making brand new wooden signs for each of the three businesses, as well as new benches for the front of their shops that have the names of the businesses carved into the backs of them. I've worked nonstop, only stopping to sleep and eat when my shoulder and arm gave out on me, but it was worth it. Delivering the gifts personally and talking to the owners, people who have been in my life since birth, was as rewarding as making it thirteen months without a drop of alcohol. We talked, I apologized and explained to them what I was going through at the time and they each forgave me easily and welcomed me back into their establishments. It was a step in the right direction and it made me feel good about myself for the first time in a long time.

"Thanks," I tell my mother. "I delivered Sal's this morning. Old man actually shed a few tears when I gave him the sign. I just have one more to finish up and deliver and then I'll be done."

My mother smiles at me and squeezes my hand.

"You're looking good, Fisher. Healthy…happy. I like the beard," she tells me with a smile.

I run my hand over my cheek and shrug. "I don't know, I've been thinking about shaving it."

She quickly shakes her head. "Oh no, don't do that. I hear scruff is all the rage with the ladies. At least, that's what it says in my *Cosmo*."

We both laugh easily.

"Yeah, well I'm only looking to make it the rage with one lady in particular, and she seems to be into the clean-shaven, suit-wearing look nowadays," I tell her, trying not to sound so depressed.

Even though I've been sequestered in the basement of my grandfather's house for the last two weeks, I've still had to run into town every once in a while to grab supplies and I've seen Lucy a few times from a distance—always with Stankford, always looking beautiful and always laughing. It should be *me* making her laugh, *me* whose hand she holds as she walks through town. I hate that every time I see her she's wearing fancy clothes with her hair and make-up all perfect. She was never more beautiful than when she was fresh-faced in just a pair of shorts and a t-shirt.

"Things aren't always what they seem, Fisher, you should know that. Look how long I went without realizing how much you were suffering? It kills me that you were in so much pain all that time and I never even knew," she tells me sadly.

"Mom, don't. No one knew, not even Lucy. It wasn't exactly something I wanted to share with people. It was a dark time and I fell apart. I hurt a lot of people and I'm glad you weren't around to witness it," I tell her.

Not only did I push Lucy away back then, I also pushed my mother away. I stopped coming out here to the house for dinner and I stopped accepting her invitations to meet in town. I was already dragging Lucy down with me, and I didn't want my mother to be affected as well.

"Speaking of Lucy, you wouldn't happen to know anything about monthly deposits into a special savings account in her name, would you?"

She looks away from me guiltily and starts fidgeting with the gold watchband on her wrist.

"M-o-o-o-m?" I drag out her name and tap my fingers against my leg, waiting for her to admit what she did.

She sighs, folding her hands together in her lap and finally looking back up at me. "Fine. Yes, it was me. I was just worried about her after you left. I overheard your father talking to someone on the phone about how she could barely pay the bills and then Trip mentioned something about a bunch of repairs that wiped out her savings account and I felt bad, so I set up an account one day when your father was out of town on business. I'm sorry, I probably shouldn't have done it, but I didn't know what else to do. I knew she'd never come to us for help, why would she? Your father has never accepted her and I've been just as bad by letting him treat her the way he does. I wanted to do something for all the hurt this family has caused her over the years."

It's hard for me to be mad at her, even though her actions royally screwed things up between Lucy and me. She was just trying to help the only way she knew how. She had no way of knowing how much it would hurt Lucy's pride to have that money given to her, making her feel like she couldn't make it on her own and that she needed help.

"It's okay, Mom. It was a really nice thing for you to do, but could you do me a favor and put an end to the monthly deposits? I'm in a little hot water right now because of them and it's not exactly helping my case with Lucy," I explain, lightening the request with a smile so I don't hurt her feelings.

"Done. I'll take care of it tomorrow," she agrees with a nod.

We sit in silence for a few moments, enjoying the sound of the waves crashing against the rocks outside that we can hear through the open window.

"I'm so happy you're doing better, Fisher. You really

do look well. I'm sure it will only be a matter of time before Lucy notices that, as well," she tells me softly with a smile.

I shake my head and lean back against the couch, glancing out the window over her shoulder to stare at the ocean. "I don't know, Mom. I just don't know what to do. I made so many mistakes with her and I hurt her so much. I just want her to see that I'm different now, that I'll never go down that path again, but every time I try to talk to her, all I seem to do is piss her off. I want a future with her. I want to love her forever and I want to take care of her. I just don't even know where to begin making things right…"

I trail off, pulling my gaze away from the ocean to look at my mother. Even though we've never been all that close because of my father, she's still always been an easy person to talk to or go to for advice. Add to that the fact that she always adored Lucy, I knew she would be the only person I could count on to help me figure this thing out.

She reaches over and grabs my hand, tugging me up from the couch.

"Come on, I want to show you something," she tells me as she leads me through the house, up the main staircase and down the hall to my old bedroom.

When she pushes open the door and pulls me inside, I pause and try to force my heart to stop racing as I look around the room. Years ago, she'd converted this room into an office for herself so she could work on the many volunteer projects she organizes. Her computer desk still sits in the corner next to the window, but the paintings and other artwork that used to hang on the wall have been replaced with shadowboxes and other framed items. A part of me wants to run out of this room so I don't have to see all of the memorabilia she's hung on the walls, but I know I can't do that. The whole point of sticking with therapy for a year was to finally exorcise all of these fucking demons. What kind of a coward would I be if I couldn't stare them down right now?

Walking slowly around the room, I look at my Purple Heart, displayed inside a shadow box along with the official letter that came with it. My shoulder injury was the catalyst to my coming home from that last tour and what I did to Lucy in our kitchen. I didn't want to leave my men behind and I certainly didn't want to leave them for something I didn't consider a "real" injury. Men were losing life and limb and I was forced to go home for a few pieces of metal in my shoulder that damaged a nerve. I was pissed that I received a medal for doing my fucking job, so pissed that I refused to attend the ceremony and shoved it into a box without looking at it as soon as it came in the mail.

Next to the Purple Heart is a framed article from our local newspaper's write-up after my first deployment on their "local boy" who went overseas. My uniform hangs from the back of the closet door and my camouflaged backpack, stained with blood from my shoulder injury, rests on the floor against the wall.

I clench and unclench my fists to keep them from shaking as I squat down and run my hand over the pack, remembering the weight of it on my back through so many years and so many deployments. All of the items in this room were shoved into a tote in the back of my closet at the house Lucy and I shared because I couldn't stand to look at them, knowing they would bring me nothing but bad memories and horrible flashbacks. Bobby told me he'd given the tote to my mother when he cleaned up the mess I'd made of my house, but I never expected her to pull them out and turn this room into a shrine, showcasing everything I'd been through. Tears fill my eyes when I think about all the men who lost their lives, men that I lived with, men that I fought with and men that became my brothers. So many lives lost and I've never understood why I got to come home, year after year. I could never comprehend why I was one of the lucky ones that wasn't shipped home in a flag-draped coffin.

Glancing above me, I see a framed picture of Lucy and I on our wedding day and I'm immediately reminded why I'm so fucking lucky.

"I'm so proud of everything you've done, Fisher and I'm so sorry for what you went through," my mother tells me as I stand back up and turn to face her. "I hope you don't mind that I pulled all of this stuff out, but I just don't think it should be hidden away. YOU should be proud of what you did, as well."

For the first time, looking at all of these things doesn't fill me with dread. I don't hear screams and explosions in my head and I don't feel the need to suck down a bottle of whiskey to make the memories go away. I served my country and did the best that I could do. I sacrificed years away from the woman I loved and it's time that I stand tall for the things I've done and be proud of what I accomplished.

My mother walks over to the closet where my uniform hangs, opens the door and pulls out a box, handing it over to me.

"Maybe what you need to do is stop worrying about what the future will bring and concentrate on the past. The only way you'll get to the end is by starting at the beginning. Maybe Lucy just needs a reminder of how it all started."

I take the box from her, sliding the lid off of the top. I can't believe I forgot about this box. I'd stuffed it at the bottom of my tote when I returned from my last deployment, determined to ignore the proof that my wife loved me enough to fight my demons so that I could find the strength to leave her. Flipping through letters, photos and sketches of most of my wood working projects, I find a journal I'd kept in high school and for a few years after. Much like the ones in the therapy journal I was forced to keep at the VA, these journal entries read more like short stories, a testament to my lifetime love of creative writing. Glancing through some of the pages, I look up and smile at my mom.

It's perfect and it's exactly what I needed. My mother is right, the only way I'm going to show Lucy that we belong together is by reminding her where we began.

Chapter 19

From Fisher's High School Journal

September 30, 2001

"I CAN'T BELIEVE you did it, man."

Holding the USMC t-shirt up in front of me, I smile when Bobby smacks me on the back and shakes his head at me.

"You heard the guy. Our country needs us, now more than ever. What happened here a few weeks ago is unacceptable. Our country, our freedom and our future are at stake. I can't just sit around here in Podunk, Nowhere and do nothing," I explain, balling up the shirt and shoving a corner of it into the back pocket of my jeans.

The Marines came to our school today to do a recruiting presentation. The only reason I signed up to go was to get out of Advanced Chemistry, but the more the guy talked, the more I listened. Not only would being in the Marines get me off of this island when I graduated in June, it would give me a chance to actually *do* something important after what happened on September 11th. This country has felt helpless and scared for the last few weeks and I've been glued to the television, wishing there was something I could do to make those fuckers pay for coming to our country and ruining so many lives.

"You're a true American hero, my friend. You know your dad is going to shit a brick, right?" Bobby laughs.

I don't give a fuck what my father thinks. I've wanted off of Fisher's Island for as long as I could remember and this is my chance.

"He told me last week he would only pay for college if I went for business economics and commuted to the mainland. I'm going to throw this shirt in his face and give him the finger when I get home tonight," I tell Bobby as we make our way to the cafeteria between classes.

The only thing that gives me pause about signing up for the military and leaving this island is my grandfather. Trip Fisher is more of a father to me than my own. Even though it was his father who founded this island, he's never cared about making more money than he could ever use in this lifetime or finding new ways to get more tourists here. He's the island handyman and lives in a small, two-bedroom cottage right off of Main Street. He's a friend to everyone and doesn't mind getting his hands dirty to help the people of this island, who are all like family to him. He's taught me how to do everything from build an addition on a house to fix a leaky faucet, much to my father's annoyance. As much as I want to get away from this place, I couldn't imagine leaving my grandfather for too long. He's been a widower since before I was born, losing my grandmother to cancer when my father was a young boy. My grandfather has mentioned to me on more than one occasion that he believes my father is the way he is partly because he never had a woman's influence growing up. Trip did the best he could, but sometimes a boy just needs the soft hand and gentle love of a mother to help mold him into a good, caring person. Since my father thinks his shit doesn't stink and rarely associates with Trip unless it benefits him in some way, I'm really the only family he has left.

Loud voices and the clanging of trays and silverware bring me out of my thoughts as we walk into the cafeteria. My name is called and high-fives are exchanged at least fifteen times as Bobby and I make our way through the room to our usual table in the back corner with the rest of our friends. Being the son of the self-proclaimed king of Fisher's Island means I'm pretty high on the popularity scale. Not to sound like a cocky little shit or anything, but all the guys want to be friends with me and all the chicks want to fuck me. I'm never without a party to attend on Friday night and I always have a girl to warm my bed on Saturday.

Flopping down on the bench at our table, a chick I made the mistake of hooking up with a few weekends ago slides up next to me and wraps her arms around my waist.

"Fisher, I feel like I haven't seen you all day," Melanie Sanders purrs into my ear. "I've missed you."

Bobby slides in on the other side of the table next to her best friend, Trish McCallister, and drops his arm around her shoulders. "Did you miss me too, Trish?"

Trish smacks his hand away, grabs her soda from the table and dumps it into his lap. "Fuck you, Bobby."

Everyone at the table laughs at Bobby's expense as Trish storms away and he grabs a few napkins to try and sop up the mess in his crotch.

Extricating myself from Melanie's arms and scooting a few inches away, I try not to wince as I move. "Sorry, babe. I've been busy. How about you run up and get Bobby a new Pepsi?"

Pulling a few dollars out of my pocket, I toss them in front of her. She scoops them up and scurries away.

Bobby laughs and rolls his eyes at me. "Well, I think that concludes the list. You have now fucked the entire female student body. I don't understand how none of these girls hate your guts."

"I've learned to be polite when I tell them I won't be repeating our time together, unlike yourself. Seriously, man, you need to learn how be a little more smooth. Making out with Angela two hours after you screwed Trish probably wasn't your best move," I remind him.

"Eh, bitches be trippin,' and all that shit," Bobby shrugs.

Movement catches my eye over his left shoulder and I crane my neck to see around him as a girl with strawberry blonde hair trips over someone's bag and flails all over the place to try and keep her tray from toppling to the ground. A few people laugh at her expense and her face flushes bright red as she hurries to an empty table and quickly sits down. She keeps her head bowed and her long hair covers her face while she picks up a fork and mindlessly moves the food around on her tray. A noise from the front of the cafeteria makes her jerk her head up and she looks right at me. Her eyes are so blue I can see the color from all the way over here. She's not like most of the girls that go to this school who barely wear enough clothes to cover their tits and ass and slap on enough war paint to put a clown to shame. I wouldn't call her gorgeous. She was more along the lines of cute with her fresh, make-up free face, tiny nose and full pink lips that she nervously licks as she continues to look at me. There's just something about her that makes my dick stir in my jeans and I don't know whether to be pissed off that some chick who is so different from my usual has caught my eye or walk over to her and try to charm my way into her pants.

She finally breaks eye contact and goes back to pushing her food from one end of her tray to the other.

"Hey, who's the new girl back there?" I ask Bobby.

He stops trying to dry off his pants and turns around to see where I'm looking.

"Ah, fresh sophomore meat. I think someone said her name is Lucy. She just moved to the island this week. Her parents own Butler House Inn."

He turns back around to face me and narrows his eyes at me. "Not your type, man. Don't even think about it."

I finally pull my eyes away from her and scoff at him. "Oh, please. Clearly, she's not my type. She looks like she might burst into tears any second now. I prefer my women to have a little more backbone and a lot more tits."

I continue to sneak glances at her every time Bobby turns to talk to someone else at our table and realize what I said to Bobby was complete bullshit. Sure, I'm a boob man and this Lucy person isn't popping out of her shirt like most of the girls here, but there's just something about her that I can't take my eyes off of. I have the urge to walk over to her, see if her voice sounds as sweet as she looks and get people to stop fucking gawking at her like she's some kind of freak show. I realize I'm a total hypocrite since I can't look away either, but at least I'm not turned around in my seat staring at her like a zoo animal like half the people in this room. No one talks to her or tries to sit with her, they just stare. I get it, it's not often we get new people moving to the island. Sure, people are always coming and going during the summer tourist months, but they're mainland people and it's like they're from another planet. They think it's "cute" that we live here year-round and they think our town is "quaint." They mess up our shit for a few months and then they go back home to their bustling cities and huge skyscrapers and laugh about the island people who never leave. Not many people come here to stay permanently, and it makes me more than a little curious about who she is and where she comes from.

While Bobby is busy talking to a few of the guys about what's going on this weekend, I take the opportunity to sneak away from the table, making my way over to Lucy.

She looks up at me in surprise when I plop down next to her and smile.

"Four."

Her long eyelashes flutter rapidly and her hand comes up to brush her hair out of her eyes.

"Um, what?" she asks softly.

"Four. The number of things I know about you," I explain, giving her my most charming smile and bringing my hand up to tick the things off on my fingers. "Your name is Lucy Butler, you're a sophomore, your family owns Butler House Inn, and you're fucking adorable."

Moving my hand in front of her, I hold it out for a handshake, wanting to see if her hand is as soft and smooth as the skin on her flushed cheeks looks. "Name's Fisher."

She stares down at my hand for a second before rolling her eyes and pushing herself up from the table. "Yeah, I know who you are. Not interested."

I don't even have time to be shocked before she grabs her backpack from the bench, slings it over her shoulder and walks away from me without another word. I can't help staring at her ass as she leaves and I also can't stop the smile that takes over my face. I'm not really used to rejection when it comes to girls. Sure, my father rejected every fucking idea I've ever had, but girls? Never happens. All I have to do is turn on the charm and I could have any girl in this room riding my dick in a matter of seconds.

Lucy Butler is an anomaly and right now, that makes me respect her more than any fucking person on this entire island. It also makes her a thousand times more appealing. I might have to put in a little work to get close to Lucy. Oh, this is going to be so much fun.

Chapter 20

Lucy

Present Day

I HAVEN'T BEEN able to stop thinking about what happened in town two weeks ago. Fisher's father's words keep popping up in my head every time I turn around. Am I in over my head? Am I just living in a fantasy where I think I can actually make this place work and keep it forever? I'm drowning in bills and I've been late entirely too often on the mortgage recently. When my parents took over this place, they thought it was an affordable mortgage and it was at the time, until the repairs and the cost of upkeep multiplied month after month. The only thing saving me right now is an inn full of guests and the steady income peak season rates provides.

Flopping down on the bed in one of the guest rooms at the cottage, I stare around the room with a heavy heart. With a different lighthouse theme in every guest room, the Fisher's Lighthouse room has always been my favorite. Decorated in several shades of blue to represent the ocean you can see from the two large windows against the main wall, it's filled with framed photos I took over the years of the lighthouse here on the south end of the island, as well as a couple of replica sculptures I've collected over the years. This room feels like home. This room *is* home. Pushing myself up from the bed, I walk over to the window and run my hand over the two-foot tall wood carving of the lighthouse that sits on the floor in between the two windows. It's a near perfect replica of the lighthouse that you can just barely see in the distance out the windows it sits in front of. I don't remember where it came from, but it's always been my favorite decoration in the house. Maybe because when I look at it, it reminds me of better times...happier times. So many good memories happened for me out at that lighthouse and all of them involve Fisher.

As I make my way out of the bedroom, I slowly walk through the rest of the inn. With eleven oversized guestrooms, it was the largest place for guest accommodations when my grandparents built it. Now that the town has grown, there are several hotels with special amenities like in-ground pools and twenty-four-hour gyms that Butler House can't compete with. That has always been what I loved about this place, though. It's not a copycat of every other hotel all over the world with the same décor on every floor and people shouting and running up and down the halls. When you come to Butler House, you come to relax and enjoy the peace and tranquility that only an ocean town can bring. You come for the old world-style design that takes you back to a time when life was simpler.

Butler House is a traditional, wooden, Georgian double house with a center stairway and two large rooms on either side – a sprawling sitting room and the registration area on one side, and a library with a side bar on the other. The entire back of the house on the first floor is taken up by the kitchen and dining area, as well as a small laundry room. In the tradition of Georgian double houses, there is a fireplace at either end of the house, one in the sitting room and one in the library. Most of the house still has the original floors, aside from the areas that had to be redone after the damn pipe burst upstairs last year, ruining some of the pine planking.

Making my way through the kitchen and dining area to the sliding glass door at the back of the house, I pull it open and step out onto Butler House's most popular feature. The veranda stretches along the entire length of the back of the house and faces the ocean. It's lined with rocking chairs, all handmade by Fisher, but I take a seat in my personal favorite, the one with lighthouses carved into the headrest. Staring out at the water, I watch as the sky around it grows darker as the sun sets.

Two guests are seated at the far end of the veranda and I smile and wave at them as they lazily rock back and forth and enjoy the view. I try not to cry as I think about this place being torn down and traded in for a modern-day resort. No one will be able to sit here to stare out at the ocean with the twinkling lights of distant ships dotting the surface. They'll be too busy splashing in the huge waterpark that will block the view and make people forget the beauty of the place they're staying. I thought when I moved here that it would just be a stopping point for me before I went off to college and eventually traveled the world. I wanted so much to see what the world had to offer, but I quickly realized that this place, my island, was all that I needed.

Well, that and the love of a good man.

Things changed and, while I might have lost that man along the way, at least I still had the inn. Now, I wonder if maybe I've been living in the past too long. I'm trying to hold on to something that will never come back to me – the popularity of an old-fashioned inn *and* the man who fulfilled all my hopes and dreams…until he didn't. Maybe it's time for me to finally let go. Staying here, being so attached to this building is keeping me rooted in the past, still wishing for things that I have no business wishing for. Staying here keeps the memories of what might have been alive and it's preventing me from moving on.

I hear the *whoosh* of the sliding glass door and turn to see Trip walk through it. He stares out at the ocean as he takes a seat in the rocking chair next to mine. We rock in silence for a few minutes before he finally speaks.

"You're a stubborn one, Lucy girl. It's always been one of the things I liked about you."

I smile at his gruff voice, resting my head against the back of my chair.

"Sometimes, though, that stubbornness can make you blind to what's right in front of you. I know you weren't happy when I took that money Fisher gave you and paid for all the repairs on this place."

I purse my lips, thinking back to that day a year ago when all I wanted to do was give up when I found out how much damage that busted pipe had done to the inn.

I was still plenty angry about the divorce alone and, when I found out half of Fisher's money had been deposited into my checking account without any notice, I was downright livid. I vowed never to touch that damn money, no matter what. Then, Trip went behind my back and touched it anyway.

"I realize you think of that money as a slap in the face, a way for him to prove he was better than you because he had more money, but you know him better than that."

I stop rocking, turning my body to face the old man. "I thought I knew him better than that, but obviously I didn't. Fine, so he didn't send that money to be mean, but the damn monthly deposits were unnecessary and cruel and you know it. He wanted to erase the life we shared, but he still had to send those stupid reminders every month for the past year. Every month, right when I think I'm finally starting to forget that he's out there somewhere, living a life without me, I get those damn deposits and it hits me all over again."

Trip stops rocking, as well, and finally pulls his gaze away from the ocean to stare at me. "Wasn't him, girl, and he didn't know anything about it until you ripped him a new asshole. He had nothing to do with those monthly deposits, even though he would have given you every penny he had for the rest of his life if it were up to him. He knew better than to insult you like that, no matter how hard it was for him not to take care of you. If I'd known how pissy you were about that damn account, I would have told you the truth a long time ago so you didn't jump to conclusions."

I narrow my eyes at him. "Trip Fisher, did you set up that account?"

He barks out a laugh and shakes his head at me. "I'm old, but I'm not stupid. You'd probably beat me with my own hammer if I did something like that. No, it wasn't me. If you think about it hard enough, I'm sure you'll figure out there's one other person in the Fisher family who always had a soft spot for you."

I stare at him quizzically for a moment before the answer smacks me in the face.

Shit.

Grace Fisher, the mother-in-law who tried her hardest to accept me when her husband hated the sight of me. She went out of her way to praise me when her husband wasn't around, checked up on me when Fisher was deployed and made sure I was doing okay with the inn. I should have known she might do something like that, but my anger with Fisher made me blind to what was right in front of me, just like Trip said.

I feel awful. I tore into Fisher at the beach two weeks ago and he had no idea what I was talking about. I blamed him for something he didn't do and let my anger get the best of me.

"He's at my house, working on some stuff in the basement," Trip says casually as he resumes rocking and staring out at the water.

"A little presumptuous of you, don't you think? What makes you think I care where he is right now?"

Trip just laughs and ignores my question. Of course he knows I care, the man is like a damn mind reader and knows I'm going to feel guilty about what I just learned and want to apologize.

I push myself up casually from the rocking chair, making a show of stretching and acting like I don't fully intend to hightail it straight to Trip's house when I step off this porch.

"I think I'll just check on some paperwork and call it a night. You gonna stay here for a little while?" I ask him casually.

He nods and gives me a wink. "Yep. Think I'll sit right here for, oh, maybe an hour or two and enjoy your view. It's the best one on the island. You have fun with your paperwork now, and don't worry about me."

Patting him on the shoulder, I turn and head to the sliding door and pull it open. Trip calls to me as I step inside.

"Spare key's under the welcome mat on the front porch."

I growl at him and slam the sliding door closed as I stomp through the house.

Irritating, meddling old man.

PUSHING OPEN THE door to Trip's house, I hear the soft cadence of music coming from the basement. I recognize the song immediately and my heart beats faster. "Storm" by Lifehouse was a song I played on repeat the first few weeks after Fisher left. I was like a teenage girl with a broken heart, listening to depressing songs while I cried out my pain against my pillow.

"If I could just see you, everything would be alright.
If I'd see you, this darkness would turn to light."

The song speaks of the person you love leaving you to drown, and it was a perfect representation of the loss I felt after Fisher left me. Listening to it back then ripped my already fragile heart into even smaller pieces. Hearing it now takes me back to that time and makes me want to claw at my chest.

I move in a daze, the sound drawing me in like it has a magnetic pull, needing to torture myself further with the softly broken words that haunted my dreams for months. When I get to the bottom of the stairs, I pause and stare at the sight in front of me. Fisher, his back to me, is in a pair of tan cargo shorts and a dark blue t-shirt, bent over something he's working on. The muscles in his arms ripple as he slides a piece of sand paper over the wood, pressing down hard to get it as smooth as possible.

His hands and forearms are covered in dust from the sanding and I think about all the times I'd sit out on our front porch and watch him do the exact same thing, completely in awe of him and the beauty he created with those hands. The same hands that worked tirelessly to make something so beautiful out of an old piece of wood touched me with tenderness and love.

I keep walking towards him, drawn to his body and his presence just like I always have been. My foot bumps against a piece of wood leaning against the wall, knocking it over, and the noise has Fisher's head jerking up in my direction.

He stares at me in surprise, his eyes traveling over my features, and I wonder what he sees on my face right now. The song is still playing, the words swirling around me, taking me back to a time when I felt lost and alone and needed him. Just…needed him.

"I will get lost into your eyes. I know everything will be alright."

His brown eyes stare into mine and I think about all the times he looked at me, really looked at me, and saw me with clear eyes, a clear mind and a clear heart, just like he's doing now. I want to tell him that I have no idea what I'm doing here, that I have no idea what I'm doing with my life and I haven't since he left. Now that he's back, I feel even more lost and confused, like I'm twisting and upside down in a wave in the middle of a hurricane. I have no idea which way is up and I can't seem to find my way to the surface.

Tossing the sandpaper down without a word, Fisher stalks across the room to me, his hands cupping my cheeks and his lips crashing down against mine before I can even blink. His tongue slides past my lips and his body pushes against mine until my back hits the stairwell wall behind me. As soon as his tongue swirls around mine, every thought flies from my mind. I clutch at the front of his shirt and pull him closer, needing more. His thighs and his hips and his stomach press against mine and the weight of his body pushing against me makes it hard to breathe, but I don't even care. I don't need air when his breath is in my mouth, giving me life.

I didn't realize how much I missed the taste and the feel of him until right at this moment. Fantasies and memories are nothing compared to the real thing. I deepen the kiss, pushing harder against his tongue, tasting peppermint and coffee and something that is so uniquely Fisher that my heart beats faster, thrilled at having it back after missing it for so long. Our mouths push and pull against each other and Fisher takes all I have to give with his lips and tongue. Our heads change positions, back and forth as his hands tighten their grip on my face, pulling my mouth harder against his so he can punish me with his lips and tongue. I remember every moment I've kissed this man; the countless times fly through my mind and I lose myself in him and forget the obstacles still standing between us. I moan into his mouth and, just as quickly as the kiss began, it ends. He drops his hands from my face and I immediately feel cold air on my cheeks instead of the warmth of his palms as he takes a few steps back from me, breathing deeply and running one hand nervously through his short, dark hair.

"Jesus, Lucy," Fisher mutters under his breath.

A flicker of the memory of Stanford muttering the same thing to me a few weeks ago floats through my mind, but I push it away. Stanford's curse was filled with shock and a touch of irritation, while Fisher's is filled with nothing but want and need.

Stanford. Shit! What the hell am I doing?

"Lucy, I—"

Pushing myself away from the wall, I edge around him and over to what he was working on, cutting off whatever he was going to say. I don't want his damn apology. If he apologizes to me right now, I will lose my shit all over this basement. I was an idiot for losing my mind as soon as I came down here, but that stupid song and this stupid man are screwing with my head. With his broad shoulders and his strong arms wrapped around me, I felt safe and secure. The light, woodsy smell of his cologne is still burned into my nostrils and the taste of his mouth is still imprinted against my tongue. My cheeks and chin burn from the scratch of his beard and I have to take a few deep breaths to stop myself from turning around to kiss him again. I have a boyfriend. I shouldn't be making out with my ex-husband, who was probably two seconds away from telling me he never meant to kiss me so forcefully, so fucking completely that I forgot about the man in my life I'm supposed to building a future with and all of the ways Fisher hurt me.

"This is beautiful, Fisher," I tell him, changing the subject and running my hands over the sign he was working on when I came down here.

He loves talking about his work and it's the best way to distract him from the giant fucking elephant in the room.

"Thanks," he replies, coming up to stand next to me, but keeping a few feet between us.

I stare at the words *Ruby's Fudge Shop* intricately carved in the middle with a beautiful, swirling design of candies and other confections surrounding it.

"I took your advice and decided to apologize with some gifts. This is the last one, and I'm hoping to finish it tonight so I can drop it off tomorrow."

Stan's Diner, The Lobster Bucket and Ruby's Fudge Shop – the three businesses he damaged last year before he left the island. It touches my heart that he listened to me and did something so thoughtful for these people.

"That's amazing, Fisher. I'm sure they appreciate it," I tell him, trying not to let this sweet side of Fisher turn my insides to mush.

I change the subject again, bringing it back to my real reason for coming here. It wasn't to kiss him and it definitely wasn't to see the old Fisher, the one who always melted my heart.

"Look, I'm sorry to drop in like this, but I wanted to apologize for the way I behaved on the beach. Trip told me it wasn't you who deposited that money, so... I'm sorry. I was a total bitch," I explain, sliding my hands into the back pocket of my shorts and kicking my toe against some of the wood debris littering the floor at my feet.

"You don't have to apologize, Lucy, it's fine. I already had a talk with my mom and she's going to stop the deposits. She just... Well, you know how she is. She doesn't know any better way to say she's sorry or to help someone out," he says with a shrug.

"Thanks. And will you tell her thank you for me? I know her heart was in the right place, but... you know, it's not really appropriate considering..." I trail off, not bothering to add, "*Considering we're divorced and I'm dating someone else even though we just made out a few minutes ago and my body is still burning, wanting more."*

"I'm glad you stopped by, actually," he tells me, moving to the corner of the room. He wipes his hands on the rag tucked in the back of his shorts before bending down and lifting the lid off of a box, rummaging around inside until he finds what he wants. Standing back up, he turns and walks over to me, holding a few folded pieces of paper out to me. "I wanted to give you these."

I take them from his hand, trying not to make a big deal when our fingers brush against each other and I have to force myself not to sigh.

"What is this?" I ask as I start to unfold the papers.

He quickly reaches out and wraps his hand around mine to stop me.

"Don't open it now. Just… you know, later. Whenever. It's just something I found that I wanted you to have."

His free hand comes up to my face and he brushes his fingertips against my cheek while my heart stutters and I hold my breath. "Got a little dust on you before. Sorry about that."

The smirk on his face tells me he isn't sorry in the least about putting his dusty hands on my face and dragging my mouth to his. I quickly take a step back so I can breathe again and his hand drops from my cheek.

I clutch the papers he gave me in my hands and continue backing away from him towards the stairs. I need some distance right now. If I spend another second down here alone with him, I have no idea what the hell I'll do, but it will most likely be something even more stupid than kissing him.

"I should be going," I tell him lamely. "Again, I'm sorry about that day on the beach."

I turn away from his stare and rush up the steps. His voice calls to me as I get to the top.

"See you soon, Lucy in the sky with diamonds."

Chapter 21

From Fisher's High School Journal

October 28, 2001

"EACH ELECTRON HAS a negative electrical charge and each proton has a positive electrical charge. The charges are equal in magnitude, but opposite in sign. So basically, they are electrically attracted to each other."

The only reason I haven't fallen asleep yet is because I could listen to Lucy's voice all day. I don't know what the hell is happening to me, but I haven't even looked at another girl in almost a month. Obviously, I've lost my mind. She's the complete opposite of almost every girl on this island. She's shy and keeps to herself, never going out of her way to be something she's not to try and fit in with the rest of the sheep in this school. She only speaks when she's called on in class and is constantly walking around with her nose buried in a book. I don't think half the girls here have read anything beyond fashion magazines, but Lucy reads *Anna Karenina* and *Gone With the Wind* for pleasure. The only time she shows a hint of personality or a little bit of snarky attitude is when she's with me, and it makes me feel pretty damn good that I can bring those emotions out of her.

On top of that, she's really smart. She's the only sophomore taking AP Chemistry and getting straight A's, to boot. When our teacher told me I'd need to get my grade up or risk not graduating in the spring, I immediately signed up for tutoring. There's no way I'm not graduating and postponing Marine basic training. As luck would have it, Lucy was on the tutor list and I made sure all of my available dates coincided with hers so that the teacher would have no choice but to pair us together.

Lucy pauses in her explanation, looking up from her Chemistry book to find me staring at her mouth instead of the page we're on. I can't help it. Her mouth drives me insane. She never wears that sticky, shiny lip-gloss shit all the other chicks paint on. Her lips are always a perfect shade of pink and she keeps them shiny enough just by running her tongue across them, like she's doing right now.

"Hey. Focus," she scolds, tapping her pencil against the book and forcing me to tear my gaze away from her mouth to stare in her eyes.

"I am completely focused. What you're saying is, opposites attract," I tell her with a wink and a smile.

I can't help it. I know it ticks her off when I try to charm her, and that's what I lov…like about her. She's the only girl in this place who doesn't climb all over me when I try to flirt.

She groans and rolls her eyes at me and my smile gets wider.

"Yes, but only in the scientific world. Why are you even in AP Chemistry if you still don't know the basic lessons?"

Moving my elbows to the table and my eyes away

from hers, I run my hands down my face and sigh. "Would you believe me if I told you I only signed up because of the hot girls in the class?"

This is the one thing that gets to me about Lucy. Okay, the one thing that gets to me more than thinking about kissing her or running my hands through her long hair to see how soft it is or squeezing her perfectly round ass. She sees right through me. Those blue eyes of hers cut into me like lasers when I try to bullshit her.

"Nice try," she tells me, tossing her pencil down and turning in her chair to face me. She folds her legs up crisscross on the chair and cocks her head to the side. "There is only one relatively good-looking girl in our class, and I happen to know she's got a very serious boyfriend that you're friends with. How about the truth?"

I hate that she always discounts herself as good-looking just because she doesn't look like every other chick in this school. She's beautiful in an all-American, girl next door way and she doesn't even realize it.

"Two," I mutter distractedly as I glance down at her legs and think about running my hands up her thighs.

She shakes her head at me in confusion.

"There are two, more than relatively good-looking girls in our class. Actually, I wouldn't classify you as *just* good-looking. I'm sure there's a much better word for how you look, but I don't think they've invented it yet," I say with a smirk.

"Can you be serious for one minute?" she asks in annoyance.

"I *am* being serious. I haven't been able to take my

eyes off of you since you walked into the cafeteria that first day," I reply softly, being honest for the first time in a long time.

I know she doesn't trust me and it bugs the shit out of me. Every day at school, she sees another girl hanging all over me, just proving that she's right to be wary of me. If she only knew that I just want to shove them off of me and hang out with her instead, that I *have* shoved them away every time the opportunity to spend time with her pops up. I've turned down dates, I've turned down blow jobs, I've even turned down parties where I'm guaranteed to get laid, just so I can spend an hour with her in the library.

"Why don't you come to any of the parties people throw on the weekends?" I blurt out, trying to steer the conversation in her direction so I don't say something stupid that will make me look like a pussy.

"I asked you first," she argues. "Why did you sign up for AP Chemistry?"

I rub my fingers against my bottom lip, something I do when I'm nervous or frustrated. Lucy makes me feel both of those things. She also makes me want to be completely honest with her. I haven't known her for very long, but I already know she would never judge me or make fun of me.

"My dad made me take it," I admit with a sigh. "Said it would look good on my transcripts for college. You know, the college *he* picked out for me, taking the classes *he* approved of. I hate math and that's all Chemistry is. I'd rather be outside, helping my grandfather fix things around the island than be stuck inside a classroom or a boardroom, but that seems to be all my dad thinks I'm good for."

She doesn't even look shocked when I blurt this out. Her eyes get soft with understanding. Thank God she's not looking at me with pity, I couldn't handle that shit.

"Well, think of it this way. Even with construction and electrical work, it doesn't hurt to know a little chemistry. So, you can secretly piss off your father by learning something that will help you do what *you* want," she tells me with a small smile.

I can't stop the loud, full belly laugh that flies from my mouth. I've never heard her curse and, even though it was only *piss*, it did something to my insides to hear her let loose like that, just to try and get me to smile.

"You want to get out of here for a little while?" I ask mid-laugh. "I'm getting claustrophobic being in this library so much."

She raises one eyebrow at me in suspicion and I laugh again. "Don't worry, Lucy in the sky with diamonds, I promise to keep my hands to myself. I thought we could take a tour of the island. I can show you some of my favorite places that no one knows about."

The nickname just flew right off the tip of my tongue and surprisingly, she doesn't give me a dirty look for saying it. I do notice her face fall a little when I mention that I'll keep my hands to myself and it makes me want to puff my chest out with pride. Lucy likes me and she *wants* me to touch her. Suddenly, nothing else matters outside of learning what makes this girl tick. She quickly agrees to the tour and we pack up our books and head outside to my truck.

Fifteen minutes later, we're climbing up some rocks at the opposite end of town. The view from the top is breathtaking, just like it always is.

"Welcome to Fisher's Lighthouse," I announce, holding my arms out from my body and spinning in a circle. "It's overindulgent and disgusting that I have to share a name with almost everything in this fucking town, but this is the one place I don't mind sharing it with."

Shielding my eyes from the sun, I stare up at the huge red and white striped structure that overlooks the ocean and Lucy does the same while I give her a little history lesson.

"There used to be a lighthouse keeper who lived inside and manned the light for the fishing boats back in the day when oil lamps and clockwork mechanisms were used. Could you imagine that? Living all alone in this lighthouse, day after day, year after year, with no one judging you, telling you what to do or getting into your business? Your only job was to make sure the boats stayed safe and got home to their families," I say wistfully as I slide my hands into the front pockets of my jeans and stare off into the distance, watching the waves crest a few miles from shore.

"Now, computers run it all and no one ever really has a need to come out here unless something breaks. So that means it's just me or my grandfather who get to walk around inside this beauty and stare out at the ocean, pretending like we're the only two people in the world.

It's the best at night, when it's pitch black and it looks like you're standing on the edge of the world. You feel like if you take one step off the rocks, you'll just drop down into nothing and disappear forever. Sometimes, disappearing sounds like the best idea in the world."

I stare out at the endless ocean, wondering why I don't feel embarrassed that I just said more to Lucy about how I feel than I've ever said to anyone else. The sun shines on my face and I feel at peace. Being at this spot, with Lucy by my side, makes that possible. She doesn't ask a thousand questions or feel the need to fill the silence with useless talk. She's content to listen to me and enjoy the quiet moment. I know what she sees when she looks at me – a cocky, popular guy that everyone wants to be around because of my money and not because of who I am. Around town, I'm the son of the richest man on the island and I have to hold myself with a little more poise and polish, but out here, on the corner of the island where no one can see me, I can just be myself. With Lucy, I can be myself – a small-town boy who really, truly loves the place he lives, but dreams of bigger and better things.

I hear her step across the gravel on top of the rocks and suddenly, her small, warm hand is sliding into my own. She entwines her fingers with mine and squeezes my hand while we both stare silently out at the water.

I'm realizing, right in this moment, that meeting Lucy *is* my bigger and better thing.

Chapter 22

Lucy

Present Day

IT'S BEEN A week since I went to Trip's house and Fisher kissed me in the basement. Okay, fine, I was an equal participant in that kiss, but I'm trying to block that part out of my mind, especially since Stanford and I have had a really great week together. I even managed to convince him to avoid downtown and stay here at the inn, not wanting to chance running into Fisher. The plan was to put some distance between us and get him out of my mind so I could concentrate on Stanford.

Too bad it's not working.

Absence is not only making the heart grow fonder, it's forcing the libido into overdrive and the guilt is driving me insane. Sticking my tongue down my ex-husband's throat one day and kissing the man I'm dating the very next makes me feel like the trashy whore Fisher's father accused me of being. I'm kissing Stanford when I still have the taste of another man on my lips, one who gets my blood pumping and makes me crazy, in more ways than one.

"What's bothering you?"

On my hands and knees in one of the guest bathrooms, I glance over my shoulder to see Ellie leaning against the doorway.

"Nothing's bothering me," I lie, going back to what I was doing.

"You only scrub toilets when you're pissed off or upset about something, so spill the beans, sugar plum."

I continue scrubbing, putting a little more elbow grease into it and blowing a strand of hair out of my eyes that has fallen out of my ponytail.

"Nothing to spill. These toilets were disgusting and since the guests are all down at the beach, I figured I'd get a head start on the cleaning so you wouldn't have to do it when you were done making lunch."

She laughs, stepping further into the room, and grabs the rag from my hand, shaking it out and holding it up in front of her.

"Right, so you just decided on a whim to use one of Fisher's old t-shirts to clean the toilets. A t-shirt I know damn well you were still wearing to bed up until a week ago," she muses.

Reaching up, I snatch the shirt out of her hands angrily and go back to work. Dammit, I really loved this shirt, too. It was one of Fisher's from boot camp, grey with the word *Marines* written across the front in black. The letters were so faded after years of washing that you could barely read them and the material was so soft I was afraid one more trip through the spin cycle would make it fall to pieces, but I still loved it. It hung down to middle of my thighs and made the best nightshirt. It also made it easier to think about Fisher and dream about Fisher and that had to stop.

I hear a retching sound followed by a little cough, and I turn around to see Ellie turned partially away from me with her hand over her mouth.

"Are you okay?" I ask, getting up from the floor and stepping to her side.

She holds up her free hand and shoos me away.

"I'm fine, I'm fine. That shirt just really smells right now. Like toilet water and....uuugghhh, toilet water. I shook that thing out and now the smell is everywhere."

I have no idea what she's talking about. I can't smell anything but the bleach I was using. She rushes out of the bathroom and into the hall, taking a few deep breaths once she's out there.

"You know, you've been acting kind of weird yourself lately. What the hell is going on with *you?*" I ask suspiciously as she bends over and puts her hands on her knees while she breathes.

I feel a little guilty that we haven't had time to talk recently. I've been busy with the inn and Stanford and trying to avoid Fisher and she's been busy with... What the hell HAS she been busy with? I know she's been here working; the clean rooms and fresh food constantly coming out of the kitchen is proof of that, but what else has she been doing that this is the first time I've seen her in a week? Ellie and I see each other every day, even when we're both busy.

She finally stands back up and shakes her head at me. "Nope, we're not talking about me. There is nothing going on with me worth talking about when there is PLENTY going on with you. Lucy, your ex-husband and the love of your life has been back on the island for a little over three weeks and I can't help but notice that you've been a lot more attentive to Stanford since that happened. You've been going out of your way to show everyone that the two of you are perfectly happy together, but I know you. I know this must be hard on you, seeing him again after all this time. You don't have to put up a front for me. You know you can tell me anything."

Leaning my back against the wall in the hallway, I close my eyes and let my head thump against the wall.

"This sucks. This really, really sucks," I whisper.

I hear her feet shuffle and she moves to stand next to me, her arm pressing against mine as we both lean into the wall.

"I don't know what is going on with me. I said good-bye to him in my mind and my heart. I let my anger take over where the love used to be and I've been fine. I've learned how to live without him. Forget three weeks, three MINUTES with him and suddenly I'm questioning everything," I tell her as I lean my head to the side and rest it on her shoulder.

"Do you know what he did last week?" I ask, pulling the journal pages out of my back pocket that I've read so many times the papers are almost starting to fall apart. I hand them to Ellie and she unfolds them and starts to scan the pages.

"Those are some pages out of a journal he kept in high school. It was from the year I moved here and we first met and then when I tutored him in Chemistry. Everything he felt, everything in his heart, was poured out on those pages and it killed me, Ellie. The way he saw me and the way he opened up to me like he'd never done with anyone else before. I remembered every moment of that time with him and it hurt so much."

I pause and squeeze my eyes closed even tighter, ashamed of the hundreds of times I've read those pages in the last week, alone in bed at night, after Stanford has kissed me good-bye and we've made plans for the following day.

"Wow," Ellie says softly as she gets to the last page and hands them back to me.

"I know," I tell her with a sigh as I refold them and shove them back into my back pocket.

"I know you're going to hate me for saying this," Ellie says softly, "But maybe it's a good thing that you remember it. Your head has been so filled with the bad stuff and he's just trying to get you to remember that there were good times, too. You two grew up together and you built a life together. It wasn't all bad, and he's trying to get you to realize that. He's a different person now, Lucy. Everyone can see it. I think he just wants you to see it, too."

"That's the problem. I DO see it. I see so much of the old Fisher that I fell in love with and it's tearing me apart."

"I think what you need is a break," Ellie suddenly announces as she slides away from the wall and stands in front of me. "Get your ass cleaned up and get out of this place. Go into town and get some fudge from Ruby's. I think some double chocolate peanut butter swirl is just what the doctor ordered."

She's right, I've been cooped up in the inn for a week and all it's done is given me more time to dwell on things. With a quick hug, I race over to my living quarters and take a quick shower, throwing on an old pair of jean shorts and a Butler House t-shirt, fastening my wet hair up on top of my head in a messy bun.

PULLING MY GOLF cart into an open parking space a few spots down from Ruby's, I immediately see the one person I'd hoped to avoid when I came to town. I should have known better. Standing here on the sidewalk, I can't help but stare at him and I'm glad I threw on a pair of sunglasses so it's not so obvious I'm checking him out. Today, Fisher's paired his usual khaki cargo shorts with a red USMC t-shirt that hugs his upper body in too many right places. On his head is a backwards Butler House baseball cap that is ratty, dirty and incredibly faded. The sight of that hat does all sorts of things to me and I have to press my hand over my heart to try and get it to stop beating so fast. I gave him that hat right before he left for basic training. He took it with him on every deployment and told me he wore it more often than the uncomfortable helmets they were given. It's been across the world and back countless times and I can't believe he still has it.

I stop ogling him long enough to realize his black, F150 truck is backed up right in front of Ruby's and I'm guessing he just got here and no one has noticed that he's breaking one of the main summer laws on the island: no motor vehicles on Main Street. It sticks out like a sore thumb in the sea of white golf carts and bicycles parked along the street. I see him struggling to pull something out of the back end of the truck and I realize why he broke the law and drove into town. He's delivering the sign he was working on when I stopped by Trip's place last week. It takes up half of the bed of the truck and there's no way he could have brought it into town on a cart.

Pushing my sunglasses up on my head, I jog over to the back of his truck and grab onto the sign across from him. I'd seen the sign almost finished and I know how much work he put into it. Seeing how absolutely beautiful it is with paint and the final coating of varnish, I don't want him to mess it up trying to lift it on his own or hurt is shoulder.

He looks up in surprise. "Hey, what are you doing here?

"It's a double chocolate peanut butter swirl kind of day," I tell him with a shrug as we work together to slide the sign out of the back.

He laughs and then pauses. "This thing is really heavy. You're going to hurt yourself if you try to help me lift it."

I glare at him before going back to work, pulling the sign out on my own before he quickly gets back to work helping.

"I've lifted things much heavier than this all on my

own for years, thank you very much."

We continue moving the sign without saying another word and I immediately feel bad for snapping at him. In one second, I managed to remind him of all the times he left me alone to do things by myself and that's not what I intended.

Holding the long, rectangular sign between us, Fisher at one end and me at the other, we walk it up onto the sidewalk and a customer leaving Ruby's holds the door open for us so we can tip it upright and get it through the door.

"Fisher! Oh, my goodness, what have you done?!"

Ruby's excited shout fills the small fudge shop as she comes running out from behind the display case and over to us. Ruby is in her late sixties and she and her husband Butch opened the store when they moved to the island after he returned from Vietnam. Ruby and I talked often while Fisher was on one of his many deployments and she gave me some good advice during that time, but we haven't spoken much other than in passing since everything happened last year. I was ashamed that she was able to make it work with her husband after he came home from the war and I wasn't.

We set the sign down on the floor in front of the display case and Ruby wraps Fisher in a big hug.

"It's so good to see you back home," she tells him softly before moving back and patting both of his cheeks.

He smiles down at her and I watch him blush as he talks about the gift he made for her.

"I just wanted to do something to make up for what

happened last year. I'm sorry I wasn't here to fix the front window. I know the sign doesn't erase what I did, but it was the only thing I could think of."

Ruby takes a moment to study the sign and I watch from the side as tears fill her eyes. It really is quite beautiful. Made out of an old piece of oak, Fisher painted it in the pale yellow and pink colors of the shop and carved *Ruby's Fudge Shop* in the middle in flowing, curly script and added wood-burned drawings of fudge, candy and other confections that are staples here in her store.

"Oh, Fisher, this is just beautiful."

She runs her hands lovingly over the sign before turning back to face him.

"The only thing we really needed was for you to get better and come back to us, but I understand why you needed to do this and I thank you. It's going to look just wonderful hanging in the front of the store."

She turns her head and shouts to the back room. "BUTCH! GET OUT HERE AND SEE WHAT FISHER'S DONE!"

A few seconds later, Butch comes through the back doors and joins us, nodding at the sign in approval. Ruby grabs my hand and pulls me around the display case, putting together a box of all my favorite flavors of fudge while Fisher and Butch begin discussing the best way to hang the sign.

Ruby prattles on about this season's vacationers and how business is going, but I tune her out after a few minutes when I hear Butch ask Fisher how he's doing.

"War changes everyone, son, there's no shame in that.

If it doesn't change you, you were already too fucked up to begin with. What's important is that you did the right thing and you found your way home."

Fisher nods, sliding his hands in the front pockets of his shorts. "I got a little lost for a while, but it helped to have something back here, guiding me back home."

I swallow thickly and blink back tears, wondering if he's talking about me or Trip or any other number of things that could have pulled him back to the island.

Butch pats him on the shoulder and nods. "Don't lose sight of that. No one understands your need to do your duty to your country more than me, but sometimes you have to figure out on your own that there are more important things than fighting a battle we might never win. Sometimes there are more important things to fight for right here at home."

Butch and Fisher both glance over at me and I look away guiltily, grabbing a piece of wax paper and helping Ruby fill the box she's started for me.

The two men talk for a few more minutes and I stop eavesdropping. Ruby sends me on my way with my box of fudge and she and Butch both give Fisher a hug before we walk out the door. Fisher tells them to give him a call when they're ready to hang the sign and he'll stop by to help as we step onto the sidewalk and into the sunshine.

"Well, I guess I should be getting back to the inn," I tell him with an awkward smile as I start to turn away.

"Lucy, wait," he says, wrapping his hand around my upper arm and gently turning me back to face him. "Since you're already here in town, how about lunch? There's no point eating dessert when you haven't had lunch, right?"

He eyes my box of fudge and I can practically see him start to drool. Ruby's fudge has always been a weakness for Fisher and whenever I brought it home, I had to hide it from him or he'd eat all of it before I could get one piece.

"You just want me to share my fudge with you," I laugh.

He shrugs. "Guilty. So, how about lunch?"

I pause, contemplating all the reasons why this is a really bad idea. I'm supposed to be avoiding Fisher, not spending more time with him to further muddle my already confused head and heart.

"I promise to keep my hands to myself," he chuckles, holding his hands up in the air.

The fact that he used the exact same words all those years ago the first time he took me to the lighthouse isn't lost on me. I don't know if it was a coincidence or if he did it on purpose, but it worked. I'm so lost in memories that I distractedly nod and let him lead me across the street.

An hour later, my belly so full of seafood that I feel like I might explode, I rest my hands on my stomach and lean back in my chair.

Fisher wisely chose the Lobster Bucket for lunch because he knows it's my favorite place to eat. Our table is littered with the remnants of the crab pot we shared, the butcher paper they threw down on the table piled high with the empty shells of king, Dungeness and snow crab, shrimp, steamed clams and muscles and a few cleaned ears of corn. I'm more than a little surprised and maybe a little sad that Fisher didn't spend our entire meal trying to charm me or make fun of Stanford in some way. We talked about the inn and Ellie and Bobby and we talked about his woodworking and the orders he's already received since coming back to the island. Our conversation was easy and friendly, exactly as it was before things went dark.

"There's no way you're going to sell Butler House, right? You love that place, Lucy. It's a part of who you are," Fisher tells me as we look out at the view and clean off our hands with the lemon-scented wet-naps the restaurant provided.

"Loving it and knowing when it's time to let it go are two different things," I tell him softly, suddenly wondering if I'm referring to the inn or him and quickly changing the course of my thoughts.

"Times have changed, Fisher. Nowadays, people want free Wi-Fi and charging stations wherever they go. They want to stay connected to the world, post selfies and tend to their crops on that stupid Farmville game," I explain in irritation. "They don't want to unplug from the world around them because they're afraid they might miss something. They don't care about the beauty of this place or the peacefulness that being here brings. They don't care about spending hours just staring out at the ocean and being amazed by what's right in front of them. They want waterparks and spas and nightclubs and I can't give that to them. I can't give them what they want anymore and maybe it's time for me to see that."

I realize I circled right back around to my initial thoughts, intermingling my feelings about Fisher and the inn until I don't know which one I'm actually referring to. He changed, but he never realized that I changed right along with him. The things I wanted and needed morphed and grew while he was away. He was so lost, and I couldn't give him what he wanted no matter how hard I tried. I can't live like that anymore, with the inn or with him. I can't keep banging my head against the wall trying to get people to see that not everything has to change, but sometimes you don't have a choice. You either change or you fail.

Fisher suddenly gets up from his seat and grabs my hand, pulling me up with him. "Come on, I want to show you something."

He drags me away from our table, quickly paying for our meal on the way out. I don't pull my hand away from his even though I should as we step back out onto Main Street and walk a few blocks to the Visitor's Center. He pushes the door open and we step into the large, air-conditioned building, walking over to a huge bookshelf on the far wall. He finally drops my hand and reaches up onto one of the shelves to grab a large, thick binder, filled with hundreds of papers. He flips it open and turns to me, holding the binder out in front of him.

"Here, look at this."

I take the binder from him in confusion, looking away from him to a hand-written letter, three-hole punched and attached inside. I scan it quickly and my mouth drops open in shock. It's a letter to the town from one of the guests of Butler House. It goes into great detail about the beauty of the inn and island and how they appreciated spending a week in an inn that was filled with friendly staff, an amazing owner and the best view on the entire island.

When I get to the bottom, Fisher flips to the next page and I see another letter, similar to the first one, going on and on about how the peace and old-charm of the inn was exactly what they needed. Page after page, letter after letter, the entire binder is filled with notes and cards about how they love that the inn is one of the few on the island that isn't overwhelmed with all the latest technology and distractions and how they hope it will never change.

Tears run down my cheeks by the time I get to the last page and Fisher quietly takes the binder from my hands and sticks it back up on the shelf.

"Not everything has to change, Lucy. Sometimes, people are perfectly happy with the way things used to be. Life just gets in the way and makes them forget for a little while," Fisher tells me softly. "My father, some of these people that come here, they've lost sight of what's important, but you never have. That binder proves that what you have here on this island is something worth keeping, something worth fighting for. You can't stop fighting, Lucy. You can never stop fighting for something you love and something you believe in."

Wiping away my tears, we head back outside and I try not to think about the fact that I'm certain he was talking about more than the inn.

Before we part ways, he reaches into his back pocket and hands me some folded pieces of paper. I should refuse to take them and just walk away, telling him to stop trying to pull me back to the past, but I don't. I accept them without a word, get into my golf cart and race back to the inn as fast as I can, where I lock myself in my room and read through the pages of our history, crying harder than I did in the Visitor's Center.

Chapter 23
From Fisher's High School Journal

THE SOUND OF the waves crashing against the beach a few hundred yards away from us as well as Lucy's soft, breathy moans fill my ear as I slowly push my way inside of her.

She lets out a small gasp of pain and I immediately stop and pull my head back to look into her eyes.

"I'm sorry! Shit, I'm so sorry. I don't want to hurt you."

Lucy smiles up at me and I can see tears glistening in her eyes from the light of the moon shining high above us. She reaches up and runs her fingers gently through my hair, over and over, while wrapping her legs around my hips and pulling me closer.

"I'm fine, Fisher. I swear, I'm fine, just keep going."

She arches up and presses her lips to mine and I have no other choice but to keep going. I move as slowly as possible, even though it's killing me. She's feels so amazing wrapped around me that I want to sink myself inside of her as hard as I can to relieve the ache that's forming in my fucking balls.

My tongue slides through her mouth as slowly as my cock inside of her and she responds immediately, moving her hips against me.

We've been officially dating for a little over seven months and I told her numerous times that I was perfectly fine doing what we had already been doing and didn't need anything more. For the first time since I lost my own virginity at fifteen, I didn't need sex to prove anything with a girl, but Lucy was insistent that she was ready. I'm not going to lie, I've wanted to have sex with her since the first moment I kissed her, but finding new and creative ways to make her come over the last seven months has been nothing short of heaven. In theory, it would have been nice to have this happen spontaneously without any planning, but this was her virginity we're talking about here. I wanted it to be special and romantic and I did everything I could to make that happen. In the center of a heart-shaped collection of Mason jars illuminated by the candles I'd placed inside each of them, I'd spread out several layers of blankets on the sand to keep it away from us. It wasn't a bed, but it was the best I could do considering we both still lived at home, her with her parents and me with my grandfather, and privacy was pretty hard to come by.

Bringing her here to the base of the lighthouse where I first realized I was falling for her made it even more special.

"I love you, Lucy. I love you so much," I whisper in her ear as we rock against each other. I'd thrown a blanket over my ass, shielding both of us from prying eyes should someone decide to come out to the lighthouse.

Her legs tighten around my hips and she pulls me

closer, moves me deeper with the muscles in her thighs. I want this to last much longer than it will. I can already feel my orgasm rushing up inside of me and I try to slow it down, but the soft sounds of Lucy's sighs and her warm breath against my ear are making that impossible. I'm as soft and gentle with her as I can possibly be, showing her as best I can how much she means to me.

Lucy's hands runs down my back until she's clutching my ass, urging me to keep going and I get completely lost inside of her. The two orgasms I gave her with my hands and mouth to make sure she was plenty ready for me before I slid into her are the only reason I don't feel like a two-pump chump. I knew I would hurt her and I wanted to do whatever I could to make it easier.

She whispers how much she loves me and how good I feel inside of her and that's the end of me thinking I could make this last. Her soft voice saying something so hot pushes me right over the edge and I moan her name against the side of her neck as I come.

After taking a few seconds to catch my breath, I slowly roll off of her and dispose of the condom in a plastic shopping bag that holds the box of Trojans I bought earlier today. Pulling her body against mine, I curl the two of us on our sides and tug the blanket up over both of us. We stare out at the Atlantic, the light from the lighthouse shimmering over the surface of the water every couple of seconds.

"I promise next time I'll last longer than thirty seconds. Jesus, you would think *I* was the one losing my virginity," I laugh sheepishly.

I feel her body shake as she laughs with me. "I told you, Fisher, it's fine. It was perfect, absolutely perfect."

I tighten my hold on her with my arms wrapped around her waist and she rests her hands on top of mine.

"Are you scared?" she whispers after a few quiet minutes.

"Not really scared, more nervous than anything," I admit.

Tomorrow, I head out for twelve weeks of boot camp at Parris Island, South Carolina. Even though it's not that far away from Fisher's Island, I'm still not going to be able to come home or see Lucy for three months. Leaving her now is what scares me more than getting my ass kicked by the Marine Corps.

"I know I've said this to you a hundred times, but I'm so proud of you, Fisher. I'm proud of you for doing what you believe in no matter what your father wants. I'm going to miss you so much, but I know you'll do amazing and you'll be back here before I know it."

I have no idea how I got so lucky. I'll *never* understand why Lucy decided to give me a chance after the reputation I've earned over the years, but I am not going to fuck this up. My friends have been giving me shit non-stop ever since Lucy and I started spending more time together and I finally got her to admit that we were a couple. Bobby is the only one who doesn't rag on me. Maybe it's because he's taken the time to get to know her, unlike most of the people in school. He truly likes Lucy and thinks of her like a little sister and he has no problem telling girls right to their face to fuck off when they make snide comments about how I'm slumming it when they see us together. Those bitches are lucky they've never said those things in front of me. I think Bobby sees how good Lucy is for me. She makes the fights with my dad more bearable and she makes me want to run back to this island as soon as I can just to be with her again. She makes me appreciate my home, because she IS my home.

"Do you think once you're finished with boot camp that you'll get shipped out immediately?" she asks quietly.

I shrug against her, resting my chin on top of her head.

"I don't know, possibly. It's all over the news that the shit is really hitting the fan over there. If they tell me to go, I *have* to go, Lucy. As much as I want to stay here with you and never leave, this is something I believe in, something I have to do."

She turns in my arms under the blanket until we're facing each other, cupping my face in her hands. "And that's one of the reasons why I love you. You love your country selflessly, and I understand that you have to do this. That doesn't mean I'm not going to miss you or worry about you or wish that you were here with me, but you need to do what you believe in, Fisher. I'll always be here, waiting for you when you get home."

For the first time since I signed on that dotted line to join the Marine Corps, I'm actually having second thoughts. Not because I'm afraid to go to war, because I'm afraid of losing Lucy. I'm afraid that once I leave, everything will change. I just need to have a little faith that we are strong enough to make it through whatever comes our way.

Chapter 24

Fisher

Present Day

J ESUS CHRIST, I'M going to puke. I'm going to throw up right here on the sidewalk.

I agreed to meet Bobby at Barney's to shoot some darts mostly because I was sick of listening to him bitch about how I need to get the fuck out of Trip's house before I turn into an old man like him. For the last couple of days, I've done nothing but pace back and forth at Trip's, wondering if Lucy read the journal pages I gave her. Did they make her sad? Did they make her happy? Did they remind her of a time in our lives when we had nothing to worry about but spending as much time together as possible?

Obviously, she either didn't read them or they didn't mean jack shit to her. Across the street, right in front of everyone, she's got her tongue down Stick-Up-His-Ass-Ford's throat. Fine, not down his throat because I'm sure such blatant displays of public affection would be beneath him, but still. Her hands are resting on his shoulders, his hands are holding respectably to the sides of her waist and their lips are fused together.

People are walking right by them not paying any attention. Don't they see how wrong that is? Doesn't it make them want to throw their fist against the wall and scream at both of them to cut that shit out?

Probably not. I guess it's just me who feels like killing someone right now.

In theory, I know it's just a kiss, but in my mind, it's like they're practically fucking right against the wall of Fisher's Bank and Trust. A kiss is intimate, it's trusting and you don't give it to just anyone, but she's fucking giving it to Staph-Infection-Ford like it's no big deal, like she wasn't clawing at my back and sliding her tongue through MY mouth and breathing heavily against MY lips a week ago.

I clench my hands into fists and count to ten when they finally break apart, Lucy giving him a small wave as he walks down the street in the opposite direction. I should walk away myself and pretend like I didn't witness this shit, but I can't. My old friends anger and rage are bubbling right beneath the surface, urging me to come out and play. I kicked them to the curb months ago when I learned techniques to express my emotions in a healthy, constructive way, but their call is so loud it's ringing in my ears.

I charge across the street, my focus on Lucy as she turns and heads down the side alley next to the bank. People call my name and wave to me, but I ignore them. Turning down the alley, I see her halfway down, covered in shadows as she heads toward the beach. I watch the muscles in her smooth legs tightening as she walks and the skirt around her ass swish from side to side as her hips sway with each step.

I move faster, slowing when I'm right behind her and I can smell her skin and feel her heat. My arms wrap around her body and I quickly turn, pushing her face-first against the wall.

She starts to scream and struggle against me and I quickly wrap my hand around her mouth and press my lips to her ear.

"Shhhh, it's just me."

She immediately relaxes in my arms, her body melting against mine and it makes me angrier. She just had her hands and her lips on another man, but the sound of my voice still turns her to jelly. It should make me happy, should make me feel good about returning to this island to get her back, but it just fills me with jealousy.

"I saw you fucking kissing him," I whisper angrily in her ear, one arm wrapped tightly around her waist while my other hand trails down her stomach to her thigh.

Lucy whimpers as my palm reaches the bare skin of her leg and I slowly slide it up and under her skirt.

She whispers my name softly, but I cut her off. I don't know if she's trying to get me to stop or urging me on and I don't give a shit about finding out right now.

"Those lips are MINE."

My hand keeps sliding up under her skirt, stopping when I reach the waistband of her underwear. My conscience is screaming at me to back away, but as soon as my hand slips under the cotton material and my fingers feel how wet her pussy is, I know there's no stopping this.

"This body is MINE and it fucking kills me that you're giving it to him," I whisper raggedly as I swirl my middle finger against her clit.

Her hands come up, her palms smacking against the building on either side of her head as I tease her with my finger.

"I can't stand seeing you with him. I can't fucking STAND to see you giving him what you used to give me."

I quickly plunge two fingers inside of her and she moans my name loudly, her back arching and forcing her ass right against my dick. I can hear the muffled voices of people laughing and talking at the opening of the alley as they walk by on the street, completely unaware of what's happening a few feet away from them. The alley is so dark that they wouldn't be able to see us even if they were looking, but hearing those voices should knock some fucking sense into me. Anyone could turn down this alley, using this shortcut to get down to the beach like Lucy was doing before I ambushed her. The thought of someone seeing us this way only makes me move faster and push harder, my body shaking against hers with the need to make her come.

My fingers slide in and out of her easily and Jesus, it's the best fucking feeling in the world. I've missed the feel of her on my fingers and the heat of her body. I've missed the soft moans and gasps that fly from her lips when I hit just the perfect spot.

"Does he make you moan like this, Lucy?" I whisper, bringing my thumb down to circle her clit, pressing my fingers inside of her as deep as they'll go.

She jerks her hips against my hand and begs for more.

"Please, Fisher… please…"

My thumb moves faster around her clit and my fingers push even deeper.

"Do you get this wet for him, Lucy? Jesus, you're so fucking wet…" I trail off as I latch my lips onto the side of her neck. My hand starts to move roughly between her legs, pumping my fingers in and out of her so hard and fast that I can feel the muscles in my arm burning. I don't think about hurting her or bruising her, I only think about marking her and leaving her with a reminder of me that sticks with her the next time she's with *him*. My lips move back from the skin of her neck and my teeth take their place, biting down hard.

Each word I speak to her reminds me of the asshole she's been spending her days and nights with instead of me, fueling my jealousy and anger to the point that I know I should back away. I shouldn't be anywhere near her when I'm this fired up, but I can't stop now that I'm inside of her.

I quicken the flick of my thumb over her clit, rubbing it back and forth, feeling it pulse against my hand as she moves her hips faster, helping me drive her closer to her orgasm.

My teeth continue to sink into the soft skin of her neck as I pick up my pace, slamming my fingers inside of her hard and deep until the sounds of people talking down the street are drowned out by the sounds of my fingers siding through her wet pussy.

I can tell by the hitch in her voice as she moans and how fast she's moving her hips against my hand that she's close to coming. I remember everything about her body, ever little nuance and sound, and I hate that she's trying to erase all of that from her mind with another man.

"You think of me when you come, dammit," I growl, my hand smacking against her pussy with the force of my fingers slamming into her so roughly and so quickly. "You see MY face, feel MY hands and shout MY name."

I slam my fingers home one last time, as deep as possible and add pressure to my thumb. Lucy comes against my hand and my name is most certainly on her fucking lips when she does.

As soon as I hear her shout my name, something inside of me snaps. The angry haze that clouded my eyes and the fury in my bones slips out of me in a rush.

I let out a shuddering breath and quickly pull my fingers out of her, moving away as fast as I can. My back slams into the building opposite her and I bring my hands up to my head, clutching my hair in my hands.

Lucy turns, rolling her body against the wall like it's boneless and takes effort for her to move. She's probably in pain. I fucking pushed her against that building because I let my anger get the best of me. I swore to never hurt her again and look what I've done. I've reverted back to an animal who can't control himself or his emotions.

"Fisher."

She says my name softly and pushes off of the wall, taking a step towards me. The glow from a nearby streetlight illuminates her face and I immediately see a red welt on the side of her neck from my teeth. I drop my hands from my hair and hold them up in front of me, shaking my head back and forth.

"No, don't. Just….stay there. Fuck, what the hell is wrong with me? I'm sorry, I'm so fucking sorry."

The soft look in her eyes instantly morphs into disgust that I'm sure mirrors my own.

"Don't you dare. Don't you DARE apologize to me!" she shouts.

Her anger shocks me and makes me feel worse. I spent all those months away from her trying to find a way to control myself and, after just a few seconds of seeing her kiss another man, I've ruined all of the progress I'd made.

"I shouldn't have done that. I shouldn't have touched you like that. I'm so sorry," I whisper, wishing someone WOULD come down this alley right now just to kick my ass.

Lucy shakes her head at me and swipes angrily at the tears on her cheeks. I made her cry. I hurt her and I fucking made her cry *again*. I want her to hit me, to scream at me and smack me and tell me exactly what kind of an animal I really am.

"You don't get it, you just don't fucking get it!" she growls as more tears fall.

I definitely get it. I get that I should have left her alone. I shouldn't have come back here, believing that I was better and could make up for hurting her by being nothing but gentle and loving with her.

"That will never happen again, I swear to you," I whisper brokenly, trying not to shed my own fucking tears in the process.

"Fuck you, Fisher. FUCK YOU!" she screams.

She turns and takes off running down the alley and all I can do is stand there and watch her go.

Chapter 25

From Fisher's Journal

March 3, 2004

"FISHER, COME ON. It's freezing! I kind of thought we'd spend our last night together doing something a little bit warmer. Maybe with less clothing."

Lucy's musical laughter tickles my ears as she tries to lighten the situation and pretend there isn't a dark cloud hovering over the two of us. She's fought back tears every time we talked about our plans for today, our last day together. It makes me love her even more than I already do, knowing she's doing everything she can to be strong so that I can walk away from her tomorrow without the distraction of worry and regret.

Tightening my hold on her hand, I pull her up the last couple of large boulders at the very top of the rock pile that lines either side of Fisher's Lighthouse. Moving behind her, I wrap my arms around her waist and hold her close, resting my chin on top of the knit cap that covers her head. We stare silently out at the dark, endless ocean in front of us, a few angrily cresting waves the only bright spots in an otherwise sea of black nothingness.

"I love this spot. I always feel like we're the only two people on earth when we come here. The entire world disappears and it's just you and me," Lucy speaks softly. I feel the vibrations of her voice travel through her back and gently rumble against my chest. Squeezing my arms tighter around her, I try not to think about walking away from her. After tomorrow, I won't be able to touch her face, hear her laugh or see her smile for eighteen long months. My first deployment right after boot camp was a measly nine months and it dragged by, so I know being away from Lucy for twice as long is going to be akin to torture.

I didn't think twice about signing up for the Marines my senior year of high school. I didn't bat an eye when I came home and told my parents that I wouldn't follow in my father's footsteps and become the next fucking king of Fisher's Island. I never regretted the rift my decision caused in my family, making my mother cry or having my father disown me. He only speaks to me when we were in public and he has to put on a good show of being a wonderful family man and supportive father. I even went along with the lie he told the island about how I moved out of their mansion on the cliffs and into my grandfather's two-bedroom cottage in town because I wanted "a new experience" before I shipped out. I didn't care about anything other than getting away from this damn island and the legacy that I never wanted.

The day I signed those fucking papers, though, I met Lucy Butler. After eighteen years of living in this one-horse town where everyone knows everyone else and the only new faces were temporary, Lucy was a breath of fresh air in my otherwise stagnant world. She didn't blow through my life like a hurricane, but she disrupted my world just the same. Lucy was more like a gentle breeze that whispered against your skin, teasing you, soothing you and forcing you to chase after it just so you could feel it again. The first time I got her to smile, I felt like the world finally made sense. The first time I made her laugh, I felt like I could walk on water. The first time she kissed me, right here in this very spot, I felt like the fucking king my father always wanted me to be.

Almost three years later, nothing has changed. I still hate everything about this town, but I keep coming back because I can't stand to feel the way I do when I'm away from her – like nothing makes sense, like I'm out there in the middle of that dark ocean, treading water all alone and trying to stop myself from sinking. Lucy keeps my head above water. She reminds me that there are still good people in this world who love you and expect nothing in return.

Given the situation in the Middle East, being redeployed was inevitable and I've been dying to get back in the action, but getting the orders still sucked and I did something really stupid that day. All I could think about was Lucy once again putting her life on hold, waiting for a man who wasn't guaranteed to return to her. She had a good life here, full of beach parties with friends, working at the inn she loved and the fun and excitement of tourist season coming up to look forward to. I had the desert and IED's, air raids and suicide bombers. We were only a few years apart in age, but a lifetime apart in experiences, and I told her as much.

It was the one and only time she ever hit me. My

sweet, shy, beautiful girl lit up with rage and called me every name she could think of after she smacked me. I chuckle to myself when I remember that night a few weeks ago and Lucy turns around in my arms, sliding her hands up to rest on my chest as she stares up at me.

"What's so funny?" she asks with a smile.

The beacon that circles around the lighthouse behind us slides over her features and I take a few seconds to memorize her face—her cheeks pink from the low temperature in the air, her silky, strawberry blonde hair spilling out from under her hat and splaying across her shoulders, her bright blue eyes sparkling as she smiles and the faint hint of freckles sprinkled across her nose.

"I was just thinking about the day I got my orders and you showed me your right hook."

The corner of her mouth tips up in another smile, and with the dim light of the moon and the steady flash of the lighthouse, I can see her eyes cloud with worry. I wanted to bring her to this spot to tell her how much I love her, and now I've screwed it all up. I can tell she's thinking that I might have brought her here to deliver the same spiel I gave her after I received my orders, the one about how maybe it isn't a good idea that she wait for me, that maybe it would be better if she moved on. Her hands clutch tightly to the lapels of my wool coat and she pushes herself up on her tiptoes so that she doesn't have to crane her neck to look me in the eye.

"Don't even think about it, Fisher. I don't care if the Marines turned you into a muscled, fighting machine, I will still kick your ass," she threatens. She takes a breath, gearing up to give me more hell and I quickly bend down and cut off her words with my mouth. Her lips are soft and cold against mine, but with a swipe of my tongue, they immediately warm and she opens for me. She moans into my mouth, moving her arms up and around my shoulders, pulling me closer. I breathe her in, committing her smell to memory so I can pull it forward every single moment I'm away from her for the next eighteen months.

Moving back, I reach behind my neck and grab her hands, pulling them between us. Without taking my eyes off of her, I remove her left mitten and toss it to the rocks at our feet, kissing the tips of each of her fingers as I speak.

"I love your laugh," I tell her, kissing the tip of her thumb.

"I love that you make me want to be a better man," I admit, kissing the tip of her pointer finger.

"I love that you support me even though what I do is hard on you," I tell her softly, kissing the tip of her middle finger.

"I love how strong and independent you are," I state, kissing the tip of her pinkie.

Reaching into my coat pocket, I have a moment of panic when I don't feel what's supposed to be in there. I finally find it shoved down into the corner and breathe a sigh of relief as I pull it out and slowly slide it onto her ring finger.

"I love the way you look at me. I love the way you *love* me. No matter what, I will always find my way back to you," I whisper, kissing the tip of her finger that now sports a diamond ring.

The lighthouse beacon circles back around at that moment and I see a tear roll down her cheek. The day we had it out and she convinced me that I was being an ass and that there was nothing she *could* do but wait for me to come home because I was taking her heart with me when I left, I told her to come out to this lighthouse whenever she was feeling sad. I told her that no matter where I was in the world, no matter what time of day, I would know she was here and I would see the beacon from the lighthouse in my mind, guiding me back home to her.

"I know we're young. Shit, I know *you're* young and I'm an old fucking man already at twenty-two, but I don't care," I tell her with a nervous laugh. "I'm already going to spend the rest of my life loving you. It would be a hell of a lot easier if you were there with me. Please, marry me. Marry me, Lucy Butler. We can travel the world, we can grow old together on this damn island, we can do anything you want. I don't care what we do or where we do it, as long as I'm with you."

I finally stop talking and rub my fingers over my bottom lip as I stare down at her, watching her examine the ring on her finger each time the light strobes across us. I don't want to picture the lighthouse in my mind whenever I close my eyes for the next year and a half. I want to picture this ring on her finger and know that she's mine, know that I have something worth fighting for, worth protecting my own ass for, worth coming home for.

"Yes," she finally whispers as a smile lights up her

face. "Yes, I will marry you, Jefferson Fisher."

I let out the breath I was holding as Lucy presses her palms to my cheeks and stares into my eyes. "Keep your head up, stay safe, come home to me, and I will absolutely marry you. Just please, come home to me."

Her voice cracks as she tries not to cry. I pull her against my chest and hold onto her as tightly as I can, wishing I never had to let go, wishing I didn't have to get on the first ferry off the island in the morning and walk away from this woman who is my everything. I take these moments to enjoy the feel of her body against mine, the brush of her hair against my cheek and think for the thousandth time just how perfectly we fit together. I experience it all and I let it consume me, I let it warm my heart and fill my thoughts because after tomorrow, I will have to shut it all off. At oh-six-hundred hours when the ferry pushes away from the island and heads over to the mainland, I will have to close my mind to the smell of her skin and the sound of her voice. I will stop being a lover and become a Marine. I will get the job done and I won't let anything distract me. Distractions can get you killed and I will do everything I can to keep my promise to Lucy.

I will always find my way back to her.

Chapter 26

Lucy

Present Day

CLIMBING DOWN THE ladder, I take a step back and stare at the front of the inn. I just finished hanging American flag bunting under all of the windows that face the street and it looks pretty good, if I do say so myself. We're only a few days away from the Fourth of July and it's always a big celebration on the island. Last night, while I was turning down the beds when the guests were at dinner, I left miniature flags for each person to hold during the parade, as well as a flyer listing the day's activities. All the businesses go above and beyond decorating their storefronts, and Main Street is lined on both sides with American flags hanging from every light post. We have a parade and a softball tournament, the businesses on Main Street set up tables giving away free samples of food and other items and the day ends with a huge beach party and fireworks show.

I spent the last week changing out the yellow and orange marigolds in the flowerbeds for red, white and blue petunias, I borrowed a t-shirt press from the souvenir shop in town and made a couple hundred Butler House Inn shirts to sell at my table on Main Street before the parade and I organized a picnic lunch order form for the guests to fill out. I planned a bunch of great menu items for them to choose from so they can grab their already-packed basket from the kitchen on the Fourth and take it wherever they'd like on the island to enjoy. Every guest put in an order.

To say I've done whatever I can to keep busy the last week is an understatement. I have so many mixed emotions going through my head and my heart that I strongly considered moving into Barney's and drinking my life away. I've tossed and turned in bed every night since the alley incident with Fisher and my frustration has been hard to keep inside. A part of me is wracked with guilt that I let things go so far with him and another part is begging for it to happen again, but I know it won't. He shut down and pushed me away and I haven't seen him since, but he did leave several more journal pages in my mailbox. I know it's his way of apologizing again for what happened last week, and it tore me up inside to read those words and remember how hopeful we both were for our future together.

I felt more guilt over the way I left things with Fisher than what I'm doing to Stanford. Even if I never speak to Fisher again, I need to end things with Stanford. He's been attending meetings on the mainland all week, so at least I didn't need to come up with excuses to avoid him so that he wouldn't see the mark Fisher's teeth left on my neck. Unconsciously I reach up and rub my fingertips over the spot where the mark has already faded away, and my pulse kicks up a notch when I remember the feel of his teeth biting down on my sensitive skin.

Dropping my hand, I close my eyes and sigh, knowing it isn't fair to myself or Stanford to continue this relationship when there will never be a future between us. I only have room in my heart for one man, and it's always going to be Fisher who occupies that space.

I didn't realize just how much I missed having him touch me until I felt the first slide of his hand up the inside of my thigh. I should have reminded both of us that I have a boyfriend and pushed him away, but I couldn't do it. I wanted his hands on me and his fingers inside of me more than I wanted to take my next breath, more than I wanted to be faithful to Stanford and more than I wanted to be smart or rational. I hate that he still has so much power over me, that I forget everything in my life but the feel of his body against mine and his breath in my ear and his hands bringing me to orgasm. It was so animalistic and hard and just... perfect. Why couldn't Fisher see how much I wanted that? Why couldn't he see that I enjoyed every minute of it until he shut down? I know his loss of control was a direct result of his jealousy over Stanford kissing me on the street, and it hurts to think that maybe he didn't really want me as much as he wanted to punish me for being with another man. I've spent the last year getting stronger, more independent and finding out who I am and, in just a few minutes in a dark alley, Fisher erased all of it. He makes me need him, he makes me want him and he makes me weak.

"Oh, sweetheart, it looks beautiful!"

Turning around, I smile at my parents, who are

standing behind me, staring up at the inn.

I join them on the sidewalk, giving them each a hug and a kiss on the cheek. My father squeezes me a little harder than usual before pulling back and smoothing my hair back from my face.

"You look tired. Are you sleeping? And you're too skinny. When was the last time you ate?"

I laugh at his concern, thinking he sounds a hell of a lot like Trip, and step out of his arms. "Dad, I'm fine. Just busy with the inn, you know how it is in the summer."

He looks away guiltily and I kiss his cheek again, trying to reassure him without words that he has nothing to feel guilty about. At twenty-one, when I saw how much of a toll the inn was taking on my elderly parents, I stepped in and convinced them to take it easy, retire, and enjoy the island without having the burden of an inn to run. I spent months slowly taking over the tasks they each handled. Eventually, they realized that I *could* do everything and, more importantly, that I wanted to. They saw how happy working here and running things made me and they reluctantly stepped back and transferred the inn to my name. I'm sure they know how much I struggle to keep the place going even if I don't share all of the gritty details with them and every time they stop by, I can see it written all over their faces that they wish they could help out more. I spend half of our visits convincing them that I don't need their help and they should never feel bad about retiring and not having extra money to give me when I'm neck deep in bills. Taking over the inn when I was in high school and having to make so many repairs on the poorly maintained building wiped out their entire savings account. Even if they had the money to give me, I would never take it. It was my decision to run the inn and it's my responsibility.

"Is Trip around? I need to ask him about a leaky faucet we have in the kitchen," dad asks, looking around the property.

"He's upstairs in the Marblehead room putting a new handle on the bathroom door," I let him know.

Dad pats me on the shoulder before disappearing up the stairs.

"Do you have a few minutes for your meddling old mother? I feel like we haven't talked in ages," Mom says with a smile.

Linking our arms together, we head across the front yard and around the back of the inn to the veranda. She takes a seat in one of the rocking chairs while I walk over to a side table and grab us each a glass of fresh, sweet iced tea from the two-gallon glass beverage dispenser that I refill twice daily.

Handing her a glass, I take a seat next to her and start sipping my own.

"Did you put fresh mint in this?" she asks.

"Yep," I reply.

"Hmmm, it's delicious."

A few silent minutes pass before she asks another random question.

"Are those new beach umbrellas down there? I don't remember them being yellow and white striped."

She points her glass to the umbrellas we stick in the sand every morning for our guests.

"Uh, no. Those are the same ones that we've used for a few years."

"Hmmm," she replies absently again, taking a sip of her tea.

"Spit it out, Mom."

She sets her glass down on the table between us and turns to face me.

"Is it that obvious?"

"I'm pretty sure you didn't stop by to talk about mint and umbrellas, so yeah, it's pretty obvious," I reply.

She looks out at the ocean and the families lying on the beach a few hundred yards away before sighing deeply.

"I ran into Fisher in town yesterday."

My stomach flips like I'm going down a hill on a roller coaster and my heart starts beating faster.

"Really? What did he have to say?" I ask calmly, not letting on that I'm dying to know how he looked, what he said and what he did.

I have a moment of sheer panic that he blurted out what happened in the alley and contemplate running inside and hiding in a closet.

"He loves you, Lucy," she says softly.

My head whips around to face her and my mouth drops open.

"THAT'S what he said?" I ask in shock.

She laughs lightly and shakes her head at me. "No, not in so many words, but I'm old and I've been around long enough to know when I'm looking at a tortured man who misses his wife."

"Ex-wife," I remind her.

She waves her hand in the air and scoffs. "Only on paper."

It's my turn to laugh. "Um, I'm pretty sure that's the only place that matters."

"You're still his wife where it counts – in his heart and soul. I can see it when he says your name and I'm wondering when you're going to see it, too," she muses.

I shake my head and roll my eyes, wiping each bead of condensation off the glass in my hands to give me something to do. I suddenly feel nervous and anxious and like there are so many emotions flying through my heart and my mind that I can't make sense of any of them.

"It's complicated, Mom. I'm seeing someone and Fisher… It's just complicated," I try to explain.

"Love isn't easy, sweetheart. I know you went through a lot with Fisher and I know it's hard for you to trust him, but he's trying. He's so afraid of doing the wrong thing. He wants to be a good man for you. He wants to take care of you and love you and I don't think…"

She pauses, taking a deep breath and trying to collect her thoughts.

"You don't think what?" I whisper, pushing her to continue.

She reaches across the table between us and grabs my hand. "I don't think Stanford will ever be the kind of man you need. The kind of man who will love you with so much passion and devotion. The kind of man who will take care of you, but also step back and let you be strong on your own."

I swallow back tears and squeeze her hand to let her know that I'm not offended by what she's saying about Stanford. I've been having the same thoughts about him myself lately, so it's not like this is news to me. Right now, I'm more concerned about the passion part of the equation between Fisher and I. It's something I want and need, but it's also something he seems to be afraid of.

"How do I know Fisher will be that man?" I ask. "He was for the longest time and I never thought anything would tear us apart. He said such awful things to me before he left the island. I can't just forget about them or pretend like none of it happened."

"Of course you can't pretend like they never happened, Lucy. They broke your heart and they changed you. I don't think he expects you to forget and instantly forgive him. He knows he has a lot of work to do to earn back your trust and he knows he has a lot of explaining to do. All I'm asking is that you give him a chance to explain. Give him a chance to show you that he never meant to hurt you."

It sounds so easy when she says it. Hand him my heart once again and trust him to take care of it. But it's not easy. It scares the shit out of me. I might be able to forgive what he said to me when he wasn't in his right frame of mind, but he's still the one who decided to end things permanently with divorce papers. He's still the one who had his hands all over Melanie and did God knows what with her while he was still wearing my ring on his finger. How am I supposed to forgive those things?

"He was a broken man, Lucy, and I know he broke you right along with himself. War doesn't just change the Marine, it changes everyone who loves him. I didn't think I could ever forgive him for hurting my baby, but seeing him yesterday and listening to him talk about you and what you mean to him… Just give him a chance."

The guilt is back in full force and I have to let go of my mother's hand, set down my glass and wrap my arms around myself to hold it together. I don't know what was going on in his mind last year when I came home and found him packing my things and he said such hurtful words to me, but I know it was bad. He'd been slowly closing himself off from me for weeks and I've always felt like a failure for not doing more for him. I tried so hard, but it wasn't enough. I would have given everything to stay and help him, but how could I when he didn't want that? I want him to be honest with me, to tell me what happened that day and help me understand why he felt like divorce was the answer to all of his problems.

I feel like a hypocrite for wanting Fisher to bare his soul when I've done nothing but alternately avoid him like the plague and seek him out only to behave like a shrew. I'm not sure if I'm prepared to forgive him for what he did to me, but I know he doesn't deserve my anger right now. We never had a problem talking until the end of our relationship. Having lunch with him at the Lobster Bucket a few weeks ago and falling right back into our old ways made me miss the ease of being with him. I've tried so hard to forget him, to move on and be happy, but as soon as he reappeared in my life, I realized letting go was impossible when I still love him. I've tried to avoid it, I've tried to pretend like I was just confused being close to him again, but I can't do that anymore.

I love him and I'm scared to death that he'll break my heart all over again.

Chapter 27

From Fisher's Journal

January 23, 2006

M Y PARENT'S 24,000 square foot home is filled to the brim with guests and caterers and I stare out of my old bedroom window watching more and more cars come up the drive to be parked by the valets my mother hired.

I tug nervously on the pale blue tie of my black tuxedo, trying to loosen it so I don't feel like I'm suffocating. My palms are already sweating and my hands are shaking, so I really don't want to add passing out to the mix. I wish I could say that it was just wedding day jitters making me feel this way, but that would be a lie. The only thing keeping me from jumping out of this second-story window is the knowledge that I'm marrying Lucy today. The problem I'm having is with all the people. So many fucking people. Since I got back from my deployment, I've avoided large groups of people, preferring to be alone working on my furniture or curled up somewhere in the house with Lucy. I can't handle all the noise, all the chatter and all the questions that come along with being around so many people.

"Oh, honey, your tie…"

I continue staring blankly out the window as my mother rushes across the room to me, fiddling with my tie and making it tighter than it was before. She runs her palms down the front of my tie to smooth it down when she's finished and then takes a step back to look at me.

"Perfect! You look so handsome, Fisher!" she moves back and buttons the coat of my tux, brushing the shoulders and the sleeves of the jacket to get rid of any lint or stray hairs while she prattles about shit I don't care about. "The guests have almost all arrived and the caterers are passing out hors d'oeuvres and champagne while they wait to be seated. Wait until you see the flower arrangements I ordered for the reception. I had blue hydrangeas and orchids flown in to match the wedding colors…"

I tune her out and try counting backwards from a hundred in my head. Even being a floor above all the guests and workers, I can still hear the hum of their voices and laughter, the clink of glasses and the slamming of doors. My ears start to ring and my head aches with so much pressure that it feels like it might explode. I want peace and quiet… I want Lucy. I need Lucy to wrap her arms around me and whisper in my ear that everything is okay.

I must have muttered Lucy's name out loud while my mom was droning on about food and decorations because she crosses her arms and glares at me, pulling me out of my thoughts.

"You cannot see the bride before the wedding, it's bad luck," she informs me.

No, bad luck is not getting the wedding you wanted, the small, intimate gathering of close family and friends on the beach at sunset. Bad luck is this circus going on downstairs with hundreds of people Lucy and I have never met before. My father was against the wedding from day one, but he certainly is playing the part of a proud father of the groom today, inviting everyone he's ever done business with and kissing ass as soon as they walk in the door. He's been parading people around "The Estate" all morning, showing off expensive artwork and the like, smiling his fake smile and laughing his fake laugh whenever anyone asks him if he's excited to become a father-in-law today.

A loud crash sounds from somewhere in the house and I instinctively cover my head and drop to the ground. I hold my breath and wait for the sound of gunfire and explosions to fill the air, but nothing comes. I suddenly feel my mother's hand on my shoulder and I shake my head to clear it, feeling like a complete idiot.

"Fisher?" she whispers nervously as I push myself up from the floor and take a few deep breaths.

I'm not in the desert, I'm in my parents' home. Every thing is fine, I just need to calm down.

"I'm fine, mom, it's nothing," I tell her distractedly as I walk around her and head towards the door. There's no point in admitting I just had a flashback. I'm pretty sure she realized that as soon as I dropped to the ground and wrapped my arms around my head.

I need Lucy. I don't care what tradition says, I fucking need to see her right now or I'm never going to be able to calm down. I need to see that she's safe and happy and hasn't changed her mind about marrying into this fucked-up family.

As soon as I get out in the hallway, I pick up my pace, jogging down the hallway until I come to the staircase leading up to the third floor. I take the steps two at a time, my heart beating faster and my spirits lifting the closer I get to the room Lucy is in. When I get to the top of the stairs, I take off running full speed, my tie flying out behind me as I head towards the opposite side of the house.

I don't even stop to knock when I get to the closed double doors at the end of the hallway. Grabbing onto both handles, I throw open the doors and step inside the huge room that my mother had set up for Lucy to get ready in. Mirrors line every wall and make-up and hair products clutter the tables, but I only have eyes for the woman standing on the far side of the room in front of a floor-to-ceiling window.

She is the single most beautiful sight I've ever seen.

I finally stop moving and start breathing again when I see her. The winter sun shines brightly through the window, surrounding her like a halo, and she looks like an angel. She IS an angel. She's my angel and she keeps me grounded and watches over me, always taking care of me. The last few months have been hard on both of us, but Lucy has never let it show. She doesn't protest when I want to stay inside the house, away from other people; she just curls up with me on the couch and tells me how much she loves me. She doesn't get scared or look at me with pity if I have a nightmare and wake her up in the middle of the night; she just wraps me in her arms, talks to me about stuff that happened on the island while I was gone and tells me she missed me.

It's a strange thing, feeling like you can't breathe without another person. Physically, I know I'm breathing and my heart is beating when she's not around, but in my soul, it feels a movie that's been paused, waiting for someone to come back into the room. When I'm away from her, I feel like my life is on hold and she's the only one who can restart it.

"Jesus… You are stunning," I whisper as I take her in from head to toe.

She's wearing a strapless white dress that hugs every curve of her body and her hair is curled in soft waves all around her face and hangs down her back. I smile, knowing that she was able to win at least one argument with my mother about this wedding. My mother thought she would look best with her hair piled up on top of her head, but Lucy refused, knowing that I love it best when it's down and natural. Her veil is attached somewhere in her hair and it hangs down her back, trailing on the floor behind her. She grabs onto the fabric of her skirt and sweeps it out of the way as she turns to face me.

I take my time walking across the room so I can enjoy staring at her. When we're standing toe-to-toe, she looks up at me and smiles.

"Does your mother know you're in here? I was given strict orders to stay away from you until the ceremony," she tells me with a laugh.

Wrapping my hands softly around her neck, I rub my thumbs back and forth against the smooth skin of her cheeks. I'm afraid to touch her anywhere else and mess up her hair and make-up, but I can't be this close to her and *not* put my hands on her.

"I don't give a shit what my mother says. I needed to see you."

Lucy's face lights up, but then it quickly morphs into concern as she stares into my eyes.

"Hey, are you okay?" she asks softly, bringing her palms up and pressing them against my chest.

I smooth a wayward curl out of her eyes with the tips of my fingers and smile down at her.

"I am now. I just needed to see you," I reassure her.

She moves into the circle of my arms, sliding her hands down and around my waist before resting her cheek against my chest.

"You're going to mess up your hair and make-up," I protest, even though I'm already wrapping my arms around her and pulling her closer.

"It doesn't matter," she tells me, squeezing her arms tighter around my waist. "Nothing matters but this, right here. None of those people downstairs matter, none of the elaborate decorations or food matters, nothing is more important than us, right here, right now. I love you, Fisher, and even though we didn't get our wedding on the beach by the lighthouse, this is still the happiest day of my life."

Kissing the top of her head while trying to avoid mussing her hair, we stand in each other's arms and stare out the window at our lighthouse, set amongst the cliffs.

"Someday, down the line, I'm going to marry you by that lighthouse. We'll just renew our vows or something,"

I tell her.

Lucy's laughter rumbles against my chest and she tilts her head back to look up at me.

"Are we going to invite your mother? Because if we do, she might try to decorate the lighthouse and invite the entire town."

I chuckle and shrug. "Maybe we can just keep it a secret and invite her five minutes before it begins. Let's say… the fifteenth anniversary of the day I finally convinced you to date me. I'll meet you at the lighthouse and you can become my wife again."

Lucy nods her head, pushing up on her toes to kiss my chin. "It's a date. I'll meet you at the lighthouse."

Just a few minutes holding Lucy and I already feel a thousand times better. I can still hear the faint hum of noise downstairs, but it doesn't bother me. I hear a door slam and I don't jump with anxiety. She makes everything better… She makes the world around me disappear until there's just the two of us and she's right, that's all that matters.

I move back and grab her hands, pulling her towards the closet on the far side of the room.

"I have something for you. I snuck it in here this morning before you came up here to get ready," I tell her as I lead us to the closet. "Close your eyes."

She complies, standing beside me with a huge smile on her face.

"I thought we said we weren't going to get each other wedding presents, Fisher. Marrying you is the only gift I need."

I let go of her hands and open the door, reaching inside for the gift I made her.

"Yeah, well, I lied. Open your eyes."

She slowly opens her eyes and they immediately fill with tears when she sees what I'm holding.

"I thought we could hang it next to the front door of our house," I tell her.

I spent the last few weeks making a sign for her. It isn't much and it's definitely not the expensive pearls my mother insisted I buy for her, but I knew Lucy would much rather have a gift that came from the heart than anything I could buy.

"Oh, Fisher, it's beautiful," she tells me as she runs her hand over the oval sign.

I carved the words "The Fisher's, EST. 2006" and beneath it, our lighthouse.

"I can't wait to hang this up at the house. And I can't wait to become Mrs. Fisher."

Setting the sign down on the floor next to us, I pull her back into my arms.

"You make everything perfect, Lucy. You're my light and my life and all I need is your love to guide me home, no matter where I go."

Chapter 28

Fisher

Present Day

"FISHER, SIT DOWN before you pace a hole in the carpet."

I stop walking and look over at Seth Michelson as he rocks back and forth in one of the chairs I made for his office during my stay here. In his mid-sixties with a full head of white hair, Seth is a Vietnam vet who's spent his free time since retiring from a steel mill living in a suburb of Beaufort, South Carolina and volunteering at the local VA Hospital. I consider him a friend now, even though I hated him the first time I met him. He counsels vets at the rehab facility operated by the Veterans Affairs Medical Center where I spent the last year of my life. He's not a certified therapist or anything, but he knows all about how hard it is to reacclimate to civilian life after being in a warzone. The VA tried pushing psychiatrists on me after Bobby dropped me off at the doors, his parting message a threat to kick my ass again if I didn't get help and get my shit together. None of the white-coats they paraded into my room had ever been to war; they all just spouted facts and figures they'd read in books and urged me to lie down and discuss my feelings about my mother. After a few weeks of violent temper tantrums intensified by the effects of the alcohol detox, Seth walked in, took a seat on my bed and didn't say a word. He sat there, lounging against my pillows until he got bored with the silence and pulled a book off of my nightstand and started reading it. It pissed me off so much that I started shouting at him. The shouting turned into another full-fledged hissy fit and I grabbed the book out of his hand and chucked it across the room. Still, he didn't say a word. I kept screaming and he started examining his fingernails until my screams turned into muttered curses and then my muttered curses turned into talking. I talked and talked until my voice was hoarse and I exhausted myself, sliding down against the wall and crumpling to the floor. When I was finished, he got up from my bed, walked over to me, gave me a pat on the back and said, "I'll be back tomorrow. We'll go for a walk."

After that afternoon, I saw Seth every day of my stay at the rehab facility. He told me about what he'd seen in Vietnam and how he coped once he got home to his wife and newborn baby girl, but mostly, he listened. If I was having a bad day and took it out on him, he'd call me on my shit and tell me to quit my bitching. If I was feeling sorry for myself, he'd tell me to stop being a pussy and think about all the good things I'd been blessed with in my life. Seth was my savior during the darkest time in my life, and with all the conflicting thoughts going on in my head over the last week, I knew it was time to take the ferry over to the mainland and see him. I spent the last hour going over the events that had taken place since the last time I spoke to him, the day I left the hospital a little over a month ago.

"So, you're freaking out that you hurt Lucy and pushed her away, ruining all of your plans of getting close to her again. Is that the gist of it?" Seth asks.

"Obviously, I hurt her. I shoved her face-first against the side of a fucking building and bit her neck. I lost control, Seth. After spending an entire year learning how to control my anger, I fucking lost it when I saw her kissing that dickhead she's dating," I explain, starting to pace again.

"I'm assuming she screamed at you? Told you to stop, pushed you away, smacked you, punched you, cursed you?" Seth asks. I can hear the amusement in his voice because he knows damn well that didn't happen or I would have included it in my explanation.

"It all happened so fast. She didn't have time to fight me, but I know she wanted to," I tell him lamely, without any real conviction in my voice.

Seth laughs. "Really? Are you a mind reader now?"

"Fuck you," I growl. "I know Lucy and I know that's not something she would have wanted from me. I turned into a fucking animal and I'm sure she hates me now, even more than she did before. She's got Mr. Perfect who probably wears white gloves when he touches her so he won't get her dirty and then she's got me who roughs her up in an alley."

Seth gets up from the rocking chair and walks over to stand in front of me. "You spent thirteen months away from her, so it's possible you don't know her as well as you thought you did. Things change, *people* change. You don't think what happened to you after your deployments changed her, as well? Changed something inside of her and made her a little stronger, a little more confident and taught her how to adapt?"

It's Seth's turn to pace and I watch him, listening to him speak. "My Mary Beth, she was a mousy little thing when I left for 'Nam. Never raised her voice, never argued… She was one of those wives who was seen and not heard, just like her mother taught her. She was the calm to my storm and it worked, until I came home a little different than how I left and I was angry all the time. She fed off of my anger and we had some knock-down, drag-out fights in the middle of the kitchen, complete with her tossing plates and glasses at my head while I ranted and raved and raged. The next day, I'd get down on my knees and practically sob about how sorry I was and she'd just laugh and wrap her arms around me. She'd say, 'Seth, fighting with you is the most fun I've had in years. If you need to let out some of your anger, I have no problem with you letting it out with me. But if you ever lay a hand on me in something other than passion, I will grab the shotgun from the hall closet and shoot your sorry ass.' "

Seth chuckles and I can't help but laugh right along with him. He stops pacing and looks at me again. "I hadn't even realized that while I was going through all my shit and I was changing into a different person, Mary Beth was changing right along with me. She realized she quite liked a little drama and excitement, as long as neither one of us was being downright cruel or purposefully hurtful. It also spiced things up in the bedroom and that's how we got three more kids."

Seth winks at me and I roll my eyes at him, pretending disgust at the talk of his spicy bedroom.

"You've told me a lot about Lucy during your time here, and the one thing you have always stressed to me is that she's strong. Stronger than anyone you know, including yourself, and that's why you felt the need to send her those divorce papers," Seth reminds me. "You didn't want to bring her down to the level of weakness that you were feeling at the time. If she's as strong as you say she is, don't you think she would've said something if she didn't want what you were doing to her? Don't you think she would've kicked your ass if it pissed her off?"

Closing my eyes, I think about every moment in that alley, even though part of me wants to forget. I think about how her sweet ass pushed back against me and how she begged for more. I think about how fast she came and my name on her lips when she did. I remember the look on her face when I pushed her away and apologized and a light bulb goes off. She was definitely pissed then, and about two seconds away from kicking my ass, but it wasn't because of what I'd done. It was because *I* regretted it. While I was wallowing in guilt because I thought I'd hurt her, she was angry because. . . shit.

Did my Lucy like it a little rough?

I shove down the thrill that thought brings me when my mind flashes back to the marks I left on her body the day I returned home from my last deployment and the way she wrapped her arms around her waist, almost like she was holding herself together, the night I forced her from our home. Every time I loosen up the grip on my emotions, Lucy is the one who suffers. I *cannot* lose control where she's concerned.

"I don't want to hurt her like I did the day I ended things. I'm so afraid of turning into that man again and lashing out at her. It's better if I stay calm and not get overwhelmed with emotions and anger," I tell him, walking over to the window to stare out at the street below.

Beaufort reminds me a lot of Fisher's Island. There are no cars racing up and down the street or people rushing around to get where they're going. Seth told me they'd deliberately chosen a small community, having had their fill of the hustle and bustle of the big city during his forty-year career at a Detroit steel mill. Up until I met Lucy, I thought that was what I wanted. To live in a big city where things actually happened, to get away from the island that was my personal hell, once upon a time. Ironically, it wasn't nearly seven years in a sandbox in the Middle East that made me appreciate the beauty of my island. It was spending a year in a treatment facility less than fifty miles away, where I could still hear the sound of the ocean and smell the salt in the air, that gave me the strength to get better. There was nothing like being *so close* to everything I've ever wanted to provide the kick in the ass I needed to get my shit together and get my ass back to the island where I belonged, where things made sense. Not only did I hate being away from Lucy, I hated being away from *my* beach, the lighthouse, our small cottage on the water and our close-knit community where everyone knows each other. Even now, it feels like my skin is filled with bugs that I want to scratch and brush away. I itch with the need to go back home to my Lucy.

"You haven't had a drink since you got back home, right?" Seth asks.

I shake my head. "No, and the crazy thing is, I'm not even tempted to have one, even with all this shit going on in my head. It feels good to be clear and focused, but even without the alcohol, I still have moments where I get fuzzy and I have to really concentrate on calming down."

"Of course you do, son. It's called PTSD, and it's probably going to be with you for the rest of your life. Forty-plus years later and sometimes I still wake up in a cold sweat and it takes me a minute to realize I'm not neck deep in a swamp of rice paddies, soaked to the bone, waiting to get my head blown off," Seth explains. "You can't keep that shit inside or it will eat you alive, as you very well know. You spent years keeping your nightmares and your problems to yourself and look what it did to your marriage. Talk to your woman, Fisher. If you want her to trust you again, you need to give her that same level of trust. You need to have faith that she's strong enough to take whatever you give her."

Seth and I spend some time wandering the grounds of the rehab facility and I talk to a few of the guys who came in right before I left. I see so much of myself in them, and for the first time in a long time, I feel proud about how far I've come since I checked in here. Seth is right; I can't expect Lucy to ever trust me or believe in me if I don't do the same with her. She needs to understand what was going through my mind while I was slowly unraveling over a year ago. Sure, the journal pages of happier times that I've been sending her are a great way to remind her how good we were together, but I can't expect her to give us a chance at a new future if I don't talk about the bad times, as well.

As much as I want to keep my anger and my jealousy as far away from Lucy as possible, I have to accept that they're a part of me. They live and breathe inside of me and I can't just ignore them and expect them to go away. I know I will never hurt Lucy like I did the day I made her leave our home, but what guarantee do I have that I won't hurt her even worse with my words and actions when those feelings take hold of me like they did that day in the alley? I want to believe that Seth is right, that Lucy would've found a way to make me stop if she truly didn't want it, but it's hard for me to see her as anything other than the sweet, shy, beautiful girl I married, no matter how much has changed since then. It's hard for me to fathom that she would want me to touch her with anything but gentleness and soft hands, but I also can't erase the sounds of her moans of pleasure from my ears, telling me that she loved what I was doing to her.

With a promise from Seth that he'll bring Mary Beth out to the island soon, I head outside and take a cab to the ferry that will take me back to the island.

I know Lucy will be busy with all of the Fourth of July events coming up, but maybe I can convince her to give me a little of her time. It's way past time for me to come clean with her.

About everything.

Chapter 29
Lucy

Present Day

"**Y**OU ARE NOT playing in that softball game today!"

"You can't tell me what to do, asshole. GO AWAY!"

I glance up from my paperwork when I hear shouting coming from the porch to watch as Ellie flies through the front door with Bobby charging in right behind her.

"I most certainly CAN tell you what to do, and you're damn well going to listen!" Bobby argues.

I've never seen Bobby so fired up before and it gives me pause. Where Bobby isn't what I would call hot, like Fisher, he's boyish and cute with his curly head of brown hair, twinkling blue eyes and easy smile. He stands even with Ellie's five-foot-ten frame and he's lucky she's not wearing heals right now or she'd be towering over him and most likely pummeling him to the ground going by the furious look on her face.

"You are not the fucking boss of me! I knew it was a bad idea to tell you!" Ellie yells, stomping right past me, not even glancing in my direction.

Bobby races behind her and I toss down my pen and follow him, wondering what in the hell is going on. Thank God all of the guests are already down on Main

Street waiting for the parade to begin and aren't getting front row seats to this shouting match.

Bobby finally catches up with Ellie in the kitchen, wrapping his arms around her from behind when she tries to leave through the sliding glass doors.

"Will you stop trying to run away from me?!" he argues, lifting her up and moving her away from the door.

She kicks and claws at his arms until he lets go and moves away, putting himself between Ellie and the door so she can't try and escape again.

"Will you stop following me? Jesus, just go away!"

"I'm not going anywhere until you agree to marry me!" Bobby shouts at her.

My mouth drops open and my eyes widen in shock. What in the actual fuck is happening right now?

"Oh, my God, will you stop?! I am NOT going to marry you, I don't even *like* you!" Ellie argues.

"Bullshit! You're in love with me, dammit, you're just too scared to admit it!"

Ellie stomps her foot like a toddler and crosses her arms in front of her. I should probably say something, try and get them to stop arguing and tell me what the hell is going on, but I'm too stunned to do anything other than stand here in the doorway.

"You are SUCH an asshole!" Ellie screams.

"You're right, I'm a huge asshole. That's one thing we agree on. I'm also not going to let you do this alone," Bobby adds.

"I am perfectly capable of doing this on my own. I've been taking care of myself since I was nineteen years old and I don't need some guy thinking he needs to marry me just because I'm pregnant!"

Whoa. What the hell?!

"Ellie?" I whisper, finally making my presence known.

She jumps a little at the sound of my voice, her tear-filled eyes finding mine across the room. I look at her questioningly and she just shrugs, swiping angrily at the tears that have started to fall down her face.

Finding out that Ellie is pregnant has thrown me completely, but finding out that she was actually *dating* someone is even more shocking. Ellie has been alone since her husband of only a year, Daniel, was killed in action. They were high school sweethearts just like Fisher and I, and when he received orders that sent him from South Carolina to Texas, they got married as soon as Ellie graduated from high school so she could go with him. She's told me countless times after a few glasses of wine that she knows she'll never love someone as much as she loved her husband. The tragic way she lost him scarred her heart worse than anything I could ever imagine, and she's kept that heart under lock and key for all of these years. I'm protective of her whenever I see a guy try to hit on her or ask her out on a date, but I also recognize that she needs to move on.

Bobby wraps his hands around her upper arms and turns her body to face him. I stand silently in the corner and let him say what he needs to say, hoping he knows what the hell he's doing. If he hurts my best friend, I will kick his ass.

"I know I'm not Daniel. I would never try to take his

place in your heart or your life, but I hope that you can make a little room for me in there and give me a chance. In case you haven't noticed, I'm completely in love with you, Ellie. I've been in love with you since the first day I met you and you told me to fuck off when I asked you out on a date," Bobby chuckles. "I want to marry you because I love you and I can't imagine spending the rest of my life arguing with anyone else but you. I'm not asking you to marry me because of the baby, I'm asking you to marry me because of ME. Because I want this, more than I've ever wanted anything else in my life."

He drops his hands from Ellie's arms and leans forward, pressing a kiss to her forehead before backing away.

"Don't say no. At least, not right away. Just think about it. You know where to find me."

Bobby gives me a nod before turning away and leaving through the sliding doors. As soon as he's gone, I rush over to Ellie and wrap my arms around her while she sobs into my shoulder. I've never seen Ellie cry, EVER, and it tears me apart to hear the anguish in her voice as she cries.

"Everything is going to be okay, Ellie, I promise. I'm going to be here for you every step of the way. If you don't want Bobby, I will be here. I'm not going anywhere," I tell her.

She lets out a groan, pulling out of my arms. "That's the problem. I DO want Bobby! He's such an arrogant ass, but he's sweet and he loves me and fucking hell, I think I'm in love with him, too!"

Grabbing onto her hand, I yank her outside onto the veranda, pointing to a rocking chair. "Sit!"

She immediately complies. Leaning my butt against the railing, I cross my arms in front of me and stare at her.

"Speak."

She rolls her eyes. "I'm not a damn dog, Lucy. Hey, aren't you supposed to be down at the parade?"

"Distraction is not going to work, missy. Explain what the hell I just witnessed in that kitchen. Why didn't you tell me you were dating Bobby?"

Ellie sighs, pulling her legs up onto the chair and wrapping her arms around them. "Because we weren't really dating, we were just sleeping together. It wasn't that big of a deal until... it sort of became a big deal. I really started to like him and I *wanted* to spend time with him. It scared the hell out of me. I kept thinking about Daniel and how I was tarnishing his memory by having feelings for another man."

Pushing away from the railing, I squat down in front of her. "Oh, honey, you aren't tarnishing Daniel's memory. Do you really think he'd want you to be alone for the rest of your life? To never experience love again and to never be happy? I can't believe for one minute that he would've wanted that for you."

Ellie brushes her hand against her cheek as more tears start to fall. "I know that, in my head I know that. The problem is that... I think I love Bobby more than I ever loved Daniel. I don't know, it's all happened so fast with him and all of these feelings came out of nowhere. I wasn't looking for love and all of a sudden it smacked me up side the head. I feel guilty because my feelings for

Bobby are so much stronger than they were for Daniel and I hate that. I hate that I'm forgetting him and Bobby is the one filling my thoughts."

Grabbing onto her hand, I give it a squeeze. "You aren't forgetting Daniel, you're just moving on, sweetie. You loved Daniel when you were both really young. You should've had more time together, but you didn't and that sucks. No one can ever take away the love you had for him, and there's no shame in falling in love again. You're older now, you've seen more of the world and life in general. You've learned more about love and you've found someone who challenges you and isn't afraid to call you on your shit. If you love Bobby, and it seems like he really loves you, why should you punish yourself by not exploring it?"

Ellie sighs, leaning her head back against the chair. "I really want to marry him, Lucy. I can't believe I'm saying that, but it's true. I can see a future with him and it makes me happy and excited. I haven't felt like this in a long time."

"I think you need to tell him that," I inform her.

"He's never going to believe I'm saying yes because I actually want to marry him. He's going to think I'm doing it because of the baby. Oh, my God, I'm going to have a baby," Ellie suddenly whispers in shock.

I laugh at the look of horror on her face. "He's going to believe you when you tell him exactly what you just told me. And when you two are living happily ever after together, you can name this baby after me as a thank you."

"I really hope it's not a boy, then, or he's going to be the girliest little boy in the world," Ellie finally laughs.

"I'm so happy for you, Ellie," I tell her honestly.

"I'm happy for me, too," she tells me with another laugh. "What about you? When are you going to get your happily ever after?"

I sigh, thinking about the things my mom said to me the other day about Fisher. I just need to get through today and then hopefully the two of us can talk. I want an explanation for all the things that happened between us and I want to be able to have a calm, rational talk with him about how I feel and what I want.

"I don't know if a happily ever after is in the cards for me, but I'm going to try," I admit.

"Does that mean you're going to kick Stanley to the curb?" she asks with an excited look on her face.

"Seriously?" I ask her in annoyance.

"What? I mean, he made you happy for a little while and I gave the guy a chance, but Lucy, he's a fucking dud. I like the way you are when you're with Fisher, that's all," she says with a shrug.

"And how is that, exactly?" I question.

"You're a little firecracker when you're with him. And yes, I just made a Fourth of July joke ON the Fourth of July. You're welcome," she says sarcastically. "I don't know, you come alive when you're around him. You aren't just going through the motions, doing what you think you have to do. You're passionate and angry and happy and crazy. You're actually *living* when you're with him. I haven't seen you do that in a while, and definitely not with Stan the Un-Man."

Ellie and I talk for a few more minutes about Fisher and I tell her a little bit about what happened in the alley without going into too many intimate details.

"Nice, Lucy likes it rough," Ellie says with a laugh.

I smack her hand and roll my eyes at her.

"That was not the point of me sharing that with you," I scold her. "The point is, Fisher thinks I'm made of glass. He thinks I'm still the same woman he married and that he has to handle me with kid gloves. He's afraid of his temper and the passion that comes with it, and I don't know how to tell him that he doesn't have to be afraid. That *I'M* not afraid and I want it. I want everything from him."

Ellie shrugs. "So how about you show him instead of tell him? Men are visual creatures. You could talk to him until you're blue in the face and he still wouldn't get it. He'd still think you were only placating him or saying what you thought he wanted to hear. Strap on a set of balls and *show* the guy that you want all that intensity and passion from him."

I mull over Ellie's advice while she helps me gather up the t-shirts to sell on Main Street. Even though Fisher and I really do need to talk about so many important things, Ellie is right. He's never going to believe that part of what I have to say unless I prove it to him, show him that I'm not afraid of his anger or his jealousy and that if he's serious about working through things, I want ALL of him this time, not just the parts he chooses to share with me.

Chapter 30

Fisher

```
Present Day
```

T HE ENTIRE TOWN, including all the tourists, has packed the small baseball field next to Barney's. The bleachers filled up quickly, so most people brought chairs and blankets and they are spread out all around the chain-link fence surrounding the field, cheering the teams on. Every year, the businesses put their names in a hat if they have employees who are going to play and the mayor draws the teams to make it fair. I really had no intention of playing this year, but a last minute ankle injury had me filling in starting in the third inning. I was team captain the last game I played in two summers ago, and let's just say it didn't go very well. My drinking had started to get out of hand right around that point and everything pissed me off, even what was supposed to be a fun, friendly competition between local businesses. I almost got kicked out of the game for shouting at my team every time they made a shitty play, but Lucy did her best to calm me down and convince everyone I was just having an off day.

To say I was a little surprised that everyone begged me to play today is an understatement. The only reason I agreed is because the team that needed me is Lucy's team and the captain is my father. He's made it a point not to let Lucy bat and threw her as far out in the outfield as she could get and still be on the damn field.

It's the bottom of the ninth and our team is losing 3-1, bases loaded with two outs. It's not looking very good for Fisher's Fireballs. If we don't get our guys home, the game is over. I thought being in the dugout with Lucy would be the perfect opportunity to talk to her, but every time I've tried, she's done whatever she could to avoid me. I realize it's not the most private place to have a deep conversation, but at this point, I just want her to smile at me and give me some sort of sign that things are going to be okay with us. We've played many Fourth of July softball games together over the years, but this is the first time I've had to hold myself back from scooping her up in my arms and cheering along with her when our team makes a good play. We were always getting yelled at in the outfield for sneaking kisses and smacking each other on the ass and not paying attention to the game. I miss having fun with her. I miss doing normal things and being the couple that everyone teased because we couldn't keep our hands off of each other. Now, I have to force myself not to rub her shoulders while she's clutching onto the fence and cheering on the team. I have to find something else to do with my hands to avoid winding her long ponytail around my hand and pulling her head back for a kiss.

"Mark, you're up!" My dad shouts to the owner of the Lobster Bucket, who was snoring at the end of the bench.

"Seriously?" I ask quietly through clenched teeth. "Mark has been up to bat four times already and each time you've had to wake him up from his afternoon nap. And he has yet to get a hit."

My father takes his ball cap off and scratches his head. "Mark is next in the line-up, so Mark better get a hit this time."

"Put Lucy in," I argue. "She can at least get us a base hit and then I'm up after that."

"Since you aren't the team captain this year, a wise decision after your behavior last time, sit down and keep your opinions to yourself," he argues back.

I'm about two seconds away from shoving my father into the dugout fence behind him when Lucy comes up next to me and puts a hand on my arm.

"It's fine if your father doesn't want to put me in," she says sweetly. "If we do end up winning, we'll just have to forfeit our victory and give the trophy to the other team. No big deal."

I watch her shrug with a cheeky smile and I try not to laugh.

"What the hell are you talking about?" my father asks in irritation.

"Oh, didn't you hear? They established rules this year on account of Erika throwing that ball at Stephen's head last year because he kept making jokes about her holding his balls when she got up to bat," Lucy informs him.

I chuckle to myself, a little sad that I didn't get to witness THAT moment between the married owners of the town's dry cleaners.

"Not only are spouses no longer allowed to play on the same team, every person ON the team must get at least one up-to-bat. Any violation of the rules results in a forfeit," Lucy finishes with another sweet smile.

"Why didn't I hear about these stupid rules?" my father grumbles.

Lucy leans up on her tip toes and snatches the baseball cap from my head and puts it on her own, pulling her ponytail through the hole in the back before grabbing a bat from the holder beside my father. "I'm sure you were too busy trying to take over the world to pay attention at the last town meeting. It's a good thing you have me."

She moves past him and out of the dugout, putting a little extra swing in her hips as she goes. My father throws his cap across the dugout and I laugh right in his face before moving to the opening so I can get a better look at Lucy's ass.

I mean, yell some encouraging words as she practices her swing.

Seriously though, those tiny black cotton shorts she's wearing have been torturing me all day and watching her lean forward and stick out her ass as she gets ready for the first pitch is making me sweat. My heart is also thundering a little harder in my chest that she's wearing my cap, something she'd always done. Even when she'd bring her own hat to the game, she'd always take it off and steal mine when she was up to bat, arguing that it brought her good luck. It was an outright lie because she never got a hit whether she wore my hat or not, but it still made me feel good to see her wearing it. She looks so fucking hot in that white Butler House tank top and tiny black shorts with my baseball hat on her head.

"Let's go, Lucy! Homerun!"

The crowd screams and cheers when they see her up to bat and now I'm nervous as hell. She played softball her senior year of high school, and let's just say she spent a lot of time on the bench. We've played in many games together since she started running Butler House, and her skills hadn't really improved, either. It didn't matter to her because she was playing for fun, but I really want her to show up my father and make him look like an ass.

The first pitch comes and flies right by her.

"STRRRRRIKE!"

"Well, there goes this year's trophy," my father mutters in irritation behind me.

"Come on, Lucy! You can do this!" I shout to her, ignoring my father.

She tightens her grip on the bat, shaking her hips a little as she gets into stance. My dick immediately wakes up in my shorts and starts panting.

The next pitch comes and she swings a second too late.

"STRRRRRIKE!"

Half the crowd boos while the other half cheers and I step out onto the dirt and yell for a time-out. Butch, who's the ump today, backs away from the plate while I jog over to Lucy.

"Shit. I forgot how much I suck at softball," Lucy laughs nervously as I approach her.

"You're doing fine," I tell her. "Just choke up on the bat a little."

Grabbing her hands, I move them up the neck of the

bat. She looks up at me and I don't remove my hands from around hers on the bat as I stare down into her blue eyes. I take another step closer to her until our toes are touching and I can feel her breath on my face.

"Keep your eyes on the ball the entire time, from the second it leaves the pitcher's hand until it connects with your bat," I tell her softly.

Sliding my leg between hers, I tap the instep of her foot with my toe.

"Spread your feet apart a little wider. You're stance is too tight."

Lucy leans into me when she moves her feet apart and I take a deep breath, inhaling the coconut scent lingering on her skin. Her eyes still haven't left mine and my hands still haven't let go of hers around the bat. I beg my dick to stay at ease and not jump up and poke her in the stomach.

"If it helps, imagine the ball is my head and you should be able to knock that thing out of the park," I tell her with a soft smile.

Her cheeks flush pink and I'm hoping it's because of my close proximity and not the sun blazing down on top of us.

"I think I got it," she whispers back, making no effort to move away from me.

"If you two are finished canoodling, can we get back to the game?" Butch asks, coming right up next to us.

We both turn our heads to see him smiling at us. He gives us a wink before pulling his face guard down from the top of his head.

I back away from Lucy and give her an encouraging smile, even though all I want to do is tackle her to the ground and fuck her on top of home plate.

"You can do this, Lucy. Eye on the ball."

I clap loudly and continue cheering her on as I walk backwards towards the dugout.

As soon as I'm in the opening of the cage, my father comes right up next to me.

"What the hell are you doing?" he asks in irritation.

"I was giving her a few pointers. Something you should have done as the team captain," I explain sarcastically, trying my best not to lose my cool since the entire team has gotten up from the bench and is standing all around us cheering Lucy on.

"You were making a spectacle of yourself in front of the entire town. She has a boyfriend, who is in the stands and no doubt saw that entire display," he says quietly with an edge to his voice. "Congratulations, you just made her look like the whore I always knew she was."

My hands clench into fists at my sides and I get ready to spew as much hate at him as I can, but someone beats me to it.

"Shut the hell up, Jefferson," my mother reprimands.

I didn't even see her come down to the dugout, but I notice she's carrying a small cooler filled with water bottles and must have been passing them out while I was with Lucy.

My father actually has the foresight to look embarrassed.

"Grace, I was just—"

"You were just, what? Making yourself look like an ass?" she interrupts him. "Keep your mouth shut about Lucy. You say one more unkind word about her and I will throw your shit out on the front lawn and you can find a new place to live."

I don't know who is more shocked about my mother's threat, my father or me. We're both wearing equal looks of disbelief on our faces, but mine is tinged with amusement that I can't quite keep contained. I smile widely at my mother and she gives me a wink before going back to passing out bottles of water.

Moving away from my father before I punch him in the face, I start clapping and shouting as loud as I can for Lucy as the pitcher finishes up a couple practice pitches.

Pressing my hands together in silent prayer, I rest my fingers against my lips and hold my breath as Lucy gets into the stance I showed her and chokes up on the bat. The pitcher winds up and throws as hard as he can. Even with the entire park screaming and stomping their feet, I still hear the loud *crack* of the bat over the noise as it connects with the ball. My hands slowly drop from my face and my eyes widen in shock as I watch the ball Lucy just hit soar through the air and into the outfield.

The entire dugout begins screaming and hugging and jumping up and down. I start to join them when I realize Lucy is still standing on home plate with the bat in her hand, staring into the outfield in shock while the runner from third is almost home.

"LUCY! DROP THE BAT AND RUN, BABY!" I shout to her with a laugh.

She jumps out of her trance, tosses the bat to the side and takes off towards first. The guys in the outfield are scrambling to get to the ball since they all moved infield when she got up to bat. They've got a long way to run since she cracked the hell out of that thing. It bounced almost to the fence line.

Our entire team leaves the dugout and we're standing along the first base line, cheering all the runners as they make it over home plate. The other team is screaming at the guys in the outfield, telling them to move their asses. Lucy rounds third when they finally get the ball and heave it infield. She slides across home plate like a pro, kicking up dust all over the place, right as the ball comes sailing in to the catcher.

"SAFE!" Butch shouts.

We all charge the mound, cheering and hollering and I shove people out of the way to get to Lucy, forgetting about the fact that we aren't together and this isn't a softball game of the past. I scoop her up into my arms and jump up and down. She wraps her arms around my shoulders and her legs around my hips and laughs as I chant her name with everyone else.

"Damn, if I'd known telling you to visualize my face as the ball would get you to hit a grand slam, I would've told you that years ago," I laugh.

She throws her head back and laughs harder as everyone pats her on the back and congratulates her.

"Luce?"

Lucy's laughter dies and her smile suddenly falls. She gently pats my shoulders to get me to put her down and I slowly lower her to the ground as her legs slide from around my waist. She untangles herself from my arms and turns to face Shit-Stain-Ford.

He grabs onto both of her hands and pulls her away from me and I immediately want to wrap my arms around her and bring her back in a jealous tug of war.

"I was going to wait to do this until later, but we might as well celebrate your win right here in front of everyone."

He gives me a quick glare that goes unnoticed by Lucy since she's currently looking over her shoulder at me. I slide my hands in my pockets and pretend like I'm not wondering what the fuck he's doing.

He starts lowering himself to the ground and I feel bile rising up in my throat as Lucy whips her head around to look at him.

"What are you doing? Get up!" she whispers frantically.

He's on one knee at this point and I suddenly realize exactly what he's doing. The prick is proposing to *my fucking wife* and I want to beat his ass more than I ever have before.

"I know we haven't known each other long, but I love you, Lucy Butler," the motherfucking piece of shit pompous asshole tells her as he pulls a light blue Tiffany's box from his shirt pocket and holds it open in front of her.

The diamond is bigger than her fucking finger and sparkles in the sunshine. Everyone gathered around home plate has quieted down and they're watching this whole shit show unfold five feet away from me.

"Will you marry me, Lucy?"

I don't bother to wait for her reply. I turn and walk off of the field, wishing I still drank. An entire bottle of whiskey sounds really good right about now, especially when I hear a loud cheer erupt from the field, most likely in celebration of Lucy's engagement.

Chapter 31
Lucy

As SOON AS Fisher walks away from home plate, I let out the breath I was holding. Thank God Bob, who owns the souvenir store, needs to take a few practice pitches so I can pull myself together and try to remember all the tips Fisher gave me instead of thinking about how much I wanted to feel his hands someplace other than on top of mine.

I've been avoiding him all day and I feel like a coward. He's tried talking to me several times, but I've made up one excuse after another and walked away from him. I want to talk to him, I really do, but I'm having a hard time thinking about anything other than sex when he's within two feet of me. It doesn't help that he's wearing his usual pair of cargo shorts that make his ass look fantastic and a three-quarter-length baseball-style t-shirt that molds his upper body and shows off all of his muscles. Every time he's been up to bat, I've been glued to the fence, panting like a dog in heat.

Instead of picturing Fisher's face as Bob winds up and throws the ball, I picture his father's arrogant mug flying towards me and I swing as hard as I can. The smack of the ball against the bat stings my hands and I stand frozen in complete shock as it flies above everyone's heads. I hear people screaming and clapping, but I don't move. I think I'm supposed to move. I'm pretty sure I'm supposed to run, but I can't stop staring at the ball soaring into the outfield. I suddenly hear Fisher scream louder than anyone else and when he tacks on the word "baby" at the end of his shout, my heart skips a beat and my feet start moving. I can't wipe the huge grin off of my face as my feet pound into the dirt and I run as fast as I can around the bases. When I'm halfway between second and third, I see the outfielders get to the ball and throw it towards home. I push my legs harder and, even though the entire team is now out of the dugout and on the sidelines, I can only see Fisher standing there, jumping up and down with a huge smile on his face.

I slide into home just as the ball zooms into the catcher's mitt and when Butch announces I'm safe, I scream through the cloud of dust surrounding me. Pushing myself up from the ground, I quickly shove my way through the crowd of people jumping and shouting around me until I find Fisher. I throw myself into his arms and he lifts me up, holding me tight. It feels like we're the only two people on the field. It feels like the last few years never happened and we're back in time, happily married and enjoying yet another Fourth of July softball game together. I take his hat off of my head so I can see his face better, clutching it in my hands behind his head. I get so lost in the moment, smiling and laughing with him, that I don't see Stanford walk out onto the field and stand next to us until he says my name.

I don't want to move out of Fisher's arms. It feels so right being wrapped up in him, feeling his heart beat against mine and listening to him laugh, just like the old days. Unfortunately, I'm technically still dating Stanford, even though I've already decided to end things with him. He's a good man and I don't want to embarrass him in front of all these people. It's bad enough I was clutching onto my ex-husband like I never wanted to let him go while he watched. I will not be the whore Fisher's father accuses me of being, and I can't figure this thing out with Fisher until I end things with Stanford.

When Fisher releases me, Stanford grabs my hand and pulls me closer to him. I take one last look at Fisher over my shoulder, trying to tell him with my eyes and my smile that I'm sorry. I hear a gasp from somewhere in the crowd around us and turn away from Fisher to see Stanford down on one knee in front of me.

Oh, no! Oh, my God, what is happening right now?!

Stanford smiles up at me and I see him reaching into the front pocket of his neatly pressed, button-down shirt. I stupidly ask him what he's doing, even though it's perfectly CLEAR what's going on, and I tell him to get up. He doesn't listen, of course, instead going right into his speech about how he loves me before he asks me to marry him. I am stunned completely stupid. My mouth is hanging open like I'm trying to catch flies and he slides the ring on my finger before I even have a chance to give him an answer. It's huge and heavy and it feels completely foreign on my finger. I immediately hate it and want to yank it off and toss it into the outfield where my ball went. Nothing makes me miss the simple quarter carat solitaire and plain gold band that Fisher gave me more than this monstrosity weighing down my finger.

I'm so busy missing those rings and wishing I'd never sent them back with the divorce papers that I'm in a complete daze. When my eyes fill with tears of regret for something I no longer have, Stanford takes it as a sign of acceptance of his proposal, jumping up from the ground and wrapping me in his arms as the crowd around us starts chanting my name again and clapping.

Why are they so happy when all I want to do is cry? I search behind me for Fisher and I don't see him anywhere. I wish he had been my voice when I couldn't speak, but why the hell would he do that when I've been avoiding him and haven't given him any solid proof that I still love him and miss him? I wish he would have told Stanford to fuck off and that I was *his*. I wish *I* could say that to Stanford right now, but Jesus, did he HAVE to do this in front of all these people? I don't want to hurt him when he's been nothing but kind and sweet to me, and I certainly don't want to embarrass him in front of the entire town by telling him I don't love him and I never will. I have no idea what he was thinking by proposing to me. We haven't even had sex yet and he thinks he's in love with me and wants to spend the rest of his life with me? Is he insane? I clutch Fisher's ball cap to my chest and my throat burns with the need to cry.

The crowd gets more and more worked up with their chanting and clapping and I'm still wondering why the hell they're so happy about this when suddenly, ice cold water is being dumped all over my head. It pours down over top of me like a waterfall, ice cubes bouncing off of my shoulders and getting stuck down the front of my tank top. I sputter and let out a few choking laughs as I wipe the water from my eyes, opening them to see the crowd completely surrounding me in a tight circle, bouncing up and down.

"Lucy, we've decided you're the MVP of today's game!" someone shouts.

"We couldn't have won the game without you!"

"Lucy! Lucy! Lucy!"

I get lost in their excitement and forget about the mess that is my life as I jump up and down with them, laughing and shouting. I feel a hand grip my arm tightly and I'm tugged out of the circle of celebration mid-bounce. I stumble as Stanford pulls me a few feet away from everyone, finally dropping my arm when we're out of earshot from the crowd.

I rub at the spot on my arm he was clutching and shoot him a dirty look. "What the hell, Stanford? That *hurt.*"

"WHAT are you doing?" he cuts me off angrily, pointing to the group of people still shouting and high-fiving.

"Um, it's called celebrating, Stanford," I reply sarcastically.

I've never spoken to him with anything other than kindness, but he's really pissing me off today. First with the proposal, and now with the attitude.

"Have you taken a look at yourself? It's indecent," he

tells me crossly.

Realizing that I'm still sopping wet from the bucket of ice water that was poured over my head, I look down at myself and see that my white tank top now makes me a contender for a wet t-shirt contest. The pink lace bra I put on this morning wasn't obvious when the shirt was dry, but now it's all you can see since the wet material of my shirt is sticking to me like a second skin.

I try to pull it away from my body, but as soon as I let go, it just slaps right back against me. I just shrug and laugh at the fact that I look like a drowned rat.

"This is NOT funny, Lucy. Everyone is staring. And those shorts? They barely cover you. You realize that when we're married you're going to have to dress the part of a proper Southern lady, not like a seventeen-year-old girl," Stanford informs me.

I really try to stay calm, but the accumulation of the day's events is wearing on me, and I suddenly feel like a dam about to burst. I forget about the fact that I didn't want to embarrass him in front of everyone, especially since that's exactly what he's doing to ME right now.

"If everyone is staring, it's because YOU'RE making a scene," I inform him. "And you JUST proposed to me five minutes ago. I didn't even give you a fucking answer, and you're already planning what it will be like when we're married?"

Stanford reaches for my arm and I twist out of his reach.

"Will you keep your voice down? My goodness, what has gotten into you today?" he demands. "You are not the type of woman who uses such trashy language."

I can't help it, I throw my head back and laugh. I laugh until my stomach hurts and I can barely catch my breath. Stanford stares at me like I've lost my mind and who knows, maybe I have? I lost my mind when I started dating this man, thinking he was exactly what I needed. All I've done for the last few months is try to be someone I'm not. I've dressed the part, I've talked the part and I've acted the part and none of it has made me happy. I've been mad at Fisher for hiding part of himself from me when that's exactly what I've been doing with Stanford. I'm not a proper Southern woman and I never will be.

"You have no idea what type of woman I am. I've been pretending to be someone that could be *worthy* of you and it's all bullshit," I tell him as I grab onto the hem of my tank top. "I like to curse, I like to be loud and I like to wear whatever the fuck I want."

Peeling the wet tank top from my body and sliding it over my head, I chuck it at Stanford's chest. His hands fly up and he scrambles to grab it, staring at me with wide eyes. Wearing nothing but my "indecent" black shorts and my pink lace bra, I tug the engagement ring off of my finger and toss it towards him, too. He quickly drops my wet tank top to catch the ring.

"I don't want to marry you. I don't want to marry ANYONE who is embarrassed by me and I can see in your eyes that you are completely appalled by my behavior. Well, TOUGH SHIT."

Throwing my arms wide, I spin in a circle, noticing that the crowd who was cheering and calling my name a few minutes ago is now trying to stifle their laughs.

"Hey, you guys! Do you have a problem with what I'm wearing?" I shout to the crowd.

"Nope."

"Hell, no!"

"Lookin' good, Lucy!"

"If I had a body like that, I'd NEVER wear clothes."

Turning back around to face Stanford, I smile at the horrified expression on his face. "I thought I wasn't good enough for you and that I'd never fit in your world. Turns out it's the other way around. YOU aren't good enough for ME. And you definitely don't fit in here."

The crowd goes wild behind me, hooting and hollering as I turn away from Stanford and walk right over to them with my head held high.

"So, does anyone have a shirt I can borrow?"

Everyone starts laughing and a few of the guys take their own shirts off and toss them towards me. I throw one on and put Fisher's wet baseball cap back on my head. I get a few pats on the back and everyone congratulates me for kicking the stiff to the curb as I walk away from them and head off the field.

As soon as I get to the fence line where the gate is, I see Jefferson standing there with his arms crossed. I should probably turn and find another gate to walk through so I don't have to deal with him, but I'm on a roll right now. If he wants to give me shit, I'm going to make him regret it.

He's blocking the gate by the time I get up to him and I have no choice but to ask him as politely as I can to ask him to move.

"You're in my way."

Okay, so polite has obviously flown the coop.

"You surprise me, Miss Butler," Jefferson tells me with a smile on his face.

I'm a little taken aback by his smile and I make the mistake of pausing instead of trying to shoulder my way around him.

"Yet another golden goose you threw away. Another man who would have tossed his money at you just like my stupid son and you ruined it. It's quite funny when you think about it," Jefferson says with a laugh. "You could have had the inn paid off with that ring on your finger and Stanford's last name attached to yours, but I guess that won't be happening now, will it? Thank you for making my job easier. Looks like Butler House will belong to Fisher Bank and Trust very soon."

I really want to tell him to go fuck himself, maybe even smack that smug look off his face, but I'm pretty sure I've made enough of a scene today. The town gossip mill will already be working overtime with the show I put on and I don't need to add beating up the king of Fisher Island to the list. I swallow all of the curses I want to throw at him and lift my chin up higher, moving around him and out the gate. There's no point giving him the satisfaction of knowing that he got to me. No point confirming that his words cut right through me and made me so angry that I want to scream.

My anger grows as I walk through town. By the time I get to the inn, I can barely focus as I strip out of my wet, dirty clothes and get into the shower. I don't want to let that man ruin how good I feel after telling Stanford off, but I can't help it. His words circle around my brain and fester until they're all I can think about.

Chapter 32

Fisher

Present Day

"SHOULDN'T YOU BE down at the beach? The fireworks are going to start soon."

I don't even glance up at Trip as he comes out the door on the small deck attached to the back of his house. I've been sitting here staring out at the ocean, feeling sorry for myself, and I plan on doing that for the rest of the night.

"I heard there was quite the commotion down at the ball game today. Is that why you've been sitting out here pouting like a toddler all afternoon?" Trip asks as he sits down on the top step next to me.

"I'm not pouting," I complain.

"There are seagulls circling overhead, waiting to take a shit on that bottom lip you've got sticking out. You're pouting."

I use my middle finger to scratch the side of my face and Trip snorts. "Your maturity level astounds me. Get off your ass, go to the beach and see Lucy. I'd like to sit here on my porch and enjoy the quiet night without listening to you sigh like a lovesick teenage girl every five seconds."

Turning my head, I glare at him and he raises his eye-

272

brow and glares right back.

"If you heard about the commotion at the game today, then I'm sure you know why there's no point in going to see Lucy," I remind him.

Trip laughs right in my face. "Since when did you turn into such a pussy? I thought Marines were bad asses who didn't take no for an answer? Last time I checked, she didn't walk down the aisle and say '*I do*' this afternoon. Strap on those balls the military gave you and go get your woman back."

It's pretty sad that my eighty-three year old grandfather needs to remind me that I have balls. I felt like I'd been castrated the minute Shit-For-Brains-Ford got down on one knee earlier. I knew they'd been dating for a couple months, but I had no idea things were so serious between her and that fuck head. I thought I had time to make her fall in love with me again, but I should have known better. She's not the type of woman that you let slip through your fingers, and I feel like an ass because Shartford realized that before me. He jumped on the opportunity that I pushed away. I have to give him credit for being smart about that, at least.

"I can't get her back when she doesn't *want* to come back," I tell him.

Trip shakes his head at me. "How can you be so smart about everything else, but so stupid when it comes to Lucy? If you'd pulled your head out of your ass and stuck around that ball park for a little while, you would've seen better fireworks than the ones they're about to shoot off down on that beach."

I turn my head to face him in confusion. "What are you talking about?"

Trip pushes himself up from the step and flicks me on the head. "Pull this thing out of your rear end and go find out."

He turns and walks into the house without another word.

I STAND OFF to the side of all the people lying on blankets and sitting on chairs around small beach fires, waiting for the fireworks to begin. This was a stupid idea, a really stupid idea. So far, I've had no less than ten people ask me if I heard what happened to Lucy after the game. Why do these people think I want to rehash that shit? Do they think I don't give a shit about her and wouldn't care that she gave up on us and moved on with someone else? When I put on a fake smile and nod at them, they start laughing and tell me how "fucking awesome" it was. Clearly, this town really hasn't forgiven me for the crap I pulled last year and now they want to torture me.

Figuring there's no point in sticking around and cursing Trip for making me curious enough to come down to this damn beach, I start to leave when I see Lucy making her way down the beach towards me, dodging blankets and chairs and barely glancing at the people who call out to her. She's looking right at me as she moves and suddenly I'm frozen in place, staring at her.

She's wearing a pale yellow, strapless sundress that hugs her torso and flows out around her hips, the hem hitting her mid-thigh. Her hair is curled in soft waves and is hanging loose around her shoulders. She looks like a warrior going into battle as she skirts around the fires and the light from the flames flickers across her face. I'm so mesmerized by how gorgeous she looks that I momentarily forget she's wearing another man's ring on her finger and she's given the heart that once belonged to me to someone else.

My feet are rooted in place in the sand as she makes her way towards me, my eyes locked to hers like I'm in a fucking trance. She finally stops right in front of me and an ocean breeze flutters through her hair, blasting the smell of her skin right into my face. My knees go weak and I shake myself out of my daze, remembering how pissed I am at her.

"I hear congratulations are in order," I tell her sarcastically.

"Screw. You," she replies, crossing her arms in front of her and cocking her hip to the side, almost like she's gearing up for battle.

I smirk just to piss her off, crossing my own arms and silently wishing she didn't look so fucking hot throwing attitude at me.

"Awww, thanks for the offer, sweetheart, but I'm pretty sure you have someone else to do that job for you now."

A muscle ticks in her jaw as she clenches her teeth. I

know I'm being a dick, but I can't help it.

"You are *such* an *asshole*," she growls.

She fucking GROWLS at me and my dick wakes up and takes notice. Why in the hell does her attitude turn me on so much? It's almost like the anger I've worked so damn hard to contain for the last year transferred over to Lucy while I was gone. While I'm doing my best not to completely lose it with her, she doesn't give a shit. She's letting her rage flow right through her and apparently has no qualms about directing it at me.

Which only makes me want to fuck it all right out of her.

"Well, you don't have to worry about dealing with this asshole anymore. You'll be married to a new one soon enough," I tell her in a calm voice, even though my emotions are raging out of control.

I want to yell.

I want to argue.

I want to pick her up, toss her over my shoulder and drag her ass back to my cave like a Neanderthal where I can remind her exactly who the fuck she belongs to.

Mine, Goddammit!

Feeling the familiar rage boiling just beneath the surface, I take a deep breath, tamp down the caveman bullshit and settle, once again, on snark. "Did you come down here to show me your ring, *Luce*?" I ask, emphasizing the horrible fucking nickname I'd heard Shit-for-Brains-Ford call her. What kind of asshole doesn't realize exactly how that sounds?

She uncrosses her arms, throws them up in the air in

frustration and makes a noise that's somewhere between a scream and a snarl. "Why are you so fucking infuriating? Maybe if you'd stuck around a little longer this afternoon instead of running away like a damn child who didn't want to share his toys, you would have seen me throw that stupid engagement ring at Stanford's face!"

I open my mouth in shock and try to speak, but all that comes out are a few unintelligible, stuttered syllables. She doesn't even give me time to make sense of what she just told me before she's off on another tirade.

"You are always running away or shutting down when things get hard and I'm so fucking sick of it!" she shouts angrily. "Sending me all those damn journal pages, making me REMEMBER and making me miss what we had and then, what? When things get a little difficult, you just give up? You just walk away without a fight? A-fucking-gain?"

"Lu—"

"SHUT UP!" she interrupts. "Just shut up and let me finish!"

My dick is about two seconds away from ripping right through the material of my black cargo shorts with each word she shouts, so I put my hands up in surrender and let her continue.

"What was the point of coming back here, making me relive all of those fucking memories if you weren't going to really put up a fight? Do you even want me or do you just hate it that someone else does? You don't want anyone else fishing in your damn pond, but you seem to forget that YOU tossed me back in that fucking water!

You always said you'd find your way back to me and you FUCKING LIED!"

She shoulders past me and storms off, away from me and everyone on the beach waiting for fireworks. Taking Trip's words to heart, I remove my head from my ass and charge after her. She's moving so fast that I have to jog to catch up with her, the darkness of the beach practically swallowing her up as she moves further and further away from the bonfires and the crowds of people. She suddenly makes a beeline for the water and splashes into the surf, ignoring me as I shout her name and follow behind her. I stop when the water is up to my shins, but she keeps going until she's beyond the cresting waves and standing chest-deep in the ocean.

"What the hell are you doing?" I shout to her as she slowly turns around to face me.

"Throwing myself back in the fucking pond, hoping you'll get the damn hint and catch me!" she yells back.

It only takes two seconds for my brain to catch up to what she's saying.

I move my feet, wading through the water as the waves crash against my waist until I make it out to her.

"So, you DO have a brain," she says sarcastically.

It's my turn to growl. "Shut up."

Grabbing onto her face, I pull her towards me and crash my lips against hers. She immediately parts her lips and moans into my mouth when I slide my tongue against hers. Moving my hands away from her face, they splash into the water and I reach for her hips, clutching onto them tightly and lifting her up to pull her against me. Her tongue moves deeper into my mouth and her legs wrap around my waist as I palm her ass under the water.

The kiss grows frantic as we move our mouths faster and push our tongues deeper. Lucy's hands slide through my hair, clenching handfuls in her fists when I bite down on her bottom lip. She rocks her hips against me and I grab onto the edges of her thong, snapping the thin strings and pulling it away from the heat of her. She looks up at me in shock before the heat returns to her eyes, burning stronger than before, and she anchors her body around mine, using the muscles in her thighs to pull me closer as she presses her lips to mine once again.

The water laps around us as I brace my feet into the sand and we sink a few inches deeper into the ocean each time the tide ebbs and flows. Reaching between us, I quickly unbutton my shorts and push them down enough to free my cock, lining it up with her body. Even submerged in water, I can still feel her slick heat against the head of my dick as I slowly inch my way inside of her.

Lucy pulls her mouth away from my lips and rests her forehead against mine, breathing heavily and rocking her hips to push me deeper.

"I will ALWAYS fucking fight for you, Lucy," I promise as I dig my fingers deeper into her hips and pull her body down a little more on my cock.

She whimpers softly and I kiss her nose and her cheeks, holding myself still halfway inside of her, taking a few breaths to calm down and get used to feeling her around me again. It's been so fucking long. Too fucking long since I was here, where I was always meant to be.

"I'm sorry I went away, but I DID find my way back to you and I'm never fucking leaving again."

Thrusting my hips hard, I push inside of Lucy until I'm as deep as I can get. We groan together, but it's still not enough. It will never be enough with Lucy.

"It's always been you. It will ALWAYS, only be you," I whisper as I shift my hips and slide in and out of her as fast as I can in the water.

Her ankles lock together against my ass and she rocks her hips against me. My hands move back to her ass and I grab it tightly, pulling her up and down on my cock. The water splashes around us with the force of our movements and I'm reminded for the thousandth time what a fool I was for walking away from her. No matter how hard I tried to shut her out when I was going through my shit, this was always where we communicated the best, where we fit together perfectly. The darkness, the pain, the nightmares, they always went away when I was inside Lucy, feeling her tighten around me and bringing me to my knees.

She grinds against me, rubbing her clit against my groin and I stop thrusting and hold my cock deep inside of her, making tight circles with my hips, the exact way I know she likes it, her whimpers and moans of pleasure letting me know that at least THIS hasn't changed.

An explosion in the sky blocks out the sound of the waves and my body jerks in Lucy's arms. My heart starts beating faster and I feel panic begin to overwhelm me until Lucy presses her hands to my face and pulls my eyes up to meet hers, even though I can barely see them because it's pitch black out here in the ocean away from everyone else.

"It's okay, it's just the fireworks," she tells me softly, pulling her body up the length of my cock and then sliding right back down.

My body immediately relaxes as another loud boom echoes around us, followed by a shower of colorful sparks far above our heads. The fireworks continue high above us, each bright explosion lighting up Lucy's face as I push and pull my cock out of her and she moves right along with me. I stare at her face, counting each freckle, and I get lost in the sparkle of her eyes reflected with every firework until we're moving faster, panting harder and clutching onto each other tighter.

She doesn't move her eyes away from mine as her body tightens around me and she comes with my name on her lips. Wrapping my arms around her, I hold her close to me as I pump and thrust and chant her name as I follow right behind her, coming harder than I have in a over a year, when I just had the memory of Lucy and my hand to get by.

Staying locked together in the water, I turn us around so we can watch the rest of the fireworks out over the water, feeling like I'm finally home, even though I've been here for almost two months.

"Fisher?" she calls my name quietly after a few moments.

Looking down at her, I'm a little surprised to find her scowling up at me. "Yes?" I answer tentatively.

"Don't *ever* call me Luce again. Ever," she answers.

I can't help the laughter that erupts from deep within my chest as I lean my forehead against hers and whisper, "Ok, Lucy in the sky with diamonds."

Chapter 33
Lucy

```
Present Day
```

"SO, WHAT YOU'RE saying is, you just used me for sex?" Fisher asks with a laugh.

I laugh right along with him, so happy to hear the sound that I can't even bother being pissed off anymore at what his father said to me earlier.

"You can thank your asshole father for that," I inform him, pulling a towel tighter around my shoulders and inching closer to the fireplace.

After our little romp in the ocean, we snuck out of the water during the grand finale. Even though we were far enough away from the crowd on the beach that there weren't any fires or lights illuminating us, I still didn't want to take the chance of someone seeing us, so we made our exit while everyone's eyes were glued to the sky in the opposite direction. We held hands and jogged through the empty town, laughing the entire way in our sopping wet clothing, thankful that everyone was down at the beach and wouldn't see us running through the streets like a couple of teenagers afraid of getting caught for doing something naughty.

Even though we did. Something very, very naughty and hot and beautiful and so amazing that my body still feels like it's on fire. My anger over Jefferson's insinuations festered all afternoon, eventually pushing me to go to the beach and confront Fisher. I'm certain my ex-father-in-law would be none too pleased to learn that he played a major role in getting us over one hurdle and pushing us to finally do something about what's going on between us.

When we got back to the inn, I grabbed us a couple of towels while Fisher lit a fire in the fireplace in the front room and we've been curled up on the floor getting dry and talking since then. It's nice being alone at the inn. Even though the fireworks are finished, people will still stay down at the beach, sitting by their fires, making s'mores and toasting the holiday.

"I'm sorry he's such a dick," Fisher says with a sigh, grabbing onto my hips and sliding me across the floor in between his bent knees. I curl back against his chest and extend my legs out straight in front of me, wiggling my toes a few inches from the fire to warm them up.

"It's not your fault. I'm just so damn tired of him bringing up money. I don't understand why he feels the need to rub it in my face that I have less than him and I REALLY don't understand how you're related to him," I explain.

He laughs, wrapping his arms around me and resting his chin on top of my head. I lay my arms on top of his and sigh contentedly when he continues speaking.

"It probably helps that I was mostly raised by my mother and Trip and they wouldn't let his asshole behavior rub off on me. Well, not completely. I'm still an asshole, but it seems like I'm only an asshole when it comes to you."

We stare into the fire quietly for a few seconds before he asks the question I know has been burning a hole in his brain since I shouted it at him on the beach.

"So, you really threw that ring back, huh?" he asks quietly.

I smile to myself and snuggle closer to him.

"I did. You really should have stuck around for a few more minutes. I also took my shirt off and chucked it at his face."

A shocked laugh flies out of Fisher's mouth. "So THAT'S what Trip was talking about when he told me I missed out on the fireworks. Please, tell me everything, in complete detail."

He continues to chuckle and I try to be irritated that he's getting so much enjoyment out of this, but it's impossible to be mad at him when I'm cozied up in his arms by the fire, nearly boneless from my earlier orgasm.

"The team dumped one of those huge buckets of ice water over my head. Stanford didn't like the whole wet t-shirt contest look and made a dig about the *inappropriate* shorts I was wearing," I explain. "He also said something about me needing to be a proper Southern lady once we're married and I lost it. I hadn't even told him that I would marry him, and he was already planning my wardrobe and telling me how to behave. So, I stripped off my wet shirt and threw it at his face and did the same with the ring."

Fisher laughs even harder and I elbow him in the ribs.

"It's not funny!"

"It's ABSOLUTELY funny! Especially because I can practically see the look on Stan-Weasel-Ford's face when you did that. His delicate sensibilities must have been mortally offended. Also, fuck him. I couldn't stop staring at your ass all day in those shorts. They were a thing of beauty."

Fisher's laugh is once again contagious and I giggle, thinking about the horrified look on Stanford's face when I stripped in front of everyone, my body warming even more knowing that Fisher had been looking at my ass during the game.

Our laughter slowly fades after a few minutes and the only sound in the room is the crackle of the fire and our breathing.

"I never slept with him," I say softly, breaking the silence.

I feel Fisher's body go rigid behind me and his arms tighten around my waist.

"It's none of my business," he mutters.

I scoff at him. "Oh, please. You've acted like a caveman every time you've seen us together and I know that's one of the reasons."

He lets out a deep sigh behind me. "You have no fucking idea how good it is to hear that. I wanted you to be happy, but I hated that someone else was giving that happiness to you. The idea that he got to have you when it's all I've ever wanted almost killed me."

"I couldn't do it, though Lord knows I tried," I tell him with an uncomfortable laugh. "All I could think about was you. All I could feel were your hands on me and your lips kissing me and I just couldn't do it. It's always been you, Fisher, I just... need you to know that. There's never been anyone else for me."

He lets out another heavy breath and kisses the top of my head. "I'm so sorry, Lucy. For everything. You have no idea how sorry I am. You were right earlier, I shouldn't have run away. I just didn't know what else to do. I was losing my mind and nothing made sense anymore."

I stay completely still and don't say a word. This is the first time Fisher has spoken of the things that happened between us, and I don't want him to stop. I want to know what was going on in his heart and his mind and why he did the things he did.

"You need to know that I was never, not once, confused about how much I love you. I was afraid of hurting you, worse than I already had. I was having the worst flashbacks of my life and I thought I was going crazy. It was getting harder and harder to separate being in the war from being back here on the island with you," he explains in a voice filled with emotion. "I know I shouldn't have pushed you away. I should have talked to you and told you what was going on, but I didn't want to put that on you. You had already done so much for me, supported me and my need to go off and leave you year after year, stuck by my side through it all without a single complaint, and I couldn't stand the thought of giving you one more thing to worry about. I hated myself and I didn't know how to get out of the darkness."

I squeeze my eyes closed to keep the tears from falling. I knew, deep down inside, that he never really wanted to shut down and pull away from me and I should be happy that he's finally admitting it, but it just makes everything hurt worse. It makes me sad for the time we lost and it breaks my heart that he wouldn't let me help him when he needed me the most.

"You were my whole life, Fisher. Everything I was, everything I did was wrapped up in loving you. We took vows – for better or for worse. Why did you think that I couldn't handle the worse? Or that I wouldn't want to?" I ask him softly. "I stuck by your side and I supported your decisions because there was nothing else for me to do. Loving you meant loving every part of you, the good and the bad, the easy and the hard. I married a Marine and I knew from day one what that would entail. I didn't go into it blindly thinking it would all be rainbows and roses. I knew we'd have our challenges, but I always thought we were strong enough to get through them. I thought you would trust me enough to talk to me when things got bad and believed in our love enough to know that it would get us through anything. I never would've left, Fisher. Ever. I would've stuck by you because that's what I pledged to do for the rest of my life."

I hear him sniff behind me, but I refuse to turn my head to look at him. If I see tears in his eyes, I will completely break down and I can't do that right now. He needs to know that I'm stronger than I was a year ago. He needs to know I can handle anything and, although I know he's sorry for what he did, he needs to know how much it hurt me.

"Even when you kicked me out of the house, I still wasn't ready to give up. I was so angry with you for pushing me away when I knew you were hurting, but I refused to let go. The things you said to me, they were nothing compared to walking into Barney's and seeing you with Melanie," I tell him, trying to keep my voice from cracking. "I knew you were drunk and I knew something was seriously wrong with you, but I still believed, even after that crap you fed me about other women, that you wouldn't go that far to push me away. You shattered my heart into a thousand little pieces that night. Seeing your hands on her and your mouth on hers... that's the only reason I gave up. The only reason I walked away."

The tears start to fall, no matter how hard I squeeze my eyes closed to stop them. Fisher moves his arm from around my waist and presses his palm to my cheek, turning my face around towards his.

He kisses away my tears, even though his own are falling just as quickly down his face and mingling with mine.

"I'm so sorry. I'm so fucking sorry," he whispers brokenly. "Nothing happened with Melanie, I swear to God, Lucy. I know you probably won't believe me, but I was having a fucking hallucination and I swear I thought she was you. I knew she felt wrong and she smelled wrong, but I wanted it to be you so badly that I didn't even care. I was beating myself up for pushing you away and I just wanted it to be you. I wanted you in my arms, telling me everything would be okay, and I kept drinking and falling deeper down that fucking black hole until nothing made sense and I just didn't care."

My heart stutters back to life at his words and I sob through my tears. The worst part about losing him was believing he'd found someone else to ease his pain. Someone more experienced than me, someone prettier than me and someone he wanted more than me. Someone who didn't remind him of his pain and his past like I did.

Fisher wipes away more of my tears with his thumb and stares into my eyes. "I should have trusted you and I never should've left you. I'm so sorry for not seeing how strong you were. I'm sorry for being weak and letting the darkness take over when I should've known you were the light and you would always make everything better."

I turn my body between his legs and hold his face in my hands. "You were NOT weak. Don't you dare say that! You went through so much and you shouldered all of that on your own. You are the strongest person I've ever met, Fisher. I'm so proud of you for what you've done. I'm proud of you for getting help and I'm proud of you for finding your way back here."

He lets out a shuddering breath and presses his forehead to mine. "I hated it. Every second I was away from you, I hated it. I was so fucked up in the head, Lucy. But I was so afraid of screwing up your life that I knew I had to stay away until I could think clearly, until I could stop imagining things that weren't there and stop being so angry all of the time."

Fisher runs his hand through my hair and kisses my lips gently.

"I can practically hear your brain working," he smiles

against my lips as he pulls back to look at me. "Talk to me. You can ask me anything. I'm not going to keep things from you anymore."

I look down and nervously pick a few pieces of lint from the towel off of the skirt of my dress.

"That night at Barney's, when you first got back to town, you told me you were just drinking sparkling water. Have you…are you…"

I trail off, suddenly feeling completely uncomfortable with this conversation, but I know it has to happen. His drinking was one of the catalysts that eventually broke us.

"I've been sober since the night Bobby dropped me off at the VA hospital," he tells me softly. "It sucked and it's been hell, but every day gets a little bit easier. It helps that I have a really good man to talk to if I ever feel tempted to drink. He kicked my ass the whole time I was at the hospital, but he's a good guy. He served in Vietnam and he understands the struggles vets go through. I don't know if I'll ever be able to have a beer again without being tempted to overindulge and for right now, I'm not going to test it. I'm taking it one day at a time like I've been taught and it's working so far."

I look up at him, staring into the clear, brown eyes that haven't been bloodshot a single time since he came back and trailing down over the face that hasn't been flushed and bloated from alcohol at any point over the last two months and I'm certain he's telling the truth. I run my hands over the stubble on his face and my heart stutters when he smiles at me and I see his dimples peeking through the facial hair.

"I'm proud of you," I tell him honestly.

He shrugs. "I'm kind of proud of me, too. It's nice not having a cloudy brain all the time and being able to see what's right in front of me and how important it is that I stay sober."

Leaning forward, I press my lips to his.

"Are you thinking clearly right now?" I whisper against his lips.

His smile widens and he closes his eyes. "The thing I've NEVER been more clear about is how much I love you, how much I need you and how I don't ever want to be anywhere else but right here with you."

I hear voices outside and footsteps on the porch. Fisher and I break apart and scoot a little away from each other as guests start filing into the inn, laughing and talking about how much fun they had down at the beach. They wave at us as they walk past and head towards their rooms.

"I should probably head back to Trip's," Fisher says quietly. "You probably have a lot of stuff you need to do around here."

Pushing myself up from the floor, I hold my hands out to him and help him up.

"It can wait until tomorrow. Stay," I tell him.

Now that I have him back, now that we've battled most of the demons living inside of our heads and our hearts, I don't want to let him go.

He leans down and kisses me quickly before pulling back. "There's nowhere else I'd rather be."

I turn and pull him through the sitting room and towards my living quarters. Tugging him into the small bathroom, I turn on the water in the shower to get it warmed up. We undress each other slowly and step under the spray of the hot water together. Fisher takes his time running a bar of soap over my body and I sigh in pleasure when he turns me around and massages my scalp with shampoo. After he rinses it out, he drops to his knees on the porcelain and gently turns my hips, sinking his mouth between my legs. He takes his time licking me and tasting me until I clutch onto his hair and beg for more, my hips thrusting quickly against his mouth. His fingers immediately join his lips and his tongue, pushing inside of me and rocking slowly in and out of my body. After so many years of pleasuring me and learning my body, he knows exactly what to do, where to touch and how to move his hands and his tongue to drive me insane. I've missed this so much that I almost start to cry when I feel my orgasm rushing through my body. I've missed having someone who knows me so completely and loves me so fully. I come quickly with a shout, my head thumping back against the tile wall as the water beats down against us and Fisher hums his pleasure against my sex.

While I pant and calm my racing heart against the wall, Fisher turns off the water and pulls me out of the shower, wrapping us both in towels from the shelf above the toilet. We walk hand-in-hand into my dark bedroom and shed our towels onto the floor before curling up under the covers on my tiny bed. Our bodies are pressed together so tightly that I'm surprised either one of us can breathe. The warmth of his arms and the thump of his heart beating against my own lulls me quickly into the most peaceful sleep I've had in over a year.

Chapter 34

Fisher

`Present Day`

Before I know it, July has flown by, as well as August. I've found my place back on this island and with Lucy, but something still feels off. I'm keeping busy with more furniture orders than ever before and I help Lucy out at in inn when she lets me. We've been spending as much time together as possible and it feels like we're dating all over again. We go to dinner, we hold hands and go for long walks on the beach and we curl up and watch movies, just like when we were married. Everything about it feels so right, but something still feels wrong.

We haven't had a deep, heart-to-heart talk since the night of the Fourth, but we've been working our way through our issues and dealing with the hurts of the past one day at a time. I've told her I love her countless times, but she never says the words back. I know she doesn't completely trust me, I can see it in her eyes, but I don't know what else to do to convince her that I'm not going anywhere and I would rather die than hurt her again. The giant elephant in the room is the yellow cottage at the edge of town that sits there dark and locked, waiting for the happily married couple who used to live there to come home. I spend the night at the inn in her living quarters practically every night, even though there's nothing I'd rather do than take her home. To *our* home, to start over and begin a new life together. I don't want to push her into something she's not ready for, but I don't know how much longer I can live my life in standstill without moving forward.

I know there's something she's holding back, something she's not telling me. I see it every time we talk and feel it every time we make love. There's almost a desperation about her that I've never seen before. She clutches onto me tighter, begs me for more and tries to hold back her tears, but I see them every time, even though she does her best to hide them. I don't know what I'm doing wrong and I don't know how to fix things. I know things will never be perfect between us, no relationship is, but it's almost like she's picking fights with me just for the hell of it. She pushes my buttons and says things that tick me off and it's like she's just waiting for me to explode, waiting for me to push her away and say hurtful things to her like I did before. I make sure to keep my anger in check and calmly reason with her about whatever stupid thing she wants to argue about, regardless of whether it's the fact I left the cap off the shampoo bottle or I forgot to lower the toilet seat. I do everything I can to prove to her that I'm not going to fly off the handle like I've done before, but all it seems to do is piss her off more.

"So, when are you kids going to shit or get off the pot?"

Lucy looks over at Trip and I just shake my head at him as I continue to eat.

He invited us over for dinner and we've been having a nice, normal conversation about the jobs he's been working on around the island and the orders I've taken the last few weeks.

"Seriously, it's getting a little annoying watching you two pussy-foot around each other. When are you getting remarried so you can start popping out some great-grandkids for me?" Trip asks casually.

Lucy starts to choke on the mouthful of food she was chewing and my silverware clatters to the plate at Trip's question. I quickly reach over and pat Lucy on the back, shooting Trip a dirty look. He sticks his tongue out at me before grabbing Lucy's glass and holding it in front of her.

She snatches it from his hand and gulps down half the glass. This old man is getting on my last nerve. He's been asking that same question every time I've stopped by to grab clean clothes, since I've practically moved out of his house and into the inn. Each time I've told him to mind his own business and that I didn't want to rush things with Lucy, but clearly he thinks rushing and being nosy is the way to get things done.

"How about we discuss why *you've* never gotten re-married?" I ask, turning the conversation back on him. "Fifty years is a long time to be alone."

Lucy gently sets her glass down and looks at Trip in wonder, holding her breath and waiting for him to answer. She's asked me that question a few times over the years and I never gave it much thought until recently. My grandfather, though annoying at times, is a good, hard-working man. He's handsome for an old guy and I've seen him flirt with plenty of women around town, so I know he's still got some spark left in him. I've never understood why he wanted to be alone for all of these years, why he never fell in love again after my grandmother died.

Trip pushes his plate away from him and folds his hands together on the table in front of him.

"Fifty years IS a long time to be alone, but I'd rather be alone with my memories than to try and fake something with another woman," he tells us.

"Why would you have to fake anything? You don't think you could love someone else?" Lucy asks him softly.

"I KNOW I couldn't love someone else," he informs her, before turning his face to look at me. "Your grandmother, she was an amazing woman. I wish you could've met her, Fisher. She was beautiful, smart, kind and she loved me more than I ever deserved. We grew up together, did I ever tell you that?"

I shake my head in silence, not wanting to ruin the moment by speaking. Trip rarely speaks about my grandmother, and it's amazing to hear about her and their relationship now.

"Yep, we were practically raised together as babies. Our parents were best friends and always did things together, so the two of us were forced to be together. Oh, she hated me when we were kids," he says with a laugh. "She was two years younger than me and I liked to tease the ever-living hell out of her. I'd pull her pigtails and chase her around the island. I didn't tell her until we were older that the only reason I did that stuff was to get her to chase me back."

Lucy puts her elbows on the table and rests her chin in her hands and I lay my arm on the back of her chair, twirling the ends of her hair in my fingers as we listen to my grandfather talk.

"It wasn't until we were teenagers that I stopped annoying her so much. Or maybe she just realized that I only did things to piss her off so she'd notice me. I'd been in love with that girl for as long as I could remember, so finding out she loved me back was nothing short of a miracle. We got married before we even finished high school and got busy starting a family as soon as we got our diplomas," he explains with a wistful look in his eyes. "It took a few years before we had your father, but it didn't matter because we sure had a lot of fun trying."

He winks at Lucy and she laughs while he continues.

"There's nothing worse than watching the woman you love slowly slip away from you. Watching her get sick, sitting by her morning, noon and night and knowing there's not a damn thing you can do to stop the hands of time from ticking by so fast it's like they're in hyper speed," Trip tells us.

Lucy wipes a tear from her eye and I move my arm off of the chair to rub slow circles against her back. Lucy knew the basic history of what happened to my grandmother, the same history and facts that I knew: they were married, they had my father and a few short years later, she died from stomach cancer. Hearing my grandfather talk so openly and lovingly about her is wonderful and sad all at the same time.

"I've never tried looking for someone else to love because I know that no one will ever compare to her. Some people can fall in and out of love and that's great for them. They can find someone else and they can move on, but I'm not one of those people. I found my soul mate when I was a child and she will always be the love of my life, no matter how many years go by," he tells us with a sad smile. "There isn't a day that goes by that I don't miss her, that I don't wish things could've been different. That I don't wish she'd been here to raise your father and make him a better, kinder man. That she could've met you, Fisher, and seen her grandson and what a strong, loyal man he turned out to be. I'm not sad about not finding anyone else. Sure, I get lonely from time to time, but I've got my memories of the love of the best woman I've ever known to keep me company. I'd much rather have those memories than try and pretend with someone else."

Silence fills the room and other than the tick of the clock on the wall above the kitchen sink, no one makes a sound or moves. I think Lucy and I are both in shock at how much Trip shared with us. Going by the fact that he's staring at his hands in silence, I think even Trip *himself* is in shock over spilling his guts all over this table in front of us. I always thought he was somewhat crazy for never finding anyone else, for never dating or getting married again, but I understand him so much more now than I ever did before.

I stare at Lucy's profile as she reaches over and quietly rests her hands on top of Trip's on the table. I look at this woman, who is my heart and my soul and my entire world, and I *get it* now. I get why Trip chose to be alone all these years. If she decides that this isn't going to work between us or that she can't trust me or love me like she did before, I know I'd rather be alone for the rest of my life than pretend to love someone as much as I do her. Every other woman would pale in comparison and my heart would never be in it. I know that I have to do whatever it takes to get her to love me again. I have to break down those last couple of walls she put up and fight for her as hard as I can.

Lucy is it for me, forever, and I'm going to make damn certain she knows that.

"Alright, that's enough sharing for one lifetime. You two kids get your asses out of here and let me watch *Wheel of Fortune* in peace," Trip suddenly announces, getting up from the table and wondering off into the living room.

Lucy and I laugh together as we watch him leave. I stand up quickly and pull her chair out for her and we shout our good-byes to him over the noise of the television as we make our way outside.

I'm not going to let Lucy keep me out. I'm not going to let her keep whatever is bothering her inside. If we're going to make this work, we're going to get through *everything* and we're going to do it together.

Chapter 35
Lucy

Present Day

FISHER AND I walk silently, hand-in-hand through town. A storm started brewing while we were at Trip's house and a few raindrops begin to fall as we make our way back to the inn. By the time we get to the end of Main Street, the couple of raindrops have turned into a full-on downpour and we run the remaining blocks to Butler House. Fisher holds the front door open for me and I race inside, shaking out my wet hair and wiping off my face as I head towards the kitchen.

It's late and Ellie turned off most of the lights on the first floor before she left for the day. The hallway leading to the kitchen is dark except for a couple of electric sconces that glow with soft lighting on the wall, guiding my way. I hear Fisher's heavy footsteps following behind me as I go and I'm tempted to tell him to go back to Trip's. That story he told us tonight was almost too much for me, hit too close to home, and I need some time alone to think. I can't think rationally when Fisher is close to me. I can't breathe for fear that something bad is looming, just waiting to ruin this little fairytale we've created the last two months. The more I listened to Trip, the more I realized this is not a fairytale. There's still something standing between us that I haven't been able to bring myself to confront him about and I can't take it anymore. Subtlety is clearly not working, because he's still holding himself back with me and we can't move forward until all of our issues are out in the open and he finally lets go.

"Man, can you believe Trip?" Fisher asks as we walk into the kitchen. I don't bother turning on the bright, overhead light as I pull open a drawer and grab a dishtowel to dry off my face and arms. There's a small lamp plugged in on the counter that gives off enough light that I can see what I'm doing.

"I can't believe he told us all of that tonight," Fisher continues as he walks up behind me and rests his hands on my shoulders.

I pull out from under his hands and take a few steps away from him before turning around. "What the hell are we doing?"

Tossing the towel onto the counter, I cross my arms and stare at Fisher. He's so Goddamn gorgeous that it takes my breath away. He still hasn't shaved, only trimming his stubble every couple of days when it starts to get out of control. His wet shirt molds to his body and I can see every line and ripple of his muscles. His hair is dripping down his face and I watch as he runs his hand through the damp strands in irritation.

"What do you mean, what the hell are we doing?" he asks.

"I mean, what the hell are we doing?!" I argue, raising my voice slightly. "We see each other every day, we're falling back into old habits like nothing has changed, but EVERYTHING has changed! We're both different people, but it's like we're trying to be who we used to be. I can't do that, Fisher. I can't be the person I used to be and neither can you."

He takes a step towards me, but I hold up my hand and step back.

"Jesus, are you trying to pick another fight with me?" he asks in exasperation. "What the hell am I doing wrong that you constantly want to argue?"

I'm so angry and frustrated with myself because he's right. I've been picking fights with him nonstop over the stupidest things, just to get a rise out of him. Just to see if I can force him to lose control and show me some of that passion he did in the alley and that night in our kitchen a few years ago. It's stupid and it's silly, but it's something that I think about constantly and I *need* that part of him. I need him to realize that I'm not going to break and I'm not afraid. I need him to see that *my* perfect man isn't one who's calm all the time and never loses his temper. I need him to give me every part of himself or this is never going to work between us.

"You're not doing anything wrong, you're doing everything RIGHT, that's the fucking problem!" I shout.

He throws his hands up in the air in annoyance and shakes his head at me. "I have no fucking idea what you're talking about right now. If I'm doing everything right, why are you so angry?"

I watch it happen right in front of my eyes, just like every time. He realizes he just raised his voice, he just lost a little bit of his calm and he instantly feels bad. His face loses its tightness and his shoulders lose their rigid stature as he slowly melts into the cool, peaceful man that he thinks he needs to be for me.

"Do you really think this is going to work between us when you can't even be who you really are in front of me?" I ask him sadly.

"Lucy."

He says my name softly and it's full of love and caring. It should warm me from the inside out, but all it does is leave me feeling cold.

"Do you know what I did the night you came back to the island and we saw each other for the first time at Barney's?" I ask him.

Bringing this up right now is either going to make things go really wrong, or really right. At this point, I'm willing to try anything to get him to stop treating me like I'm a piece of glass.

Fisher shakes his head, but doesn't say anything.

"I brought Stanford back here and I did everything I could to get him to fuck me," I inform him.

My eyes flicker to his hands, slowly clenching into fists at his sides, and I continue.

"I straddled him, I ripped his fucking shirt and clawed at his skin, begging him to give me more. I wanted him to give me *everything*. I wanted to erase you from my mind and from my body. I wanted him inside of me so I could stop thinking about *you* all the damn time!"

Fisher knows I didn't sleep with Stanford, but I never went into detail about other things we did because it didn't feel right to torture him with that knowledge.

I see his chest rise and fall rapidly and his nostrils flare while I throw all of this stuff at him, fully aware that I'm poking the beast and trying to get him to show his damn face.

"I let him put his hands on me, I let him touch my breasts and I let him slide his hands between my thighs until he—"

Fisher is on me instantly, his arms wrapping around me tightly, pulling my body roughly against his.

"Stop… just fucking stop," he begs on a ragged whisper.

His eyes are wide with jealousy and anger and his chest bumps against mine each time he takes a deep breath. I can see him mentally counting in his head, trying to calm down, but I won't let him.

"NO! You fucking stop! Stop treating me like I'm going to break and like I can't take what's going on inside of you!" I shout into his face. "I let another man into my life! I let another man touch what should have only been YOURS! Does that piss you off?"

"YES!" he roars right back at me. "YES, it fucking pisses me off and you know it! Why the fuck are you doing this to me?"

His arms are banded so tightly around me that they shake with the anger he's barely keeping in check.

"I'm doing this because I'm sick and tired of you hiding this from me! I can't handle you thinking that I can't take your anger or I can't stomach you losing control with me!"

He shakes his head back and forth in denial. "Stop, please, Lucy. I can't do that with you. I can't hurt you like that. Why do you think I stayed away for a year? Why do you think I pushed you away to begin with? I can't be that person anymore."

I untangle myself from his arms and push him away roughly.

"Don't you get it, Fisher? You ARE that person. I know you aren't cruel, I know you would never physically hurt me, but I also know that this Zen bullshit where you refuse to let anyone ruffle your damn feathers is not you. You're passionate and full of life and you're hotheaded and get angry and jealous. It's who you are and who you've always been. How do you expect me to be with you when I can't be with ALL of you? Did it ever occur to you that I WANT your passion? That I've been pushing your buttons lately because I want you to let go?"

He runs his hand through his hair again in frustration.

"I let go with you once and I *hurt you*. I left *bruises* on you, Lucy. I destroyed our fucking marriage because I couldn't control myself!" he argues.

I can see the guilt all over his face and it all clicks into place. Why my entire world fell apart right after he came home from his last deployment, why he started drinking more and talking to me less.

"Do you really think you hurt me the night you came home from that last deployment and fucked me against the kitchen wall?" I ask in shock.

He winces at my words and I can tell he honestly believes his loss of control that night is what cost us our marriage.

"Oh, my God, you do," I mutter, taking a step closer to him. "If you would've talked to me instead of internalizing everything, I would've told you that it was the hottest damn experience of my life!"

He scoffs and looks at me like he doesn't believe me, so I continue, moving closer until I can touch him. I run my hands up the front of his wet shirt, clutching it in my hands.

"I have *never* wanted you more than I did at that moment. Do you know what it's like to know that your husband wants you so badly that he can't spend another second outside of your body? That you're all he thinks about and all he needs and he doesn't have to speak or explain it, he just needs to claim you and own you, bruise you with the force of his need for you?"

I take another step closer until my body is pressed up against his.

"If you'd talked to me, you would've known that I loved seeing those bruises on my hips. I loved knowing that you wanted me that badly and I was sad when they disappeared, especially since you wouldn't even look at me, let alone touch me by that point."

He closes his eyes and tilts his head back and I keep going, closing my eyes right along with him and thinking about another night when he made me feel alive and wanted.

"And that night in the alley, a few months ago. You have no idea how much I wanted you. How much I needed your hands on me and how much it turned me on that you were jealous and you wanted to mark your fucking territory. Did you hear me begging for more? Did you hear me scream your name while I was coming? *You're* the only one who makes me feel that way."

My eyes fly open in surprise when my body is suddenly whipped around. I gasp in shock when Fisher pushes his body against mine and my hips bump into the kitchen table. He slams into me and I have no choice but to bend over the table and smack my hands down on top of it. He's right behind me, his chest pressed against my back as he breathes heavily in my ear.

"Goddammit, Lucy, what the hell are you doing to me?" he growls. His hands fly underneath my skirt and he rips my panties right off of my body.

"I ALWAYS want you so much that I can barely breathe from it. All I think about is fucking you until I forget about everything but how it feels to be inside of you."

I hear the button of his shorts fly off and ping against the kitchen floor as he rips them open. I whimper when he flips up the skirt of my dress and I feel the heat of his groin pressing into my ass and his cock sliding through me.

"Tell me you want this," he demands. "Tell me you fucking want me like this."

I arch my back and push myself against him until his cock is right at my opening.

"I want this," I pant.

"I *need* this. Show me how much you want me,

please," I beg.

He clutches onto my hips, pulls his body back and slams inside of me so hard that the table legs screech against the floor. He lets out a roar and I moan, clutching onto the edges of the table as he begins pounding into me.

"I'm fucking claiming you, Lucy," he mutters as his cock ravages me from the inside out.

"Yes, yes, yes," I chant with each slam of his hips against my ass.

He leans over me, sliding one of his hands between my legs and circling my clit with the tips of his fingers as he continues fucking me relentlessly.

"You are MINE and you will always be mine," he whispers harshly against my ear.

"Don't ever fucking hide from me again," I tell him as I thrust my hips forward against his fingers. "I need you. I need all of you."

His fingers circle faster and his thrusts become harder. The table rocks beneath us, and if I cared about anything else but the orgasm creeping up on me, I'd worry about the legs giving out and us crashing to the floor and waking up the entire inn. The hundred-year-old kitchen table is practically the only piece of furniture in this place that Fisher didn't build and its stability should probably be a cause for concern.

I forget about the table as Fisher takes me, claiming me just like I wanted, my body spiraling out of control at the knowledge that he's finally letting go and giving me all of him. His hips smack against my ass rapidly and his fingers start tapping lightly against my clit until I'm clawing at the table and moaning so loudly I'm sure breaking the table isn't what's going to wake everyone up.

With one incredibly hard thrust that shoves my body roughly against the table, I realize I might have jinxed us. I hear a snap, followed by a crack and then Fisher's arms wrap around me when I start to tumble forward as two of the table legs break in half, causing the whole thing to crash to the floor in a heap of pieces.

We both stare unmoving at the mess on the floor and before I can even manage a laugh at what we've done, Fisher is turning my body and pushing me up against the counter, his cock never leaving my body. I slap my hands against the granite and hold on tight as he resumes fucking me like we didn't just destroy an antique table. I forget about the mess and let go of the worry over what the hell I'm going to tell people when they ask what happened to the table and just enjoy the pleasure Fisher is giving my body with each slam of his cock inside me.

He keeps one hand on my hip as his other hand slides back between my legs to resume the sweet torture with his fingers. Each gentle tap of his fingers against my clit sends waves of pleasure through me that are so strong it makes my legs start to shake and my hips move erratically as I reach for the release that's right within my grasp.

"Every time I'm near you, I want to fuck you until I forget everything," Fisher growls into my ear.

His hand tightens on my hip as he helps pull my body back against his cock with each hard thrust. The upper half of his body is pressed tightly to my back and I can feel his heart pounding against me as he pants against the side of my neck.

"Your body was fucking made for me, Lucy. Say it again. Tell me you want me to take you like this."

He stops moving and holds himself still inside of me, waiting for the words I can barely form with the pleasure coursing through me.

"Fuck me harder. Don't stop. Please, don't stop," I beg.

I barely get the words out before he's pulling back and slamming inside me harder than before, his growls and moans and muttered curses filling the room as he gives me everything he has.

His pleasure-filled voice in my ear, his fingers between my legs, his cock working tirelessly in and out of me and the sound of the rain falling against the roof all come together to create a symphony of pleasure through my body that I couldn't stop even if I wanted to. I tumble over the edge and my body clenches around Fisher's cock as I come. His hand quickly moves from my hip and presses against my mouth, muffling my screams as my orgasm rips through me.

He follows right behind me, slamming his cock deep one last time before holding himself still inside of me. He buries his face into the back of my neck to muffle his own curses and shouts as he comes. His hips jerk against me as the tremors of his orgasm shoot through him until we both collapse against the counter, panting.

The rain continues to beat against the side of the inn and the room is suddenly lit up with lightning as Fisher keeps his weight on top of me while we catch our breath.

He finally speaks after a few minutes.

"Don't worry, I'll build you a new table. And Lucy?" he asks.

Pressing my cheek against the cold counter to cool it off, I reply to him with a sigh.

"Yes, Fisher?"

"Never, ever bring up Stan-Dick-Fuck-Ford in front of me again."

He kisses the back of my neck before pulling himself off of me and I can't hide the huge smile on my face as I turn and wrap my arms around him.

Chapter 36

Fisher

Present Day

"**W**HAT IN THE fuck happened to the kitchen table?" Bobby asks in surprise, holding Ellie's hand as they stare at the mess on the floor.

Lucy and I share mischievous smiles over the rims of our coffee cups while we lean against the counter.

"Oh, you know, something slammed into it. Repeatedly," I tell him with a shrug as Lucy smacks me lightly in the stomach while I try to contain my laughter.

"So, anyway, how are you guys doing? How are you feeling, Ellie?" Lucy asks, changing the subject and busying herself with pouring Bobbie a cup of coffee and heating the teakettle for Ellie.

When Bobby told me a few months ago that Ellie was pregnant, I came close to punching him in the face. Even if Ellie hasn't been my biggest fan after what I did to Lucy, she's still like a little sister to me, and I didn't really like the idea of my best friend knocking her up and not giving a shit. I was more than a little surprised to find out he was in love with her and the feelings were mutual, even though it took Ellie a little while to admit it. Lucy has been pushing her all summer to tell Bobby how she feels and she finally did it a few weeks ago. Bobby immediately

313

bought her a ring and proposed to her the right way, getting down on one knee and telling her how much he loved her instead of demanding she marry him because she's pregnant.

While Ellie and Lucy talk about pregnancy, morning sickness and what Ellie's plans are for the wedding, Bobby jerks his head towards the door and we leave the women to talk while we head out onto the veranda.

Kicking back in the rocking chairs with our coffee cups, both of us prop our feet up on the deck railing and stare out at the ocean.

"I can't believe you're going to be someone's father," I tell Bobby.

"No shit. I'm going to be responsible for shaping someone's mind and for being his or her role model. I can't believe no one made me get a permit for that shit."

We share a laugh as we sip our coffee and stare out at the haze over the water. Most of the summer tourists have started leaving the island now that we're getting ready to enter into hurricane season. The sky has been more overcast lately and thunderstorms have been popping up sporadically all over the place. It won't be long until the entire island will need to start inclement weather preparations. September on an island smack in the middle of a hurricane zone meant dragging out the sandbags and storm shutters and taking all of the patio furniture inside.

"Things with you and Lucy seem good," Bobby muses, fishing for more information.

I've kept him as up to date as I could these last few months, not wanting to get into too many intimate details, but he knew I'd been concerned about Lucy keeping something back from me.

"They're really good," I tell him, unable to hide my smile. "We had a good... talk last night."

I keep the chuckle to myself and tell my dick to stay calm when I think about what happened in the kitchen the previous evening. Jesus, how many months did I spend feeling guilty about that night I came home from my last deployment? It was the reason I started spiraling out of control, so certain Lucy hated me for what I'd done. I was such an idiot. Having her yell at me and push me and force me to lose control with her was scary as shit, but it was the best fucking thing that could have happened between us. She's right, we've both changed and there's no going back to who we used to be. I can't be afraid with her and I can't treat her like the quiet, shy girl she was when I married her. She's the strongest fucking woman I know and she proved that last night. I feel freer and calmer than I have in a long time. I was absolutely holding myself back from her and it wasn't fair to either of us. I never want her to think I don't crave her so fucking much that I lose all sense of control. I might need time to myself every once in a while to work through my memories of the war, but I will never hold back any part of myself from her and I will always be open and honest about how I'm feeling.

"I'm glad you guys have worked things out, man. It's good to see you happy again," Bobby tells me.

"It's good to BE happy again," I tell him with a smile. "What about you and Ellie? Did you guys set a wedding date yet?"

Bobby face lights up at the mention of Ellie's name and I'm still amazed by that shit. I never thought he would settle down and I'm a little ticked he never told me the crush he had on Ellie since she moved here might actually be something real.

"She wants to wait until after the baby's born. I hate waiting that long, but I get it. She's worried about fitting into a wedding dress and she wants to be able to have fun. You can't have that much fun at your own wedding when you're pregnant," Bobby explains.

I'm happy for him, I really am, but a part of me is sad that Lucy and I never had children. We talked about it a lot when we first got married. We talked about how many we would have and what we would name them and how we would raise them completely different from how my father raised me. As the years wore on, the talk of babies fell by the wayside and neither one of us brought it up again. I couldn't stand the idea of her being pregnant and having to raise our child practically alone, since I was never guaranteed to be here with her for more than a year at a time. I couldn't saddle her with something like that when I never knew when or if I'd ever get out of the military. I know I should be grateful that we didn't have children to witness my breakdown when everything went to shit. I can only hope that since we're both still young and we have a lot of years ahead of us, there's still time and it's still something she wants.

"I still can't believe everything is falling into place for both of us. This is fucking nuts," Bobby says with a laugh.

"Now I just need to convince Lucy to let me help her out with the inn."

Bobby laughs even harder and shakes his head. "Good luck with that. Not going to happen."

I roll my eyes and take a sip of my coffee. "I can't let her lose this place, Bobby, especially to my fucking father."

"You also can't just fork over money and expect her to be okay with that. She will cut off your balls and shove them down your throat."

She didn't react very well to my mother sending her money every month, especially thinking it was from me, and according to Trip, she was so pissed that I sent her a lump sum after the divorce that she refused to touch it.

"What the hell am I supposed to do, just sit back and watch her lose her dream? Her family's business and the place that makes her happy?" I ask him.

"I don't know, just don't do anything stupid like go behind her back and pay off the mortgage. I can already see the wheels turning in your head and that will NOT end well for you, my friend," Bobby informs me.

I don't tell him that I was already thinking of doing just that and pretending like I had no idea when she found out. Last night, we broke down every wall left between us, though, and I'm not about to screw it up by lying to her right off the bat.

"She made enough money this summer to keep the place going through the winter, so I have some time to come up with a plan," I let him know.

"You'll think of something. You have to think of

something. Ellie wants to have our wedding right here on the veranda. No pressure or anything," he tells me with a smile.

"Speaking of weddings, when are you going to give Lucy those damn rings you've been holding onto for a year?" he asks.

I reach into my pocket and finger the diamond solitaire and plain gold band that I've carried around with me ever since she sent them back with the divorce papers.

"Soon. Definitely soon. I just want to make sure the timing is right and she actually WANTS them back," I say with a shrug as I remove my hand from my pocket.

"She loves you, of course she'll want them back."

I shrug again. "She hasn't said it yet, so who knows."

I don't tell him that it's killing me not to hear those words from her. I know her actions have more than proven that she loves me, but I need the words. I need to hear her tell me she's still in love with me so that I know without a shadow of a doubt that she wants this. That she wants everything. I can't blame her for not trusting me completely, but I hope what happened last night goes a long way towards proving to her that she can put her faith in us again.

"Hey, do you remember that sign I made for Lucy as a wedding gift? The one that said *The Fishers* on it?"

Bobby nods, taking a sip of his coffee.

"When I stopped by the cottage, it wasn't hanging next to the door. I went there a few weeks ago to look for it and couldn't find it. I even looked all around the inn and it's not here, either. I wanted to surprise Lucy by hanging it back up at the cottage and asking her to move back in there with me."

Bobby sets his coffee cup down on the table between us and gives me a sheepish look. "You're not going to find it anywhere."

I look at him in confusion and he continues. "The day you sent Lucy the divorce papers, she sort of went a little nuts. Ellie got her drunk and drove her out to the cottage. Lucy pried the sign off of the wall and proceeded to beat the shit out of it with a hammer."

"Yikes," I reply.

"And then she lit the pieces on fire."

"Oh, Jesus," I mutter. "So much for THAT surprise."

Bobby laughs and pats me on the shoulder before pushing himself up from the chair.

"You're a romantic asshole, I'm sure you'll think of something else. I need to get Ellie and head over to the mainland. She's got an appointment for one of those fancy 3D ultrasounds in an hour. I guess the machine Doc Wilson has here on the island isn't good enough for the first look at our little munchkin."

We shake hands and I tell him to have Ellie call Lucy after their appointment to let us know how it went.

Bobby heads inside the house and I finish my coffee, wracking my brain for ways to convince Lucy that I truly love her, I'm not going anywhere and that I want to spend the rest of my life with her.

Chapter 37

Lucy

Present Day

"I CAN'T BELIEVE it's already the middle of September," I grumble, burrowing myself closer to Fisher under the covers. "I miss summer."

Fisher laughs, wrapping his arms around me and squeezing me tight.

"According to the weather report, today is going to be one of the last hot, sunny days for a while. You should take advantage of it," he tells me.

"I'm planning on it," I inform him as I slide my hands down the front of his bare chest, across his stomach, and run my fingers teasingly above his groin. "I'm meeting Ellie down at the beach and we're going to lay around like bums all day."

I wrap my hand around his quickly thickening length and he groans, tossing his head back on the pillow. I take my time sliding my hand up and down his cock as his hips begin thrusting up to meet me, enjoying the sounds that he makes as I tease him by moving my hand fast and hard and then slowing it down, barely grazing him with my palm.

After the night in the kitchen when he finally let go, the last few weeks with Fisher have been nothing short of amazing. We've christened every room in the inn more than once. We've had hard, fast sex with most of our clothes on and we've taken our time, stripping each other and slowly making love. He talks to me when he's having a bad day and he's started to open up to me about his time overseas, what he saw, what he did and how those things affected him in return. He let me run my fingers over the scars on the back of his shoulder and kiss each spot marked by the shrapnel that imbedded in his skin after he finally told me about how he sustained his injury. My heart broke for him learning that men he considered brothers were killed during the explosion and I understand now why he was so angry when he came home, feeling like the injury wasn't 'real' enough to warrant a ticket stateside.

I love him more and more each day that I spend with him, but something keeps me from saying the words. They're on the tip of my tongue every time he looks at me, every time he touches me and every time he shows me how much *he* loves me, but I still feel like I'm waiting for the other shoe to drop. I felt like the luckiest girl in the world the first time I fell in love with him, and it feels like a dream that I've been able to do it a second time. How many people get a second chance at love with the only person they've ever held in their heart?

Pushing aside my negative thoughts, I slide on top of him and straddle his waist. Fisher moves his hands to my hips and helps me lift myself up so I can position him right where I need him. I slide down slowly on top of him until he's seated fully inside of me. I begin rocking back and forth on top of him, pressing my hands against his chest to help give me leverage. He brings one hand up to my face and holds it in his palm, staring up at me as I ride him, moving slowly and letting my need for him consume me and erase everything else from my mind. I'll never get tired of these moments with him, when all we have to do is look into each other's eyes and feel our bodies moving as one and everything else melts away, leaving just the two of us without a care in the world.

My orgasm comes fast and hard, even though we're moving slowly and taking our time. I lean down and press my lips to Fisher's, kissing him with all the love that I have as I come. He wraps his arms around me and slowly lifts his hips off the bed, pushing in and out of me at a languid pace until his own release takes hold of him and he jerks his hips against me, coming with my name on his lips.

I collapse on top of his body, rolling off of him to my side after a few minutes and resting my head on his chest. As his fingertips lazily trace patterns on my back, I blurt out something that has been on my mind for years.

"Why didn't you ever write to me?"

His fingers still on my back and I hold my breath, waiting for his answer. We've spent a lot of time talking about the past and how all the things he said to me the day everything fell apart were lies, but he never mentioned the letters. I'd like to believe that he was lying when he told me he didn't want to write to me, but he's never given me any explanation about those words he threw at me.

With a deep sigh, he goes back to running his fingers over the skin of my back.

"I DID write to you. I just never sent them," he admits softly.

Lifting my head from his chest, I turn and stare at him in shock.

"For every letter you wrote me, I wrote one in return. Then, I'd read through them and realize how depressing and pathetic they sounded and I couldn't bring myself to send them," he explains. "All I could write about was how much I missed you, how much I needed you and how much I hated being away from you. I knew it was hard enough on you being here all that time with me so far away and I didn't want to make it more difficult. I also didn't want you to worry about me and a lot of the stuff I wrote would've freaked you out. I detailed my days and the shit I saw and you didn't need to read about that. You didn't need to know those things. It would have just been worse each time I went back."

I tilt my head to the side and shake it back and forth. "You should've sent them. You should've shared those things with me. All this time, I honestly thought it didn't bother you being away from me so often and that you didn't miss me as much as I missed you."

He cups my face in his hands and stares into my eyes. "I'm sorry. I'm so sorry. I hate that I made you feel that way. I hate that I never let you know how much it killed me to be away from you. I hate that I made you second-guess everything I felt for you."

Pulling one of his hands away from my face, I kiss his

palm before pulling his hand against my chest. "No more secrets, promise me. Whatever you're feeling, whatever you're thinking, you have to share it with me. We have to be open and honest with each other about everything."

He leans forward and kisses my lips. "I love you and I promise."

I curl into his side and rest my cheek on his shoulder. He continues to whisper words of love to me as my eyes grow heavy and I drift off to sleep. The alarm on his cell phone wakes us both from a sound sleep an hour later.

"What are you doing today?" I ask as he slides out from under the covers and grabs his clothes from the end of the bed.

"Oh, you know, just some running around. What time are you meeting Ellie? Want me to pack you guys a lunch or something?" he asks, quickly changing the subject.

He's done that a few times lately when I've asked him about his plans for the day. I know he's hiding something, but even when I flat out asked him what he's up to, he changes the subject. I even caught him digging through the attic a few weeks ago and he looked like a kid caught with his hand in the cookie jar when I went up there to see what he was doing. I can't really be mad at him when I've been keeping a little secret of my own and I instantly feel guilty about making him promise to never keep anything from me. It's something that will fix all of my problems, but will undoubtedly piss Fisher off, so I'll leave him to his secrets until I'm ready to divulge my own.

Fisher finishes getting dressed, leaning across the bed to give me a kiss. "I'll pack a few things in a basket for you guys and leave it on the kitchen counter. Don't forget your sunscreen and if you wear that hot, red bikini, keep it on until I get home."

He kisses my nose and I laugh as he pushes himself off the bed and heads out the door.

"I HATE YOU so much right now. Why do you have to look so hot when I look like a whale?" Ellie complains.

I just came in from the water and I'm standing in front of her drying off while she stares up at me in disgust from her beach chair.

I took Fisher's suggestion and went with the red bikini, even though I've secretly hated this thing ever since I bought it on a whim. I don't think I have the body to pull it off, but when he saw it in my dresser drawer last week, he started drooling and asked me to model it for him. Let's just say this red bikini didn't stay on for more than a couple of seconds that day, so it's starting to grow on me.

"You don't look like a whale, you're pregnant and beautiful," I remind her. "And you're barely showing, so quit your bitching."

I spread out my towel next to her and flop down on my back, closing my eyes and letting the sun warm me and dry off the rest of my body.

"Did you tell Fisher about Stanford yet?" Ellie asks.

I squint open one eye and glare up at her. "No. And I thought I told you we weren't going to discuss this until I made a final decision?"

Ellie shrugs and rests her head back against her chair with her face turned up towards the sun. "I wake up puking every morning, I get up seventeen times to pee at night and my fiancé uses baby talk to speak to my stomach. Please, give me something to live for. This is exciting and we SHOULD be talking about it."

I sit up on my towel and cross my legs in front of me.

"It is kind of exciting, right? I mean, this isn't a completely insane idea, is it?" I ask.

"Hell, no! I mean, when you first told me Stanford called you with a proposal, I laughed my ass off and almost got on the ferry to the mainland to kick his ass, but I really do think this is going to work," she tells me.

The thing I haven't told Fisher is that I've been in contact with Stanford. After I broke up with him and pretty much embarrassed him in front of the whole town, he left the island with his tail between his legs and I didn't hear from him again until a few weeks ago. I felt a little bad at first about the way things ended, but then I remembered the shit he said to me. Fisher also set about wiping all traces of him from my mind, so pretty soon it was like Stanford never even existed.

Getting a call from him out of the blue was a shock. When he told me that he quit working for Fisher's father as soon as he got back to the city, it threw me even more. He overheard the things Jefferson said to me that day at the ballpark and there had been some other questionable things Jefferson had said and done in the time that Stanford worked for him that made him uncomfortable and forced him to realize that the man was not to be idolized. He quit and had a job with another, larger corporate bank with locations nationwide within a week.

He felt bad about the way we parted and he still wanted to do whatever he could to help me with the inn. I immediately distrusted him and assumed he was trying once again to buy the place from me, but he had a better idea. His new company specialized in small business loans and he asked if I would consider refinancing the mortgage on the inn with his bank. I politely told him no and tried to explain to him that having to deal with my ex-boyfriend for the duration of my loan would be almost as bad as having to deal with my ex-father-in-law. I ended the call and assumed that would be the end of it. Within an hour, the president of the bank was calling, giving me his assurance that my account would be serviced by another loan officer and that Stanford's name would only be on the paperwork as the referring party for commission purposes. He went on to explain that they were committed to keeping the small businesses in America afloat, giving them the lowest possible finance rates permitted by law. I really didn't want to believe that there might be a chance to save Butler House without having to crawl on my hands and knees and beg Fisher's father, but it was hard NOT to believe it when the bank sent me a draft of the paperwork. The interest rate is almost seventy-five percent less than what I'm paying now with Fisher's Bank and Trust and it would cut my monthly payments almost in half.

"When are you going to tell Fisher?" Ellie asks.

I shrug and look out at the ocean. "I don't know. When is it ever a good time to tell the man you love that the guy you were dating is the one who is going to make your dreams come true?"

"Never," Ellie informs me.

"Awww, keeping secrets already? Tsk, tsk, that's never a good thing."

Whipping my head around, I stare up at the one person on this island I hate more than Fisher's father.

"I think you made a wrong turn. The skank beach is a mile that away, Melanie," Ellie says, pointing to the left with a sweet smile.

"You're one to talk, getting knocked up before you're married," Melanie sneers.

Ellie continues to smile as she lifts both of her hands in the air and gives Melanie two middle fingers.

I push myself up from the ground, feeling much more comfortable being eye-level with Melanie than having to look up at her, but I quickly realize how bad I look standing next to her and immediately want to wrap a towel around me. The red bikini I'm wearing made me feel sexy until I stood next to Melanie with her long legs, fake boobs and flat, toned stomach. The white string bikini she's wearing consists only of three triangles precariously concealing her goods and doesn't help my confidence much, either.

Every time I see this woman around town, all I can

think about are Fisher's hands on her ass and his mouth pressed against hers that night at Barney's. He swore to me that nothing happened between them, but I still have to swallow a few times to keep my lunch down where it belongs just thinking about that night.

"I have no idea how you do it, Lucy," Melanie says with a shake of her head.

I sigh and take the bait, even though I know better. "How I do *what*?"

Melanie laughs and brushes her long, perfect, shiny blonde hair off of one shoulder. "How you managed to get the richest, most eligible bachelor on the island to propose to you, kicked him to the curb and then got that hot piece of ass ex-husband following you around like a puppy. I'd say you must be good in bed, but that's obviously not the case since Fisher practically *begged* me to fuck him and give him a taste of what he was missing."

White-hot rage flows through me and I don't even think about my actions. I raise my arm and smack that smug look right off of her face. She yelps loudly, causing a few vacation stragglers enjoying one of the last nice days at the beach to sit up and take notice.

"Daaaaaamn," I hear Ellie mutter softly, but I don't pay any attention to her.

"You are a skanky piece of trash and the only reason Fisher went anywhere near you a year ago is because he was drunk," I shout, not caring that people can hear me.

"You are a BITCH!" Melanie screams.

"At least I'm not a scheming whore who tried to steal someone else's husband!" I fire back.

"I didn't steal anything! He CHOSE me, and you just can't stand that, can you? You weren't good enough for him and you couldn't satisfy him, so he chose someone who could," she argues.

"Nice try. I happen to know nothing happened between the two of you, so give it a fucking rest already," I tell her with a roll of my eyes.

She laughs right in my face and leans in closer. "You keep telling yourself that, sweetheart, and maybe one day you'll believe it. He was so angry and full of rage that night, and you just walked away from him. Don't worry, sugar. I took care of your man after you left, right in the bathroom at Barney's. When he fucked me against the wall, he shouted MY name when he came, not yours."

My heart starts beating frantically in my chest and I bite down on the inside of my cheek, trying my damnedest not to cry. I will not cry in front of this heartless bitch or give her any indication that her words are killing me and making me doubt Fisher in any way.

"Jesus, LOOK at you! Do you honestly think he'd want you when he could have me?"

I start to lunge for her when I feel a pair of arms wrap around me from behind, dragging me away while Ellie jumps up from her chair and starts screaming at Melanie.

"Lucy, calm down, baby," Fisher tells me.

I jerk out of his arms when he gets me far enough away from Melanie that I won't be tempted to punch her in the nose with my fist this time.

My pride and my heart have both cracked in half and my head is filled with memories of things I'd rather forget. I hate Fisher for making me look like a fool with Melanie and I hate Melanie for throwing it in my face and for making me doubt everything I thought to be true. I hate *myself* for being so fucking weak where both of them are concerned, but at least I didn't keep my mouth shut with Melanie. She can wear my handprint on her face for the rest of the day as a reminder to stop fucking with me.

I let the tears fall while my back is to Melanie and Ellie is still ripping into her.

"Hey, what happened?" Fisher asks softly as he reaches for me.

I step away from him and swipe angrily at my tears.

"Don't. Please, just don't right now," I beg him.

I feel inferior and I feel worthless and I hate that I'm questioning my own worth. I hate that I feel like I'm back in high school all over again, wondering why the king of the jocks and the hottest guy in school wants anything to do with me. I'm a grown fucking woman and I feel pathetic for letting Melanie get to me.

I start walking away from Fisher and he tries to grab onto my arm, but I jerk it out of his grasp. "No! Just please, leave me alone right now!"

He realizes I'm serious and he stops trying to follow me. As I start moving faster and run up the veranda stairs to the inn, I hear him begin to shout.

"What did you do? What the FUCK did you say to her?!"

I race through the sliding door and run up to my room, the tears coming fast and hard until I can barely see.

Chapter 38

Lucy

Present Day

"YOU'RE GOING TO have to talk to him, Lucy. You can't keep avoiding him," Ellie tells me a week later while we hang the storm shutters on the front of the inn.

After Fisher got the story from Ellie that day, he ran into the inn and found me curled up in the fetal position on the bed, crying so hard I could barely breathe.

"You know she's lying, Lucy. Please, God, tell me you know she's lying. I swear to you, NOTHING happened between us. Baby, please, you have to believe me. I don't know why she's doing this."

I didn't say a word to him. I couldn't. I wanted to throw myself into his arms and tell him that yes, I knew it was all a lie and that I loved him and of course I believed him, but I just couldn't do it. Melanie made me feel like a fool and ugly and worthless and it hurt so deep down in my soul that I couldn't make the pain go away. Nothing Fisher said could make it go away, either, and he finally listened to me when the only words I could get out through my sobs were the ones telling him to go and that I needed time.

He's called every day since then and stopped by multiple times, and while I haven't refused to see him, I haven't spoken to him, either. I've allowed him to do all the talking, listening silently while he begged, pleaded, and apologized. He swore over and over that nothing happened between him and Melanie, but I just can't get her words out of my head. She talked about his anger and his rage and him fucking her against the wall and it was too much. It was too much like what Fisher and I shared and I don't know how to get past that. I don't know how to see past those words and find the truth. I don't want to be one of those foolish women who automatically believe their man when he says he didn't cheat, especially when there's so much evidence to the contrary. I'm not stupid and I refuse to let anyone make me feel that way. It's bad enough I don't feel like I'm woman enough or good enough for Fisher, I don't need to feel like I'm not smart enough, as well.

I was finally forced to talk to him last night when he came storming into the inn, pissed off and more than ready to fight. He'd found out about my phone call with Stanford and he was definitely not happy.

"How in the hell could you keep something like that from me?"

"I wasn't keeping it from you, I was waiting to see if it panned out before I said anything."

"Jesus, you've been ignoring me for a week for something I didn't even do when the entire time you've been going behind my back with your ex-boyfriend!"

"I wasn't going behind your back with anyone! I was doing what I needed to do to make sure I didn't lose the inn.

This has NOTHING to do with you!"

"It has EVERYTHING to do with me! I was your fucking HUSBAND and you wouldn't let me help you with the inn, but you're going to let THAT schmuck bail you out?"

"That's exactly why I WOULD let him bail me out, because he isn't my husband and it's not something he feels like he HAS to do."

"I don't HAVE to do it either, I fucking WANT to. I love this place just as much as you do. Dammit, why can't you just let me take care of you for once? What's mine is yours, don't you see that? I love you and I WANT to do this for you!"

We went round and round for over an hour, neither one of us willing to give in. When he tried bringing up the Melanie situation again as a way to steer the argument away from the inn, I finally stormed out of the living room and locked myself in my room.

"Am I bad person for not believing him when he tells me he didn't sleep with her?" I ask Ellie softly as I step down from the ladder and stand next to her. "I feel like the worst person in the world. He was going through so much when all of that happened and he's done so much to get better and be a better person and I can't let go of this hurt. I can't let go of this one little thing."

Ellie wraps her arm around me and I rest my head on her shoulder.

"It wasn't a little thing, though, it was a big thing. Even if he didn't fuck her—which, I'm telling you right now and I've told you a hundred times before, HE DIDN'T—it was still a big thing. It broke your trust in him and when you break a woman's trust, it's hard to get it back," Ellie tells me. "You aren't a bad person, Lucy, you're a woman with a big heart. You loved him more than anything else in the world and he pushed you away no matter how hard you tried to keep him close. I think it's time for you to decide if you can let all of that go and let him heal your heart once and for all, or if you're going to let it stay broken."

I lift my head off of her shoulder and run my palms up and down my face. I feel like shit and I know I look like shit. I've cried myself to sleep every night that Fisher hasn't been here with me. I want to believe him; I don't want to let Melanie have the last word and get the satisfaction of knowing that she tore us apart, but I don't know how to do this. I've been with one man my entire life and it's something beautiful to me. Even though Fisher was far from a virgin when we first slept together, I've always been confident that he was faithful to me. In the back of my mind, I've always had those little worries and doubts that every woman has from time to time that maybe he'd find someone better, someone prettier, but I never let them take over and he always made me feel like I was the only one he would ever want. A few choice words from Melanie and all of that is shot to shit.

I put away the ladder and leave the rest of the storm shutters for another day while Ellie heads over to Bobby's house and I go inside to do a little work on the website, switching out the summer rates for the winter rates. As soon as I sit down at the computer, I hear the front door open and see an older couple walk inside with a few suitcases.

It's not unusual for us to get guests once the season is over. Some people don't like the crowds and prefer to be on the island when it's quiet and peaceful, but I checked the schedule this morning and we don't have any new guests coming until next week.

I get up from the computer and move around the desk to greet them.

"Hi, my name's Lucy, welcome to Butler House," I tell them with a smile, holding my hand out for each of them.

"Thank you," the woman tells me. "This place is absolutely beautiful. I'm so sorry, but we don't have a reservation. Will that be a problem?"

We only have one other couple staying here at the moment and they are checking out tomorrow.

"It's definitely not a problem," I tell them as I gesture towards the front desk and head back around it, pulling up the registration page on my computer. "How long will you be staying?"

They share a look before the man rests his elbows on top of the desk and smiles at me. "This was kind of a spur-of-the-moment vacation. Is there any way we can pay for a week and then play it by ear after that?"

I nod, typing that information into the computer. "That's no problem at all. Each of our rooms has a different lighthouse theme and a view of the ocean. We serve breakfast, lunch and dinner every day and even though it's off-season, all of the businesses in town will be keeping their summer hours for a few more weeks."

I hand them a brochure with a list of all the attractions on Main Street as well as the ferry schedule to and from the island.

"You probably saw the horrible red shutters we've started putting up on the front of the inn, sorry about that eyesore," I tell them with a smile. "We're getting into hurricane season, so we like to get a head start on making sure everything is ready, just in case."

"I saw on the news there were a few tropical storms brewing in the Gulf. Do you guys get many hurricanes here?" the man asks as I print out his registration information and slide it across the desk with a pen for him to fill out.

"We actually haven't had an official one blow through here for about twenty-one years. Mostly we just get a few bad storms," I explain.

I can barely remember the hurricane that hit the island when I was nine years old. I was here visiting my grandparents that summer and all I remember was racing around, helping them put up the storm shutters and hiding out in the library with a bunch of candles lit all over the place after we lost electricity. I was too young to remember much else, but from what I've heard from people in town since then, it wasn't as bad as it could have been and the island didn't get too much damage, thank God.

The gentleman finishes filling out the paperwork and hands it back to me. I grab one of the room keys and slide it over to them. Unlike large hotel chains, Butler House uses old-fashioned skeleton keys for each of the rooms.

Attached to each key with a ribbon is a small card welcoming the guest to the inn along with the name of the room they're staying in.

"You'll be staying in the Cape Hatteras room," I tell them. "If you go through these doors you'll see a central staircase. It's right at the top, the fifth door down. If you'd like to leave your suitcases here, I'll have them brought up in just a few minutes."

I look down at their form and quickly memorize their names.

"I hope you enjoy your stay at Butler House, Mr. and Mrs. Michelson," I tell them with a smile.

Mr. Michelson returns it and nods at me, wrapping his arm around his wife's shoulder. "Please, call us Seth and Mary Beth."

Chapter 39
Lucy

Present Day

S ETH AND HIS wife, Mary Beth, have been here for two days and, while I enjoy talking to my guests and getting to know them, Seth has gone a little overboard with the personal questions. Whenever I try to ask him about his life, he turns things around and asks me about mine. I don't know what it is about him. Maybe his age, his kind face, his understanding eyes? Whatever it is, I've found myself pouring my heart out to him on more than one occasion.

Mary Beth went into town to do some shopping and Seth offered to help me fold towels at the dining room table. I refused his help repeatedly, telling him there was no way I would let a guest lift a finger to help with laundry, but he's a persistent old man. He followed me into the dining room, sat down at the table and started folding. He ignored me when I tried giving him a bunch of suggestions of other things he could do on the island, just smiling up at me and continuing to fold until I had no choice but to sit down and let him help.

"So, what do you do for a living, Seth? Aside from push your way into doing manual labor when you should be relaxing?" I tease him as I grab a towel out of the laundry basket and shake it out.

Seth chuckles, resting a folded towel on top of the pile he's already made on the table. "Well, I've been retired for a few years now, so I spend my spare time volunteering as a counselor."

I smile to myself, not really shocked by this admission. Within just a few hours of meeting Seth, we were drinking coffee and I was spilling my guts to him. He's friendly and easy to talk to and I can definitely see him counseling people.

"At the VA Hospital on the mainland," he adds, not meeting my eyes when I stop what I'm doing and stare at him.

Well, isn't that just a strange coincidence? A counselor who volunteers at the same hospital where Fisher spent the last year suddenly shows up at the inn when Fisher and I are having problems?

I clear my throat in irritation and Seth finally stops folding to look at me.

"I know, I should have said something when we first checked in, but I didn't want to make you nervous," he tells me with a soft smile.

"Definitely something you should have mentioned before I talked your ear off," I tell him in annoyance, thinking about all the things I told him about my relationship problems with Fisher. "So, you worked with Fisher I assume?"

He nods, folding his hands in his lap. "I did. I was the only one he *would* work with for quite a while. Probably because I can be just as stubborn and pig-headed as he can."

Seth laughs, but I don't find anything about this funny, so I just cross my arms angrily. He leans forward and pats my arm.

"Now, now, don't be cross with me, or with Fisher. He has no idea I'm here. He called the other day wanting some advice and I decided it was time to take him up on his offer to see the island," he explains. "And to meet the woman he talked my ear off about every day for a year."

I shift uncomfortably in my seat. This man knows everything about Fisher and probably myself, as well. He knows what Fisher went through the year that he was away from me and I'm sure Fisher spoke to him about a lot of things that I probably shouldn't now about. Personal things, confidential things. Things I'm suddenly dying to know about, but I don't feel right asking. If Fisher wanted me to know what he discussed with his counselor, he would have told me himself.

"Isn't there some sort of doctor/client confidentiality rule you're breaking by being here with me right now?" I ask.

Seth laughs and shakes his head. "I'm not a doctor, I'm just an old war vet myself who has nothing better to do with his time than spend my days at the VA trying to help men who were just like me."

I nod in understanding, but I still don't feel right talking to him about Fisher without Fisher knowing and I tell him that.

"I don't think Fisher will be very happy knowing that you're here, divulging personal information about him."

Seth shrugs. "I'm sure he's going to be a little pissed off that I've been here for a few days and didn't tell him I was coming, but I plan on giving him a call later tonight and getting together with him. I wanted to spend some time alone with you before I did that. Fisher has always known that I'd want to speak to you at some point and he's made it perfectly clear that I'm free to talk to you about anything we discussed during his stay at the hospital. He doesn't want there to be any secrets between the two of you, but some things, well, they're just a little hard for him to talk about on his own."

I'm already well aware of that fact. The times we've talked over the last few months about what he experienced overseas were very difficult for him. He'd get choked up talking about friends he lost, he'd have to stop and take a few calming breaths when he told me about scary situations and the dreams that still haunted him to this day. I'm suddenly back to feeling horrible about pushing him away over a couple of stupid comments from a woman I despise. All of the pain he suffered, all of the tragedy he lived through and the choices he had to make to protect the freedom of people back here at home who have no idea what those men and women are living through day in and day out makes my issues and my insecurities feel small and pathetic.

"I'm not going to bore you with my opinions about Fisher's character or how far I think he's come since I met the ornery little shit at the hospital," Seth explains with a smile, pulling a thick manila folder out from under the pile of towels that I didn't even see him place there. "I think it would just be better for you to read it in his own words."

Seth passes the folder over to me, pushing it into my hand with a smile when I reach for it tentatively. "It's okay, it won't bite you. When Fisher and I first started talking, he told me that he used to keep a journal when he was younger. I suggested he start doing that again. There were things that he was having a hard time remembering and I knew writing them down might help. He wanted to remember everything he'd done, even though he knew it would be hard. He understood that the only way for him to get better would be for him to relive every moment of his breakdown."

Placing the folder in my lap, I run my palms over top of it. I've read his journal pages from when we were younger, and his words and the way he saw me and our relationship were nothing short of beautiful. I'm scared to death that what's in this folder will cut me in half.

Seth gets up from the chair, resting his hand on my shoulder as he walks by. "To get to the good, sometimes you have to live through the bad."

He walks out of the room, leaving me alone. Taking a deep breath, I hug the folder to my chest and get up from the table, moving into the library to curl up in a chair in the corner, next to the fireplace. With a shaking hand, I open the folder and pull out the first page, filled with Fisher's neat, block handwriting.

I start to read and realize it's about the day he came home from the last deployment and we had sex in the kitchen. We've already talked a little bit about how disappointed he was in himself for the way he behaved with me, and I did my best to convince him that he did nothing wrong. Seeing how he felt tortured that night makes me press my hand to my chest to stop the ache. He watched me sleep and traced his fingers over the bruises he'd left on my hips, crying with hate and anger at himself. He started to have a panic attack, thinking he'd hurt me and that I'd hate him and when he went to the bathroom, he had a horrible flashback.

My hand moves to press against my lips and I cry silent tears as I read what was going through his broken mind on a night when I went to sleep so happy and fulfilled and woke up the next morning with a husband who wouldn't look at me or touch me.

I flip the page and move to the next journal entry, the day I came home to find him packing my things and ordering me out of our house. It's like reading a fictional thriller as he talks about hearing the explosion of bombs and creeping through the house looking for an enemy that wasn't there. My cracked heart breaks in half as I read about how he crawled through our bedroom, believing with everything inside of him that he was back in the desert, fighting for his life. I cry harder when I read that I startled him when I came home and he reached for a gun that wasn't attached to his hip. He was so afraid he would hurt me, so afraid he would never be able to separate reality from his flashbacks, that he didn't know what else to do other than get me away from him where I'd be safe.

I read the words he said to me in anger, as well as the words he chanted in his head the entire time he was shouting at me, and I'm crying so hard I can barely see the page by the time I'm done.

"We're done, this is over. I'm packing your shit and you're leaving."
I'm sorry, I love you, please forgive me.

"Everything is fucked up, don't you get that? It's ruined, all of it is ruined and you need to fucking leave."

I'm so sorry, I love you, please forgive me.

"You need to get a life."

I'm sorry, I love you, please forgive me.

"All those sad, pathetic letters."

I'm lying, don't believe me, please don't believe me. I loved your letters, I kept them all and I cherish every one of them.

"I prefer women with a little more experience."

I don't mean it. I don't mean any of it. Knowing I'm the only man who has ever been inside of you makes me feel like a fucking king and the luckiest man alive. I'm sorry, I love you, please forgive me.

"It doesn't get better when I come home to you. I hate this life."

I'm lying! Every word is a lie. I love our life and I wouldn't change it for anything in the world. I love you, I love you, I love you.

I quickly turn the page over, unable to see those words anymore through my tears, unable to stand the pain he must have been going through when he said them. The next page doesn't get any easier. It's later that night at Barney's. The reason why I've been avoiding him the last week, and the reason why I can't let go of my own hurt and anger.

I've never known the exact order of events from that night. I knew he got drunk at Barney's, I knew that he thought I was Melanie, I knew he went on a rampage through the town and I knew Bobby knocked him out and dragged him to the ferry, but I never knew exactly how it all happened. Now I do, and it makes my stomach cramp and my chest physically ache. I read exactly what he was thinking and feeling and hoping for and I want to die from the pain in my heart.

Maybe it's Lucy. Maybe she ignored everything I said to her and came back to me. I know it's wrong and she shouldn't be here, but I just need her right now. I can see her one more time and then I'll leave and I'll walk away.

She doesn't feel the same and she doesn't smell the same, but none of that matters. Her legs straddle my thighs and I clutch onto her ass, pulling her closer so she doesn't change her mind and walk away.

I don't like her voice. It's not the same soft, sweet cadence that always makes my ears tingle and my heart beat fast. It's probably because my heart died and there's nothing inside my chest but a shriveled up, useless organ. This voice is shrill and annoying. Lucy is changing right before me, but I don't care. It's my fault, anyway. It's my fault she's different and doesn't feel the same or smell the same. I changed her, I hurt her…all my fault.

She doesn't taste the same and I hate it. I want my Lucy, not this drunken, morphed version of her.

I hear angry shouts and the shuffling of feet and the Lucy on my lap speaks again and it makes me wince. I want to tell her to stop talking like that. Stop talking

in a different voice, stop smelling different, stop
feeling different...just stop it. Be MY Lucy. I need
MY Lucy.

I'm not a hero, I'm not a good man, I'm not a good
husband...I am none of those things and they need
to see that.

The papers and the folder flutter to the floor as I lean forward, wrapping my arms around my waist to try and hold myself together. I'm crying so hard I can barely breathe, each ragged breath I take in making my chest hurt and each tear that falls making my eyes burn. He loved me so much and, even during his darkest time, he never lost sight of that. I let a few words from a woman who means NOTHING to me make me lose my faith in him. I'm such a coward and a fool. I had the proof of his love right in front of me this entire time and I refused to believe it. When you've been hurt once, it's so hard to let go and not be afraid you won't be hurt again. I should have trusted him, I should have believed him and I should have taken the love he gave me, wrapped it in my arms and never let it go.

I think about the journal pages he gave me himself, his memories of when I tutored him in Chemistry and how he flirted with me and only had eyes for me and became the sweet, strong amazing man that I fell in love with.

The day he proposed and how nervous he was, how scared he was of leaving me and how I gave him something to fight for, live for and come back home for.

Our wedding day and the crash of glasses in his parents' home that caused him to panic, sending him running to find me and breaking tradition by seeing me in my gown before the ceremony. How he couldn't calm down until he saw me, held me and told me he loved me and how we promised to renew our vows at the lighthouse on the fifteenth anniversary of when we started dating.

The fifteenth anniversary that is only a few weeks from now.

A howling wind outside rattles the windows, making me hop up from the chair and quickly wipe the tears from my eyes. The sky that was slightly overcast this morning has now turned pitch black with swirling, angry clouds. The trees that line the street in front of the inn are flopping from side to side with the force of the wind.

I quickly grab the folder and the papers from the floor and race out of the room, turning on the small television set on the counter in the kitchen, listening to the newscaster report on the quickly changing weather.

"Tropical Storm Vera has made an unexpected turn and is now bearing down on the coast of South Carolina. With damaging winds measuring up to forty miles per hour in some places, we're asking everyone in our viewing area to take precautions and begin hurricane preparations. While this storm hasn't yet been upgraded to a hurricane, it's still a good idea to be safe. We'll keep you posted on Vera, so stay tuned."

Chapter 40

Lucy

Present Day

THE LIGHTS FLICKER as I try to call Fisher for the fifth time, still with no answer on his cell phone or at Trip's house. I've tried Bobby and Ellie's cell phones, as well, and neither of them are picking up, either. I finish gathering the wireless LED lights, checking the batteries as I place them around the first floor of the inn while making sure Seth and Mary Beth know to stay away from the windows and in a central part of the house, just to be safe. I hear the front door fly open and slam shut with the force of the wind and I race out of the living room, hoping it's Fisher.

My footsteps falter and my hope falls when I see Trip securing the deadbolt and shaking the rain from his hair.

"Don't look so disappointed to see me, Lucy girl," Trip mutters.

I rush over to him and give him a quick hug. "I'm sorry, I thought you might be Fisher. I've been trying to call him for the last hour, but he's not picking up."

Taking Trip's coat from him, I shake off some of the water and hang it on the coat rack next to the door. I glance out into the driveway and notice Trip's SUV parked there.

"It must be getting really bad out there if you drove. You never drive," I comment.

"It's really kicking up. I wanted to stop over and make sure you were doing okay here. Haven't seen Fisher since first thing this morning," Trip tells me. "I'm sure he's fine."

Trip doesn't sound convinced, and it doesn't make me feel any better. Fisher always answers his phone no matter what he's doing, and I hope he's just avoiding my calls. I don't like the idea of him being out in this storm. I don't like the idea of Trip being out in it, either, even though it was really sweet of him to check on me.

"You shouldn't have gone out in this, you could have just called," I tell him as I watch him rub his left shoulder and wince. "What's wrong with your arm?"

He shakes it out and gives me a smile. "Eh, I just bumped it on the car door when I got out and the wind took hold of it, it's nothing."

I watch him with concern for a few minutes, noticing that his face is flushed and he doesn't look like he feels well. He shoos me away when I try to help him walk as I lead him into the library and introduce him to Seth and Mary Beth.

They shake hands and everyone but me takes a seat. I can't sit still, not until I know Fisher is somewhere safe and dry.

"Figured it would be better to wait out the storm here in a much bigger place. With that wind, my little house sounded like it was about ready to be blown off into the ocean," Trip says with a laugh. "What's the news saying so far?"

"They still aren't categorizing it as a hurricane, but that wind is really getting bad," I tell him.

There's a loud knock at the front door and Trip and I share a hopeful look before I run back out to the front room. When I see Fisher's mother hovering on the other side of the door, shielding her face from the wind and rain, I quickly unlock the door and have to brace myself against it as I hold it open for her to enter. Water and leaves come flying into the house, covering the floor as she rushes inside. I slam the door behind her and put the deadbolt back on.

"Grace, what are you doing here?" I ask as she wraps me in a wet hug before handing me a large basket.

"Running around to as many residential homes as I can, passing out supplies. Being the head of the Storm Emergency Committee means my work is never done," she says with a laugh. "Thank goodness this was my last stop. You don't mind if I stay here for a little while, do you?"

I peek inside the basket to find bottled water, batteries, flashlights and some snacks.

"Of course not! This is wonderful, Grace, thank you so much. Come on into the library, everyone else is in there right now," I tell her, leading the way.

"I hope you don't mind, but I grabbed your mail on the way in. The mailbox door was blown open and I was afraid you might lose some things," she tells me, handing me a stack of letters and bills that are slightly damp.

I take them from her, handing the basket over to Trip as she sits next to him on the couch. Trip and Seth begin assembling the flashlights while Mary Beth and Grace make their introductions.

Pacing around the room, I flip through the stack of mail to give myself something to do. When I come to a large, white envelope with Fisher's handwriting on the front, my heart plummets to my feet. There is no return address and no postage, so he didn't mail the envelope. It looks like he just stuck it in my mailbox at some point after I got the mail yesterday. It looks so much like the envelope that the divorce papers came in that I'm afraid to open it. Had I finally pushed him too far? Is he tired of waiting around for me to get my shit together? I move away from everyone else while they are busy chatting about the storm and force myself to tear open the envelope and pull out the single sheet of paper inside.

Dear Lucy –

I'm sorry for so many things. I don't even know why I'm saying it to you again, because saying the words isn't the same as showing you. Right now, I'm showing you how sorry I am. I'm sorry for never sending you a letter before now. You deserve a thousand letters telling you a thousand different ways how much I love you and how much you mean to me. I know you're afraid and I know you're worried, but everything will be okay. We were meant to be together. We were meant to fall in love on this island and to spend the rest of our lives together… it was fate. The photo inside proves that.

There's a light that guides all of us to where we're meant to be. You're meant to be with me, Lucy. Please… be with me.

I love you. Always.

Fisher

My eyes fill and I'm honestly surprised that I have tears left in me to shed at this point. Reaching back inside the envelope, I pull out the photo he mentioned. My hand flies to my mouth and I gasp, the letter and the envelope falling from my hand. Staring at the photo in my hand, I almost can't believe what I'm looking at.

Both Trip and Grace walk over to me when they realize I'm crying. Trip pats me on the back and Grace wraps her arm around me, looking over my shoulder to see what has gotten me so upset.

"I was wondering if he'd give that to you," she tells me softly. "I found it in one of my photo albums a few months ago."

Trip looks over my opposite shoulder and chuckles.

"Well, Goddamn, would you look at that? I forgot all about that. Wasn't that the year of the big hurricane?" he asks Grace.

Grace nods. "It was. You took Fisher with you that day to make sure none of the residents needed help with their storm shutters. I was worried sick when you guys never came back."

"Got way too bad out there for us to try and make it back to your end of the island," Trip muses. "We ended up stopping right here at the inn and hunkering down with everyone else."

I finally find my voice and tear my gaze away from the photo.

"What the hell is this? Will someone please explain this to me?" I ask in a shaky voice, waving the photo back and forth in front of them.

Trip guides me over to the couch and I sit between him and Grace. He takes the photo from my hand and stares at it for a few seconds before handing it back to me.

"Fisher was eleven the year of that hurricane, so that would have put you around nine, right?" he asks.

I nod silently, urging him to continue.

"It was the last year you came to visit your grandparents here at the inn. As soon as we pulled into the driveway, that huge weeping willow uprooted and fell right behind my truck. By that time, the drainage system was overloaded and the water in the street was about shin-deep, so Fisher and I ran up to the porch and your grandparents ushered us inside and brought us right in here to this library," he explains.

I stare down at the picture in my hand and trace my fingers over the two children sitting in front of the fire with big smiles on their faces. Me and Fisher, ages nine and eleven. It's almost too hard to believe. I don't remember this picture being taken and I barely remember being here during that hurricane.

"The electricity went out shortly after we got here. Your grandparents kept the adults occupied by stuffing them full of food and passing out board games. You were upset and scared about the storm and no one could get you to calm down," Trip tells me. He pauses to cough and runs his hand over his chest. His forehead is dotted with sweat and I don't like the look on his face.

"Trip? Are you okay?"

He bats my hand away when I try to press it to his forehead to see if he has a fever.

"Stop fussing over me, Lucy girl, and let me finish this story," he complains. "Where was I? Oh, right, so Fisher had this piece of wood he was carrying everywhere with him at the time, trying to carve something out of it. I had my toolbox with me in case anyone had any problems, so he took out what he needed, grabbed your hand and sat the two of you down over there in the corner by the fireplace with that big piece of wood."

Trip points over to the corner and we both stare for a few seconds in silence as I try to remember before Trip continues.

"Fisher started whittling away at that wood and you calmed right down. You curled up next to him and watched him work for hours. He explained everything he was doing like you were his student and he was teaching you how to whittle. Your grandmother even fetched him some paint and he let you help him paint it when he was finished."

I sniffle and wipe the tears from my eyes as Trip speaks and a quick flash of a memory from that day skates through my mind. I remember being sad because I was leaving the island the next day and I wanted the boy to make me something I could take home with me.

"All in all, we were probably stuck here for about eight or ten hours. When the storm finally passed, you started crying when Fisher and I got ready to leave. Fisher gave you what he'd carved and your face lit up like a Christmas tree," Trip says with a laugh. "I wish I could remember what the hell it was he made."

Another memory hits me and I gasp. I see him handing me the finished product. It's red and white and beautiful and I'm so happy that I helped him make something so amazing.

Snatching up a flashlight and turning it on, I get up from the couch without a word and race to the stairs. I take them two at a time until I get to the top, running down the long hallway until I reach the door to the Fisher's Lighthouse room, throwing it open and bursting through the doorway. I stop right inside the room, my heart pounding so hard that I'm certain it might pop right out of my chest. The wind and the rain beat against the side of the house as I slowly walk over to the windows in the middle of the wall on the far side of the room.

With a tentative hand, I reach out and run my palm down the side of the red and white wooden lighthouse that I've been drawn to since I found it in the attic when my parents and I first moved here. I dusted it off and stuck it right here in this room that very first day when I was sixteen years old. I would come in here almost every afternoon and sit in front of it, staring at it, touching it and loving it for reasons I never understood.

Another memory assaults me and I remember my parents telling me that I couldn't take the lighthouse home with me because it was too big and wouldn't fit in our suitcases. I cried almost the entire way home from the island.

Dropping down to my knees, I lift the two-foot tall wooden lighthouse from the floor. I see another flash of a memory in my mind and I have to know if it's real. Tipping the lighthouse upside down, my face crumbles and I sob, seeing that it was, indeed, real. In the same block script that he writes in now, just a little larger and a little messier, are carved words that make my thundering heart ache.

I hope someday you find your way back here.
If you do, I'll meet you at the lighthouse.

I cradle the lighthouse to my chest and rock back and forth. How can this be happening right now? The promise he always made me about finding his way back to me and the words we said to each other on our wedding day when we spoke of renewing our vows and how we'd meet each other at the lighthouse… he carved those same words to me into a wooden lighthouse when he was eleven years old. It doesn't seem possible, and yet, it is. I have the proof and the photo and the story from Trip and Grace and my little snippets of memories to reassure me that it's all true and it really happened.

"I found my soul mate when I was a child and she will always be the love of my life, no matter how many years go by."

"We were meant to fall in love on this island."

"You were meant to be with me."

The words Trip spoke when he told us how much he loved his wife and the words that Fisher wrote to me in his note swirl through my head faster than the wind and the rain outside.

Placing the lighthouse on the floor, I jump up and race out the door and down the stairs. Reaching into Trip's coat pocket, I grab the keys to his SUV and I'm already racing out the door and into the harsh, biting wind and rain just as everyone comes into the front room and starts screaming at me to come back.

Chapter 41
Lucy

Present Day

I TRY CALLING Fisher again as I slowly make my way through the flooded streets in town, but all I get is a voice recording telling me that all systems are down. Tossing my phone across the seat angrily, I flip the wipers from low to high and lean forward against the steering wheel, trying to see better.

I drive past every business on Main Street, I drive by Barney's, I drive by the beach and I drive by Trip's house, but I don't see Fisher's truck anywhere. The storefronts were boarded up as soon as the storm started picking up earlier this afternoon, and I'm the only idiot out on the streets right now.

A trip to Bobby's house produces the same results, but when I get to Ellie's, I see both her and Bobby's cars parked in the driveway. Her house is on a hill right in the middle of the fork in the road that splits Main Street into two separate streets and one of the few houses that doesn't sit directly on the beach. Aside from the inn, which is a huge structure, and the evacuation center, Ellie's house is one of the safer places to be right now since it's further inland than anywhere else, and I'm glad that she and Bobby are holed up in here instead of his beachfront cottage.

I pull the SUV up behind their vehicles and make a mad dash up to the house, noticing that Ellie's hurricane shutters are wide open and smacking against the siding. Finding the front door unlocked, I start shouting their names as I move through the house, but I don't get an answer. The faint sound of snoring comes from the finished basement that she uses as an extra living room, so I quickly make my way down the carpeted stairs.

I find Bobby and Ellie curled up together on the couch, fast asleep. While I'd normally find the sight in front of me so sweet that I'd immediately want to snap a picture of it with my cell phone, I don't have time for that now.

Saying both of their names softly so I don't scare them, I rush over to the couch and shake Ellie's shoulder. She jerks awake and stares up at me in confusion, rubbing the sleep from her eyes.

"What's going on? What time is it?" she asks in a raspy, sleep-filled voice.

Bobby yawns and stretches behind her, blinking his eyes open and staring up at me with the same confused look as Ellie.

"Have you guys seen or heard from Fisher today?" I ask them frantically as they both swing their legs down the front of the couch and sit up.

"What time is it? Jesus, what *day* is it? Why the hell are you sopping wet?" Bobby asks with another yawn as he stares at my wet clothes, which are dripping all over the floor.

I'm about ready to shake the shit out of them both if they don't get with the program.

"What is WITH you two?" I ask in irritation.

"Sorry, I was up every hour last night throwing up. Every. Hour. From nine last night until nine this morning," Ellie explains. "We moved down here on the couch this morning to watch a movie once it finally passed. We must have fallen asleep."

Bobby looks down at his watch. "Shit. We've been asleep for like seven hours."

He starts to joke with Ellie and I lose it.

"PAY ATTENTION! HAVE EITHER OF YOU SEEN OR HEARD FROM FISHER TODAY?!"

They stop laughing and look at me in shock.

"Uh, he stopped by here this morning, right before we fell asleep on the couch. Jesus, Lucy, what's the big deal? You've been ignoring him for a week, what's another day?" Bobby asks sarcastically.

Ellie punches him in the arm and tells him to shut up and he immediately apologizes.

"The big deal is that we're in the middle of a hurricane and I can't get ahold of Fisher!" I yell.

Bobby jumps up from the couch. "Are you fucking kidding me? We've been sleeping through a hurricane?"

He races up the stairs, Ellie and I right behind him.

"Jesus Christ!" he shouts as soon as he gets to the top of the stairs and looks out the windows in the kitchen. "Did I completely miss the news that we were getting a hurricane?"

Ellie comes up behind him and slides her hands

around his waist, standing up on her toes to look over his shoulder at the rain and wind beating against the window.

"I guess now we know my basement is soundproof," she mutters. "Dammit, there goes my hydrangea bush."

We all watch as the bush in question flies right by the window.

"SHIT!" Bobby suddenly shouts, moving out of Ellie's arms and reaching for his cell phone on the counter.

"The phone lines are down," I tell him. "What's wrong?"

Bobby ignores me, trying to use the phone, cursing again when it doesn't work.

"Shit, motherfucking shit!" he yells, tossing the phone on the counter. "No one else has heard from Fisher, either?"

Panic overwhelms me as he rushes to the hall closet, throwing the door open and quickly digging through a collection of scuba equipment. Bobby has slowly been moving his things into Ellie's home since they got engaged. Her house is larger than his cottage and there's plenty of room here for a new baby as opposed to his tiny bachelor pad cottage.

Pulling an empty bag off of the middle shelf, he curses again as he throws the bag angrily against the wall.

"What the hell is going on, Bobby?" I ask nervously.

"When Fisher stopped by here this morning, he asked to borrow some scuba equipment. It was cloudy, but there weren't any reports of a storm coming in," he explains as he paces back and forth in the small kitchen. "He wanted to get in one last day of diving before the

weather started turning bad. I told him I was too exhausted to go out with him and that he should give me a few
hours to catch up on some sleep. He fucking knows better
than to dive alone, that son of a bitch!"

My hand flies to my mouth and Ellie immediately
comes up to me and pulls me into a hug.

"He probably didn't go, Bobby. I'm sure he's just
holed up somewhere waiting out the storm," Ellie
explains.

"That bag is the one I keep filled with HIS equipment, Ellie. It was there this morning when he stopped
by. I told him to let himself out because I couldn't keep
my eyes open anymore, and that I'd call him when I woke
up. He must have taken it when I wasn't looking."

Ellie squeezes me tighter, still trying her best to convince us that Fisher is fine.

"It's okay, there's no way he would've gone diving in
this storm," she reassures me.

"If he was down under the water, he might not have
known the storm was coming until he surfaced," Bobby
tells us.

"I drove by the dive hut and his truck wasn't there.
Would he have gone anywhere else? That's where you
guys always dive," I tell him, my stomach churning with
dread.

Bobby stops pacing and runs a hand through his hair.
"He's been a fucking downer and out of sorts all week. I
told him I'd keep the entire afternoon open so he could
take his time and enjoy the underwater scenery, clear his
head. He mentioned something about wanting to dive

somewhere different, somewhere that reminded him of you, whatever the fuck that means."

There's a light that guides all of us to where we're meant to be.

I pull out of Ellie's arms and race for the front door.

"LUCY! You can't go back out in this storm," she shouts.

"Lucy, just WAIT! I'll go with you!" Bobby yells.

I ignore them both, moving as fast as I can through the storm, holding my arms over my face, battling the wind and the rain to get to Trip's SUV.

THE ONLY REASON I know I'm heading in the right direction is the beacon of light that circles around in the sky, shining bright even through the torrential downpour. I'm driving faster than I should, considering I can barely see a few feet in front of me. Trip's SUV rocks from side to side with the force of the wind and bounces up and down along the gravel drive that takes me up to the lighthouse. The sight of Fisher's truck parked about a quarter of a mile from the lighthouse, right in front of the walkway that leads to the beach, has me throwing open the door and racing to the driver's side window. I peer inside, finding it empty, and I take off through the ankle-deep puddles, not even bothering to shield my face as the rain batters against my skin.

I scream Fisher's name as loud as I can as I follow the walkway, running in between the giant rock formations. The water has moved so far inland that there is only about a hundred yards of beach left where there is usually at least three times that. I continue screaming for Fisher, but the wind blows the sound right back at me. The waves crash angrily onto the shore, one right after another, pounding against the sand like God himself has come down and is slamming his fist into the beach.

Shielding my eyes, I blink rapidly, trying to see through the rain hitting my face, but it's no use. I can't see anything beyond the waves. A shift in the wind switches the direction of the rain so that it's beating against my back instead of my face and I can see a little more clearly. I try to hold my sopping wet hair away from my eyes as the wind whips it in every direction. Quickly scanning the beach, something not too far down catches my attention. My stomach drops and I take off running, falling to my knees in the wet sand. Resting in a puddle on the beach is a backpack and harness with the two air tanks packed inside. The same type of pack that Fisher wears when he dives.

Why would he do this? Why would he come out here, even if he didn't know about the storm? He's been diving all of his life, so he knows how dangerous it is out here by the lighthouse. The current is unpredictable near the rocks and there have been numerous accidents over the years involving people who chose to ignore the warnings because they wanted to see what was down at the bottom of the ocean near the lighthouse. He knows better, dammit!

The crashing waves inch closer and closer to me and I know I need to get off of this beach, but I can't move. My body is frozen in place when something bright yellow tumbles around in the wild crest of the wave that just battered the beach. The object floats on top of the quickly advancing water as it ebbs towards me, getting lodging in the sand as the water leaves it behind and goes back out to sea. I crawl on all fours across the wet sand, tears and rain blurring my vision. I grab the yellow and black scuba fin from the sand, cradle it to my chest and scream as loud as I can at the angrily churning ocean.

Chapter 42

Fisher

I KNOW I shouldn't be diving in this area, especially alone, but I needed to be here, needed to be somewhere that reminded me of Lucy since I can't actually *be* with Lucy right now. I know she needs space to figure things out, but all this time away from her is killing me. How am I supposed to convince her that we're meant to be together if I can't touch her and kiss her and show her how much I love her? Sticking that note and picture in her mailbox first thing this morning was my last ditch effort.

The random, gurgling *whoosh* of my breathing apparatus forcing air into my lungs every few seconds is the only sound filling my ears at the bottom of the ocean. It's calm and peaceful and, other than Lucy, it has always been the one thing that helps clear my head when I'm distracted or feeling uneasy. I love being down here, sharing space with nothing but fish and coral. I lost track of time as soon as I submerged myself, but going by the faint beep of the alarm on my tank signaling I only have about thirty minutes left of air, I've been down here for quite a while. Even though I've already gone through almost four tanks, I'm still not ready to surface. I don't want to come up and deal with the reality that I'm still waiting for the woman I love to decide if I'm worth the risk. I want to be worth it to her, dammit.

Everything was going so perfectly. We got past so many hurdles that I never imagined anything else could possibly fuck it up. I'd been sneaking away from her every chance I got to work on our cottage, fixing the bedroom door I kicked open the day I lost my shit and Bobby helped me paint and move the furniture he'd put into storage for me after I went to rehab back into the house. I wanted to surprise Lucy, to drive her out to our home, get down on my knees and beg her to be my wife again. I wanted to give her the wedding rings I still carry everywhere and ask her to spend her life with me and to love me forever. I'd finally gotten everything finished the day she went to the beach with Ellie and fucking *Melanie* decided to spew her bullshit.

I should've spent more time talking to Lucy about what *didn't* happen that night at Barney's. I should've done everything in my power to reassure her that she has been the only woman for me since the first time I kissed her. No other woman could ever compare, and I wish she could see herself the way I do. I wish she could see how beautiful and perfect she is to me. When Ellie repeated the shit Melanie said to Lucy, it's the first time in my life I've ever wanted to strangle a woman. Melanie, with her fake tits and fake hair and her feelings of entitlement about everything around her make her the ugliest person in the world to me.

The rage I turned on her erased that haughty look

from her face for the first time in my memory. Melanie cried like a baby, but I didn't feel a bit sorry for her. She's gone through so many husbands that I don't think she has any idea what true love really is. I fucked her once in high school and the bitch is so convinced of her own appeal that she truly believed I was pining away for her ass almost fifteen years later. One drunken mistake last year that lasted less than five minutes was enough to convince her that I was ready for seconds. I told her in no uncertain terms that I wouldn't fuck her again if she were the last woman on earth. I reminded her that it's ALWAYS been Lucy and it always will be, and I told her if she didn't stay away from both of us, I would make her life more fucking miserable than it already is. She tried to apologize, but I told her to fuck off. She'd already done enough damage, and a few words of contrition weren't going to fix anything.

Lucy made offhand comments about not being pretty enough or good enough for me when we were younger, but I never imagined she would still carry some of those insecurities to this day. I didn't realize what happened at Barney's would still be festering inside of her, just waiting for a chance to boil over and ruin everything we'd worked so hard to build. Why didn't I spend more time explaining to her what was going through my head that night? We talked about it once and I foolishly thought that was enough. I should have known her better. I DO know her better, dammit, and I should have realized she'd need more from me. A woman who believes her man has cheated on her doesn't get over something like that easily, no matter how many words of reassurance you throw at her. I should have held her face in my hands and looked into her eyes and told her NO ONE could ever make me forget the vows and promises I made to her. Even when I was half out of my mind with flashbacks and whiskey, the very thought of being inside another woman was enough to make me physically ill.

I also can't let go of the betrayal I felt over Lucy going behind my back and talking to that fuck face ex of hers to make a deal to save the inn. Naturally, my father was the one to share that little tidbit with me when he found out through whatever investment grapevine he keeps his ear glued to. I don't understand why she refuses to trust me or accept my assistance, but more than willing to put her faith in *him* and allow *him* to help her. All I've ever wanted to do is protect her and make sure she's happy, why can't she see that?

It's being here, under the water, where everything is calm and beautiful, that helps me realize it's all trivial bullshit in the grand scheme of things. I almost lost her forever. Do I really want to engage in a pissing contest with her ex? Does it even matter where the money comes from, as long as she gets what she wants? And what right do I have to bitch about her lack of trust, considering I served her with divorce papers and left her twisting in the wind for an entire year after I broke her fucking heart?

When the alarm on my tank starts beeping frantically, I set aside my thoughts and kick my legs through the water, beginning my assent up to the surface. The closer I get, the less calm the water becomes. I can see it churning angrily far above my head and I wonder what the hell has been happening up top since I've been down here. It takes a lot of extra effort to kick through the water and the current is so strong that it keeps trying to push me back down and twirl me around. I start to panic a little, realizing I don't have much air left in my tank. Using every ounce of muscle I have in my body and with the help of the fins on my feet, I kick and practically claw my way to the surface, my head popping out of the water just as a giant wave crashes over top of me and pushes me back under. I tumble around, ass over end, and it takes me a few seconds to right myself and figure out which is up.

What the fuck is happening? I'm far enough away from the shore that there shouldn't be any waves like that out here.

I kick off as hard as I can again and I'm prepared when I pop above the surface and another wave comes at me. I start swimming to shore as fast as I can, trying to stay on top of the waves instead of letting them overtake me and push me back under. The sky is almost pitch black above me and rain and wind batter the surface of the ocean all around me as I swim. I spit the regulator out of my mouth and grit my teeth, the muscles in my arms burning with each stroke I make through the swirling, angry water.

It takes me twice as long as normal to make it to the shore and when I do, I collapse face first into the sand, realizing I lost both of my fins somewhere in the water. The wind and rain beat so hard against me that it's a struggle to even get up on all fours, especially with the heavy weight of my tank and harness system on my back. I quickly unbuckle myself from the pack and slip it off of me, letting it drop to the sand as I continue crawling across the beach, panting so hard that I almost can't catch my breath. My legs and arms are screaming at me to take a break, but one look over my shoulder tells me I need to keep moving. I've never seen the ocean so crazy and I can't believe I had no idea what was happening up here on the surface while I was down below.

Pushing myself up to my feet, I stay hunched over, covering my face as best as I can from the wind and the bruising rain to try and see where I'm going. Looking up, I notice the current pushed me a long way from where I parked my truck in front of the walkway to the beach. I'm not about to try and make a run for it when I'm closer to the lighthouse. Digging my feet into the sand, I move my body as fast as I can against the wind, finding the small walkway that will lead me right up to the door of the lighthouse.

It takes me several seconds of cursing and struggling to get the old, rusted door to open and when I do, the wind rips the doorknob out of my hand and slams the door against the side of the structure. I hustle inside, using my bodyweight to pull the door closed behind me before collapsing in a heap on the black and white checkered floor. I stay on my back, trying to catch my breath and staring up at the spiral staircase that winds around and around to the very top of the huge lighthouse. Trip and I retiled the floor years ago and added a heating system to the place in case tourists wanted to come out here in the off-season and look around, and I am more than thankful that this building is somewhat finished inside. The floor is smooth and dry and isn't filled with puddles and there isn't water dripping down on top of me like you'd have in some other, older lighthouses. We've reinforced this place as much as we could over the years and even with the howling wind and rain beating against the side of the building, I know it can withstand anything.

Panic starts to overwhelm me when it hits me that this is the start of a hurricane. I have no idea where Lucy is or if she's safe. I don't care what the hell it's doing out there or how dangerous it is, I can't stay here for more than a few minutes to take a breather. I have to get to my truck and get back to the other side of the island to Lucy. My wetsuit is starting to feel like it's suffocating me, so I quickly unzip it and slide my arms out, pushing it off my body until I'm wearing nothing but my swim trunks. Within seconds, the motorized sound of the light turning at the top of the structure comes to a halt. The room is pitched into darkness, but thankfully, the back-up generator kicks on and the sconces on the wall flicker back to life, bathing the room in soft light. Unfortunately, the generator isn't powerful enough to keep the heat going and my skin quickly chills. Thankfully, Trip is a romantic at heart and always makes sure there are a few clean blankets left on a small table by the door for couples that want to come out to the lighthouse, curl up together and enjoy the view. Grabbing one from the pile, I wrap it around myself, cupping my hands around my mouth and blowing warm air against my chilled fingers.

I hear something that sounds like a scream coming from outside and I stop rubbing my hands together to warm them up and strain my ears, listening harder, but all I hear is rain beating against the side of the lighthouse. I shake my head and pull the blanket tighter around my body.

I hear another scream, this one louder than before, almost like the wind carried it right here into the building. Stepping over my wet suit in a pile at my feet, I move towards the door, thinking there's no way anyone else is out in this weather. If there's someone out there as stupid as me, however, I can't just stand here and not help them. I think about putting my wet suit back on to protect me from the elements, but it would take me forever to get that thing back on my body. Another scream rips through the wind and the rain and whoever is out there sounds like they're in a world of pain. I don't have time to do anything other than toss the blanket from my shoulders, push open the door and race back out into the storm.

Chapter 43
Lucy

Present Day

I NEED TO move. I need to get off this beach, but I can't. My throat is raw from screaming into the wind and my face burns with the force of the rain pelting into me, and still, I don't care. The tide gets closer and closer to me as I kneel here in the sand, screaming and crying and cursing the storm, but I don't move. I want to be swept out into that ocean. I want to let the water take me out to sea and drown me in guilt in misery. The water rushes up around my legs as the brutal waves keep pounding against the surf and my knees sink deeper into the sand each time the water races away. My flimsy t-shirt is plastered to my skin, my sopping wet jeans are molded to my body and my hair flies around my face, whipping against my raw cheeks and stabbing into my eyes. I'm so cold from the wind and the rain and the biting ocean water that my body shakes and my muscles scream in pain.

I think I hear my name on the wind and I sob, hunching over, still clutching Fisher's fin to my chest, squeezing it as hard as I can, wishing it was *him* in my arms and not some fucking piece of rubber. I angrily toss the fin into the ocean swirling around my legs and I lean forward, my hands sinking into the water and the mushy sand. I start crawling mindlessly into the surf as waves crash into my arms and chest. There's nothing left in me to get up to my feet and walk. I crawl and I sob, smacking my hands down into the angry tide, dragging my knees through the water and sand, choking on my tears and the repeated splash of salt water against my mouth and nose.

I hear my name again, louder and filled with fear and I pause, staring down a giant wave headed right for me. I should stand up, I should run, but there isn't time and I don't care. Go ahead and swallow me up, go ahead and spit me out into the sea... I don't care. I close my eyes and hear my name screamed with so much pain that it makes my already broken heart split off into even more pieces as the wave crashes over top of me. My hands and my knees are suddenly ripped away from the beach. My shoulder slams into the sand, my head scrapes against pebbles and seashells and I'm tumbled around and around, upside down and inside out as I swallow huge mouthfuls of water. I don't even try to fight against the ocean, just allow my body to go limp and let it take me wherever it wants to go. I'm dizzy and I'm numb and I have no idea which way is up as my body continues to be tossed around like a rag doll. I automatically open my mouth to breathe when my chest gets tight and panic overwhelms me. Water fills my lungs instead of air and I start to thrash against the pain in my chest. My brain is still fighting to live even though my heart wants nothing more than to die.

Something hard and strong and warm, so different

from the cold ocean water, wraps around my waist and yanks me backwards. I claw and fight, trying to get it to let go of me and just let me stay here, under the water, but it refuses. It tightens its hold on me, squeezing me hard as it continues to pull and pull until my head suddenly breaks the surface. I cough and sputter and cry, spitting out water, the pain in my chest exploding as cool air fills my lungs. My body is hefted right out of the water until I feel arms under my legs and around my back, cradling me to strength and warmth that I instantly recognize.

I close my eyes through the dizziness and disorientation as my body is jostled, not even caring about the wind and rain still hammering against me until it suddenly stops and I feel nothing but heat and the sound of the wind is no longer ringing through my ears, but becomes muffled. Coughs wrack my body all over again as a blanket is wrapped around me and strong hands pat and rub my back, helping me lean forward to spit out more water, and I suddenly hear the voice that I thought I'd never hear again.

"Lucy, my Lucy, what the *hell* were you doing?"

My head jerks up and I'm met with Fisher's worried, tear-filled eyes as he stares down at me and begins smoothing my wet hair off of my face before running both of his palms over the top of my head, and cupping the back of it in his hands.

"I didn't think I would get to you in time. Oh, my God, I almost lost you," he whispers in fear. "That wave went over top of you and I almost lost you."

TARA SIVEC

I throw myself against him, wrapping my arms around his shoulders, my sobs echoing around the room when I feel his strong arms encircle my waist and pull me as close to him as possible. He's so warm and real and alive that I can't stop crying. I pull back a little, just enough to be able to see his face. His beautiful, wonderful face that I can't imagine never seeing again, never touching again or never kissing again.

"I love you, I love you so much," I tell him with a raspy voice as the tears fall down my face, mixing with salt water.

He lets out a shaky gasp, sliding his hands to my cheeks and holding my face in his palms. "You have no idea how much I love you, Lucy. No fucking idea."

I nod against his hands, my lips quivering with the tears that continue to fall. "I do. I know, I've always known, I just didn't want to see it. I see it now and I'm so sorry. I should have believed you, I should have trusted you. I love you, Fisher. With everything I have and everything I am."

His sobs join my own and he pulls me roughly back to him. I'm seated in his lap, cradled in his arms as he rocks us back and forth on the floor of the lighthouse. He only lets go of me long enough to wrap the large blanket around both of our shoulders, before pulling me back to the warmth of his chest.

"You're my light, Lucy," he tells me as I run my hands over his face, his shoulders and his chest, still trying to convince myself that he's real and he's here and I didn't lose him. "You are always the light in my darkness. You're the reason I'm alive, you're the reason I'm here and you're the reason I breathe, every day."

He kisses my nose, my cheeks and my forehead before pressing a gentle kiss to my lips.

"I kept my promise. I found my way back to you and I will ALWAYS find my way back to you, no matter where I go, forever," he vows.

"Please, don't leave me, ever again," I beg him. "I love you. You are everything to me. I don't care about Melanie, I don't care about the inn, I don't care about *anything* but being with you and loving you for the rest of my life."

He wipes the tears from my eyes before closing his own, resting his forehead against mine.

"There never has been, nor will there *ever* be anyone but you, Lucy. How could anyone possibly compete with you?" he asks me. "You've been in my heart since I was eleven years old. You are the calm to my storm and I never should've pushed you away. I should've recognized how fucking strong you are, how strong you've *always* been. Walking away from you was the worst mistake I ever made. I can't live without you, Lucy, I can't. Please, come back to me. Marry me. Love me. Grow old with me. I can't do this without you."

I kiss his lips, lingering against his mouth.

"I can't come back, because I never left. I never left," I whisper against his lips. "I've always been here, waiting for you to come back to me."

Fisher leans our bodies sideways, reaching for his wet-suit. He drags it across the floor with one hand, refusing to let go of me with the other. He unzips a small pocket on the chest of the suit and pulls something out of it. Bringing his hand between us, I look down and find my engagement and wedding rings resting in his palm.

My eyes grow blurry with tears all over again when I see them sitting there.

"I've carried these with me every day since you sent them back to me. I don't want to hold onto them anymore," he tells me as he grabs my left hand and slides them on my ring finger.

He brings my hand up to his mouth and presses a kiss over top of the rings.

"I love you for being so strong."

He flips my hand over and kisses my palm.

"I love you for waiting for me to come back to you."

He wraps his hand around my wrist and pulls me against him, kissing me with love and passion and promise.

"I love you for meeting me at this lighthouse, even though you took ten years off my life," he tells me with a grin.

He leans his head to the side and kisses my cheek, moving his lips to my ear.

"Most of all, I love you because you're Lucy," he whispers against my ear. "*MY* Lucy."

As the storm rages around us, nestled on the floor of the lighthouse on top of the pile of blankets, Fisher slowly removes the wet clothes from my body. He touches and kisses and runs his hands over every inch of my body, whispering words of love after each kiss. He holds himself above me and I wrap my legs around his waist, pulling him down on top of me, wanting to feel his weight and his strength. I will never get used to the sensation of him entering me for the first time, how full and loved and wanted he makes me feel. Our love spans so many years and is filled with so many memories, I could never imagine another day without him and I say a silent prayer that I will never have to.

Fisher and I move together slowly, holding each other tightly with the wind and the rain beating against the lighthouse.

The same lighthouse that brought us together when we were children.

The same lighthouse that helped me see the kind of man Fisher really was when we were teenagers.

The same lighthouse where our future began as adults.

It wasn't too long ago that I thought our story had come to an end. Turns out, it was only beginning.

Epilogue

Fisher

Six weeks later…

WITH THE SUN setting in the distance, I stare down at Lucy with a mixture of love and sadness. Tears fill her eyes and I know we're both feeling the exact same way. We're on the beach, in front of our lighthouse with my mother, Ellie, Bobby, Lucy's parents and Seth and Mary Beth off to the side, and a minister standing in front of us as I slide those rings back on her finger where they belong.

The last few weeks have been a whirlwind of emotions, and we went back and forth about doing this today, not sure if it was right when there was one person missing. One person who had always supported us and would be happier than anyone that we'd found our way back to each other and finally got our small, intimate wedding in front of our lighthouse.

"I now pronounce you husband and wife. Again," the minister says with a smile. "You may, of course, kiss your bride."

I wrap my arms around Lucy and lift her up against my body, kissing her with every ounce of love I have inside of me. As our family and friends clap, I press my mouth to her ear.

"I love you, Mrs. Fisher," I whisper.

"I love you more, Mr. Fisher," she replies softly.

Setting her down on the sand, we walk hand-in-hand to the water's edge. I pick up the sky lantern from the sand and Lucy pulls a lighter from down the front of her dress and lights the square block of wax attached to the inside of the paper balloon. We hold onto it for a few seconds before lifting it up together and letting the wind carry it away, out over the ocean. Wrapping my arm around her shoulder, I pull her close and we watch the light from the luminary float higher and higher above the water until it disappears into the clouds.

"You know he's really pissed right now that we're getting all sappy," Lucy says with a shaky laugh as she swipes the tears off of her cheeks.

"He is absolutely calling me a 'little shit' and shaking his head at me," I laugh with her, blinking the tears out of my eyes.

Jefferson 'Trip' Fisher, Sr., my grandfather and the only father I've ever truly known, died from a massive heart attack the day of the hurricane. Nothing has been the same since he's been gone and the only thing keeping me from breaking down is the woman in my arms next to me. Lucy knew something was wrong with him that day and she's been beating herself up ever since for not getting him to a hospital. I've done everything I could to convince her that there was nothing she could have done in the middle of a hurricane, and it's not like Trip would have let her do something, anyway. He was a stubborn old man and the one thing giving me solace right now is that he's finally reunited with the love of his life.

"They're finally together," Lucy says softly, mirroring my thoughts as she continues staring up at the sky.

"He's probably already pissing her off, complaining about things that need to be fixed in Heaven," I joke.

She laughs and the sound warms my heart. I turn her to face me and hold her face in my hands. In a simple, long-sleeved white dress with her hair hanging loose around her shoulders and a white flower tucked behind one ear, she's more beautiful to me now than she was on our first wedding day. Keeping our promise not to tell my mother about this until right before the ceremony, Grace Fisher, in her usual fashion, clucked her tongue at me when she saw that we were both barefoot and I was wearing a casual pair of khakis rolled up to my shins and an untucked white button down shirt. She wisely kept her loving mouth shut when we told her this is what *we* wanted and she should just go with it.

"I love you. So much," I tell her softly. "I miss him, and I wish he was here to see this, but I know he's up there, cheering us on."

She nods, resting her hands on top of mine on either side of her face. "He was so proud of you, Fisher, don't ever forget that."

I hear a throat clear behind me and we turn, both of us more than a little surprised to see who's standing next to us, especially since he wasn't invited.

"Fisher... Lucy," my father says with a nod in both of our directions.

He holds up a large, wrapped package and hands it to

Lucy. "I hope you don't mind, Bobby said he was supposed to give this to you after the ceremony, but I wanted to do the honors."

Lucy takes the package from my father. It's the wedding present I made for her and I was having Bobby keep it hidden until the ceremony was finished. I have no idea what he's trying to pull and I can't help but be a little on the defensive and protective of Lucy. I don't want anything ruining this day for her.

I wrap my arm around her waist and pull her securely into my side as she slowly rips the paper off of the present. She gasps when she sees the sign I carved. When I found out she trashed the sign I'd made her on our first wedding day, I knew I would make her a new one if she ever agreed to marry me again. I'm actually happy that she got rid of that first one. We're starting over, beginning again and this sign, with a new date, signifies that.

"It's beautiful, son," my father tells me softly as he stares down at the sign in Lucy's hand as she lovingly traces her fingers over the letters.

"Welcome to the family again, Lucy," he tells her with a smile. "I know an apology will never suffice for the way I've treated you over the years. The way I've treated both of you. But for what it's worth, I'm sorry. I'm ashamed of the way I've behaved and I'm even more ashamed that it took the death of my father to open my eyes. I hope one day you can forgive me. I don't want…"

I watch his eyes fill with tears as he pauses and clears his throat. I'm dumbfounded and I've suddenly forgotten how to blink.

"I don't want to leave this earth with any regrets when my time comes. Right now, I have entirely too many and I want to change that. I'm proud of you. I'm so proud of both of you," he tells us with a sad smile before walking away from us and back over to the group standing a few feet away.

"What in the hell just happened?" Lucy whispers as we both stare at my father while he chats easily with Lucy's parents.

"I have no fucking idea," I whisper back.

My father has been quite friendly since Trip passed away. Lucy had the wake and the ceremony at the inn and my father helped with everything, telling her to relax and not to lift a finger. He bragged about her and Butler House to everyone who walked through the door and pointed out every piece of furniture I'd made for the inn, praising my skills and telling everyone how proud he was of me. When I asked my mother about it, assuming he was just trying to showboat and be the center of attention, she told me he was grieving in his own way and wanted to make up for the past. It was nice hearing him say such good things about me, but I still wasn't inclined to invite him to our wedding.

Maybe he finally realized what a shitty son he'd been or maybe he saw how devastated I was when I lost Trip and realized I wouldn't grieve that way when he dies. Maybe he finally realized that the love of family and friends is the only thing that will truly sustain you through life, or maybe the letter Trip left behind was the kick in the ass he needed. When I read the letter Trip wrote to all of us on the day of his funeral, I watched my father cry for the first time in my entire life. Trip apologized to my father for the loss of his mother and for not doing everything he could to give him enough love to make up for her not being there. He told my father he would haunt him for the rest of his life if he didn't stop making the same mistakes he did, and to be proud of me and accepting of Lucy. Then, he royally pissed Lucy off by enclosing the 'paid in full' deed to the inn, telling her that she better stop rolling her eyes and just say thank you. He told us that if we were reading that letter, we damn well better not be sad because he was finally where he belonged, with the woman he loves, and that he hoped we had finally stopped being idiots, gotten our shit together and gotten remarried. Every time we've waffled about whether we should continue with our wedding on the anniversary of our first date, all we had to do was think about that letter and know we were doing the right thing.

Whatever is going on with my father right now, I can only hope it continues because he has a whole new generation to be there for and to love and cherish.

Getting down on my knees in the sand, I hold onto Lucy's hips and press my lips to her stomach.

"There's hope for you yet, little one. Your grandfather might actually turn out to be a decent human being by the time you get here," I speak softly.

Lucy laughs and runs her fingers through my hair as she smiles down at me. I stare up at her as the wind ruffles her curls and the sun forms a halo behind her, reminding me yet again that she is my angel and the child she carries inside of her is just the beginning of the amazing future we're going to have together on this island. We no longer have to worry about the security of the inn, Ellie and Bobby can get married on the veranda just like they planned, our children will be born close together and will obviously grow up to be best friends, and Lucy and I can grow old together in the place where our story began, but will never, ever end. Rumor even has it that Melanie got her hooks into Stanford and they've fallen madly in love, so that's two less annoyances Lucy and I will ever have to worry about. I'm sad that Trip will miss out on meeting his great-grandchild, but maybe my father really is turning over a new leaf and he can be a better grandfather than he was a father.

"Thank you for meeting me at the lighthouse," I whisper.

Lucy pulls me up from the sand and wraps her arms around my shoulders, smiling at me through the tears.

"Thank you for finding your way back to me."

The End

To stay up to date on all Tara Sivec news, please join her mailing list:
http://eepurl.com/H4uaf

Acknowledgements

Thank you to my amazing beta readers Stephanie Johnson and Michelle Kannan. Thank you for being excited whenever I ask you if you want to read something, thank you for catching things that I completely miss and thank you for being wonderful friends and readers.

Thank you to my editor, Nikki Rushbrook, who isn't afraid to call me a heifer and tell me when something absolutely sucks. You always enhance my stories in such a way that I could never do alone and I'm so thankful for you.

To my publicist, Donna Soluri – you complete me. Thank you for talking me down from the ledges...all the ledges.

Thank you to Shelly White Collins for telling me about the song "Storm" by Lifehouse. This song MAKES this story and I'm so glad you suggested it!

Thank you to Steve and Maggi Myers for answering all of my scuba questions! I hope my constant texting wasn't too annoying.

Thank you to Danielle Torella of Pushy Girl Paintings for the awesome drawings of Lucy and Fisher's signs! Thank you for dealing with my crazy ass and for making them so much more than I imagined!

Thank you to all of the blogs who take time out of their busy schedules to share teasers and cover reveals and purchase links and all of the other thousands of things you do to help authors. Your support is never ending and it means the world to me.

Thank you to the most amazing author friends a girl could ask for – Jenn Cooksey, Beth Ehemann, Jasinda Wilder and Jenn Sterling. Thank you for your friendship, your support and your encouragement. I love you all more than words can say.

Last but certainly not least, thank you to every man and woman who fight for our country. Thank you for your selflessness and for your dedication to our freedom. Thank you for leaving your families to protect us and thank you, from the bottom of my heart, for your service.

CPSIA information can be obtained at www.ICGtesting.com
Printed in the USA
LVOW04s1912010515

436906LV00014B/1001/P